Acclaim for Sarah P. Blanchard's debut novel

Drawn from Life

"**Blanchard delivers a twisty thriller and memorable cast** in this spirited debut… [An] expertly plotted thriller powered by twisty suspense and memorable characters."
—BookLife

"**A skillfully executed story of suspense** with compellingly complex characters….A well-crafted thriller about memories regained."
—The Kirkus Reviews

"**Beautifully written**…a mesmerizing tale [with a] gripping narrative and psychological depth."
—Online Book Club

"**Exudes a palpable sense of conviction,** carrying readers effortlessly into the intricate world of her vibrant characters and the ruggedly beautiful landscape of North Carolina."
—The Bookview Review

"**A psychological thriller worthy of placement alongside** the novels of the masters in that genre: Stephen King, James Patterson, Lee Child, Gillian Flynn…"
—Reedsy Discovery

"**Blanchard's finesse for teasing out the complexity** of human relationships is a highlight and makes this novel compelling, suffusing the writing with profound depth."
—The BookLife Prize

GRABTOWN

a novel

Sarah P. Blanchard

Grabtown

Content warning: depictions of murder, fire, kidnapping; discussions of human trafficking; brief descriptions of pornographic material and child sexual abuse materials.

October 2025   Eagle Ridge Press
Second Printing
ISBN   979-8-9996922-0-7 paperback
979-8-9996922-1-4 ebook

For Rich and Phil,
always

But, then, my legs begin
trembling, that shaking wild thing they sometimes do,
And, I want to run wild somewhere. In a
greenfield wild somewhere. Somewhere away
From here. Away from where it happened.
Somewhere where it never happens. Never.
Where we all run. Free. And.
Everywhere is, where we run, always green.

—from "Tell Me" by Frances Driscoll
Seaglass Picnic: with a Splash of Post-Traumatic Stress

PROLOGUE

Metal presses in from three sides, cold and unforgiving. The fourth side is wood, rough-cut planks that give you splinters if you bump against them. Twelve-year-old Elena sits with her bottom on hard smooth steel and her back against a corrugated metal wall. She shifts a little in the dark, trying to get comfortable. Sharp ridges dig into her shoulder blades through the thin t-shirt, now damp with sweat and fear.

The container smelled at first of oil and jet fuel, with an underlying earthiness of leather and wood. But now it mostly smells like them—three small unwashed bodies, plus the acrid stench from the plastic bucket they cannot empty.

Cuatro dias, she thinks. Four days they've been traveling. Or is it five?

She switches on their only working flashlight and sweeps its beam across what she's come to think of as their prison cell. The wooden crate still dominates everything, squatting in the center of the shipping container like a sleeping giant. The crate's bulk stretches nearly to the ceiling, almost to the side walls.

Elena and her sisters are living in the small space between the crate and the container's rear doors, eight feet by perhaps five feet. She can touch both the crate and a door if she stands and stretches her arms out. She does this often, to reassure herself that the walls aren't closing in.

At first, she was terrified the crate would shift position on the smooth floor. Slide back on takeoff, perhaps, crushing them against the container's doors. Now she knows it's securely bolted to the floor so the precious cargo in the crate, whatever it is, isn't damaged.

She should switch off the flashlight and save the batteries. Instead, she stares again at the crate's shipping labels, studying the details she missed in their first excited hours aboard the plane. Yellow and white papers in a plastic sleeve, sealed with clear tape and stapled to the wood. Many words are printed in English, which she recognizes but cannot yet read, and in some other language that uses unfamiliar characters.

Ten-year-old Carmen presses closer to her big sister. Elena can feel how thin her sister has become. They are rationing the granola bars, but Carmen barely eats anymore. After two days in the desert and however long they've been in this box, she's barely able to hold her head up.

Carmen's whisper is hoarse from tears. "Elena, ¿Cuando vamos a llegar?" She's asked this a zillion times: When will we get there?

"Pronto, mija," Elena murmurs, but the words taste like a lie. She's been saying "soon" for several days now.

Yesterday, Sofia, the youngest, stopped talking entirely. She sits now with her knees pulled to her chest, her mostly empty backpack clutched against her stomach. In the flashlight beam her eyes are wide and glassy, staring at nothing. Carmen offers her little sister a drink of water from their last jug, but Sofia only twists her head away.

The container's air vents are Elena's new obsession. Four of them, high on the walls near the ceiling. They let in a little air but almost no light.

Sofia whispers, "Necesito usar la cubeta." The first words she's spoken since yesterday.

Elena helps her sister to the corner where they've placed the white bucket, now nearly full and reeking. The smell makes her gag, but she holds the flashlight steady while Sofia uses the bucket, then wipes herself with a small scrap of newspaper from a thin pile on the floor.

As Sofia returns to sit beside Carmen, the flashlight stutters and Elena switches it off. In the darkness, every sound is amplified: the scratch of fabric against metal, the rustle of their few remaining granola bar wrappers, the quiet slosh of water as they pass around the jug.

Their container shudders. Elena feels the plane tilt and hears the whine of machinery. Pressure in her ears tells her they're descending, about to land—but this time, her heart doesn't jump with excitement. They've been through this before. The landing, then the rumble of cranes, the lifting and swaying, the voices outside giving commands in languages she doesn't understand.

"Otra vez, nos están moviendo." she tells her sisters. Her voice is flat, defeated. They're being moved again.

Through the ventilation holes, she can hear men shouting, but not in Spanish or English. The words rise and fall in a fast, clipped rhythm, nothing like the warm vowels of home. The container lurches, and all three girls brace themselves against the wall. No one whimpers this time.

"¿A dónde dijiste que vamos?" There's no hope in Carmen's voice, it's just another rote question.

"America." Elena says automatically, but the word feels hollow. She tries a few words of English. "To live with Tía Rosa."

But something's gone wrong. Mamá had assured them the trip would take no more than a day, but they've been traveling too long. The man who helped them climb into the container had spoken Spanish, yes, but with an accent she didn't recognize and a smile she didn't like.

The container settles with a thud and Elena hears the rumble of engines starting up. Different engines, this time. Bigger, louder, with a deeper vibration that makes her teeth ache. The sound grows more insistent. They press their hands to their ears.

"Escuchen," Elena says, but her voice cracks. "Otro avión." The third plane, by her count. How many flights does it take to get to Galveston, Texas?

They brace themselves against the acceleration and Elena's stomach lurches.

The engine noise settles into a steady drone. Though she knows Sofia probably won't eat, Elena distributes their remaining granola bars, two each. She no longer tells her sisters stories about hamburgers and pizza, or schools with smiling teachers and rooms with windows.

In the darkness, with only the drift of stale air through the ventilation holes and the steady drone of engines to keep them company, Elena holds her sisters close and tries not to think about the symbols on the crate or the strange languages she's heard.

Elena begins to cry.

CHAPTER ONE

Cassie

Cassie rubs her scalp with both hands until she feels her hair bristle like burnt-black grass. When she was a kid, that gesture would have drawn an eyeroll from her twin sister Ana and an exasperated headshake from their mother. But Cassandra Masterson and Anastasia Prescott are nearly forty, and their mother died four days ago.

Two hours after Marla Bousquet's funeral, Cassie sprawls on the green plaid sofa in the rambling Connecticut farmhouse she grew up in. Nursing a cooling mug of coffee and more grief than she's prepared to deal with, she's waiting for Ana to return from delivering a carload of flowers to a local nursing home.

So many flowers. They'd filled the small Congregational meeting house with a thick, humid fragrance. Lilies, carnations, gladioli, roses, chrysanthemums. And a handful of black-eyed Susans, looking like a child had plucked them from a roadside ditch. An odd choice for a funeral, Cassie thinks. Someone else must have known how much their mother loved black-eyed Susans.

An empty fist of sadness spreads through Cassie's ribcage. She flops back into the threadbare cushions, resigning herself to tears, but her eyes remain dry. Nothing comes—no tears, no clarity, no escape.

She'd thought the funeral service would hand her a sense of peace so she could move on. But all she's accomplished so far is to swap her pantsuit for shorts and a T-shirt, power up the living room's tower fan against the sultry heat of summer, and collapse into the cushions.

Her hip vibrates. Startled, she props herself up on an elbow and fumbles her phone from a rear pocket.

Marsh's voice crackles through static, warm and familiar. "Hey, beautiful. I'm about to head out to LAX. How's it going? God, I miss you already."

The small hairs on her forearms lift, responding to the strong pull of his voice. It's disorienting, hearing her husband's California charm in this house. In their eighteen years together, he's been here exactly once. Which was the last time she was here, too, more than a decade ago.

But why is he calling? He's promised her one uninterrupted week to help Ana clear out their mother's house. To mend a few fences, maybe make peace with her sister. Cassie's already feeling unmoored. She isn't ready for his voice wrapping her in its smooth, no-worries velvet.

She stands and pads barefoot to the front window, searching for signal. Cell reception is laughably bad here in this dead-end corner of an old Connecticut mill town, where narrow gravel roads snake between rocky hills and mosquito-infested swamps.

The smell of her mother's old house—musty blankets, disinfectant—clings to everything, following her to the window. She wrinkles her nose. "Okay, I guess. I just got back from the funeral."

"Oh, babe." His voice drops to that tender register she remembers from their early days. "I'm such an ass. I should've asked about that first. How are you holding up?"

She rubs tired eyes, surprised by the genuine concern. This is the Marsh who used to bring her soup when she was sick, who'd massage her feet after long days at her writing desk.

"It was a funeral. The usual." If she tries to explain the sadness, he'll worry and tell her to cut the visit short.

"I wish I knew what that meant." He lets out a self-deprecating laugh. "I'm terrible at this stuff, aren't I? Death, grief—I never know the right thing to say. I'm sort of glad I missed it, but I know I should've come with you. Should've been there for you."

The vulnerability in his admission catches her off guard. "It's okay. I know Hong Kong's important."

"Not more important than you." He's offering that little-boy earnestness that used to make her melt. "I keep thinking about you in that house, with all the memories. And Ana, giving you grief." He pauses. "I'm worried about you, babe. You get so lost in your own head sometimes."

She's too tired to argue. And it doesn't matter what she says, Marsh will hear what he wants to hear. At the moment, his concern feels genuine, though he's preoccupied with overseeing the delivery of a rare Lamborghini Miura—one of only twelve ever made—to a demanding Chinese billionaire. An oligarch, he'd said with theatrical mockery, mimicking the man's accent until she'd laughed despite herself. The buyer is insisting that the owner of Masterson's Exotic Motors be

13

present at the Hong Kong airport to supervise the uncrating of his precious car.

She checks her watch. His flight from LAX is scheduled to leave in a few hours.

"It's only six days," he's saying, and she pictures him smoothing his sculpted beard with a thumb and index finger, the way he does when he's nervous. "The container was off-loaded yesterday. So I check it for damage, get it through customs, schmooze the buyer for a few hours on Saturday—you know how these guys love the dog-and-pony show—talk with a couple other clients on Sunday, and head back that night." He pauses. "Actually, I could try to get home a day early. Maybe switch my flight and catch a Saturday night red-eye, go straight through to Boston or Hartford and join you there for a few days. What do you think?"

Through the dusty window, Cassie glimpses a basket of red geraniums hanging from the roof-edge above the front porch. Her mother's most cherished plants, four large pots evenly spaced beneath the roof overhang where they catch the rays of the afternoon sun. Mindful of the heat at this time of year, her mother always gave the flowers a thorough soaking each morning. Cassie wonders who's watering the geraniums now.

"Babe? You still there?"

"Sorry, I'm here. Just…taking it all in." She catches up to what he's been saying. "No, don't change flights. I'm fine."

His voice softens again. "I can only imagine. That house holds a lot of history for you."

"Yes."

Beside the porch steps, two dogwood trees flank the gravel path running from the house to the unpaved driveway. Near the end of the driveway, there's a woodlot where a farmer collects sap from a grove of sugar maples each spring. It's late August now, but thin blue plastic tubing still hangs in haphazard coils from the massive maple trees lining the dirt road.

She shifts her eyes back to the porch's white railing, with its peeling paint and coating of gray-brown road dust. One picket is cracked and two are missing. *Everywhere I look, something is broken.*

"Cassie?" Marsh's voice pulls her back. "I was asking about Ana. How's she treating you? Still playing the grieving daughter who was always the favorite?"

There it is again, the familiar jealousy disguised as protection.

"She's fine. We're fine."

"I just don't want her laying some guilt trip on you, okay? Making you feel bad because you weren't there as much as she was." His voice gets that reasonable quality that always makes her doubt herself. "If she really cared, she would've invited you to visit more often instead of hoarding your mother to herself."

"Marsh—"

"Are you sleeping okay? You have your Xanax, right?" The concern is genuine but tinged with something else. Control, maybe, or the need to fix things he doesn't understand.

"We've been over this. I'm okay."

"I know, I know. It's just—" He chuckles a little. "I can't help myself. I see you hurting and I want to swoop in and make it better. Very caveman of me, I know."

Despite everything, she almost smiles. This is the Marsh who won her over—the successful businessman who could poke fun at his own intensity. Who made her feel precious and protected.

He says, "Do you think you'll have time to write? What are you working on?"

"Jeez, no. I haven't even had time to think." She'd told him that a few extra days here in her childhood home, with no WiFi and few other distractions, would give her a chance to concentrate on writing a new story. The truth is, she hasn't even unpacked her laptop. And her creativity evaporated months ago.

"That's okay, babe. Sometimes you just need to let the well refill, you know?" His voice hardens slightly. "Just remember how much we've invested in giving your mom the best care possible. Extra homecare nurses, specialists, that adjustable bed we rented—Ana seems to think we're made of money."

"I *know*. We've been over it before." The sharp impatience in her voice surprises them both.

She bites her lip at the overstep. Now she's crossed some invisible line. Hearing his quick intake of breath, she braces for the shift. Marsh can be so mercurial, it's hard to keep up.

"Dammit, Cass, I can barely hear you. You're breaking up." His voice has changed, all the warmth gone. "Find a better goddamn signal or call me back on the landline. But not now—make it four o'clock, after I get to the airport."

He pauses. "Did you hear me? Say it back, so I know you got it."

Her familiar rush of submission fights with something more resistant. "Four o'clock, your time. Yes, okay, that's seven my time."

The line crackles again and she thinks they've lost the connection. No, he's still there.

"Just be careful, Cass." Now he's almost pleading. "I know I sound paranoid, but that house—it's not good for you. All those old ghosts, your sister stirring up ancient history. Don't talk to anyone you don't have to, okay? Get through the week and come home to me.

"Or you could come home early," he adds hopefully. "Maybe switch to an earlier flight—Sunday or Monday instead of Tuesday?"

"Not a chance, Marsh. Sunday's the estate sale. Ana needs me for that. And I'm thinking of staying on a few days longer, maybe."

And just like that, the steel is back. "That's a hard no, Cassandra." He's switched to The Voice, that steely tone of command that makes the heat rise on the back of her neck as if he's grabbed her there, pulling her in for a hard kiss. Like he did the last time they had sex, three nights earlier when he spread his long fingers and gripped her skull hard, bringing her mouth down to his crotch. Insisting on one last romp before her 5:00 AM flight to Hartford, when all she wanted was to sleep off the extra wine he'd poured for her at dinner.

"You have commitments here, Cassie. To me. To us. Get yourself home on schedule."

The line goes dead and she's left staring at the phone. Did the call get dropped, or did he hang up? She should have managed a "miss you" or a "love you too," but the moment passed too quickly.

She exhales sharply and turns away from the window. That's the thing about Marsh—he can make her feel like the most beloved woman in the world one moment and like a small, disappointing child the next. Nearly two decades together, and she still can't predict which version of him will show up.

Enough. It's time to begin what she's agreed to do, help her sister clear their mother's very cluttered house.

Downstairs: dust-caked rugs, the sagging sofa, stacks of *National Geographics*, cheap tote bags hanging on cup hooks by the door—all destined for the landfill. Upstairs: clothes, photos, costume jewelry, scarred furniture, closets full of who knows what.

Ana will save only a handful of photos for herself and ask the estate-sale people to clear out the rest. Cassie briefly considers shipping the mahogany guest-room chest back to Palos Verdes but then imagines Marsh's scowl.

Her eyes fall on her mother's ancient black rotary phone, perched on the little telephone desk in the front entry—maybe she'll keep that as a stage prop for the gritty, darkly humorous, mid-century play she'll write someday. Maybe.

She paces the living room, dropping books and knick-knacks at random, until she stops at a shelf lined with photos. Mom and Dad, impossibly young on their wedding day in 1981. Then the twins at two: Angelic Ana beams at the photographer but Cassie scowls and shrinks from the camera.

Even then, I wanted to be anywhere but where I was.

She begins assessing the rest of the room, creating a mental checklist. Donate this, recycle that, discard everything else. Discard, discard, discard.

The front door swings open with a sudden burst of sunlight and heat. Cassie jumps slightly and trips over a braided rug, feeling a quick pang of guilt. She wanted her sister to find her hard at work, perhaps taking down curtains or sorting clothes—anything but drifting aimlessly or crying into the sofa cushions, which she's already done plenty of.

Ana drops her purse on the sofa. Smudged mascara rims her green-brown eyes, and her cheeks shine with dried tears. "Oh my god Cassie, the crowd. I didn't know half those people, but they all knew Mom."

Cassie shrugs. "You live and work seventy years in one small town, you get a long funeral line." That sounds unfeeling so she tries again. "Mom knew a lot of people. Helped a lot of people."

"Yeah. People remember their physical therapist even when they forget their doctor's name." Leaning against the back of the sofa, Ana toes off her kitten heels and plucks her navy linen skirt away from her thighs. "What was I thinking? Pantyhose, in this heat. Ugh." She kneels in front of the tower fan. The air tousles her shoulder-length hair, pale cornsilk threaded with gray. "And no AC. Who's gonna buy this place?"

"Someone with lots of money, who falls in love with an old farmhouse in a backwater town. They'll gut it, probably, and put in mini-splits for AC." Although Cassie hasn't been home for years, the thought of someone else living here hits with a quick sadness that she tries to mask. "It was good to see Jonathan and Julie today, even for a few minutes. Did Jules get away okay?"

Straightening up, Ana turns her back toward the inadequate fan and lifts her skirt to let the air travel up her legs. "Jonathan hustled Julie out early, while we were still in the receiving line. He's taking her for lunch so they can have some daddy-daughter time before she flies back to Chicago. Her flight's at 3:30."

She retrieves her phone from her purse, taps and scrolls quickly. "And I got a text from Scott in Edinburgh. He sends his condolences, says he's sorry he couldn't be here to say goodbye to Gramma. All's well, he's loving the city, et cetera."

Cassie feels a tug of what-if wistfulness. She's never wanted children and hasn't paid much attention to her only niece and nephew, but still. "You've launched them well, you and Jonathan."

Ana frowns a little, but her voice remains neutral. "They're good kids. We had a lot of help from Mom. And Jonathan's parents, of course."

She doesn't say, "And you've helped too, Cassie," because it wouldn't be true. Cassie hasn't been any more present in her niece and nephew's lives than she was in her mother's, these past twenty years. Does she even know what they're studying? Architecture and engineering, maybe.

Ana's saying, "It hasn't hit me yet, losing Mom only a week after the kids left for school. I've been living with her, I watched her fade away, and still somehow, I didn't expect her to ever really die. It's the finality of it, isn't it? I keep expecting her to come out of the kitchen or walk in from the garden."

She sighs and shakes her head. "Next week, I'll step back into my normal boring life in West Hartford. Go to the office, plan the athenaeum fundraisers, decorate our house for the next holiday. But now there's this huge empty hole. My mother's gone, my kids are in college. Nothing will be the same."

Cassie's too detached to offer appropriate comfort. She watches her twin push back a stray lock of yellow-gray hair and feels an unusual twinge of envy.

No color tints, fasting, or skinny shots for Ana. She's apparently never been at war with her comfortably padded mom-body. With guilty satisfaction, Cassie notes the sweat stains beneath her sister's armpits. It's a rare blemish in her sister's usual composure. Anastasia, the first-born twin. The unshakably competent big sister, moving through the world with deliberate care and an eagle eye for disorder.

Cassie's spent her entire life, nearly forty years, trying not to be like her twin sister.

Ana says, "Sorry it took me a while to drop off the flowers. There were so many, I had to make two trips."

"Were they happy to get them?"

"They seemed to be. Oh, I nearly forgot." Ana walks out to the porch and returns with a cluster of black-eyed Susans in a brown stoneware pitcher. "I felt a little embarrassed, giving these away to a nursing home. They're so pitiful-looking. Do you know who brought them? Here." She thrusts the pitcher at Cassie. "They can go on the kitchen table, I guess. Or I'll dump them in the woods if you think they're too ratty."

"They're okay. I like them." Cassie carries the pitcher into the kitchen and sets it in the center of the wide oak table, then pokes at the stems to see if she can make them stand a little straighter. In the jungle of green leaves, her fingers touch a small card, limp with moisture. She wipes it off on the seat of her shorts and deciphers the uneven handwriting:

Marla, you've done well. Godspeed. Carl

It's a strange thing to write on a funeral bouquet. Did their mother have a boyfriend that no one knew about? Cassie feels the ghost of a smile touch her face. She tucks the card into her back pocket and returns to the living room.

Ana's still talking funerals and flowers. "A strange custom, isn't it? Donating all those strong-smelling lilies and gardenias to old people who're going to have their own funerals soon. I hate the scent of gardenias, don't you? They always smell dirty, sort of musty. I can't see why—" She stops abruptly, her shoulders sagging. "I'm babbling. Sorry."

"It's okay." Cassie hesitates, then moves near and stretches a little to wrap her taller twin in a stiff hug. They stand uncomfortably close until Ana steps away.

Cassie breaks the awkward silence. "At least they get to enjoy Mom's flowers, right? They won't see their own."

"I guess," Ana says uncertainly. "Okay, I've got to get out of these things. Back in a sec." She picks up her shoes and hat and disappears up the stairs.

When she returns, dressed in khaki shorts and an oversized pink tee knotted at the waist, Cassie's busy dumping stacks of magazines and paperbacks into two boxes labeled RECYCLING. She holds up a yellow booklet, no bigger than a thin paperback novel. "Ana,

22

look. A phone book from the year we were born." It's titled *1985, Winslow, East Winslow, Coulterville, Graves Parish.* "The current one's over there beneath the phone, so why'd Mom save this one?"

"She saved everything from the year we were born, newspapers to napkins. The bigger question is, why does the new phone book even exist? I can't believe someone's still printing them."

"Because people here still have landlines, I guess." Cassie retrieves the current directory from beneath the phone's permanently tangled spiral cord. "The cell coverage sucks."

"Cassie, please. Just keep the latest book and toss the old one. We don't have time to examine everything page by page." Ana wraps a scrunchy around her hair and pulls it up into a high pony. Selecting an empty carton, she heads back upstairs. "I'm going to start on the shelves in my old room. Maybe you can put together more of those banker boxes?" She points her chin at a stack of flat-packed cardboard.

"Okay." But when Ana's out of sight, Cassie takes the two phone books to the kitchen table. She sinks into a chair and sets them side by side.

The newer one is only slightly thicker than the one from 1985. Winslow and surrounding villages certainly haven't expanded much in four decades. The directories have nearly identical covers, featuring photos of black-and-white cows grazing in a field of golden dandelions and impossibly green grass.

In 1985, she remembers, Winslow was a town of barely eight thousand people. And the flanking villages—Coulterville on the west and East Winslow, bordering Rhode Island on the east—were less than half the size of Winslow proper.

Graves Parish, on the northeast edge of Winslow, hasn't been a real town for nearly a century. Even in 1985 it was nothing more than an artifact, a smudge on a byroads-and-bygones map. Now it must be only a few stone foundations beside a weed-covered path, eroded by storms and overtaken by the forest.

The phone book is another artifact. When Cassie was little, your phone book was your lifeline, how people found you before Google and PeopleSearch. Such a quaint concept, allowing—expecting—the phone company to publish your name, address, and phone number in a free directory for everyone to see.

Here, phone books are still a thing because many people still have landlines. So yes, these numbers get published in the little free book. Which is also chock-full of local advertising and large-print information about fire and police and social services.

In Marla Bousquet's house, a phone directory also served as a message board, its front and back covers filled with random handwritten notes, their mother's way of taking notes or starting a shopping list. Her unique cursive covers every available space on the front and back of both directories, old and new. Her distinctive scrawl squeezes along the edges and inside the white patches of clouds and cows, the spontaneous life notes of a quiet, considerate woman who preferred to scribble in the phone book rather than ask a caller to wait while she searched for a notepad.

Planting an elbow on the kitchen table, Cassie leans her chin on one hand as she runs a finger over words on the cover of the old directory, deciphering *broccoli bread peppercorns Kleenex white vinegar cider vinegar.* White vinegar for cleaning, cider vinegar for pickling, because cider vinegar has the milder flavor.

She finds *6/7 Monday – Marge, The Talisman. Overdue?* which meant her mom might have been in trouble with the head librarian at the Winslow Public library. Marla wasn't a fan of Stephen King or Peter Straub—the British cozies were more her style—so maybe it was Keith, their dad, who'd borrowed that year's best-selling fantasy-horror novel.

Cassie puzzles over two other notes: *AJ loafers?* and a cryptic reminder to *Call C. Androski,* with a local number written large on a cow's pale flank. She knows who AJ was, their mother's closest girlfriend from way back in sixth grade, but she draws a blank on C. Androski. She checks the white pages but can't find a listing for that name.

Another note, written in bright purple on a fluffy white cloud, looks more recent. *Baby aspirin—ask Grace.* Dr. Grace Gorham, she remembers, was the cardiologist who'd set up her mother's heart bypass operation after her first stroke, nearly a decade ago.

She feels the heaviness swell again in her chest. Isn't she done with weeping? How on earth will she survive the week if something so insignificant as an old phone book sets her off?

She rubs her face with a rough hand and tosses the '85 directory in a recycling box. Done and dusted, just a relic from the past.

But curiosity tickles again, so she retrieves it and thumbs through the inside pages, looking for old familiar names and addresses. She finds teachers, shop owners, neighbors, Ana's basketball coach.

Her sister's steps sound on the staircase and there's the muted clatter of a box being set on the floor in the front hall. "Cassie," Ana calls, "come give me a hand with these collectibles. We need to figure out if there's anything worth adding to the estate sale, or if it's all going to charity."

Poking her head through the kitchen doorway, Ana frowns at the sight of her sister, still sitting at the table.

Cassie holds up the older phone book. "Ana, did you see all of Mom's old notes in here?"

"Yeah, she did that to every phone book we ever had." The frown deepens. "Come on, Cass, we need to get rid of this stuff."

"I can't believe Graves Parish is still labeled as a town. See?"

Ana sighs and gives in, propping a hip against the wall and crossing her arms.

"Do you remember," Cassie muses, "that Halloween when we were eleven? When Dad walked us through the woods to the lost village. At night, with flashlights. There was nothing there but old chimneys and cellar holes. It was really spooky. Remember how mad Mom got when she found out? She said Graves Parish used to be called Grabtown. It was a place where bad things happened to naughty kids, especially girls. We had nightmares for a week."

"Wow, you're going way back." Hunching her shoulders in a small shiver, Ana pushes herself away from the door frame. "Dad said there used to be a big barn up there, where all the kids hung out when he was young. It burned down, I think, before we were even born."

She glances at her watch. "Come on, Cassie. Put that down. I can't do all this by myself."

CHAPTER TWO

Cassie

Head deep in the refrigerator, Cassie pokes through a stack of cold cuts and casseroles dropped off by neighbors. Nothing looks appetizing, so Ana uses the landline to call Winslow's lone Thai restaurant for takeout.

Ana eats quickly but Cassie merely picks at her dinner, choosing white wine over pad thai. They talk about nothing important, thinking their separate thoughts and gazing occasionally through the kitchen windows as the sky darkens into twilight over farmland and wooded hills. Then Ana clears space on the table to sort bills and bank statements while Cassie pours herself a third glass of wine and plucks the petals from a broken-stemmed black-eyed Susan.

Cassie remembers the note she found in the vase. "Ana, do you know someone named Carl? Carl with a C. Maybe a friend of Mom's." She fishes the wrinkled card from her pocket and pushes it across the table.

Ana removes her tortoiseshell glasses and pinches the bridge of her nose with a thumb and forefinger. "There was a Carl in fourth grade. I think he moved away."

"Why would someone from our fourth-grade class, who moved away, write 'you've done well' on a card for Mom's funeral? I don't remember anyone named Carl coming through the receiving line."

Ana shrugs. "Maybe he's a PT patient that Mom helped. She had a lot of patients over the years. They sent her thank-you notes and cards at Christmas. A few of those people made some great recoveries. She always told us about her successes." She drops her eyes to the pile of papers but doesn't put her glasses back on. "Cassie, please. We need to talk."

"What about?"

"The estate sale. Getting this house on the market."

"Can't that wait? It's stuffy in here. I'll be on the porch." Ignoring her sister's frown, Cassie empties the last of the wine into her glass, switches on the porch lights, and picks up the 1985 phone book.

Hands full, she pushes the screen door open with a hip. It bangs hard behind her, and she feels a twinge of guilt because she's neglected to ease it closed. She hears again her mother's frequent entreaties. *Please, Cassie! Don't let it slam.*

The quick threat of tears rises again but she swallows hard and sets her glass on the porch railing.

Out of long habit, she inspects the cushions on the wicker chairs before sitting. Finding neither bird deposits nor bat droppings, she chooses a chair and settles in with bare feet curled beneath her and opens the dog-eared phone book to the P's.

Her mother's best friend, AJ Porter, had been first a news reporter, Cassie remembers, and later a legal aid attorney working in Manchester. AJ died in a car crash when the twins were sophomores in college, Ana nearby at UMass and Cassie far away at UC-Berkeley.

She finds several Porters, including a *Porter, Agnes J.,* on Turnbull Road. The number has a Graves Parish exchange, placing her just east of Winslow proper. In the margin of the page is a note in their mother's handwriting: *4-14-2004 Deceased. Car accident.* Three small red hearts filled the space beside the terse words.

AJ's name was Agnes? I don't think I knew that. She was always just AJ, Mom's weird friend.

Cassie didn't attend AJ's funeral. She'd been too far away, too busy with studies, and too poor to travel. Also probably too muddled with drink, drugs, and whatever man had captured her attention at the time. She can't remember if Ana went. Probably, because that's what Ana would do.

Another feather of guilt flutters, this time layered with a heavier resentment. AJ had been a near-constant presence in the twins' young lives, especially right after their parents' divorce when they were in middle school and their mom needed someone to keep an eye on them after school or drive them to their dad's apartment for weekend visits to Boston. AJ lived in a little cottage on the other side of town, but she often stayed here overnight to help with breakfast and getting the girls off to school when their mother worked an early shift at the hospital.

Marla had urged the twins to call her best friend Auntie AJ. Easygoing Ana was fine with that; she followed all rules and most of their mom's suggestions. But Cassie refused to own the embarrassment that was AJ, with her odd limp, clunky shoes, and unpopular ideas about raising teenage girls.

The limp was because of AJ's clubfoot, their mother explained. Not anyone's fault, just something she was born with. "It's why I became a physical therapist,"

31

Marla had said. "So I can help people with challenges like Auntie AJ's."

When the twins got their first cell phones at fifteen and the internet became a thing, AJ began monitoring their social lives closely. With Marla's approval, she switched her lectures from nutrition to the perils of sex, drinking, and drugs. Ana accepted the guardrails, focusing her energies on getting good grades and making the cheerleading squad. But Cassie chafed against every rule, channeling her resentment into class-skipping and binge drinking.

Thinking now of those years, Cassie feels her face grow warm. *Poor AJ, and poor Mom. It's a wonder we all survived, I was such a hot mess. I'm still a hot mess, but I've learned to hide it better.*

Automatically reaching for her wine, she takes a mouthful but it's gone warm and sour. She spits it into an azalea and sets the half-full glass back on the railing.

Turning the phone book's pages, she picks annotated names at random. One note explains that Martinson, Matthew K. *died 12-28-99.* Another scribble informs Cassie that the Hanrahans *moved to Cincinnati 4/06.*

Next to the name Desjardins, James R., is a different note: *GONE 8-14-85.*

That's odd, she thinks. *Why GONE? Why not DIED or MOVED?* She flips quickly through the pages but finds no other mention of someone being *GONE.*

Gone where? Perhaps he'd gone missing. Or it's something that shouldn't be mentioned, like prison. Cassie squints at the page but the numbers have gone small and blurry. She takes another sip of wine and gazes out over the lawn, where twilight has settled and fireflies glide over the grass. She watches them float into the dark trees beyond the driveway, flickering on and off like glowing sparks rising on invisible smoke.

The screen door opens halfway, and Ana pokes her head out. "I made a pot of Earl Grey. Do you want some?"

"No, I'm good."

The door opens wider as Ana carries a cloth tote bag and a mug onto the porch. She leans the tote against the house's dusty gray clapboards, sets her mug next to Cassie's wine glass on the railing, and drags a second wicker chair across the warped floorboards. "The katydids are crazy loud tonight, aren't they? Doesn't that mean a storm's brewing?" She lifts her damp hair from her neck with both hands.

Cassie isn't interested in insects or weather. "It's summer in New England. There's always a storm brewing somewhere."

But the cacophony of insect noise is hard to ignore. There's nothing like this in southern California, and Cassie's oddly pleased she still remembers their names and sounds: the bell-like chime of crickets, the three-note thrum of katydids, the rising rattle-chime and falling buzz of cicadas. The enduring soundtrack of all her childhood's summer nights.

"Have you heard from Marsh?" Ana asks.

Cassie squirms a little in her chair. "He called earlier, before you got back. He's sorry he had to miss the funeral. Sends you his sympathy." The small lie is automatic, part of the veneer she's constructed over the past two decades. "The cell signal was sucky. I'm supposed to call him back tonight on the landline, but I think I'll just wait until morning."

"Won't he be angry?"

"Eh," Cassie shrugs. "Probably. I'll deal with it."

"You mean you'll put up with it." Ana's voice sharpens. "He's a bully, Cass. The passive-aggressive kind, so it's harder to spot. He's kept you away from us and—"

"That's not true." Cassie's eyes drop to the tote bag. "What's in there?"

Ana is silent for a moment, as if deciding something. She sighs and reaches for the bag. "Something with your name on it. I think Mom left it for you." She pulls out a stack of paper an inch thick, bound with a pair of crisscrossed rubber bands.

Cassie frowns. "A manuscript?" She reads the title page aloud. "Working title: Common Justice. A novella by AJ Porter. March 9, 2001, Winslow, Connecticut."

At the bottom of the page there's a note in their mother's handwriting. Red ink, all caps: FOR CASSANDRA BOUSQUET – CONFIDENTIAL!

"Where did you find this, Ana?" Wondering if her words sound a wee bit slurred. "And why did Mom write only my name on it?" She lifts her hands, palms up.

"Maybe because you fancy yourself a writer." Ana bypasses Cassie's outstretched hands and drops the manuscript so it lands with a slap on Cassie's bare knees. "It was in a lockbox on the top shelf of her closet, beneath a ton of old bank statements."

Cassie's eyes narrow. "Did you—"

"Are you accusing me of reading something Mom left for *you?* Really, Cass." Ana looks offended. "Though I did put new rubber bands on it. The old ones were so brittle, they broke into pieces."

Cassie holds up both hands in a conciliatory gesture. "I'm not accusing you. She pulls off the bands, sets the title page aside, and quickly scans the first several sheets.

She looks up, puzzled. "The story starts in the summer of 1985. It looks like AJ wrote a murder mystery, set here in Winslow. A farmer named Jimmy Desjardins got shot. But—" She frowns, remembering her mother's note in the phone directory: *Desjardins, James R. GONE 8-14-85.*

Cassie flips back to the beginning and begins reading. Three pages in, she's forgotten that her sister is still sitting beside her.

Ana waits quietly for a long moment, watching Cassie read and listening to the overlapping rattle of the cicadas. Then she rises and carries her cold tea into the house.

CHAPTER THREE

AJ

COMMON JUSTICE
A novella by AJ Porter

~ 1 ~

Did Jimmy Desjardins realize what was happening in those final, fleeting seconds?

That was just wishful thinking on my part. It was too quick. No time for questions. No bargaining, no explanations, no regrets. Maybe he felt a flicker of surprise or a quick confusion of fear. But then came the blast and nothing else mattered.

Most people knew Jimmy as a farmer. Those people considered him a little reserved, but friendly enough. His farm was the one you visited when you wanted to watch a cow being milked or a calf getting born. Some people said he wasn't a particularly good farmer, but that's not a reason for murder. When he was alive, I knew him the way I knew most of my back-roads neighbors, by a nod and a "howya doin" when we crossed paths at the feed store or the gas station. I learned way more about him after his death.

***

Jimmy lived just east of Winslow, Connecticut, an old mill town straddling the Pennatucket River in the state's northeast corner. Outside of the town's business district, it was mostly swamp-Yankee territory, hardscrabble farms carved from the woodlands and marshes of a rural New England that always seemed stuck in the landscape and mindset of an earlier time.

This area had a celebrated past. Go way back, and you'll find a flourishing population of indigenous peoples. The Nipmucks, mostly, but also Mohegans and Pequots to the south, Narragansetts and Wampanoags to the east. In 1676, many of their villages were obliterated in the devastating conflict the English called King Philip's War.

Thousands of native people were slaughtered, starved, or sold into slavery. Only fragments of the culture and language persisted, mostly in the place names of the lakes and rivers: Quaddick, Quasset, Natchaug, Quinebaug, Mashantucket, Mashamoquet, Wappoquia.

The town of Winslow is named for the colonial commander-in-chief who was largely responsible for that slaughter. But older names persist, and the river flowing through Winslow is called the Pennatucket, meaning "freshwater fishing by the hills." Which it still is, mostly because the state stocks it with trout every year.

Back in colonial times, timber harvested from Winslow forests built merchant schooners and trade ships. During the Civil War, wool from the town's sheep farms and weaving mills created uniforms for the Union Army. In the 1930s and early '40s, the town was still bustling with lumberyards, foundries, shoemakers, and textile factories. Freight and passenger trains arrived daily in the busy Providence & Worcester railroad yard.

But after World War Two, cheaper labor sucked the manufacturing jobs away—first to the South, then overseas. In 1955, a catastrophic flood washed away most of the remaining mills along the Pennatucket. Now it's thirty years post-flood but Winslow still hasn't figured out how to create a new prosperity. Most people who are born here leave as soon as they can. Those who stay usually hang on because, like Jimmy, they've inherited a small business or the family farm.

Or they've deliberately chosen a quiet community where no one questions how you make your money or live your life. Small towns are great for scolding the kids who throw too many snowballs, but not always good at acknowledging bigger problems. "Live and let live" could be Winslow's motto.

In 1985 Winslow, most news traveled wirelessly, unofficially by the usual gossip mill and officially by a low-power, daytime AM radio station. That's where I worked, radio station WWCT, 1360 on your AM dial. I was their afternoon news announcer and very first girl reporter, which sounded exciting until you realized the entire news department consisted of Mike, the news director; me; and one stringer, a high school intern named Tony who picked up odd assignments on weekends and after school.

It was entry-level journalism, but even after three years I still felt a small thrill every time I flipped on the mic and told my listeners about an accident or a house fire. Or the latest pronouncements of the town manager or the Winslow Rotary Club. Because that mundane stuff was part of the job, too. Reassuring everyone that today was just a normal day and nothing bad happened while they were sleeping or working.

Except when it did.

A little after eleven on a blistering hot Wednesday morning in August, Winslow's farmers were working fast, trying to get their second-cut hay baled and put up in their barns before the next thunderstorm arrived. The air was sticky and fragrant with the scent of new-mown grass, mixed with the everyday odors of cow manure and tractor diesel.

That's what I noticed first on that Wednesday morning, the warm earthy smell of the hayfields.

Heading east into Winslow to start my noon-to-six shift at WWCT, I drove along Turnbull Road with the windows open to catch a breeze. At the crest of the hill where the woods ended and Turnbull joined Cherry Valley, I let the Chevy idle for a few minutes admiring the view.

Below me was open farmland, two hundred acres of green hayfields and greener pastures cross-hatched by old stone walls. A sparkling creek ran beside the road and, midway down the valley, a white farmhouse sat among its assorted barns and outbuildings. A small herd of black-and-white cows grazed beside a long, low milking barn.

In the freshly cut hayfield just this side of the cow pasture, a new-looking tractor pulled a baling machine, both John Deere green. Every thirty seconds or so, a hay bale popped out the back end like a giant string-wrapped biscuit. Most of the field had been baled but there was still a section where the raked hay lay in a long, neat row, waiting for the sharp tines of the baler's pickup reel.

In early autumn when the hills flame red and orange, photographers swarm these roads for their best calendar shots. But that day, my Chevy was the only car on the road and I was in no hurry. I took a few minutes to look away from the valley, half a mile uphill to where a rocky cow pasture met the trees of a hilltop woodlot.

At the edge of the woods was an old barn, a relic from an earlier century. Its original wood siding had been patched with bare, weathered planks, but high up beneath the eaves it retained traces of old paint, a dark rusty red. When the morning sun caught that barn and the hills exactly right, the whole landscape glowed with brilliance. It was that kind of glorious summer morning, and I remember wishing I'd brought my Kodak.

I have no idea how long I sat there. Four or five minutes, perhaps. Long enough for the scene in the valley to change.

As I pulled away from the stop sign, I saw a dark-colored pickup at the bottom of the slope. It was parked off the road, tipped a little sideways in a shallow ditch at the edge of the hayfield. The green tractor had stopped nearby and now sat driverless.

A tall, lean man wearing typical farmer's clothes—faded jeans, long-sleeved denim shirt, orange trucker's cap—stood between the pickup and the idling tractor, about twenty feet from the pickup's passenger door. I saw him raise an arm to his mouth, as if taking a drag on a cigarette. Then he pointed toward the old barn on the hill, maybe giving directions or pointing out a landmark.

My car was halfway down the slope when I heard an explosion. Like the thunder of a truck's backfire, but louder. The man lurched sideways. He twirled in a clumsy half-pirouette and collapsed.

Echoes of the blast pinged off the hills as the pickup lurched forward, rear tires spinning in the dirt. It fishtailed, then caught traction and leaped onto the asphalt. Seconds later it shot over the creek bridge and turned right onto a side road, heading north and away from town.

The man lay in the hayfield, legs splayed at odd angles. Nothing moved except my Chevy, which continued to carry me sedately downhill toward the hayfield.

A whisper of fear touched the back of my neck. That blast wasn't a backfire. It was gunfire. He'd been shot.

I tightened my grip on the steering wheel, swallowed the fear-whispers, and took the necessary actions to get my car the rest of the way downhill to where he lay.

He lay on his right side. One arm was folded beneath what remained of his ribcage, and the other hugged his chest like he was trying to hold it together.

I stopped on the side of the road and scrambled out, trying to sort out what had happened.

His name came to me. Jimmy Desjardins, one of the many farmers who lived near Winslow. His place was a little larger than average, a couple hundred acres. He grew hay and cow corn, some for his own cows and some to sell. He had maybe two dozen milkers and half that number in the heifer herd.

As if that mattered.

His glass-blue eyes were open, fixed on something distant. He had short yellow-gray hair, three-four days of gray beard-stubble, and skin so leathery he might be any age, but I thought he was about forty. His face was creased with hay dust, dirt, and a lot of blood, bright red and wet.

The number one cause of death among farmers is machinery mishaps. But Jimmy hadn't been run over by a silage chopper or crushed in a tractor rollover. He'd been killed by an explosion that shredded his denim shirt and pulped his chest, opening his ribs to the summer sky. What would do that? A shotgun, maybe.

Blowflies move fast in summer heat and a few had already found him. I swatted them away, kneeled in what I hoped wasn't blood, and touched his left arm.

"Hey," I said. "Are you okay?"

Which was absurd because he was obviously dead. Shock was doing funny things to my mind. I felt it, knew it, and still I took hold of his left wrist. No pulse.

Come on, AJ, my brain prompted. You took CPR. What are the ABC's of rescue? A is for Airway. So check the airway. B is for Breathing. What the hell is C?

Circulation! C is for circulation. Circulation means blood.

There was plenty of blood but the airway was gone. I can't check A for Airway so how can I find B for Breathing and C for Circulation?

I sat back on my heels and scanned the field, panic rising like the bad taste of bile. Where's our first-aid instructor? Hiding behind the tractor, taking notes on my performance? Is this an unannounced field test?

Something moved in the ditch and I jolted to my feet, swiveling to scan the fields again.

Where's the killer? Don't hang around, AJ! Run!

It was only a rabbit, frozen into momentary stillness beneath a stand of goldenrod.

Then I saw a wisp of smoke rising from the short dry grass a few feet away. A small flame flickered from the tip of a still-burning cigarette. I moved quickly, stomping it out and stubbing dirt over the butt.

Nearby, the idling tractor was still chugging rhythmically in the way of heavy machinery interrupted in its work. I stumbled to it, grabbed the steering wheel, and pulled myself up onto the footstep to switch off the ignition. In the sudden quiet, a red-winged blackbird trilled.

I stepped down again, swaying a little because the sky and earth were threatening to swap places. Back at my car, I leaned both elbows against the hood and pulled in deep breaths, trying hard not to vomit. The world steadied and my brain kicked into a better gear.

I needed a telephone.

The closest house, other than Jimmy's, was the Jellniks' place, a few minutes beyond the bridge and halfway around the next bend. The same way the pickup had gone.

As I'd hoped, Shirley Jellnik was home with her kids. She came to the screen door with a baby on one hip and two older girls peering from behind her jeans. Her eyes grew big and her welcoming smile faded when she saw the blood on my white shirt and best navy slacks, the clothes I saved for interviews.

She paused a second, then urged me into her kitchen. I eased in sideways, trying not to touch the doorframe. "I'm okay," I assured her. "But I need your phone. There's been a— Someone's been killed. It's Jimmy."

I almost said, There's been a murder. But I didn't know that, did I?

"Oh!" Her big round eyes got bigger and rounder but she recovered quickly, pointing her chin at a pale yellow wall phone near the fridge. She carried the baby out of the room, sweeping the older girls out with her. I grabbed a damp dish towel from her counter and scrubbed at my hands, hoping to minimize blood on the receiver and, absurdly, thinking I should buy her a new one.

Winslow has a small police force—a captain, one sergeant, three patrol officers—but their jurisdiction was limited to the central business district. Jimmy's farm was outside the district's borders so my call landed at the state police station, Troop D barracks in Danielson, twelve miles away. The nasal-voiced dispatcher, whose name I probably heard but promptly forgot, had me repeat everything twice.

Name, location, what I saw, when I saw it. Name and location were easy but everything else had gone fuzzy. My brain had stalled again, stuck on that vivid, technicolor image of Jimmy.

The dispatcher assured me someone would pick me up at Shirley's. "I got a trooper on the way right now, Miss Porter. You stay put, please. Hold on a sec."

She paused and I heard voices in the background. Then she was back. "Miss Porter, can you give me more information on the vehicle? You said it was a dark color. Like dark blue, or black? What make? Whatever you can give me, please."

I hesitated, fiddling with the tangled phone cord. I couldn't remember—was there a badge or logo on the truck's tailgate? Ford or Chevy, Dodge or GMC? "Ford, I think. But I'm not sure. Black, or dark blue."

She jumped over my words with her next question. "Stepside or fleetside?"

I closed my eyes, trying to visualize the pickup's side panel from when it fishtailed out of the field. "Uh, it was a long body. So—fleetside. What Ford calls a styleside."

"Like an F-250? Or one of those little ones, like a Ranger?"

"Bigger. Full-size. Half-ton, maybe three-quarter."

"Did you get the plate?"

"No, I was too far away." Then, wanting to be helpful. "But I think the plate had white numbers on a dark background. Maybe black. But it didn't look like a Connecticut plate. Something else."

"So, out-of-state."

"Maybe. I don't know. Just an impression I had."

I bit my lip, hearing Gran's voice. *Don't guess, Agnes Juliet! Don't go making stuff up. If you don't know, just say so.* Guessing worked okay for me in school—all those multiple-choice exams—but not now, not with a killer on the loose. What a hackneyed phrase, killer on the loose—

The dispatcher wasn't done. "Anything else you remember about the truck? Dents, paint, special mirrors? Carrying anything in the bed? We're getting a BOLO out."

"Sorry, it was just a pickup. Nothing special."

"And the driver? Can you describe the driver?"

"I told you, I only caught a glimpse. Like a silhouette."

"About how tall was he?"

"Shit, I don't know. Tall enough to drive a truck."

I bit my lip again. Watch your mouth, AJ. Sarcasm and potty mouth were surefire ways to get canned from a radio job, even when you were off-air. I had a history of skating close to both.

The dispatcher abruptly quit interrogating me. "Okay. Ernie's coming to pick you up at Jellniks' house. Stay right there. Don't go back to the scene on your own. Don't touch anything."

I looked at the blood on my hands and clothes, the phone's receiver, Shirley's dish towel. Too late.

CHAPTER FOUR

AJ

~ 2 ~

I made my second phone call to Mike Gorman, my boss at WWCT. He wasted no time getting to the point.

"Dammit, AJ, I need you back here!" Mike never indulged in small talk, and I appreciated that. As a veteran newsman who prized hard facts over superficial glaze, he was known for his steely focus. Yet now, with the biggest news story Winslow had seen in two decades, his normally steady voice was edged with frustration.

"Sorry, I'm stuck here at Shirley's." My voice was rough, my throat dry. "This is going to run long. And no, I don't know exactly how long. I'll need to go to the barracks and give them a statement."

When news of the murder came in over the newsroom's police scanner ten minutes earlier, Mike's first instinct was to grab a cassette recorder loaded with fresh D-cell batteries and race to the scene. But someone had to stay in the newsroom to field calls, monitor the police scanner, and go on-air with the hourly newscasts. Abandoning the news desk for more than an hour during a daytime shift meant pre-taping a newscast or asking Keith Bousquet, our afternoon deejay, to read.

Keith already had enough to juggle: spinning LPs, delivering live and taped commercials, announcing sports news, reciting the station ID and weather at prescribed intervals, and updating the handwritten log for each segment of his show. He counted on our newscast to take over the airwaves for a few minutes at the top of each hour so he could prep the next hour's music, sports, and commercials.

Neither Mike nor I wanted to drop more work on Keith.

"Sorry," I told my boss. "I have no choice. Maybe I can call in a report from somewhere." Though I wasn't sure where the somewhere would be. There was a pay phone at the police station, but would they let me use it? I'd be reporting on a crime I'd witnessed firsthand, which raised a conflict-of-interest question.

There was also the matter of Jimmy's blood smeared on my car's seat and steering wheel. Would the police let me drive it from Shirley's house to the barracks? Or would it be seized as evidence and held for days, maybe weeks?

"I'll get back to the newsroom as soon as can, " I promised him. "But I can't go to the studio in these clothes. I need to clean up and change."

"Clean up? Why?"

"There's blood."

"Ah." His voice faltered, but he recovered quickly. "Hold on. There's something on the scanner." The staticky hiss of the newsroom's police-band radio filtered through the Jellniks' phone line. "They're setting up roadblocks on 395. And all the state roads."

Interstate 395, our crucial north-south artery, ran parallel to the Rhode Island border through eastern Connecticut from New London to Worcester,

Massachusetts. A roadblock in this region required coordination across three states.

He added, "They're searching for a dark blue or black fleetside Ford pickup with out-of-state plates. Is that what you saw?" His voice was muffled now. He'd probably tucked the receiver between ear and shoulder, tweaking the scanner dials as he took notes.

My throat constricted. Yes, that's what I'd reported. But I'd been guessing on the model and color. Maybe other things, too. What if I was wrong and the killer sped away while everyone hunted for the wrong truck?

"Yeah," I muttered. "I hope I got it right."

"What'd you say, AJ?"

"Nothing. I'll call you later."

"When you're at the barracks, put your reporter hat back on and see if you can squeeze any info from the guy on desk duty. It's probably Billings."

"I'm going there to give a statement, Mike. Not get a story. Trooper Billings won't spill anything to me. I can't function as a reporter on this, I'm a witness."

"Then what *exactly* are you getting paid for?"

That should have hurt but I was too numb. I could only repeat, "But I'm a witness. There are rules."

"So don't act like a reporter, AJ. Just talk to him. Try a new angle. Be charming." He hung up.

I stumbled away through Shirley's mud room and found a cramped laundry room, where a wicker basket was piled with clean folded diapers and a pair of dozing kittens. Leaning over a plastic laundry tub, I stared into a small square of mirror.

The reflection was startling. I recognized the sharp chin, plain brown hair, and overgrown eyebrows—

those were all me, same as always. But behind my silver-rimmed aviators, a pair of very dark eyes with huge, fixed pupils stared back. I looked like a humanoid alien. Something that wandered out of the woods, got tangled in a clothesline, and woke up lost in Shirley's laundry room.

Classic shock symptoms, I supposed. What did the first-responder training recommend? Tea and cookies, maybe.

I scrubbed my hands in the paint-stained sink and slapped cold water on both cheeks. Wiped my glasses with a tissue and tried to tame my unruly hair with a futile finger-combing. The cowlicks won, as they always did, but the familiar actions helped kickstart my brain.

In the kitchen, a familiar song was playing on the Jellniks' tabletop radio. Madonna's sultry lines, about being touched for the very first time, confirmed that Keith—a big Madonna fan—had just begun his afternoon deejay shift.

Shirley appeared in the doorway between kitchen and living room, her face etched with worry. Her arms were empty of baby but the older girls still flanked her like silent sentries. She gestured toward the table. "Please, AJ. Sit down. Can I get you a glass of water?"

"Thanks, water would be great. I won't sit, though, I'm too…dirty. I don't want to mess up your chair."

At the sink, Shirley's voice rose above the rush of running water.

"It's just terrible, Jimmy getting shot right here, practically in our own backyard. I mean, there's stupid hunting accidents every fall. But that's not what this was, is it? Though I didn't know him very well."

She spoke fast, in that jumbled way that people do when unexpected tragedy upends their day. "You know, sometimes I take the girls for a walk up the road past his farm. We love watching the new calves, in the spring. Jimmy always says we should stop in so the girls can watch the four o'clock milking. But I never let them go into the barn alone, of course—"

She paused. "Because—well, you know," she finished lamely.

"What do you mean—"

Madonna was cut off mid-lyric and my boss's voice, heavy with self-importance, boomed from the radio.

"Police across three states," Mike intoned, "are searching for a suspect in the murder of a man in Winslow this morning. Residents are urged to stay off the roads."

He was using his big-news voice, the same tone I'd heard when Reagan ordered the marines out of Beirut or the Democrats nominated a woman vice presidential candidate. Earth-shattering stuff.

"Moments ago," he continued, "a man was shot and killed on Cherry Valley Road—I repeat, Cherry Valley Road in Winslow. Police in Connecticut, Massachusetts, and Rhode Island have set up roadblocks, looking to apprehend a full-size, dark blue or black Ford pickup with out-of-state plates. Police warn the driver is armed and dangerous. The victim's identity is being withheld until the next of kin can be notified. Anyone with information, call nine-one-one or the Connecticut State Police hotline immediately. More details at noon."

I hoped I was right about the truck details. It was now 11:45 and, unless they nabbed a suspect quickly, we *wouldn't* be hearing more details at noon. I finished my water and set the glass down with a clink on Shirley's counter.

A man's heavy knock rattled Shirley's back door. Ernie Walters, our town's resident state trooper, had arrived to escort me to the police station. Standing six-five and powerfully built, his normally cheerful demeanor was subdued beneath a Smokey Bear hat, usually tilted back just enough for his smile to be visible—a smile that was missing today. Ernie always looks a little hunched over from bending down to speak with everyone shorter than him.

We'd spent twelve years of school together, acquaintances more than friends. He'd been the popular sports jock, I was the antisocial loner who cut home-ec to hang out with the geeks and dweebs in chess club. Now he wore his trooper's uniform—gray shirt, navy tie, charcoal pants—as comfortably as he'd worn his black-and-gold basketball uniform ten years earlier.

His face was tight with worry. "Hey, AJ. You doing okay? Looking a bit worse for wear." He turned to Shirley. "Mrs. Jellnik, maybe you have something that AJ can wear? I'll need to bag up her shirt and pants." He glanced at my scuffed loafers, the regular right one and the custom-built left. "And your shoes, too. Then we need to go. I'm your ride."

Shirley and I exchanged looks, comparing sizes. I was two inches taller and quite a bit smaller through the hips—she had three kids to my zero—but whatever replacement clothing she could offer was fine by me. I glanced down at my best navy slacks, the knees stiff with drying blood, and swallowed back a taste of bile. I forced a tentative smile for Shirley's benefit.

"Of course," she said. "I have some clothes I was planning to donate anyways. I'm not sure about the shoes. Maybe some sandals? Can you—" Her eyes slid away from my crooked left foot. "You know, maybe strap them tighter."

She shooed her girls back through the doorway and returned minutes later with a ruffled flower-print shirt and a pair of baby-blue capris cuffed with lace. They were two sizes too large and nothing I'd ever choose, but I wasn't about to protest.

Next she dug out a pair of worn Birkenstock sandals. Also too big, and incapable of holding my orthotic insole, but they'd do if I didn't have to walk far.

In the cramped laundry room, I changed out of my bloody clothes and tossed everything, including loafers and the tea towel, into the paper bag Ernie held. The orthotic insole went into my handbag—he didn't need that, did he?—and followed him to his gray Crown Vic. He held the passenger door open and I felt almost like a celebrity.

"I get to sit in the front?" I said. "I thought you put everybody in the back, behind a screen."

"Nope, no screen. If you were a suspect, I'd cuff your hands behind you and belt you in. But I'd still put you here in the front, where I can keep an eye on you. We only put a person in the back if there's another trooper to ride back there with them."

"Oh. The cop shows have it wrong, then."

"Yup. For this state, anyway." At the end of Shirley's driveway, Ernie swung the cruiser left instead of right.

"We're not going to the barracks?"

"Not immediately. Detective Androski wants you back at the scene first. He's the man in charge."

At the hayfield, Ernie pulled off the road behind three other black-and-whites, their engines idling and blue dome lights quietly spinning. Opposite, a gray unmarked sedan and an ambulance occupied the only spot of shade beneath a solitary oak tree. A trio from the volunteer rescue crew clustered awkwardly around the ambulance's hood, two chatting quietly and the third standing a little apart, smoking. Waiting for the medical examiner's nod to remove Jimmy's body.

The EMTs likely recognized Jimmy as I had, in the usual small-town manner of sharing weather forecasts, helping neighbors capture an escaped cow, or exchanging gossip at a fire department fundraising dinner.

Now that Jimmy was gone, what would happen to his farm? I'd heard his wife wasn't a farmer. Who would care for the livestock, fix the fences or harvest the crops? Perform the twice-daily rituals in the dairy barn, the milking, feeding, and barn-cleaning. Farmwork doesn't end just because someone dies.

Ernie and I climbed out and leaned our butts against the hood of his cruiser, staring across the field and squinting against the searing midday sun.

Thin metal T-stakes, pounded into the ground, were strung with yellow-and-black crime-scene tape, forming a perimeter around Jimmy and his tractor. Two men, one in a blue shirt and tan pants and the other in gray coveralls, crouched beside the body. Beneath a white tent, a cluster of other gray-suited technicians busied themselves with cases and cameras arranged on folding tables.

Everything else remained unchanged, rectangular bales of hay still scattered across the field and goldenrod still arching gracefully over the roadside ditch. Ignoring the sweat trickling beneath Shirley's flowered shirt, I focused on the minute details I might have overlooked. Tire marks where the truck had spun on the grass, how the victim had landed when the blast ripped through him. Things like that.

I didn't know how many lifeless bodies I'd have to see before the scene of a violent death no longer smacked me in the gut, but I knew I wasn't there yet. During my three years at WWCT, I'd seen a couple of fatal auto wrecks and once I glimpsed the charred body of an old man pulled from a house fire. Horrific as those had been, murder by shotgun was far more visceral.

Shifting weight off my left foot, I shivered a little despite the heat. Ernie placed a steadying hand on my shoulder. "How you holding up?"

That was the second time he'd asked. Despite Shirley's donated clothes, I must have looked a mess. "Okay, I guess."

He followed my gaze over the field. "You knew him?"

"Everybody knew him, sort of. It's Jimmy Desjardins. This is his farm." I pronounced it as Jimmy had, duh-JAR-din, the locally accepted way of mangling his French-Canadian surname.

Ernie's hat dipped in acknowledgment. "We still need to notify his wife and have her confirm identity. Don't put his name out there yet, okay?"

He didn't have to tell me. Every news reporter knew not to release a fatality's name before the next-of-kin was notified. That's just common courtesy.

He glanced across the field. "In a minute Detective Androski's gonna come over here and get your account. Where you were, where Jimmy stood when he got shot. Where the truck went. What you gave us before, plus any other details you can remember.

"And while you two talk," Ernie added, "I'll arrange to have your car brought from Shirley's place to the barracks. We need to check it for prints and other things. For comparison and elimination. It shouldn't take long."

My turn to nod. Of course they'd comb through my car. Blood stains on the seat and steering wheel were clearly visible. At the very least, they'd want pictures to corroborate my statement. Print-matching would be easy; they already had me on file from when I'd renewed my press pass last April.

In rural Connecticut, the State Police handle far more than just highway patrol, and all the troopers are trained in basic investigative techniques. So it didn't surprise me that Trooper First Class Ernie Walters would be helping with this investigation.

Connecticut had no county government to speak of, so the SP handled nearly all law enforcement for about 50,000 people spread across 400 square miles. The troopers' roles often stretched into full-on detective work for run-of-the-mill stuff like burglary, larceny, firearms violations, domestic abuse, and property crime. When a crime was more serious or the usual troopers needed help, the investigation got kicked up to the Eastern District Major Crime Squad. Those detectives tackled the big stuff and worked with federal agencies on cases of organized crime, trafficking, kidnapping, felony assault, murder.

Detective Carl Androski, the barrel-chested man crouching now beside the body, had recently joined the Major Crime Squad after a move from Cincinnati. I'd talked with him only once, a month ago after a big drug bust involving an organized crime ring that was trafficking cocaine and heroin from Providence through eastern Connecticut to New Haven.

Androski, with his mild brown eyes and an offhand manner that some misinterpreted as slow or dull, wore his prematurely gray, military-short hair like a badge of gravitas—a façade to bolster the friendly-uncle demeanor. I knew he was only mid-thirties but the rapidly receding hairline added a decade to his looks.

As he strode toward us across the field, the weight of my own attire struck me—Shirley's frilly shirt and baggy capris, the clumsy oversized sandals. Would anyone take me seriously?

"Detective." Ernie nodded to Androski, touched his hat, and stepped away.

"Hello, Miss Porter." Like everyone else, Androski usually addressed me as AJ but that day I was Miss Porter. "Let's find some shade, okay?"

We crossed the road and stood beside his unmarked cruiser, beneath the oak tree. "I'm sorry for all of this," he said. "It must've been a big shock for you.

But now we need your help. Walk me, please, through what you saw. Every little detail."

I began recounting the scene again but he interrupted. "You felt for a pulse. On which wrist?"

"His left. I was kneeling behind him and reaching over his back. Trying to avoid the—" I swallowed hard. "The blood. His chest was…gone."

"I understand." His face softened. "Even though you thought he was dead, you checked for a pulse?"

"Instinct, I guess. I've had some first responder training."

"We found blood on the tractor's steering wheel."

We both glanced at my now-clean hands. "It was Jimmy's. I grabbed the steering wheel after I checked his pulse. The tractor's engine was still running so I had to climb up the step to shut it off."

"Why did you do that?"

"I couldn't stand the noise."

Nodding, he fixed his gaze on the spot where the pickup had parked. Small orange flags marked where tires had flattened the grass. "When the pickup left, did it go straight away or did the tires spin?"

"The tires spun, just for a second. It slid a little sideways."

"Probably not a four-wheel-drive, then."

A detail I hadn't thought of. "I guess not."

"Was the truck at all familiar? Have you seen it before?"

"I don't think so. It was just an ordinary pickup. I was pretty far away."

"People personalize their trucks. Roll bars, pipe racks, towing mirrors, a tool box in the bed. Anything like that? On a farm truck, the older ones, there's maybe dents or rust. Any distinct sounds? Maybe a loose muffler, the engine sputtering."

"No, nothing."

"How well did you know the victim?"

"I saw him around town. That's all."

"And you saw no one else? No other vehicles near the farm?"

"No one. No vehicles." I'd said this several times.

"Do you think the driver saw you?"

A chill prickled my arms.

"No." I turned to look up the hill toward the stop sign where I'd sat yesterday morning, so long ago, admiring the view. "I was coming out of the shade, beneath the trees at the end of Turnbull. The truck drove away while I was still pretty far off. He'd have had to turn completely around to see me." At least I hoped so.

Androski looked to where I indicated, then swept his gaze east along the ridge to the old red barn.

"What about over there, by that barn? There were reports last week of vandalism up there. Graffiti, trash. Signs of a campfire."

"The Grabtown barn? I didn't see anyone up there."

Androski leaned in on that. "Grabtown. Why's it called that?"

"You don't know about that? It's famous."

"Indulge me. I've only been here a few months, and the local troopers handle the misdemeanors. Something has to get bumped up to a felony before it lands on my desk."

"It's just a nickname. There was a whole village up there, years ago, called Graves Parish. Now it's just a couple of trails through the woods, some old foundations, and that barn. On the maps it's still Grave's Parish but most people just call it Grabtown. That's where local kids go to party."

He raised a questioning eyebrow.

"There's a big hayloft, and a shed, where Jimmy used to store things like extra hay and tractor parts. The local kids mess around in there because it's remote, there's no houses nearby. They break the hay bales apart, then climb up on the beams and jump down into the loose hay."

"Isn't it locked? How do they get in?"

"There's nothing to lock, the doors fell off ages ago. The town took over the property for back taxes. Everyone says it's a hazard, it should be demolished. Except the historic preservation society wants to restore it, but they don't have any money so it just kind of sits there. And if they pull that barn down, the teenagers will just find another one. There's plenty of places like that around here, old barns and sheds no one's using anymore."

"Anybody ever start a fire or break a leg there? Get smothered under a pile of hay?"

"When I was in eighth grade, a high school girl killed herself there." My voice caught a little. I hadn't thought about Brenda in years.

He frowned. "But the name Grabtown?"

Did I need to spell it out?

"Because of what happens there. It's kind of a rite of passage, for the boys anyway. They take their dates there, scare them in the dark, grab a feel, and maybe get laid."

"You grew up here, then. So you know what went on up there."

Was he suggesting I'd been one of those girls getting grabbed? What did this have to do with Jimmy's murder? I bristled. "Only from what people say. I didn't date much in high school. Too busy working."

Changing gears, Androski pressed. "Anyone you can think of who might want to kill Jimmy Desjardins?"

"Sorry, no."

Thunder rumbled distantly, warning of a possible storm. The hairs on my arms prickled again, charged by static or dread.

He walked us back across the road and asked Ernie to drive me to the barracks.

To me he said, "We'll get a statement typed up for your signature and then you can go. We should be done with your car by then, too. Thanks, AJ."

At least I'd get my car back sometime today.

***

Cassie stops reading to puzzle over a red-penciled comment at the bottom of the page: *Good foreshadowing—I can see it clearly*, with a winking smiley face drawn in. It's clearly more of her mother's handwriting, but why was she providing editorial feedback? Their mom was a physical therapist, not a writer or an editor. The only things Cassie had ever seen her mother write, aside from her case reports, were family newsletters and an occasional letter to their congressman.

She turns pages and discovers more notes, line edits in blue pencil and margin notes in red. As a high school sophomore in '01, Cassie doesn't remember AJ working on a book. But AJ had apparently written this—about a real murder?—and her mother had apparently helped edit it.

How strange it is to read, too, about their father Keith in his early-days job as a disc jockey. He'd always said he loved that job. And it must have suited him, she thinks. His quick-talking voice and all that enthusiasm, bordering on hyperactivity. She imagines him sometimes as a lovable, distractable hound dog, trying hard to stay on the trail but ready to follow any kid with a cookie.

After Cassie's ADHD diagnosis, her dad was the most sympathetic member of her family. Now she feels a stronger compassion for him, a young father-to-be struggling with new responsibilities in a small-town job that paid shit. And compassion also for their mother, pregnant with twins.

Staring at the page she's just read, Cassie touches the name Androski. That's the name her mother wrote on the front of the old phone book. It must have been this guy, Detective Carl Androski of the State Police Eastern Regional Crime Squad.

Is he also the Carl who brought the black-eyed Susans to Marla Bousquet's funeral? AJ's story pegged his age at mid-thirties in 1985, making him in his mid-seventies now.

She moves through the manuscript, skimming rapidly. She finds more editing notes from her mother and then her mother's name in the text, not just once but several times. But it's impossible to tell what's really happening without reading it in sequence.

The last chapter ends as AJ seems about to interview someone. An unfinished novel. Is it even worth reading?

She returns to the end of the second chapter and dog-ears a corner to mark her place, then squares the stack and stands.

"Ana, look what—"

But Ana is gone.

CHAPTER FIVE

Cassie

Cassie stands, swaying a little, and lifts her wineglass from the railing. It's teeming with small gnats or fruit flies attracted to the warm wine she's forgotten to drink. After pouring the dirty liquid into a flower bed, she carries glass and manuscript inside.

Ana props her reading glasses on top of her head and begins feeding pages into a paper shredder next to the kitchen table. She raises her voice over the grinding. "I hope I wasn't making too much noise while you were working. Maybe you can turn AJ's novel into a play and get famous."

Cassie's too preoccupied with what she's just read to catch the sarcasm. "Ana, let me tell you about it—"

Ana's stuffing pages in, too many and too fast. The effort brings a sheen of sweat to her face, and a hank of damp hair has escaped its scrunchy. The machine grinds, jams, whines.

Cassie frowns at the noise. "Turn that thing off, would you?"

Ana pulls the plug and begins yanking out jammed paper. "So yeah, go ahead, tell me about AJ's story. Or should I just read it myself?"

"So back in 1985, there's this murder—"

"Actually, forget it. I don't have the time. *We* don't have the time. But there you are, reading some stupid story—"

Cassie catches up to Ana's anger. "Whoa, hey. What's this about? I know you're pissed with me about never being around —"

Ana starts a retort but Cassie talks over her. "Please, Ana, listen. It's about Mom. I need you to understand. AJ's story opens with the murder of this farmer, here in Winslow. And Mom was helping AJ write it or edit it or something. But she's in the story, too. As a character."

"Mom? What was she, the murderer's secret girlfriend or something?" Ana's anger has been sidetracked but her attention is split. She's still fiddling with the shredder.

Wanting to explain this to Ana sharpens Cassie's focus. "It takes place in 1985, while she was pregnant with us."

She waves the manuscript to hold her sister's attention. "I've only read the first few pages but it starts out with this guy, Jimmy Desjardins. A farmer, here in Winslow. He was a neighbor, a real person. Until he got murdered."

She grabs the 1985 phone book from the table and shows Ana where she's bent back the pages to highlight the D's. "See where it says 'gone'? Mom wrote that note in there."

Ana sits back, one hand holding a fistful of confetti strips, but now she's listening. Her forehead knits into a small frown. "Mom and Dad never said anything about that."

Cassie carries her phone to a front window. "I think it's real. I'll Google it." She taps, swears, and stabs at the Search icon while Ana pulls more fragments of financial records out of the shredder.

The browser is maddeningly slow but after several seconds of scowling and muttering, Cassie finds what she's looking for.

"Got it. Here's a story in *The Manchester Journal-Observer*, August 18, 1985." She clears her throat. "'Police continue searching for one or more suspects in the murder of a Winslow man, 42-year-old James Desjardins, who was killed four days ago while working on his farm on Cherry Valley Road.' With a shotgun, it says." She scrolls. "Here's another article, on the one-year anniversary of the murder. Nothing new, police are still looking. That's all there is. Looks like they never found the murderer."

"A shotgun?" Ana's frown deepens. "But I don't understand. What's Mom doing in the story?"

"I don't know yet. And it looks like the second half is missing."

"But why did Mom leave it for you—"

"Dammit, Ana. I don't know. Here, read it yourself." Cassie drops the stack of loose pages onto the table. The pile slides and scatters, sending several sheets onto the floor. Some of Ana's bank records catch the draft and slide off the table.

"Damn it, Cassie." Ana's anger flashes again as she drops to her knees, chasing statements. "You're so careless! Now everything's a mess. No, I don't want to read it. Mom left it for you, and I don't care what you do with it. Toss it or burn it. Or, sure, go ahead, steal AJ's story and turn it into your own project. Make money with it, sell it, whatever. Just leave Mom out of it, okay? You've stolen enough from her already." Her eyes fill with tears. She rolls into a sitting position, her back against a table leg. She's clutching bank statements to her chest with one hand and swiping at her nose with the other.

Suddenly contrite, Cassie crouches to scoop scattered papers into an untidy pile. Sorting AJ's story from Ana's paperwork, she squares the pages on a corner of the kitchen counter and anchors the stack with a pepper grinder.

"Ana, I'm so sorry." Cassie kneels on the wide wooden planks of the kitchen floor beside her sister and now she's crying too, a full torrent of tears that run in rivulets down the creases of her face and dripping from her chin to the floor. They bump shoulders awkwardly and Ana slings an arm around Cassie, who sags into the embrace.

"I'm trying to get this right," Ana wails. "But I've never done it before. It's impossible, nothing's right, and there's too much to do. I miss her so much and I feel like I'm just flailing around. And I miss her, did I say that?"

"Yes." Cassie can't think of anything else to say so she repeats it through her own weeping. "Yes. Yes." She's silent then, holding her twin who's not so much a twin as a big sister, and they rock a little together until both have run out of tears.

It's been years since they've held each other like this, not since first grade or maybe kindergarten. Maybe younger.

After several minutes, their tears have eased to hiccups and sniffles. Cassie crawls from beneath the table as Ana stands to locate a box of tissues.

Ana blows her nose, passes a tissue to her twin. "We need to sort this out, okay? This thing between us."

"Now? It's after eleven. I'm too tired. What time tomorrow are you meeting the estate-sale people?"

"At ten. I'll sign a contract and they'll explain the process. I think I know how it works but maybe you should talk with them, too. And it's only, like, 8:15 California time. You can't be tired."

"No, but I bet you are." On her feet now, Cassie leans against the gray Formica countertop, a wadded up tissue still in one hand. "Okay, then," she sighs. "What did you mean about me stealing from Mom? I never stole anything from her. Not that I recall, anyway. Well, maybe some M and M's."

"No jokes. Please, Cassie." Ana's red-rimmed eyes slide away from Cassie's face and she falls silent. Abruptly, she heads for the kitchen and busies herself with the teakettle.

"Her love," she says over one shoulder. "That's what you stole. The love you never seemed to return. Her time and attention. And money, too. Money for college, that you said you'd repay but never did. Did you know she took out a second mortgage on the house so you could go to Berkeley? Then you dropped out, and didn't tell her for months."

Cassie stiffens, then runs a hand through her hair, pulling the short strands upright. Her first instinct is to fight back, to think of a snarky retort. Instead, she pushes herself away from the counter and follows Ana to the stove. "I was too embarrassed," she admits. I meant to pay her back, I just couldn't. I spent everything on rent and a car. And then— Well, she never said anything, so I figured it was a gift."

"Mom kept working for three years after she'd planned to retire, just to pay it off. Did you know that?"

"I thought she wanted—" But the truth is, Cassie has never thought much about what her mother wanted. She'd spent her tuition money on rent, yes, but also alcohol and drugs, parties and clothes.

Have I always been that selfish?

Ana pulls two teabags from a box of chamomile. "We all tried so hard with you, Cass. I know it was tough for you in school, the ADHD and whatever else they diagnosed you with. But even earlier, when we were, like, four or five, you'd wake up every day angry at the world." Ana's not yet ready to forgive.

"You came into a room," she continues, "and it was like a tornado landing, sucking all the air out. And all those small cruelties. Like when Sara MacDonald showed you her bruised hand. Instead of sympathizing, you grabbed it and squeezed."

Cassie colors. She steps away and falls silent, remembering the sting of being diagnosed with the disorders in second grade. Getting pulled out of class twice a week for counseling or therapy, whatever they called it back then. A special class for dysgraphia because she had trouble learning to write, and a weekly visit with a psychologist for a newly identified condition, oppositional defiant disorder. The other kids called her a psycho.

Being a twin was supposed to give her a permanent best friend in the lunchroom, but even Ana shunned her for most of third grade.

Cassie rubs her scalp again. Hard, using both hands this time. She slides her palms down over her face and pauses for a moment, eyes closed behind her spread hands. The familiar frustration rises but she pushes it back and drops her hands with a small sigh. "I couldn't help it, Ana. You know that. It's just who I was, I don't know why. But I've grown out of it. That's what my therapist tells me, anyway. I put all the anger into my writing now."

But there it is again, the lie. She hasn't written more than a few pages of a story or script in more than a year. She has boxes full of first pages, first scenes and unfinished script treatments.

You can't be a writer if you don't write.

She'd had that one well-received story in *The Atlantic* more than a decade ago, a few years after she met Marsh. She's often thought that's why he wanted to marry her, the brightest new light on the national literary scene. Then, nothing else published or even finished to her liking. Somehow, she's toppled into a black hole. A grand fugue of suspended animation that writer's block doesn't begin to describe.

Cassie starts again. "Marsh thinks—"

"Marsh thinks what?" Ana abandons the teakettle and turns toward Cassie. "That you've been bullied by your family? That we're toxic? Because that's what I remember you said to me, years ago."

Cassie takes another step away and frowns. "When did I say that?"

"On that phone call, three years ago. Just before AJ died. When Mom invited us all out here for a nice family reunion. We ate barbecue in the back yard and toasted s'mores on the fire. Rented kayaks at the lake—"

"We couldn't come, you know that—"

Ana's words roll over Cassie's protests. "Mom even invited Dad and Melanie, who drove all the way from Chicago in that big stupid RV of theirs. They had a terrible time turning that thing around in the driveway. Backed over the mailbox, actually, and everyone laughed after AJ got done being furious. But you and Marsh? You couldn't be bothered."

Ana stops for breath.

Cassie's voice wavers. "Marsh worries about me, Ana. About where all that anger came from when I was little. He reads all these articles about childhood trauma, and he thinks—he wonders—if maybe something happened that I don't remember. Or that I've blocked out." Her eyes slide away, fixing on a stack of empty boxes in the far corner of the kitchen. "He says it would explain a lot."

Ana's hazel eyes widen, then narrow in suspicion. "'Something happened?' Like what?"

"I don't know. Maybe...maybe someone hurt me? When we were kids?" Cassie's voice gets smaller. "He's not trying to blame anyone. He just wants to understand why I was so angry all the time. He says it's not normal for a little kid to have that much rage unless—"

"Unless what?" Ana steps closer and grabs Cassie's shoulders, forcing her to look up. "Cassie, listen to yourself! Who was supposed to have done that? And when, for gods' sakes? We were together all the time. That's completely insane."

"I don't know who, or when. I know it sounds crazy, but—"

"It doesn't just *sound* crazy, it *is* crazy. He's messing with your head." Ana's voice rises. "I get it, okay? You were an angry kid because you had learning disabilities, and the other kids were cruel. Because the teachers didn't know how to help you. Because you felt different and frustrated and misunderstood. It scared you, and I get that. That's enough trauma, without inventing some boogeyman molester. He's gaslighting you, Cassie. Or he's projecting. Maybe *he's* the damaged one."

Cassie falls silent, trying to sort through Ana's words and her own blurred confusion. Part of her knows Ana is probably right. But Marsh was so gentle when he'd brought it up, so concerned. He'd held her while she cried out her old frustrations, stroking her hair and telling her it wasn't her fault. That she was brave for surviving whatever had happened.

"Why on earth did you marry that man, anyway?" Ana demands. Her face is just inches from Cassie's.

The question hangs in the air like a sour fog as Cassie tries to find words. "He made me feel special. He took care of me, at a time when I'd bottomed out. I'd dropped out of school, I was getting evicted—"

Ana frowns and steps back, releasing her sister's shoulders. She drops into a chair, the teakettle forgotten.

Cassie follows her to the table and tries again, her voice gaining strength as she talks of her early days with Marsh. "He was so different from anyone I'd ever dated."

"Older. Lots older."

"Well, yeah. But he didn't *seem* twelve years older. We listened to the same music, watched the same movies. He was successful, and he introduced me to successful people. We'd go to these amazing restaurants and he'd tell me stories about his clients that had me laughing until my ribs hurt. He *listened*. He made me feel like I was the only woman in the room."

She pauses, lost in earlier memories. "And he believed in my writing when no one else did. Everyone else was telling me it was shitty, that I should give up and get a real job. But Marsh read my stories and said I had real talent. He said I just needed time and his support to develop it."

She didn't mention how that early encouragement had gradually shifted into suggestions for improvement, then earnest corrections, then not-so-gentle critiques that left her second-guessing every word.

"And he had money," she continues stubbornly, "so I didn't have to work. I could spend all my time writing. And he had contacts. Other writers, editors, agents. He'd throw these incredible parties, and suddenly I was moving in a crowd of successful people. People who seemed to take me seriously."

She leaves out how the wonderful parties always seemed to deteriorate into more-fabulous-than-you competitions among Marsh's wealthier friends. How, later, the little bags of white powder came out and everything looked bright and promising again, just for a little while. Until the successful people gradually stopped returning her calls and she learned that some of Marsh's contacts weren't at all what they'd claimed to be.

"It was all so easy," she continues quietly. "The months slipped away, months became years, and I sort of stopped thinking about traveling back east to see family. Vacations in Tuscany and Rio were easy; visits to my family became...complicated."

She sometimes wonders what signal she'd given to Marsh, something that told him that this distance from her mother and sister was what she wanted. Because she'd never really wanted that, had she? It just sort of happened, like so many things in her life with Marsh. Bills paid, house cleaned, dinners arranged — all without her having to lift a finger.

Ana returns to the stove and switches off the teakettle. She speaks into the pause. "So tell me a little more about Marsh. You said he grew up in Rhode Island, right? How'd he end up in California?"

"His family's from some little town not far from here, just over the line. He doesn't remember his father, who disappeared when Marsh was little. His mom got married again and his stepfather was really rough on him. I met his mom once. She came to our wedding, but then she died about a year after that. There's a couple of older brothers, Conan or Conrad and...I've forgotten the other one. They had some kind of falling out, years ago. Marsh never mentions them."

Cassie takes a mug from Ana and pulls two chairs from the table. They sit, fanning the hot tea and sipping gingerly.

"He doesn't like talking about his past," Cassie adds. "Says it's better to focus on the future."

"Well, he still sounds like a damn manipulator," Ana declares. "Making you doubt your own memories, your own family. Keeping you isolated out there while he fills your head with theories about imaginary abuse. Can't you see what he's doing?"

Cassie sighs. "I don't know, Ana. Sometimes—"

The phone shrills from its table by the front door. Both women startle, and Cassie's tea sloshes. She reaches for a napkin and their eyes lock.

"Speaking of the devil," Cassie says weakly. They trade glances.

It rings again, assaulting the quiet. Ana protests, "It's eleven-thirty." But she's already taken a step toward the phone.

Cassie raises her voice. "Leave it, Ana. I'll call him tomorrow. He's probably at a layover in Honolulu, halfway to Hong Kong. He'll be pissed because he wanted me to call this evening and I forgot. He'll leave a message on the answering machine."

Ana stops but her hand still hovers. The lifetime habit of a dutiful daughter, wife, professional woman. She shakes her head. "He can't leave a message. It stopped working so I disconnected it. I should've bought a new one—"

"There must be a volume control for the ringer. Maybe on the bottom of the phone?"

They remain motionless. After ten jangling peals, the ringing stops.

Ana lets out a breath. "Bedtime." She pivots for the stairs, her tea forgotten. "We'll get back to this tomorrow, okay?"

"Yeah, tomorrow," Cassie agrees, though she isn't sure what Ana means by "get back to this tomorrow"— the work, or their conversation, fraught with so many years of hurt and misunderstanding.

She's suddenly very tired, feeling again the weight of too much alcohol or something else.

But she can't sleep yet. AJ's story is waiting upstairs.

CHAPTER SIX

AJ

~ 3 ~

Ernie dropped me off at the squat brick building that housed the Troop D barracks, the regional unit of our state police force. Built in 1903 to provide living quarters as well as office space and holding cells, the three-story brick building sat in a sloped parking lot of cracked, uneven asphalt. Four temporary office units, essentially house trailers, had been squeezed in behind the main building.

At the front desk, Trooper Billings introduced me to Carlos Reyna, a fresh-faced uniform who led me upstairs and down a narrow hallway to a small room with three chairs, a desk, a typewriter, and a tape recorder. A few minutes later, Androski joined us. He took the third chair and sat silently as Reyna began the interview.

"Name and address, please," Reyna instructed.

"Agnes Juliet Porter." I added my address.

He lifted an eyebrow. "But you go by AJ."

"Yes."

I hadn't yet found a way to change it legally. No court clerk that I knew would allow a woman to call herself "AJ" without a legal battle, requiring money I didn't have.

"And where do you work?" he asked.

We went again through the familiar questions. I thought I was using my best radio voice for the recording, but when Reyna re-played it for me, I sounded hesitant and a bit shaky. I considered asking for a do-over but decided I didn't care enough.

After Reyna left to transcribe the statement for my signature, Androski escorted me back downstairs to his office, a space only slightly larger than the interview closet. He moved a teetering pile of papers from a chair to the floor.

"Please, sit. Mainframe upgrades," he explained. "Once we iron out the bugs, everything will be transferred to disk. Or so they tell me. Until then, we're stuck in the dark ages, drowning in paperwork."

He settled into his desk chair and leaned back a little. "AJ, I need to remind you we're in a bit of a peculiar situation here. You're a reporter, but you're also our primary witness to what appears to be a serious felony. Our only witness. How do you plan to handle that?"

"I'll be all right—"

He interrupted. "Let me be clear. You're in a tricky position. We have to handle this carefully so there's no conflict between witness and reporter, okay? I don't want anything to come up that a defense attorney could use to argue for a mistrial. Assuming, of course, we charge someone and this goes to trial."

He added a scowl for emphasis. "We need you to stay hands-off with your news reporting. You can't be an active reporter, poking around and asking questions. I don't even want you *reading* this story live on air, because that makes it sound like you're the reporter. If you're getting paid to cover this story, it's a conflict."

"You're saying I can't do my job." A rotating fan described its half-turns on top of a bookcase, but the room still felt uncomfortably warm.

"I'm saying that your boss, or someone else, has to do the interviews, write the stories, and record them in his voice. Then it's okay if you play the tapes in your newscasts." He flattened his hand on a stack of folders as if swearing on a bible. "Promise me you won't have your name attached to any news reports about this murder. We need you to be a completely unbiased witness. Otherwise, any testimony you give can be questioned or even tossed out. It's called 'fruit of the poisoned tree.' If we had evidence, your testimony wouldn't matter as much, but right now you're all we've got."

He threaded a pencil through his fingers, waiting for me to assure him I wouldn't sink the testimony he needed.

I tried to work out what he was saying. Until I finish testifying—at a potential trial with an unknown date for a suspect who hadn't yet been caught—Androski wanted someone else to report on this story? That meant Mike would have to do all of it. *Every day we run a story about the murder, he'll have to leave a batch of pre-recorded tape cartridges for me to play on the afternoon newscasts. And he'll need to be on call 24/7 to handle potential updates and developments.*

If I were Mike, I'd promptly fire me and hire someone else.

"Another thing," Androski continued in a milder tone. "I know it's nearly impossible to keep things quiet around here. People know you witnessed Jimmy Desjardins getting killed. We still don't know who did it, or why, and everyone wants answers. That's only natural. They're gonna be jumpy until this guy is caught.

"But you're facing more than just the challenge of deciding what airs in the next newscast. Until we can figure out who's involved, I need you to keep a low profile. Don't discuss this case with anyone. Please, don't go anywhere alone—not just because we'll need you to appear as a witness, but also for your own safety.

"And don't let any other reporters coax you into talking to them about it. No talk shows, no interviews. Just stay unavailable, okay?"

Going out alone? Talking to people I don't know? But that's my job. I didn't know what to say so I gave him a half-nod. Then I stood, assuming we were finished.

But he wasn't done. "Jimmy Desjardins' place. Have you ever been inside his house or the barns?"

I sat back down. "Inside his house, no. The milking barn, yes. My grandmother took me there a couple of times when I was little. Jimmy and his parents invited kids in sometimes to watch the milking."

I didn't mention the Grabtown barn. Technically, that one belonged to the town.

Androski glanced at his watch. "We're notifying his next of kin. There should be a trooper talking with his wife right now."

"Can we—sorry, can *Mike* say you've ID'd the victim?"

He scowled. "No questions, AJ. You're a witness. Keep out of it."

He placed both hands flat on the desk, indicating yes, now we were done. Trooper Reyna appeared at the office door with my typed statement and Androski waved him in.

"It must have been a terrifying experience," Androski said sympathetically, perhaps for Reyna's benefit. "I'm sorry you got caught up in this mess. Stay safe, AJ. Don't do anything reckless."

He added, "We're releasing your car. Ernie even offered to clean it up a little. You're good to go."

After scrawling my signature in several places, I found a pay phone near the front desk and called Mike, letting him know I'd be at the radio station in twenty minutes. When I summarized what Androski had said about building a wall between reporter-me and witness-me, Mike snorted, grumbled, and grudgingly said he'd figure it out somehow.

Waiting outside for Ernie to bring my car around, I felt the wind pick up. Black clouds climbed higher in the sky and a few fat drops of rain spattered down, hissing as they struck the hot asphalt.

I thanked Ernie for wiping the blood off the seat and steering wheel but didn't ask when I'd get my custom-made loafers back. I'd probably have to file an insurance claim to get those replaced.

I absolutely did not stop to chat with Trooper Billings at the front desk.

***

Cassie sits back and rubs her eyes. She remembers AJ's clubfoot and the clunky shoes she always wore, the specially made loafers and high-top sneakers.

Mom went into physical therapy so she could help people like AJ. That was Mom, saving the world, one body part at a time.

Can she turn AJ's story into the script for a play? Not easily; the settings are mostly outdoors. A screenplay, then. The streaming services are always looking for new content. Murder mysteries and historical fiction pull good market share, and the tropes are certainly popular—quiet little town, spooky old barn, farmer killed in a hayfield.

It could work, assuming there are some clever plot twists. And someone solves the murder in the end.

CHAPTER SEVEN

Cassie

Early Thursday morning, Cassie stands on the front porch, curling her bare toes against the weathered planks and trying to clear the sluggish, top-heavy fog in her head.

Overnight showers washed the air clean, settling the dust on the dirt road and replacing sticky humidity with a fresh breeze. She takes a deep, slightly shaky breath and recognizes the green-earth fragrance of the geraniums in their hanging baskets. They look a little wilted, and she realizes the porch overhang prevented last night's rain from reaching them. Their mother's geraniums are decades old, and it would be a shame to neglect them now.

There's a watering can on the floor at the far end of the porch. She fills it at an outside spigot and gives each basket a good soak, then plucks a few spent blooms. Wondering, who will take Mom's geraniums?

Ana the nurturer, probably. Every autumn since college, Ana has spent a weekend here at the farmhouse, helping their mom ready the gardens for winter. Trimming shrubs, mulching, and bringing the potted plants inside for shelter against the cold. Not just the geraniums, but all the tender perennials—Gerber daisies, begonias, African violets.

The geraniums and African violets always spent their winters on a small table in front of a living room window, close to where AJ and Marla set up the Christmas tree each December. For Cassie and Ana, the childhood smell of Christmas wasn't only spiced apple and gingerbread, it was geraniums. Not the fragrance from the flowers—the blooms are scentless—but the earthy green smell of the plants themselves. Standing near the base of the stairs on Christmas morning, wearing their flannel nightgowns, faces bright with delight, they'd smelled those geraniums before anything else.

Maybe she and Ana could share them now. Sort of a peace offering, two plants each. But she'd never get hers on the plane, and how would geraniums heal the chasm that still yawns between them?

Cassie can't believe she told Ana about Marsh's hurtful accusations of abuse. It must have been the wine talking.

She doesn't really believe anyone in her family abused her, does she? That's absurd. Marsh was just being Marsh when he said that, always so protective of her. She knows he was raised in a rough family, where trust was a rare commodity. He was probably speaking from his own experience, though he'd never admit it.

Still, she should've kept her mouth shut.

In the kitchen, her sister is toasting bagels. Their mom's old countertop radio is tuned to WWCT and Cassie hears the rapid-fire, boyish chatter of the morning DJ. She thinks of their father sitting there in a small glassed-in studio like the current announcer. Speaking into an old-fashioned microphone, playing vinyl LPs on a pair of turntables. That was his job for the first two years after they were born, before he got the advertising job in Boston. Before their parents' marriage began its long, slow slide into separation, then divorce.

Ana asks brightly, "Do you want to be part of the estate sale discussion this morning, or just stay in the background?"

"Background, please. You've set it up, you know what's in the house. I can take some boxes of clothes to the donation center while you're doing that."

"Coffee?"

"Yes, thanks."

There will be no time to air their issues this morning. They'll just have to remain civil and get the work done.

Cassie's loading boxes and bags into her rented Volvo when Ana appears on the porch, shading her eyes from sunlight reflecting off the car's windshield. The day will heat up quickly.

Ana says, "Are you going to call Marsh back this morning?"

"I should, shouldn't I? Though I have no idea where he is now or what time it is there. Where's a good place to call from? Does Winslow finally have a decent coffeeshop with WiFi?"

"Several, believe it or not. The whole business district has Wi-Fi. That's why I never installed a hotspot in this house. Jonathan and the kids know they can call on Mom's landline, and I was catching up with emails and texts by going into town for an hour or two each afternoon while the visiting nurse was here." Ana slides the bagels onto plates and hands one to Cassie. "It was nice, actually. No distractions. I did a lot of reading while Mom slept. When she was awake, sometimes she asked me to read to her. She loved her Agatha Christies."

It's another tiny window into her sister's relationship with their mother. Cassie feels again the hollow touch of regret, seasoned with old-fashioned envy. She never read aloud to their mother. Never even thought about it.

I could have done a Zoom call and read to her, while she was bedridden. Marsh and I could've paid to have a WiFi hotspot installed…

Cassie grabs her laptop case along with her phone and the car keys. Maybe she'll find a quiet café where she can work on a few story ideas.

She unloads three boxes at the donation center's small warehouse on the edge of Winslow, then heads into town. When was the last time she was here? Twenty years, at least. Then, the business district consisted of a cluster of struggling stores and small diners. She remembers a bakery, an A&P, a butcher shop, an Army surplus store, and the Bradley Playhouse, a century-old vaudeville theater featuring third-run movies for three dollars. Antique stores had come and gone along Front Street, alternating spaces with donut shops and vacant storefronts. Cracked pavement and a multitude of potholes testified to the town's general state of disrepair in the 1990s.

But at some point in the past two decades, Winslow found a measure of prosperity. Cassie drives slowly along Front Street, noting that nearly all the shops have been refurbished and repainted. Signs advertise yoga and pottery classes, home décor and art studios. A craft brewery and a new bookshop advertise Saturday afternoon open-mic music and poetry readings. Cafés offer vegan options, fresh-ground coffee, and pizzas made with fresh figs and balsamic drizzle. The Bradley's bright new marquee features comedy shows, musicals, and dance recitals.

Cassie parks the Volvo in a freshly paved lot and walks along the path to the riverside park where the Pennetucket River still flows past the squat brick building that houses the radio station and on down through the business district. Where there used to be only a narrow strip of worn grass and weedy gravel hugging the riverbank, there's now a broad green lawn with a Victorian-inspired bandstand, paved bike paths, historical plaques and outdoor sculptures set beside well-tended flower gardens.

The footbridge over the falls has been rebuilt and widened, with separate paths for walkers and cyclists. The original low wooden railings have been replaced with five-foot-high bars of polished steel, the gaps filled with wire mesh to keep children and animals from falling through to the rushing water below.

Halfway across the bridge Cassie pauses, resting her hands on the smooth handrail. She looks down into the turbulent water below the dam, then upriver to the smooth surface of the millpond. From thirty feet up, the water looks cool and inviting, but she knows there are rocks just below the surface. After a heavy rain, the current is strong near the dam, and the falls are especially treacherous. Caution signs have been posted along the shore and a yellow cable with floats, strung across the river fifty yards upstream, warns kayakers to turn for shore before the current drags them over the dam.

She continues over the bridge and up a short, steep hill to find an unexpected bonus: not one but two coffee shops right in the center of town. Both advertise freshly ground coffee, lattés, cappuccinos, award-winning homemade pastries, and free WiFi.

"The pandemic," the teenage barista says as she hands Cassie a latté and a warm croissant. She's wearing a skinny black tank top, leggings, ballet slippers, lots of facial hardware, and full-sleeve tattoos. Feeling suddenly old and stodgy, Cassie realizes that she's old enough to be this girl's mother. Old enough, even, to be a grandmother.

"Come again?" Cassie says.

"You asked what happened," the girl explains brightly. "The way the town changed. I read this thing online. During the COVID lockdown, people discovered Winslow. They wanted to get out of Boston and Providence, so they came here." She's got a rough South Boston voice so Boston renders as Baaw-stuhn and Cassie suspects she's relating her own experience.

"Housing's way cheaper here," Southie adds. "And hey, if you can live here but work from home, and you can still pull down a big-city salary, well, it's a no-brainer, right? But city people want all their stuff, too. Restaurants, parks, healthcare. Good schools. The town smartened up and put in fiberoptic for WiFi, and here we are. It sounds kinda morbid, but yeah, if you think about it, it's all because of COVID. Weird, huh?"

Cassie carries her coffee and croissant to a vacant table with charging outlets and a window view of the playhouse across the street. Pulling out her cellphone, she figures the time in Hong Kong. Ten AM Thursday in Winslow, Connecticut, means ten PM Friday in Hong Kong. It's the perfect time to call Marsh, but her mind skitters away from deciding what to say. Resolving to finish her latté before calling, she muses instead about the barista's words.

Nothing like a global pandemic to drive people to the countryside. Cassie knows many people in the west-coast arts world who suffered terribly from the lockdown—from the awful isolation and financial hardship, if not from the ravages of the disease itself. It's hard to relate, because she and Marsh experienced only minimal disruption. They simply stayed home in his big house in Palos Verdes. She mostly lounged by the pool, organized their grocery deliveries, and occupied the rest of her time with writing. Trying to write.

But if she's being honest, the left-coast people aren't really her friends. When she told a few of them about her mother's death, only a couple sent texts or emails. No one bothered to send an actual sympathy card. Was that not a thing anymore? Only one person, a producer whom she'd once helped re-write a spec script, sent a bouquet to the funeral. Or, she assumed, his assistant sent it.

But what did she expect? She didn't mention her mother's death to everyone. How could she work that into conversations about story pitches and the art center's autumn gala? It didn't seem relevant to anything in that life.

Now, after only a few days back in Connecticut, it's her California life that feels unimportant, unreal. Out of sight, out of mind.

And why am I so reluctant to call my husband? Don't I miss him?

She swallows the last of the croissant, finishes her coffee, and pulls her laptop out of its sleeve. A small black device also slides out and she remembers Marsh telling her that he'd bought her a new high-capacity storage drive. It's about the size and shape of a credit card but ten times thicker, with a short cable and a rubber coating to protect it against damage. Four terabytes of memory, he'd said. Loads of room for videos and high-res photos.

He's always buying extra hard drives for his business, filling them with hours of detailed videos depicting vintage cars. Custom-built car parts, repairs and restorations, how-to videos for potential buyers and new owners.

She knows the storage devices are vital for his business, but she doesn't really need all that storage space for her writing. All she has to keep track of are a few notes and revisions for other people's scripts, an album of photos, her research notes for a couple of unfinished projects, and the beginnings of stories that never go anywhere. There's plenty of room on her laptop; she doesn't need a megaton of extra storage. She slides the little hard drive back into her laptop case and picks up her phone.

She stares for a moment at his contact icon, then pulls up her favorite photo of him, an unexpectedly great candid shot she snapped outside a ski lodge in the

French Alps three years ago. She touches the image with a light finger, studying the deeply tanned face and dark eyes, the sculpted goatee and wind-tousled hair. Everything about him oozes confidence and style, a successful international businessman at the top of his game. The man who made her feel like the center of his universe, at least in the beginning.

She's caught him at a good time. The flight went smoothly and he's all set to sign paperwork and oversee the Lamborghini's uncrating at the port tomorrow morning. Then he'll put in a few gallons of gas, hand-wash it, and give it a brief test-drive. Then he'll drive the new owner, escorted by a hand-picked security detail, six and a half miles to the billionaire's private residence, a magnificent hillside estate just outside Hong Kong. Most people would never drive a car like that—way too valuable—but Eric Li is definitely a flaunt-the-wealth kind of buyer and Marsh is determined to make a great impression.

"I wish you could be here with me, Cass. It'll be incredible—wining and dining with one of the wealthiest men in the world." His voice carries that boyish excitement she used to find so endearing. "You'd love Eric's art collection. He's got a Monet in his foyer that's worth ten times your average house."

She hears his enthusiasm and, just for a moment, she does want to be there with him. Dressed in something sleek and casually elegant, dining on whatever extraordinary delicacies the ultra-wealthy prefer, instead of sorting through moldy magazines in her mother's dusty farmhouse. "Next time. Take lots of pictures, okay?"

"If they'll let me. These oligarchs can be touchy about photos." He laughs, that warm chuckle that used to melt her defenses. "But hey, the stories I'll have to tell you when I get back."

Oligarchs. My husband does business with oligarchs. She pushes down the uncomfortable thought and congratulates him on the sale of yet another wildly overpriced collectors' item. This is, after all, how Marsh pays for their very comfortable life in Palos Verdes.

"So Cassie, how's everything in beautiful downtown Winslow?" His mood is genuinely upbeat. "I tried calling your mother's landline last night. Were you out painting the town red?"

"Sorry, I must've been asleep. We had a late dinner and I was exhausted."

"No worries, babe. I figured you needed the rest." He pauses. "I hope you can get everything wrapped up soon and get home to me. Are you bringing anything back? Please tell me you're not bringing back one of those pottery monstrosities."

She winces. Her mother's wedding present to Cassie and Marsh nine years ago had been a tall stoneware pitcher with an elaborately swooped handle. Crafted by a local potter known for incorporating straw and feather designs into his raku creations, it weighed nearly four pounds empty. Cassie had found it intriguing, but Marsh called it "aggressively ugly."

She'd used it as a flower vase a few times before their housekeeper dropped it on the tile floor. Rosa had apologized profusely, but Cassie noticed how she glanced at Marsh before fetching the broom.

"No pottery," she says now with forced lightness. "But I did find something interesting. Mom's friend AJ wrote a novel. A novella, actually."

"Really? What's it about?"

"It's a murder mystery. I think it's based on a real killing that happened here, near Winslow, back in '85."

Marsh goes quiet, long enough for Cassie to wonder if they've been cut off. She tucks her phone between ear and shoulder and plays with her napkin.

He coughs suddenly, startling her. When he speaks again, his voice has lost all its warmth. "Sorry. Got something caught in my throat. So, who got killed?"

The shift in his tone makes her stomach tighten. "This local farmer, Jimmy Desjardins. Apparently, AJ saw it happen while she was driving to work. I think I could write a good adaptation, maybe a series. Four or five episodes exploring—"

"Who killed him?" His words are clipped, businesslike.

"I haven't gotten that far yet. I've only read a couple of chapters, and the ending is missing. Maybe AJ never finished it. I looked online but couldn't find much about it. I don't think anyone was ever arrested."

"Doesn't sound like much of a story then, does it?" His dismissive tone stings. "I mean, if they never caught the killer. But fine, bring it back with you. I'd like to see it before you try to do anything with it." He pauses. When he continues, there's something almost urgent in his voice. "But don't show it to anyone else. Not until we've had a chance to look at it together. If it doesn't work, we'll just quietly shelve it."

"Ana needs to read it too, since our mom's mentioned in the story. I really think this could have potential. I could rework it, change the names to protect—"

"No." The word cuts like a blade. "You're not listening, Cassandra. Don't show it around and *definitely* don't show it to Ana. She wouldn't recognize a good story if it slapped her in the face, and I don't trust her to keep her mouth shut."

The familiar condescension toward her family makes her bristle. "Marsh—"

"Look, if this thing has any real value, you'll want to protect it. Keep it close to your vest until we know what we're dealing with. If it's just some delusional fantasy by a lonely old woman who watched too much *CSI*, we'll toss it. Or maybe we can salvage something— keep the small-town setting but do something more commercial. A rural horror flick, maybe, like *Clown in a Cornfield*. That could sell well."

"I'm not going to write some teenage slasher—"

"Okay, then. Just drop it, Cassandra." His voice sharpens to a familiar edge of command. "Do you hear me? Don't go digging around for the missing pages, and don't push back on this."

She resists the urge to protest or ask questions, which would only make him angry.

His voice shifts again, softening slightly, but the steel remains underneath. "Look, if there's something worthwhile there, I'll be happy to help you develop it. With producer credit, naturally. But right now, you've got nothing, and we both know how you can get carried away with projects that go nowhere. So just finish what you have to do and come home, okay?"

She tries to unclench her jaw enough to respond, but the line has gone dead. She stares at the phone, a familiar mix of confusion and hurt washing over her. How does he do that—make her feel cherished one moment and diminished the next?

Marsh has always positioned himself as a patron of the arts, generous with praise for other people's creative work. He offers encouragement for her ideas, but that's always followed by a thousand cautions about the embarrassment of failure. He claims he's protecting her from disappointment, but she's beginning to wonder if he's more interested in protecting himself from her potential success. At dinner parties and gallery openings, he loves introducing her as "my wife, the writer" to new acquaintances and potential clients—but she suspects that's only a setup to redirect the conversation toward his own interests in theater, contemporary art, and vintage automobiles.

After someone inevitably asks "Oh, what do you write?" and she stumbles through her usual vague response about literary fiction, and mentions her one story in *The Atlantic* from more than a decade ago, she's left standing beside him in an increasingly awkward silence. He never helps fill those moments; never suggests she's got other projects in development. Instead, he'll smoothly transition to discussing his latest acquisition—a rare '67 Shelby Cobra, or tickets to some exclusive art auction—leaving her feeling like an afterthought at her own introduction.

But he's never actively tried to steer her away from a story before. And why did he say "we'll just shelve it"? This isn't his project, it's hers. The presumption rankles, especially paired with his dismissive suggestion about turning AJ's story into some commercial schlock. If she chooses to develop this project, whatever it turns out to be, she absolutely will not let it become a formulaic horror movie.

A slow heat spreads in Cassie's chest as frustration crystallizes into a small hard knot of resentment. She gathers her things, suddenly wanting very much to get home and lose herself in AJ's story. To remember what it feels like to read something that matters.

***

She parks her rented Volvo beside Ana's Subaru, in front of the small carriage house their mother used as a one-car garage. There's an unfamiliar SUV near the front door. As she steps onto the porch she hears muted voices from inside the house and realizes Ana's still talking with the estate-sale people. Cassie slips through the screen door and up the stairs, carefully avoiding the squeaky end of the third step, to her old bedroom, the one at the front of the house with its narrow, iron-framed single bed pushed against the wall beneath a sloping ceiling.

She's feeling the familiar thrill of discovery that fueled her happiest moments in childhood, the anticipation of returning to the delicious pleasures of a half-read story. She closes the door, remembering to jiggle the knob to be sure it's secure. No door hangs exactly square in this house. Several, including this one, are likely to swing open or closed on the merest whisper of a draft. Cassie remembers adding an extra hook-and-eye to it when she turned thirteen and needed absolute privacy, but someone had removed that extra hardware.

Cassie piles pillows against the wall and curls up on the patchwork quilt with AJ's manuscript. She turns to chapter four and wonders how far she can get before Ana realizes she's come home.

CHAPTER EIGHT

AJ

~ 4 ~

The worst of the storm skirted Winslow, dark clouds threatening a downpour but ultimately delivering only a brief shower. I arrived at the radio station at three-thirty, with just enough time to cobble together the four o'clock newscast.

At the front desk, WWCT's bright-eyed office manager, Peggy Moran, was organizing log sheets into the August binder. Transmitter and antenna readings, plus all the aired segments—news, sports, commercials, public service announcements, music, talk—had to be entered into the log to confirm FCC compliance, and to prove that commercials had aired when they were supposed to. The daily logs were sacrosanct, and Peggy was their keeper.

Peggy also handled accounting and payroll. It was a lot of responsibility for a nineteen-year-old fresh out of secretarial school, but she probably found this easier than caring for six younger siblings.

When she saw me, she leaped up from her binder and three-hole punch. "AJ, hi, Mike told me you'd be late. Everything okay? Did you hear about the murder?"

She seemed not to know that I'd witnessed it. "Yes," I said. "Sorry, no time to talk." I pointed at the wall clock over her desk and kept walking down the short hall to the newsroom.

"Hey, AJ," she called behind me, "don't forget about the picnic on Saturday. I signed you up for a side dish, okay? Maybe potato salad?"

"I'll make tabouli. Got it, yup." I gave her a thumbs-up.

Peggy was our self-appointed den mother. It was a difficult role, given that she was young, single, pretty—and what my Gran used to call well-developed—in an office of quip-prone, ego-driven men. More than once, I've wanted to take her aside and suggest that she buy her sweaters and skirts one size bigger. With a lower hemline or a higher neckline, say.

She'd probably just take offense and short my paycheck. It's not worth the risk.

Mike was stuffing a notebook and the day's newspapers into his backpack, ready to leave. He nodded toward the news desk where the boom mic stood sentinel beside a taller-than-usual stack of sound-bite cartridges.

"That's what Androski wants, right? I taped three versions of the story so it's in my voice, not yours. And I sent it to the wire services, so you'll probably get calls from other stations and probably the papers. Just refer them to me."

I nodded, relief mingling with jealousy. Mike's workaround would keep me employed for now but the fact that he'd shared the murder story—my story—with the syndication services filled me with a quiet resentment. And there was nothing I could do about it.

"And I rescheduled your interview with Sean McCarthy for Friday at two-fifteen. I hope that works."

Damn. I'd completely forgotten my afternoon interview with the town manager. I should've handled the rescheduling myself, from Shirley's house.

Mike handed me his to-do notebook and today's tickle file, our daily calendar folder where we store the keep-for-future-updates stories. "Here's the afternoon assignments and tonight's meeting agenda. I'll make the police and fire calls at 4:30 so you don't have to."

He hoisted his backpack over a shoulder, then paused to look me up and down. "Hey, you look a little off-color. Are you coming down with something?"

I just saw a guy get shot-gunned to death on my way to work. But I'm fine, really.

I tried for levity, dredging up the jokey voice we used for newsroom banter. "It must be the clothes." I spread my hands with palms up, inviting jokes or disparagement. "What Shirley Jellnik thought I should wear to work today."

He wasn't listening. "Hey, about the witness conflict thing? Don't worry, I'm sure it's just for a few days, until they catch the guy. We'll figure it out." He sounded like he was trying to convince himself. "Maybe Tony can help. He can sit with you, do some live lead-ins just on those stories. He'll be delighted to get some real air time."

Tony Scott was our part-time stringer/intern, a nerdy teenager whose voice hadn't yet figured itself out. He helped out on weekends by writing human interest stories and high school sports reports. Mike hadn't let him go live on-air yet but occasionally Tony got to do a wraparound, taping a lead-in and a tagline for a sound bite that we included in a slow-day newscast.

The words popped out before I could bite them off. "You're giving my job to Tony?"

Mike shrugged and raised his eyebrows, asking me to understand his perspective. "Dammit, AJ. Look, I'm stuck. My second-in-line can't cover our biggest story? You can't call the police for updates, and I can't send you to interview Androski or the prosecutor when they arrest someone. You can't go to a press conference or sit in the courtroom when it goes to trial, except to get up there on the stand and be their lead witness. I'm still figuring this out, okay?"

"None of that may happen. They don't even have a suspect."

"Then it will drag on forever and fall into cold-case status, but meanwhile you're still their primary witness and you still can't do anything with it. That's no good. Best-case scenario, they find the guy fast and he confesses. Then there's no trial and they won't need you to testify."

He softened his tone. "Just please stay safe, okay AJ? I'm relying on you to help me solve this."

Did he mean solve the work thing, or solve the murder? Before I could ask, the door closed silently behind him. What exactly was Mike relying on me to do? Stay away, as Androski had warned? Or somehow chase the story without risking my position as a credible witness?

Mike had taken a gamble when he hired me, the first female reporter at WWCT. He said he chose me not for outperforming the other candidates but for having the "acceptable vocal delivery" he demanded. "You're not squeaky or shrill like most women," he'd said. "Your voice is almost as good as a man's."

He offered it as a compliment, but I saw it as a constant challenge to prove I could punch above my weight. To be not just "almost as good as a man," but better.

For all Mike's vanity—those expensive haircuts, the dental work, the manicures, and his perfect tan—he was an efficient newshound. He arrived at five every morning to greet Winslow with the day's first newscast at six. Then he made dozens of calls, recorded interviews, and churned out story after story, chasing leads with a singular focus that always left my own efforts feeling secondary. After his noon roundup, I took charge of the newsroom while he juggled story leads and schmoozed with cops and politicians. The news was his life, even when personal chaos—like his recent divorce, his second—intervened.

I felt like a journeyman compared to Mike. I craved the rush of being the one to break a story, but I knew I could never fill his size-twelve shoes. He was the headline creator while I was stuck covering the mundane: Rotary Club meetings, school board sessions, petty thefts, minor accidents, layoffs at the cable factory. I'd become good at my job, but I had no illusions about being indispensable. I could be easily replaced by anyone with half the skills and a voice "as good as a man's."

Mike Gorman was the man. I was just AJ, girl reporter.

Shaking myself out of these thoughts, I sat down and began sifting through the tickle folder, trying to find some clarity amid the pile of notes and news clippings.

On the other side of the soundproof glass separating our newsroom from the control studio, Keith lifted a hand from the control board and mouthed something. I pointed at the speaker on the newsroom wall, reminding him to use the intercom, which doubled as an on-air monitor, typically playing WWCT's live broadcast when it wasn't needed for room-to-room communication.

Billy Joel's "Piano Man" cut away, replaced by Keith's thundering faux-newsman voice on the inter-studio monitor. "Here's WWCT's own ace correspondent, AJ Porter!"

I jumped to turn down the monitor's volume control.

Keith was doing his Walter Cronkite impersonation, giving each syllable a slow, basso profundo importance. "At WWCT," he intoned, "we report all the news that is the news, all the time, everywhere. Where it happens, when it happens, before it happens."

He could be annoyingly childish on a good day, and this was not a good day. "Not cool, Keith. You'd like to cover the next murder, maybe?"

I shivered at my own words. Would there be another murder?

He abandoned his attempt to channel Uncle Walter. "Nope, nada, no way. The sight of blood makes me puke. Okay, I get it, this is not the time for my world-renowned improv skills." I heard him sigh. "How're you doing, AJ? Mike said you saw it happen."

His kindness surprised me. Keith was thirty, two years older than me, but I always thought of him as just a kid. A constant prankster, he was always ready with smart remarks and dumb adolescent humor. Once in a while, though, a flash of intelligence slipped through, and I suspected a sharp intellect lurked beneath the façade. Which was probably why he and my good friend Marla were still married after five years.

"I'm okay, I guess." Not true but it would do for now.

"I heard it was some farmer out on Cherry Valley. Do they know who was killed?"

"His name's Jimmy Desjardins. Older guy, maybe forty?"

"Oh, shit." Keith pushed his boom mic aside and scrubbed a hand over his eyes and mouth. "Jimmy's related to Marla, some sort of distant cousin. She's going to fall apart when she hears that. Her mom told me they spent a couple of summers on his family's place when Marla was a kid. He's a little weird, not the brightest bulb, but why the hell would someone want to kill Jimmy?" His mobile face sobered. "I'd better give her a call before she hears it from someone else."

"I'm sorry, Keith. I didn't know they were related. I'll call her, too, right after I do the four o'clock."

Keith glanced at his wall clock and cut off the intercom, switching back to the on-air monitor as "Piano Man" faded. He adjusted his headphones, flipped his mic on, and launched into a fast-paced, joke-riddled live commercial extolling the virtues of a local appliance store. He looked strained, but resolute. The show must go on.

I turned my attention to the stories and sound-clip cartridges Mike had arranged for the four o'clock newscast. He'd been leading with the murder, of course, and so would I for the rest of the afternoon.

There was also a piece on the continuing construction problems of Winslow's new water treatment plant, a short preview for tonight's board of ed meeting, a report on plumbing repairs at the local animal shelter, and a couple of state stories pulled off the AP's teletype feed.

I had less than eight minutes to proofread and pre-read the stories for 4:00 PM. I set aside the tickle-file assignments and focused on the current stories in front of me.

When the AP Radio national news began, I swung my chair into place at the front desk, slotted Mike's first cartridge into the tape deck, and slipped on my headphones. Three minutes later, Keith cut the AP feed and punched up the station ID, followed by the news intro jingle. I positioned the boom mic, yodeled briefly to clear my throat, and watched the second hand count down on the big wall clock. I flipped on the mic switch and my stomach did its own small flip.

I crossed a couple of fingers, vowing to remain steady and professional.

"Good afternoon. It's 79 degrees at 4:03, and I'm AJ Porter with WWCT's four o'clock report, brought to you by Pierre's Place, your family restaurant on the corner of Church and Front Streets.

"State police continue their search for a suspect in the shooting death of a Winslow farmer. WWCT News Director Mike Gorman has the details." I punched the green button on the cartridge deck and let out a breath.

I thought I was doing pretty well. No fumbling fingers, no quavering voice. No lingering visions of a dead body in a hayfield.

The newscast took all my attention. I read the next story and the next one after that. Pulled out the first sound-bite cartridge, pushed in the next. Introduced the halfway commercial and followed that with weather, stocks and a Red Sox update, wrapping up just as the second hand ticked straight up to 4:10:00. Keith flashed me a thumbs-up as he spun his turntable into another Madonna selection.

The pace of newsgathering picked up between 4:00 and 5:00, as always. Mike's to-do list directed me to chase down a local angle on a state budget story and dig into the teachers' salary controversy in a nearby town.

I also fielded calls from other reporters who'd seen the murder story on the AP feed. Those took time but were easy to handle, as I simply referred all the inquiries to Mike's home phone or the state police.

Then it was time to tape our bird feed, the state news that came in by satellite from the Connecticut Radio Network in Hartford. The phone rang at the appointed times with the weather and closing stock-market numbers. I taped each segment, wrote short intros, did a quick rehearsal reading, shuffled everything into order, and went on the air for the twenty-minute day's wrap-up at 5:00 PM.

At 5:23, I assembled yet another five-minute newscast and recorded it for Keith to play at six. Then I stuffed a tape recorder, notebook, and microphone into a duffel bag and headed home, exhausted.

CHAPTER NINE

AJ

~ 5 ~

Driving home along the narrow back roads toward Cherry Valley and the scene of the murder, I was imagining the metallic stink of blood. But it wasn't imaginary.

Half-way home, I pulled over and cranked down all four windows to clear the air of my car's lingering coppery smell. I remembered Ernie telling me he ran a rag over the steering wheel and seat after they tested for prints and blood, but I knew I'd still have to do a thorough cleaning to get the fingerprint powder and dried blood out of the seams. I made a mental note to buy Lysol and bleach.

I slowed down when I got to Jimmy's hayfield. No cars, no people, no body. A ribbon of yellow police tape still sagged from the metal T-posts, but there was nothing else visible from the road to suggest what had happened here. The tractor, baler and hay bales were gone. A neighbor must have finished the work and hauled everything away.

My stomach growled, reminding me I'd missed lunch. I stepped on the accelerator and put the hayfield in the rear-view mirror.

The shake-shingled gray cape on Turnbull Road was the only place I'd ever lived. It first appeared on the town's tax map in 1890, not old enough to land on the historical preservation list in a town where at least half the houses are pre-Civil War, but plenty old enough to regularly bust my repairs budget. The floorboards were gently warped and all the doors hung a little crooked. Most of the rooms were small and low-ceilinged; Gran's big woodstove took up so much of the kitchen that her 'sixties-era avocado-hued fridge had to live in the pantry, a long narrow closet of cupboards and wainscoting.

There were three rooms down and two up. For more than twenty years, it had been just Gran and me living here. As a child, I'd slept in a long narrow room upstairs under the eaves. Gran had her bed in the former dining room and we shared the single downstairs bathroom, built first as a cold-storage room off the kitchen.

When Gran passed and the house came to me eight years ago, I moved downstairs into her old bedroom. I bought a new TV and added a microwave in the pantry, but otherwise left everything else pretty much the way it had been. I kept her saggy sofa, rag rugs, and Formica countertops not only because they reminded me of her, but because I'd just replaced the roof and had to pinch pennies.

Gran was gone but her cat was here, perched on the front porch railing. Pippin was a sleek little runway model of a cat, long-legged and lean-bodied, with mouse-gray fur, a white tuxedo bib and four perfect socks. The bell on her collar chimed as she leapt from the railing to the porch floor and began speaking in her own personal dinner-demand language, a rumbly purr interrupted by loud mewing. She began twining around my legs as I headed for the front door.

In the kitchen, I dumped kibble in her bowl, then went back to the front door and locked it. I didn't usually bother locking doors while I was home, but Jimmy's murder made everything feel different. I was sure many of my neighbors were doing the same.

In the bathroom, I started the shower and tossed Shirley's clothes in the trash. Just as I climbed into the clawfoot tub and tugged the plastic curtain closed around it, the phone rang. I heard my answering machine click as it picked up the call.

It was Marla. "AJ, please answer if you're there." I heard her pause, then sigh. "Ohmigod, I can't just talk to your stupid machine. Keith told me Jimmy's dead and you saw it happen. So please please please pick up! Dammit, AJ, this is important."

Shit. I'd forgotten to call her. Marla was my best friend from nearly forever. Today her cousin had been murdered and how had I forgotten to call her?

The hot water finally came on full blast and sent me scrambling for the faucets. I vowed to myself that I'd call her the moment I got out of the shower.

***

Ten minutes later, wrapped in Gran's blue cotton robe and preoccupied with wiping fog from my glasses, I walked out of the bathroom and yelped. "Marla! What the hell?"

She jumped up from a kitchen chair, spilling Pippin off her lap. "Sorry, AJ, but your back door was open. I had to come over, I couldn't just talk to your stupid answering machine again. I got worried when you didn't pick up."

"I'm so sorry about your cousin—" I thought of Marla's pregnancy. "Are you okay? Is Keith still at work? Is something wrong?"

"I'm fine, they're fine. It's not about me, I'm here for you, AJ. I heard about the shooting. And…what you saw. I can't imagine how horrible."

Her kind words, meant to comfort me, didn't quite fit with how she looked. Her late-summer tan wasn't quite covering the ashen pallor of her face and the dark circles beneath both eyes. There was the tiniest whiff of vomit beneath the minty toothpaste smell of her breath. I chalked that up to her recent bouts of morning sickness.

Marla was four months pregnant with twins but you wouldn't know it to look at her. She was one of those tall, fit, athletic women who always looked pulled-together, even in today's baggy tee-shirt, cut-offs, and those clunky Dr. Scholl's sandals she liked.

I hadn't seen her since Sunday morning, when we'd done our usual three-mile jog-walk along Winslow's river trail. Marla had talked non-stop about her latest ultrasound. She'd been beside herself with worry because she hadn't felt the babies move yet, and one of the twins appeared to be smaller than the other. It was still early days, her doctor had told her. No need for concern. Results from an amniocentesis showed everything looked normal and she'd just have to be patient, which was not Marla's strong suit.

Now she held out her sturdy physical therapist's arms and folded me into a bear hug. Her shoulder-length honey-brown hair plastered itself to my still-damp neck and I felt the contours of her body pressing against me, grounding me with sudden warmth and a new awareness of the lives she carried inside. I wrapped my arms around her and pulled us closer. On the floor, Pippin rumbled an ecstasy purr and rubbed herself against our bare ankles.

Marla winced, easing back. "Sorry, I've got a sore shoulder. A patient, an older man, lost his balance on the stairs. I think I wrenched my rotator cuff trying to save him from a fall." She held my shoulders for a moment and peered into my face with her wide-set hazel eyes. I swiped a hand across one cheek and managed a weak smile.

"You were successful," I said. "Right?"

"Doing what?"

"You saved him from falling. Your patient, this morning."

"Well, yeah. But it wasn't this morning, it was yesterday. I took today off. I'll be okay in a day or three, but what about you? Are you okay? Oh dammit, that's a stupid thing to say. Of course you're not okay. That must have been a *terrible* thing to witness."

Four other people had asked me that question today and I hadn't wanted to answer. Finally, with Marla holding me up, I could speak truthfully. "I'm not exactly okay, not yet. But I'll get there. And now I really have to get ready for work."

"Of course. Get dressed." She gave me a gentle push toward the bedroom. "Shirley called me. That's how I heard." She kicked off her sandals and plopped onto my bedspread, belly down, propped up on her elbows. "She said you came into her kitchen looking positively white. Like a ghost, she said."

Pippin jumped up beside her, purring and swinging her tail in Marla's face. She leaned on one elbow to rub the cat's ears.

I said, "I'm not surprised you heard it from Shirley first. I'm sure the whole town heard it from her."

"She told me there was blood on your clothes, so she had to give you some of her things to wear. I'm so, so sorry, I can't imagine how awful that was."

My mind skidded away from the details. "Yeah, not a picnic." I pulled on gray slacks and a yellow camp shirt. "Sorry, I can't think about that right now."

"Have they caught anyone?" She plucked at my chenille bedspread as the cat began kneading it with her front paws. Marla and Pippin, they're the reasons it's practically threadbare.

"No, not yet." I fished the orthotic insert from my handbag and slipped it into a jogging shoe.

She rolled over and sat up. "Where's your loafers?"

I explained about the blood, and the police taking my shoes for evidence.

"That sucks. You should be able to get those replaced. I'll write a statement for insurance if you need it."

"Thanks. Hey, have you eaten? I'm scrambling eggs."

"No, I'm good. We're eating dinner at my mother-in-law's tonight. The good news is, Ryan's not invited so I can spend the evening away from my husband's creepy buddy." Ryan Jones was a friend of Keith's who worked construction in Vermont. Recently laid off, he'd shown up at their house two weeks earlier, offering to help Keith renovate the upstairs in their old farmhouse to create a second bathroom and a nursery for the soon-to-be-born twins.

She added, "The bad news is, Keith's mother doesn't serve wine. And her cooking's terrible. Everything's fried or overcooked. I didn't think anyone could ruin asparagus, but then I met Janet. And she's always trying to fatten me up. Ugh." She pointed a finger toward her open mouth and stuck her tongue out in a gagging motion.

"Marla, you're pregnant. You shouldn't be drinking wine."

"Yeah, I know. It's just one glass, once in a while."

This was a bone of contention between us. In our sophomore year of high school, she'd been a heavy drinker. One of those super-cool party kids looking for popularity in a bottle. I didn't see much of her that year because I was a timid wallflower mouse, not a fun-and-games girl. That was also when Gran suffered her first stroke and needed me to help more at home.

It was only after Marla met Keith in her junior year that she'd straightened out and ditched the booze and pot, mostly. Though stress at work or home still sent her back into the package store for a bottle of wine or a six-pack.

She trailed me into the kitchen and perched backwards on a wooden chair while I dug out a frying pan and two eggs, keeping one eye on the wall clock. In twenty-five minutes, I had to be on the road or I'd be late for the school board meeting.

I turned on a burner and threw a handful of chopped spinach and onions into the pan with a pat of butter. "Marla, I'm sorry about Jimmy. I didn't know he was family. You never mentioned him. That must be hard—"

"Nah, it's fine." She shrugged. "We weren't close. His father and my mother were first cousins, so I guess that makes him my second cousin. Or something else, maybe once removed? Anyway, except for that one summer when he worked at the horse camp, I barely knew him."

She stared out the kitchen window at the big maple in my backyard. A tire swing hung there, its rope frayed and gray with mildew. She was thinking, maybe, about all the times we sat out there in the shade, taking turns on the tire and drinking lemonade as we compared dreams, listened to music, and complained about boys.

I slid eggs onto a plate and ate quickly, thinking about the summer camp where Marla and I met. Eighteen years ago, we were horse-crazy ten-year-olds sharing an unshakable conviction that heaven could be found on the back of a pony. It was an awesome time but by the end of summer, we'd both had enough of shoveling manure and getting stepped on by bad-mannered horses.

I'd forgotten Jimmy had worked at that camp. I couldn't conjure him now as he must have looked then, in his mid-twenties. The only image in my head was of the forty-something man I saw get shot-gunned to death a few hours ago.

"I sort of remember him," I said. "He helped feed and clean the stalls, right? And he rode along on some of the trail rides."

Marla frowned. "Yeah, but he was a horrible rider. Too heavy-handed. Always running his horse too fast, trying to impress all the girls." She picked up a dish towel from the counter and folded it neatly in quarters. Changed her mind and folded it a different way. "AJ, did anyone see you this morning? When it happened, I mean. Maybe someone in the truck? Were there any other witnesses?"

"No. At least, I don't think they saw me. I really hope not."

"So the police have to rely on what you saw. And you didn't see who shot him?"

"All I saw was a vague shape. Some guy in a dark-blue pickup, or maybe it was black. I'm not certain about the color, actually. The sun was in my eyes."

"So whoever—" She ran her tongue over dry lips, then chewed on her lower lip for a moment. "Whoever killed Jimmy is still out there somewhere. Do the police think it's drugs?"

"Marla, I really don't know. We can speculate all we want. But really, what good does it do?" I was losing patience. "Sorry. My nerves are kinda shot."

She went a little on the defensive. "All I meant was, maybe the killer was on PCP or something. The police should warn us about that, shouldn't they?"

I swallowed the last bite of egg and carried my plate to the sink. "How can they possibly know without catching him? And I'm not supposed to talk about it, okay? I'm a witness. *The* witness." I glanced at the clock again. "Look, I've got to run. I've got a meeting to cover."

"Right, sorry." Marla stood and moved toward my back door. She paused, one finger tapping the doorknob. "Look. Can I call you tomorrow morning? I have a favor to ask. It's important. But I have to explain first."

"Sure. Or I can stop by your place for coffee."

She shook her head quickly. "No, I'm working tomorrow. Only half a day, but it's a morning shift. I'll be off at noon, but then you'll be at work."

"Call me around ten when you have a break," I told her. "I promise, this time I'll pick up."

***

Cassie sets the manuscript down and stares unseeing out the window.

She knows her mother had been popular in high school. Marla Ferguson, later Marla Bousquet, was a cheerleader and the senior class treasurer. But also a heavy-drinking party girl? And according to AJ's story, she also drank, at least occasionally, while she was pregnant with Ana and Cassie.

That just doesn't fit with the mother that Cassie knew. She can't recall her mom ever asking for more than a occasional glass of wine at dinner. No cocktail parties, no Sunday afternoon martinis like some of her friends' parents.

But Marla had obviously read AJ's manuscript, because there are several red copy-editing corrections in these chapters. A few misspellings, a misplaced semi-colon. And one blue-ink note, a circle around the tire-swing paragraph and that classic comment: "Nice imagery."

No wonder Mom and AJ were always so worried about my drinking. It runs in the family.

Cassie glances at her watch and listens for movement or voices downstairs. Silence. Maybe she can squeeze in one more chapter.

CHAPTER TEN

AJ

~ 6 ~

Wednesday evening's school board meeting, held in the middle school auditorium, promised to be a routine affair. The seven board members, four men and three women, sat at a long table on the small stage like judges at some quiet tribunal. On the floor, an audience of thirty or so people perched in small clusters on hard wooden seats. Their buzz of agitated conversation fell away into an uneasy silence as I entered.

I patched my tape recorder into the PA system and chose a seat at the far end of the front row. Setting up, I kept a wary eye open for anyone wanting to ask me about the day's events. People straightened their postures, fidgeted with their printed agendas, and slid their glances past me. No one approached me.

Such meetings are usually yawn-inducing. That night, however, I spent the first twenty minutes twisted sideways in my seat, keeping an eye on everyone. Wondering if the killer was there in the auditorium, breathing the same stale air. Was it the business-suited man who stood frowning over a clipboard at the back of the hall? Maybe the acne-scarred guy with restless fingers, scratching his chin. Or the angry-looking blond woman in the second row, whose thin-lipped smile never quite reached her watchful eyes.

Which of these could kill a man in cold blood?

Thirty people barely qualified as a crowd, but I've always been wary of large groups and that shotgun blast still echoed in my ears. Sitting there in a room full of strangers—all of them certainly aware by know that I'd witnessed Jimmy's murder—I felt exposed.

But I couldn't do my job in constant state of hypervigilance, so I made a conscious effort to pay attention to the meeting, occasionally punching the record button to capture a pithy comment about teacher salaries or gym renovations. We were three weeks from the start of school and several parents were there to complain about the new transportation schedule, which had some kids riding the bus for more than an hour each way. Others wanted to speak their minds about the high cost of football uniforms.

Their voices rose and fell in familiar cadences. It was all very civil. No one spoke out of turn. No one swore, yelled, or brandished a weapon.

An hour after the meeting began, the board adjourned to go into executive session and decide about the applicants for two teaching vacancies.

I caught up with the chairman on my way out and asked him to call me later with the names of the new teachers so I could write up that story.

Then I slipped out the side door before anyone could pepper me with anxious questions or share their own fears.

No one followed me to the radio station.

Mid-week, Winslow went dead quiet after sundown, when the traffic lights changed to a slow blink of red and yellow. WWCT goes off the air at 9:30, so the building and parking lot were deep in shadow when I got there just before 10:00. I parked my car close to the entrance, in the small glow of two pale lights flanking the front door.

I sat in my Chevy for a few minutes, gathering thoughts and wits.

The ten-car lot was partly enclosed by a chain-link fence that kept vehicles from falling down a steep slope into the Pennatucket. In the dark, I could see only the wavering reflection of a streetlamp on the falls. I could hear it, though—a low, muted roar as it spilled over the twenty-foot dam onto the rocks below.

Thirty feet above the falls, slung on rusty cables strung from concrete piers, a footbridge linked the riverbanks. Like a thread connecting two worlds, the bridge had been built eighty years earlier to provide easy access to the mills for workers living on the far side of the river. In the daytime, the falls and footbridge offered a great photo op, if you cropped out the abandoned factories on the east bank. At night, the dimly lit footbridge and the riverside park were favorite hangouts for Winslow's homeless and anyone else seeking the cover of darkness.

One night, I'd found a ragged man curled up by the entrance of the radio station, sheltering from the rain. When I gently roused him, he moved on without complaint. I'd never felt unsafe working there alone.

That night, though, I was jumpy. Every shadow seemed to shift when I glanced away.

Enough stalling. I locked my car and wedged the keys between my knuckles for the short walk to the building's entrance. I quickly unlocked the front door, slipped inside, and checked twice to be sure I'd locked it behind me.

Breathing through my mouth to stay as quiet as possible, I moved directly to the newsroom and turned on all the lights. I snugged the blackout curtains tighter across the big plateglass window that looked out on the parking lot and street, then moved room to room, flicking switches as I checked the sales room, manager's office, breakroom, restroom, mechanical closet, and control studio.

I'd never realized how many potential hiding places there were in such a small building. How many dark corners could conceal someone who knew exactly where to find me.

Gradually, work displaced worry. On the reel-to-reel machine, Mike had left two public-affairs interviews for me to edit, so for the first hour I cut actualities—the recorded voices of newsmakers—into fifteen- and twenty-second chunks, then transferred them to continuous-loop tape cartridges. I wrote the lead-ins to those stories, plus three versions of the bus-route story from the board of ed meeting.

Next, I sorted through the long roll of newsprint spit out over the last several hours by the teletype machine and found a couple of business stories with local angles that we could use: a change in federal milk support prices, the repair schedule for a bridge on the interstate.

Taking a break, I boiled water for a cup of instant coffee and puttered a bit, waiting for the school board chairman's call. If he neglected to phone in by eleven as he'd promised, I wouldn't hesitate to call him at home.

All the town officials knew how persistent I could be, and they were pretty good about returning my calls.

The phone rang at 10:40, but it wasn't the school board chairman. It was Androski.

"Mike told me I'd probably find you there." His voice sounded tired. "You always work this late, AJ? Alone?"

"Yeah, most nights. Part of the job." I wanted to say, "How often do you ask the male reporters that question?" But I gave him the benefit of the doubt, chalking it up to his concern for my safety as a witness, not as a fragile female.

"You have something for me, Detective?"

"I assume you're asking about the Desjardins murder, which you should not be asking about. But I'll let it go. And no, we don't have anyone in custody." He paused, perhaps reconsidering what he'd planned to say. "What I'm going to tell you is not for the news, is that clear?"

"Clear." A small adrenalin jolt bubbled up, every reporter's response to a hint of confidential information.

"Okay, but this is off the record. I'd like to give you some details from forensics, and I need you to tell me if anything doesn't fit with what you saw. Don't add anything and don't speculate. Got that?"

My hopes fell, but curiosity remained. "Okay."

"Desjardins was killed with a ten-gauge shotgun from three or four yards away. What I don't get is how the shooter, who you say never got out of the truck, maneuvered the barrel of a shotgun out through the passenger-side window, in just a few seconds, without

Desjardins seeing it in time to duck. So, please think. Are you sure the truck doors never opened?"

I was stuck on his words, "who you say never got out of the truck." Were they questioning what I'd told them?

I said carefully, "The truck doors did not open. Not the driver side, not the passenger side. Did you find a shell case?"

"No."

"It's in the truck, then." He said nothing so I went on, "I don't think Jimmy ever saw the gun. He was turned away, waving a hand like he was pointing at something on the other side of the field." I thought of something else. "He had a cigarette in that hand. Shoot—did I mention that earlier? It was burning in the grass. I stomped it out."

Androski grunted. "No, you didn't mention that. And yeah, that explains the cigarette butt. We were hoping the killer left it." He paused. "I guess we should be glad the valley didn't catch on fire."

I ignored his tired sarcasm. "Have you found the truck?"

"Still looking."

"How much of this can I use on the air?" Then I knew I'd overstepped.

"There is no *you*, AJ. *You* can't use any of it. Tell Mike to call me in the morning and I'll let him know what *he* can use." He cleared his throat. "One more question. What do you know about Jimmy Desjardins' business connections? How he makes his money."

"He's a farmer. He sells hay locally. And I assume he sells his raw milk to the co-op, like everyone else."

"Okay, that's it. Stay safe." He hung up, leaving me to wonder about the possible business connections of a murdered dairy farmer.

What should I do with these bits of information? I didn't want to get in trouble. But if I could show Mike I was contributing something to the story, maybe I could keep my job. I rolled my chair to the writing desk, switched the Selectric on again, and began tapping keys. All caps, the standard for read-aloud journalism.

POLICE HAVE IDENTIFIED WEDNESDAY'S MURDER VICTIM AS WINSLOW FARMER JAMES DESJARDINS. SOURCES SAY HE WAS KILLED SHORTLY BEFORE NOON BY A SINGLE DISCHARGE FROM A 10-(TEN) GAUGE SHOTGUN FIRED AT CLOSE RANGE. STATE POLICE CONTINUE THEIR SEARCH FOR A SUSPECT IN A DARK BLUE OR BLACK PICKUP WITH OUT-OF-STATE PLATES.

Mike would hear the same details from Androski in the morning. It shouldn't matter that it came first from me. I'd still be a credible witness, right?

The phone rang again. The school board chairman gave me the info about the new hires and I dashed off the last of the night's write-ups.

I rinsed my coffee mug in the bathroom sink and switched off the overhead fluorescents. The newsroom was silent and dark, with only the soft glow of dials on the electronics to light my way out. I reached for the drapery cord to open the curtains at the front window.

Something rapped softly against the building. I heard two taps, then three. Then two more.

The radio station's plate glass windows were supposed to be soundproof, but this small noise seemed to be coming right through the wall. It was barely perceptible, noticeable only because all the newsroom machines had gone momentarily quiet. I held my breath, but heard only the beat of my quickening pulse.

Then it came again. A tapping, then a persistent scratching, like something outside was trying to scrape away the mortar between the bricks. Trying to get in.

Heart pounding, I flattened myself against the wall beside the still-closed curtains. Summoning a scrap of courage, I reached up and yanked hard on the cord.

Dim light flowed in from the parking lot and street beyond. Just outside the glass, a pale jellyfish shape hung from a boxwood bush. A white plastic bag was snagged on a branch. As thunder rumbled, wind caught the bag and slapped it against the wall. It ballooned upward again as the branch trembled and scraped against the bricks.

I exhaled and surprised myself with a yawn, which seemed the best way to shake off an adrenalin rush.

I finished locking up. With only a moment's hesitation, I stepped outside and pulled the plastic bag from the bush, breaking off several offending branches in the process. I unlocked my car and tossed the debris onto the back seat.

After checking, of course, to be sure no murderers or monsters lurked there.

At home, I locked all the first-floor windows, wedged a wooden chair beneath the unreliable latch on the front door, and retrieved Gran's old shotgun from the pantry cupboard.

She'd bought it used, when I was nine or ten, to scare coyotes and raccoons away from her chickens. Only a little four-ten Mossberg with a pitiful three-shell capacity, it didn't have anything close to the power of the ten-gauge used to kill Jimmy Desjardins. But one of those little shotshells would still take down a human intruder, if the shooter aimed well.

The last time I'd fired Gran's gun was in April, when Keith, Marla and I spent an afternoon at the rod and gun club, shooting clay pigeons. Now, feeling guilty that I hadn't touched it in months, I gave the chamber and barrel a quick rub with a rag and a few drops of gun oil. I leaned it in the corner of my bedroom, thinking: *What else would Gran do?*

Returning to the pantry for the box of shells, I loaded the shotgun's chamber with a single shell and filled the magazine with two more. Made sure the safety was on and stood the gun carefully in a corner of the bedroom.

I lay in bed for a long time, wide awake and waiting for sleep but finding only a continuous replay of death and blood. At some point, the open-eyed memories morphed into a host of vivid nightmares, layering embellishments on the original event and looping over and over, refusing to change or end.

Sometime in the deepest dark, with thunder rolling above the rafters and lightning stabbing through Gran's muslin curtains, Pippin vibrated herself into a tight ball against my chest, and the dreams faded.

CHAPTER ELEVEN

Cassie

It's nearly two on Thursday afternoon by the time Cassie begins stacking dozens of old gardening magazines into a single tower. She straightens the pile, then tries to lift it without spilling everything to the floor. Thinking, *Me and my big mouth. I never should've told Ana what Marsh said on the phone this morning.*

When Cassie had shared Marsh's response to the news of AJ's novel, Ana exploded. Cassie's never seen her sister so angry.

"Marsh said he doesn't trust *me*? And he ordered you not to talk to anyone, including me, about AJ's story. Our *mother's* story. Unbelievable." Ana is moving kitchen chairs aside to drag a pair of area rugs out to the porch, having declared her intention to give the rugs an old-fashioned cleaning by draping over the railing and beating them with a tennis racket she found in the garage. The front door's propped open with one of their mother's gardening boots. Dust motes float inside and out, swirling in beams of afternoon sunshine that flow through windows and doorway.

Ana begins rolling up one end of a frayed Persian rug, punctuating her efforts with sharp words. "What's he scared of? That we'll learn something scandalous about Mom or AJ?" She goes next to hoist a heavy end table, grunting a little with the effort. "Hunh. Your husband's a bully. He's supposed to freaking support you, not tear you down."

"He's not—" The magazine tower abandoned, Cassie heaves a box of books onto a growing stack near the door. "Ana, please. Set that thing down so we can talk."

Ana drops the end table with a small thump and turns to her sister, planting her hands on her hips. There's a smear of dirt on her forehead and larger stains on both bare knees.

Ana wears her industry like a martyr's badge, Cassie thinks. *As if to demonstrate how hard she's working while I've done nothing but lounge around reading.*

Cassie rolls her eyes at her sister's self-righteous stance. "For chrissake, Ana, why are we doing this?" She swings an arm wide. "I thought the estate-sale people would handle all this. Or we can call the neighbors, or hire some furniture movers. I'll pay."

"With Marsh's money?" Ana snaps.

For once, Cassie doesn't bite. "You're making yourself crazy, Ana. Don't do that. And we don't have to have the estate sale this Sunday. Let's put it off a week or two."

"But you're leaving on Tuesday."

"I'll stay longer. A week, two weeks. As long as you need me." The moment she says it, Cassie realizes it's true, she does want to stay longer. Though it means putting up with Ana's bossiness and Marsh's likely anger.

"Really, Cassie? I doubt your charming husband will allow that. He'll crook his finger and away you'll go." Ana slumps onto a stool. "Oh shit, I'm sorry.

Really. It's just that Marsh is the elephant here and every time I think about him, yeah, I get crazy. I wish you could see what I see. You're dying a slow death with that life. With him." She glances at her watch and shoves an escaped lock of gray-blond hair back under her Red Sox cap. "It's two-thirty. Did you even have lunch today?"

"No, I was reading and sort of lost track of time," Cassie admits. "I'm not hungry." Cassie sinks onto the sofa and runs her fingers through her short, dark hair. She doesn't have to look in a mirror to know she's due for a roots touch-up. Time for a change, she thinks. Time to drop her public persona, the goth-adjacent schoolgirl with all its life-sucking black draped over a fashionably scrawny frame. Espresso-dark hair, bruise-dressed eyes, washed-out skin. Marsh loved the damaged-waif look she'd rocked so effortlessly in her twenties and thirties. But it doesn't pair well now with the crow's feet and sun-darkened, leathery skin that comes with years spent beneath a harsh desert sun.

She wonders idly what Marsh would say if she follows Ana's lead and quits coloring her hair. She could stop starving herself, too. Eat a little more protein, ease off on the alcohol and Xanax. She'd put on a few pounds, sure, but maybe the headaches would go away.

What will Marsh say? But she doesn't have to wonder, he'll be disgusted and angry. *He'll say I'm letting myself go. That my sister's a bad influence.*

Ana is still staring at her, eyebrow pulled high on her forehead. "Do you want to stay longer? I mean, that would be great. But seriously, can you do that?"

Cassie shrugs. "Sure. I don't have anything important on my calendar."

This is true, though Marsh has promised their attendance at several events he's supporting. A gallery opening a week from Friday, a fundraising gala for the local police on Saturday, and something else to do with an art museum. She can't remember the details. But those are Marsh's obligations, not hers. All he needs is a well-behaved, stylish female at his side. It doesn't have to be her. She's never liked that part of her life, the dress-up glamor-posing he insists his business demands.

Let someone else be his escort for the evening. Any one of his wealthy clients would be delighted to lend him a piece of arm candy or two for an evening, or longer.

Cassie lifts her chin, decision made. "Yes, I'll stay another week. So don't sell my bed on craigslist yet."

She doesn't want to think about what will happen when the week's up, or when Marsh learns of her changed plans. She offers a small smile to Ana, who's hooked her bare feet around the rungs of the stool and seems to be regarding Cassie with new eyes.

"Then I'll stay, too," Ana declares. "I'll have to sort out the staffing at the law office, but that shouldn't be a problem. We'll just ask the temp to stay on an extra week or two. Jonathan's got it under control. Do you want me to cancel the estate sale?"

"Maybe just push it back a week. That will give you—us—some breathing room."

They're interrupted by a knock at the front door. Cassie glances at Ana, who gives an I-don't-know shrug.

"Please, no more casseroles," Cassie mutters.

Three more raps, confident but not demanding. Through the screen door, Cassie can see a wisp of a woman on the porch. She's all sharp angles and brown, sun-weathered skin, balancing a stack of mismatched plastic take-out containers with one hand like an offering. Her other arm cradles an egg carton against her chest. In the driveway, an old green pickup idles. It's missing its tailgate and there's a large brown hound sitting in the driver's seat, panting through the open window.

"You must be one of Marla's girls," the woman says when Ana opens the door. Her voice carries the familiar flat vowels of rural New England, worn smooth by decades of use. "I'm Dotty Kellerman, from down the hill. Brought you some real food."

Ana steps through the door. After a moment's hesitation, Cassie follows, closing the screen door carefully so it doesn't slam. She moves to Ana's shoulder and takes in their visitor. Dotty looks to be in her seventies, with wiry steel-gray hair pulled up in a messy top-bun and sharp blue eyes set in a face that's seen plenty of weather. Her jeans are stiff with grime and old paint, her sandals are held together with duct tape, and her sleeveless t-shirt proclaims "Polite as Fuck" in faded purple letters.

"That's very kind of you," Ana says as Dotty hands over the plastic boxes. "Would you like to come in? I could make some coffee—"

"Nah, thanks. Too nice a day to be inside." Dotty shifts the egg carton to her free hand. "These are for you, too. Nice fresh butt-nuggets from my girls." Cassie suppresses a startled chuckle, earning a smile from Dotty. "Unwashed, so they'll keep longer. And that's quinoa salad and falafel. Figured you might be sick of all the tuna casseroles and Jello molds by now."

"You figured right," Cassie says, earning a sharp look from Ana.

Dotty grins. "You must be Cassandra. Your mother always said you were the truthful one. Said Ana was the diplomat and Cassie was the one who'd tell you your barn was on fire." She cocks her head a little and looks sharply from one to the other, first Cassie and then Ana, as if waiting for some acknowledgment to her comment.

Finding nothing in their faces, she leans against the porch railing. Apparently settling in. "I just wanted to let you know how much we're all missing your mother. She was special."

Ana steps around Cassie and sets the containers on the wicker table. "We think so, too." She adds a smile. "And thank you, we appreciate this so much. Mom always said your chickens laid the best eggs."

"That's the truth. They do. But that's not why I'm here." Dotty's eyes grow serious.

She frowns and her mouth moves as if she's shifting a piece of gum from one jaw to the other. She turns a little away from them and reaches two fingers into her mouth. Cassie realizes she's adjusting a set of dentures, getting ready to say something important.

"Stupid teeth," she mutters. "So, yeah, I wanted to pay my respects. I couldn't make it to the church service but I wanted you girls to know how we all felt about your mother. She was something of a legend, you know."

Cassie feels Ana tense beside her. "A legend? How?"

"Maybe that's not quite the right word." She shrugs. "And maybe she never told you about it. That would be just like Marla, to stay quiet. Some secrets have to be kept a long time." Dotty glances around, as if debating whether she's already said too much. She lowers her voice. "You know, a town gets set in its ways. When things are mostly working okay, it just goes humming along. People turn a blind eye to the parts that don't work so well. Live and let live, that's what people around here think. We learned that in the sixties and seventies, didn't we, when all sorts of new people showed up, thinking they'd invented back to the land. Live and let live," she says again. "We're pretty tolerant. If you work hard and show up at town meeting once a year, go to church sometimes and pitch in to keep the volunteer fire department running—well, we think it's all good."

The sisters exchange glances, wondering if there's a point to the rambling.

Dotty shifts a little against the railing. Her eyes narrow, furrows deepening in her brow. "See now. In the early 'eighties, a little before you two were born, there was this—this situation, with a man who lived out in Graves Parish. Where the old village was, what they call Grabtown. You know what I'm talking about?"

Cassie nods.

"Some folks knew," Dotty goes on, "what was happening but nobody wanted to get involved with the cops. You know how it is here with the old families, everybody's related to everybody. Sometimes the law can't handle certain problems."

She pauses, studying their faces. "Your mother, though—she had a way of making problems disappear. She made us safer, I can tell you that."

"What kind of problems?" Cassie asks.

"The kind that shouldn't be talked about on a front porch," Dotty says firmly. "But the kind that needed handling, all the same. Your mother understood that."

She straightens and rubs her hands on the seat of her jeans, as if her palms have gone sweaty. "Anyway, I just wanted you to know—a lot of families around here owe Marla Bousquet a debt they can never repay. She was a real protector, that one. Fierce as a mama black bear when she needed to be. And AJ, too. The two of them…" Her voice trails off and she shakes her head a little in obvious admiration.

Ana and Cassie glance at each other in confusion.

"Sorry, I don't think we know what you mean," Ana says.

"I expect not. You didn't need to, not when you were kids. That's the point." Dotty hands the egg carton to Cassie. "She did what she did so you girls could grow up safe. Other kids, too. But now that she's gone, well— it seems right that somebody should tell you what kind of woman raised you."

The old woman turns to go, then pauses at the top of the porch steps. "Oh, and girls? If anybody comes around asking questions about the old days, about things that happened back then—you don't know nothing about nothing. That's not being dishonest, that's being smart. Some stones are better left unturned."

She's halfway to her idling truck before either sister finds her voice.

"Wait," Ana calls. "Mrs. Kellerman? Dotty—"

But the old woman just waves without turning around, her duct-taped sandals slapping against the gravel. Hauling the driver's door open, she elbows the dog away from the steering wheel and climbs in.

They watch Dotty's truck making its slow way toward the road, small puffs of dust kicking up behind the rear wheels.

Cassie says, "What the hell was that all about?"

"I have no idea. But she clearly thinks Mom walked on water."

Cassie flips open the egg carton and makes a face. "Ewww, unwashed butt-nuggets. Just what I've always wanted. Random sizes, all different colors, thoroughly coated in chicken shit."

Ana grins at her twin's discomfort. "I'm sure she means well."

***

Cassie pushes a stack of threadbare kitchen towels into a trash bag and plops down onto a kitchen chair. Her face feels damp and gritty with a mix of perspiration and dust. She longs for a shower but it's only three o'clock and she's promised Ana another hour of sorting and carrying.

"Ana," she says, "we need to talk about AJ's story. But we can't do that until you start reading it, too. I've been thinking about what Dotty Henderson said. There's something important here, Ana. Not just because there's a story I might be able to use, but because it's our history. It's about Mom and AJ, who they really were before we were born. Mom left this for us, so she wants us to read it. Don't you want to know?"

Ana looks up from her perch on the stool where she's been sorting papers and labeling manila folders. Credit Cards, Mortgage, Hospital Records, House Repairs. She puts down her felt-tipped marker and examines a broken nail.

"I don't know," Ana admits. "I'm not sure I want to know a different version of Mom. I love her just the way she is. Was. I don't want to spoil that. And how do you know AJ's story is even true? Is she a reliable narrator?"

"Yeah, we should keep that in mind. But you should at least start reading what I've read. We haven't found the second half, anyway. If it even exists."

"Okay, I'll start reading. But not now. Later, after dinner." Ana squares her shoulders.

"Great. So what should I do next?"

"Christmas ornaments. They're stacked in the closet in AJ's old room. What used to be your room."

"First, it was the nursery. Hey, do you know who constructed the shelves and desk in that room? It was Ryan Jones, a friend of Dad's from way back. He lived here for, like, three weeks when Mom was pregnant with us."

Ana blinked. "I did not know that."

Cassie grins. "It's in AJ's story. See, I know something you don't." Feeling oddly happy about this, she picks up an empty box and trots upstairs.

The holiday ornaments, some in their original boxes and some in clear plastic bins with red and green tops, are stacked at the very back of the unlit closet. The space is narrow and deep, stretching back into a crawl space beneath the eaves. Cassie drags out dusty boxes in ones and twos, setting them on the bookcase and the desk, until she can see the back of the closet.

Propped in a far dark corner, there's something that looks like a rifle. Pausing with one fist holding a coiled tangle of extension cords, Cassie can see a wooden stock and the glint of light on dull steel.

She sets the cables aside and reaches far in, wrapping a hand around the cold barrel of the gun. Holding it steady, she carefully slides the last large boxes away from the corner of the closet. Moving slowly, deliberately—wondering if it's loaded—she lifts the gun from its precarious resting place.

It's not a rifle but a bolt-action, single-barrel shotgun, coated with dust and a lace of incipient rust near the trigger guard. She locates the safety lever and ensures it's locked, then brings the gun into the light of the room's one tall window. She removes the two-shell magazine clip, empty, and eases the bolt back to inspect the chamber, also empty.

She can't find a serial number, but there's a maker's mark on the underside of the barrel near the receiver.

O.F. Mossberg & Sons, Inc. New Haven, Conn., U.S.A. Model 185 K-A. 20 GA.

An involuntary shiver runs up her spine. It's AJ's shotgun. I was just reading about it.

She hasn't handled a gun in years, but the smooth walnut stock feels comfortable in her hands. It brings back memories from the year she turned fifteen, two years after their parents' divorce. Most weekends, their dad would drive down from Boston to Winslow for regular visits. One Saturday, trying to find a shared interest with two teenagers who had little in common with him or each other, Keith took his daughters to a deserted field and taught them to shoot tin cans off the top of a hay bale with a small shotgun like this one. The girls quickly grew bored and Keith never suggested they go shooting again, but Cassie still remembers the safe gun-handling lessons he'd drilled into them.

She doesn't remember what gun they used. Maybe it was this one.

Now she raises it to her shoulder and adjusts her left hand on the barrel, her right hand on the grip. Keeping her index finger outside the trigger guard as she's been taught. Pointing the muzzle toward the window, she lines up the bead and knife sight on a fence post near the garage. She breathes in, then out, and mimes a trigger squeeze.

What did it feel like for Jimmy Desjardins' murderer to line up the sights and pull the trigger for real?

"What the hell are you doing?"

Cassie jumps but her safety training kicks in and she swings the muzzle down toward the floor before pivoting toward her sister. Ana's standing wide-eyed in the doorway, one hand clutching the door frame like she's about to push off and flee.

"Sorry," Cassie says. "It was in back of the closet, behind the Christmas decorations. I think it's AJ's gun. She mentions it in the story."

"Dammit, Cassie, I didn't know there was a gun in the house. But yeah, this was AJ's room. So I guess it was hers." Ana lets go of the door frame and approaches, keeping a wary eye on the weapon. "My god, is that the shotgun that killed Jimmy Desjardins?"

"No. That was a ten-gauge, lots bigger than this one. But AJ mentions this one, too. Her grandmother bought it to scare raccoons away from her chicken coop. You really need to read the story, Ana." Cassie sets the gun on the patchwork quilt covering her bed and picks up a small box labeled BUBBLE LIGHTS. "I've been working on the holiday stuff. See?" It comes out a little defensively. It's not her fault she got sidetracked.

Ana's still staring at the gun. "I wonder if we need to turn that over to the police. The probate court makes a big deal out of locating and securing guns after someone dies. Jonathan will know. That's one advantage of having a husband who's a lawyer."

"I didn't know you were so leery of guns. Don't you remember that time when Dad and AJ took us shooting? We were what, fifteen? He borrowed a twenty-two from his dad, and I think AJ brought this one. I didn't have the patience for it, but you were a good shot. You went back with Dad several times, right? After I got bored."

"Maybe I did, but guns scare me. Mom hated guns, remember? I'm surprised AJ's shotgun is still here."

Wanting to pull Ana's attention from the gun, Cassie stands the weapon in a corner behind the desk and returns to the closet. She ducks her head and peers in. "There's one more box in here. And a whole lot of dust."

She sinks to her knees, reaches into the dark recess, and emerges with a small, lidded carton labeled 3-TAB

FILE FOLDERS. Someone has crossed that out with red marker and written below, ANASTASIA BOUSQUET 8-31-2001 CONFIDENTIAL! The box feels heavy enough to hold a small book. It's sealed with gray duct-tape, frayed and curling at the edges.

"This one's for you, Ana." Cassie sits on her heels, wipes the box with the hem of her tee shirt and offers it to her sister. "Want to guess what's in it?"

They lock eyes, one twin standing and the other kneeling.

"I can't believe Mom hid this from me for so long. From us, I mean." Ana sighs and takes the box. "Whose idea was this, do you think? AJ's or Mom's?"

"Both, probably." Cassie scrambles to her feet. "You've got to admit, it's pretty clever. Can't you just see them hatching a scheme to get the two of us working together? AJ writing the story, Mom editing it. So we'd know it was a collaboration. Then they hid the two halves and sat on it for decades. Saying nothing to anyone else, just speculating together maybe about how someday we'd be here together, cleaning out the house after they were both gone. Though I don't think AJ planned to die in that car crash."

She pauses. "Ana, do you think they were lovers? Mom and AJ. I know they were close since, like, eighth grade. After Dad moved out, AJ was here all the time helping Mom. It's not something you want to think about when you're, like, fourteen. But then, after we left for college, AJ sold her place and moved in here and…"

Ana's mouth forms a half-smile. "Cassie, you once claimed to be in the advance guard of the pansexual revolution. This has only just occurred to you?"

"Hey, it's our Mom we're talking about." Cassie raises an eyebrow. "But you've known for a while, haven't you?"

Ana shrugs. "I guess. Does it matter?"

"Well, no, of course not. But it's just one more thing I wish I'd known. How much they meant to each other, I mean. Here I've been thinking they were just really good friends. But now…" Cassie turns to the bookcase where she's stacked her half of the manuscript.

She hands Ana the first six chapters. "Which is why you need to start reading, Ana. Right now."

"So we're knocking off work for the day?"

"If I don't have a shower, I'll scream."

"Well, we certainly don't want that happening." Ana pushes her lower lip forward and blows her breath up into a lock of straw-and-pepper hair that's escaped the baseball cap. "Okay, fair trade. Let's see how far we get in two hours. I'm a fast reader." She places the box on Cassie's bed. "But no spoilers, okay? And no reading ahead. You have to finish the rest of your chapters before you start on mine."

For the first time in weeks—years?—Cassie grins at her twin. She holds up her right hand and crooks a pinky, then arches her back and pushes her slender chest forward. "Pinky-swear or bust trust?"

Ana laughs. "I haven't thought of that in years!" She glances down at her own ample breasts. "Better do a pinky-swear. If we bust-trusted, you'd get bounced out the window."

CHAPTER TWELVE

AJ

~ 7 ~

The thunderstorm that should have cleared the air on Wednesday night never materialized, so the same stale, humid air lingered into Thursday morning. I slept later than usual, waking at seven-thirty only because Pippin was kneading my pillow and humming like a lawnmower, wanting breakfast.

As I filled her bowl with kibble, I listened to yesterday's messages on my answering machine. Marla's, plus three others. One was from a woman I knew only slightly, who begged me to call her back with "the true details" about "the hideous atrocities." Plural, as if one murder wasn't enough. A man's voice left a number that I could call for counseling by a sympathetic, certified Christian therapist. The last message was from an anonymous woman who invited me to sign up for a concealed-carry class and hinted that she could help me buy a handgun, quick and cheap. I cleared everything and re-set the machine.

I'd fed the cat, but I needed milk and coffee for my own breakfast. That meant a trip to Roland's General Store.

A fixture in Winslow since 1892, Roland's was a true mom-and-pop store without a whisper of gentrification, so stereotypical it looked like a movie set.

Built from local lumber with wide oak floorboards, there was a big porch in the front with rocking chairs and a wood-frame screen door that slammed your butt when you forgot to catch it.

Inside was a long, narrow counter topped with hammered tin and crammed with all the key impulse purchases: maple sugar candy, jawbreakers, miniature Tootsie Rolls, cough drops, and a rack of balsa-wood airplane kits. In the walk-in cooler at the back of the store, sides of beef, pork, and venison (in season) hung beside cases of Coors, St. Pauli Girl, and 'Gansett.

Along with essential produce and canned goods, the store stocked one of everything else you might need: axe handles and hinges, barn boots in odd sizes, greeting cards, umbrellas, assorted fuses, plumbing supplies, ammunition, motor oil, livestock feed, and nursing bottles for newborn lambs as well as humans.

Paul Roland, well into his seventies, was especially proud of his meat counter. He ground the burgers fresh each day, always mixing a bit of beef fat into your venison so the leaner meat wouldn't stick to a frying pan.

Over the years, Roland's has survived supermarket competition, clueless tourists, beer heists, hurricanes and blizzards. The milk was always fresh, the seasonal produce always local, and the gossip always current.

Walking in, I heard the WWCT jingle introducing Mike's eight AM news summary blaring from a brown Bakelite radio perched beside the adding machine.

I'd been hoping for a "suspect apprehended" headline, but the only new information about the murder was what I'd typed up the night before, identifying the weapon and the victim.

As the morning's first customer and the murder's key witness, I braced for questions from Paul and his wife Evelyn, but they seemed more eager to share their own ideas about why Jimmy Desjardins got shot.

I asked Paul for a half gallon of two-percent.

"Morning, AJ. I've got some in here somewhere." He crouched beside the dairy case and non-sequitured from milk to murder. "Jimmy was land-poor, you know."

Evelyn's softer voice chimed in from the produce bins where she was sorting green beans. "Yes, and that wife of his. My money's on her."

Here was an opportunity. Maybe I could gather information without acting like a reporter.

"Oh?" I strolled toward the coffee shelves. "I didn't know. Land-poor how?"

Paul straightened to his six-three height and placed a carton of milk on the counter. "Well. He inherited that farm from his parents about twenty years ago, did you know? Those fields along the road, and all the way up the hill to where the old village used to be. He never had the money, though, to run it properly. Tractors broke down, the milking barn needed a new roof. It's always something. But he was stubborn. Hanging on, still farming it the way his parents and grandparents did. Wouldn't sell a single acre, even back a few years when we had a housing boom and land was going for twice what it is nowadays. Land poor, like I said. Too much land and not enough money."

A "housing boom" in Winslow meant maybe a dozen new houses, tops.

Evelyn added, "He had more than his share of bad luck, too." A foot shorter than Paul, stocky like him but with a quicker way of moving and speaking, Evelyn had the local habit of dropping unnecessary words and syllables. "Equipment breaks, you get sick. Milk prices fall but meanwhile, feed costs go up."

"And then his parents got sick." Paul found his wire-rimmed glasses on the counter and tucked them into a tan shirt pocket. "They were bed-ridden for months before they passed on, and Jimmy was looking after both of 'em. Couldn't tend to the cows and had to hire a man to do the milking. You do that, you never get caught back up."

"But he had a wife. Couldn't she help?" I chose a one-pound can of Hills Brothers Drip.

"Nah, she didn't come along until later." Evelyn dumped the culled green beans in a bucket. "Understand, Jimmy didn't marry 'til just three years ago. And he always was funny about girls, even when he was in school."

I was confused. "You mean he's gay?"

"Oh, no." She wiped her hands on her pink apron and began re-stacking a pile of white onions. "I don't think so, anyway. Just real shy. Always kept to himself. Working all day, no time for socializing. But then he turns forty and marries a woman almost twenty years younger, who hates farming. It made no sense. You met her?"

"I think I saw her once or twice in the co-op. I thought at first she was his daughter."

"No, no kids. Good thing, I guess, not having extra mouths to feed. She's Charlotte Collier, from up in Southbridge." Evelyn pulled a rag from her apron and moved along a shelf, wiping invisible dust from spaghetti boxes.

Paul totaled my purchases at the front counter, his long fingers moving rapidly over the adding machine keys. "Jimmy was an only child, real quiet and none too bright. Our eldest, Gary, was in primary school with him. Jimmy got as far as eighth grade, I think, then stayed back twice. The moment he turned sixteen, his parents pulled him out. They needed him on the farm. You want a bag? No charge." He shook open a wad of white plastic printed with the red Caldor logo.

"Thanks." I thought of something. "But the tractor Jimmy was driving looked new. And his baling machine."

"Yeah, that was kinda strange," Evelyn said. "He came in here last spring boasting about this wicked new John Deere he bought. In the same breath, he's complaining about all the loans he's got to pay off. Charlotte's brother is in real estate. I think he fixes private loans, too, and maybe Jimmy got tied up with that. He said he was hoping to bale enough hay this summer to pay it off. He'd a done it, maybe, if Charlotte ever lifted a finger to help."

"Evie," Paul cautioned, "that's not for you to say." He headed toward the back of the store.

"It's true," she insisted. "She wouldn't even drive truck so he could load up the hay wagon. The most she'd do was cook a little. She says she's a city girl." She shook her head. "And she's always been after him to sell up and move closer to town. Developers would love that farm, good flat land in the valley. But he loved it there. He was never gonna sell."

She smoothed a crease in her flower-print dress, pushed a curly tendril of white hair off her brow, and glanced out the store's wide front window. A car slowed, then drove past.

"Jimmy was a sad case." Her voice dropped. "And I think he maybe owed a lot of money to some bad people. Not just Charlotte's brother, but others too."

I lowered my voice to match hers. "Who?"

She walked it back. "I don't know, I'm just guessing. Another thing, I think there's a big life insurance policy. Charlotte told me once that she'd be set for life if he kicked the bucket."

"She probably inherits everything anyway."

Evelyn nodded. "And she won't have a problem with selling the farm to the highest bidder. I don't think she's shedding tears."

I picked up my purchases and thought of something Androski had asked me. "Evelyn, what do you know about Grabtown? How the barn got that name."

"Oh, that goes back to the 'thirties, when there was still people living up there in the old village. It's all gone now, except for that barn. But if you go back even further, before the war, Graves Parish was a good-sized village. Had a dozen houses, a gristmill, even its own schoolhouse."

I didn't ask which war. Evelyn could've meant World War One, the Civil War, the War of 1812, or the

American Revolution. There's a lot of history in these hills.

She rubbed her dust rag over the bakery case. "So, Grabtown. When the economy crashed in 1929, all the factories closed up. It was soup kitchens and breadlines for everyone. Milton, that was Paul's dad, owned the store back then. Once a week, he took groceries up to Graves Parish in his Model T. He let people pay on credit. If they were really bad off, he gave them food anyway.

"Whenever Milt made a delivery, a dozen starving kids ran out of the woods and swarmed his truck, grabbing at everything they could get their hands on. He started calling it Grabtown, and it stuck. Now the village is all gone except for that one barn. And the town took that for back taxes."

"Gran never told me that story," I said. "Or maybe I wasn't listening. All I knew about Grabtown was from high school. It's where boys took girls at night to spook them. A girl'd get scared in the dark and grab a boy's arm. Then the boy 'saved' her from the scary stuff, and he grabbed her."

Evelyn snorted dismissively. "Well, yeah. That too. And now the barn's a real danger. It's not just teenagers I worry about, it's the younger ones, too. The town should tear it down before someone starts a fire and a kid gets killed. Kids are smoking cigarettes and lighting fires all the time up there. With all that dry hay and old lumber, it's a tinderbox."

Evelyn followed me out onto the porch. She paused there and placed a hand on my arm, glancing back through the screen door before continuing. "Talking about that barn reminded me of something else about Jimmy. Years ago, when he was maybe nineteen or twenty, he came in here one day with an old camera hanging around his neck. I think he said his dad brought it back from Germany after the war. Jimmy was learning to use it."

That war I could identify, World War Two. I wasn't sure where this was going, but I nodded to encourage her.

"Anyway," she said, "There was a tourist family came in the store. Mom, dad and two little girls, the oldest about eight. They're going up and down the aisles. Then suddenly the dad's shoving Jimmy out the door and yelling. Said Jimmy was taking photographs of the girls. The older girl said he gave her a candy bar and told her she was the prettiest thing he'd ever seen. She said he'd like to put her picture on the cover of a magazine."

"Wow. What happened next?"

Evelyn's face flushed pink. She glanced left and right, reassuring herself we were alone on the porch. "Paul hustled Jimmy out fast. Told him in no uncertain terms to learn some damned manners, respect people's privacy and keep the camera in his car, or he'd call the police. Paul didn't mean it, of course, about calling the police. It was just Jimmy being Jimmy. He probably thought he was paying the girl a compliment. I don't think he understood why anybody'd be offended."

Evelyn broke off as a rusty white pickup pulled into the parking lot next to my Chevy. She took a step away, tidied her hair, and smiled at the stoop-shouldered gentleman making his way along the concrete walk.

"Morning, Harvey. How's the weather treating you? That hip doing okay?"

Driving home, I wondered about the man whose murder I'd witnessed. The Rolands had suggested one of the oldest motives for Jimmy Desjardins' murder — money, by way of insurance or inheritance. They'd also given me a short list of who could benefit from his death: his widow Charlotte and her land-developer brother. And maybe a loan shark, ready to place a claim against the estate of a slow-to-pay farmer.

What should I do with that information, tell the police? But everything I'd learned, the police probably knew already. And I didn't want Androski to think I'd been investigating.

I could tell Mike, though. That would score some brownie points and maybe I could keep my job.

***

Cassie turns over the last page of Chapter Seven, rises from her desk, and stretches. Her bedroom has gone cool with a late afternoon breeze blowing through the open window. A cold front moving through, perhaps. She switches off the overhead fan but leaves her window open.

Now that they've found the last chapters, Cassie's feeling a deep sense of urgency to get to the end. She's picked up on AJ's worry about the killer, but she's also beginning to share Ana's concern about what they're about to learn. Not only about their mother, but about the town they all grew up in.

So how reliable is AJ as a narrator? Cassie's assumed, up til now, that the story is accurate. Filtered, of course, through AJ's eyes and mind — but essentially true.

159

What if it's really just a fanciful tale of what-if, using made-up dialogue and real people as pawns to play out a fictional fantasy?

She still doesn't know why AJ wrote it. And what are they supposed to do with it?

CHAPTER THIRTEEN

AJ

~ 8 ~

Digging into people's private business leaves me feeling a little queasy but digging in real dirt always makes me happy. By nine-forty-five that Thursday morning, I'd weeded a row of wax beans, tilled a new bed for a crop of fall spinach, and set four pink beefsteak tomatoes on the kitchen windowsill to finish ripening. The day felt almost normal.

Marla called promptly at ten, just as I'd finished drying a sinkful of dishes.

Her voice was hushed, barely above a whisper. She didn't bother with a hello. "Have the police arrested anyone yet? It's been almost twenty-four hours." I heard conversation in the background and remembered she was calling from work.

"I don't know. I don't think so." As I spoke, Detective Androski's voice was replaying in my head: Don't talk about it, not even to family and friends. "I don't know any more than what's on the news. I'm not really in the loop on this one."

I expected her to remind me that I was a news reporter, it was my full-time job to be in the loop. But all she said was, "Good, there's still time. I need a big favor. Can you help me?"

"Sure. But please, don't ask me to throw you a baby shower. I am awful at those things. Completely useless—"

"No, not that. Something else." There was more noise in the background. Marla paused, inhaling sharply. "Oh, god," she whispered. "Okay, this isn't working. I need to talk to you in person. People keep walking by. This was a bad idea, trying to talk about it on the phone. When are you off work tonight?"

"I'm free after the six o'clock news. No meetings tonight."

"Meet me by the footbridge at six-thirty, okay? That bench by the dogwood trees. And don't say anything to Keith or anyone else. That's a pinky-swear, AJ." She hung up.

She'd sounded worried. This was something way more serious than a poorly managed baby shower. Was there a problem with the pregnancy?

She'd sworn me to our highest level of secrecy, so I'd simply have to wait until after work.

***

When I got to the newsroom a little after noon, Mike was propped against the counter by the reel-to-reel machine, reading *The Hartford Courant*. He looked up and beamed an electric smile.

"Hey, AJ. Guess what? I just got a call from Channel 14 in Portland, Maine. I'm on their shortlist for a reporter's position, with a shot at weekend anchor after six months. They want me back for a second screen test and a final interview."

I knew he'd been putting out feelers for a new job—he was always doing that—but I had no idea he'd gotten to the interview-and-audition stage.

"That's terrific. When's your interview?"

"Next Wednesday at two. I can manage things here through the eight AM summary, but then I'll need to leave right after. Can you handle the rest of the morning shift, say from nine o'clock on?"

"Sure, I can be here, but—" I felt a frown pinch into shape. "What about coverage for the Desjardins story? If something breaks while you're not here. They might need me to go to the barracks and ID someone."

He shrugged dismissively. "If they arrest someone and call you in to identify him, tape a newscast or two and leave it for whoever's on air. If there's no arrest, there won't be anything new, so..." He spread his hands. "...then there'll be nothing to report. I'll ask Tony to back you up. Use him however. Make calls, write stories. It's just for one day."

"And speaking of that," I began. I filled him in on what the Rolands had told me about Jimmy's wife and money troubles.

Mike eased down to sit on the counter. "Okay, maybe that will fit with this other thing I want to talk to you about."

I took the chair at the news desk and gave him my full attention.

"AJ, I want this Channel 14 job so bad I can taste it. Remember, when I move on maybe you can move up. Wouldn't that be cool? You'd be the first-ever girl news director at WWCT. Maybe the first in the whole state."

"Woman," I said automatically. "Or female. That works, too. Woman or female, not girl."

He waved a hand, dismissing my comment. "Whatever. The point is, you can't get promoted unless I get another job. I need to prove to the Portland people what a hotshot investigative journalist I am. And I need your help."

"I could come in earlier every day. Do the eleven o'clock and—"

"I've got something else in mind. And I promise we'll keep you clean for Androski, okay? Anything we learn about the Desjardins murder, we'll hand over to the cops. Hey, maybe we can even solve this case for them."

"But how—" My mind was racing. I'd been worried about getting fired, but now Mike was talking about a promotion. Would the station owner agree to a female news director? George Grayson was so conservative.

I pulled my attention back to the conversation. "I can't just walk up to people and ask questions. Androski will be furious if I screw up his case."

"AJ, just listen. You've lived here all your life. You know everyone and people trust you. So I've got this idea." His voice turned persuasive. "I was talking with this guy Zach Stollman, a reporter at *The Nutmeg Insider*."

I must have looked confused because he added, "That new glossy out of Hartford? It's a monthly, they do in-depth pieces on state issues. Zach's doing a story on why small family farms are in trouble. The economy, the cost of feed and fertilizer, interest rates, et cetera. He'll be in town tomorrow morning. I gave him your name and told him you could introduce him to people, help him figure out who he should talk to."

"That's easy. Local farmers, the co-op farm store, the manager at the milk processing plant. Maybe the slaughterhouse in Plainfield. But—"

"You could start with Jimmy's wife."

"What, Charlotte? She's not a farmer."

"Zach does the Q and A, you tag along. He talks about farming, she says nothing of consequence, then he adds a couple questions about the murder. He gets a hard-luck profile for his farm story—or maybe not, doesn't matter. Then I follow up on the other stuff, and we see where that takes us."

"Does Zach know I can't ask questions about the murder?"

"I told him. But surely you can still talk about farming and the economy."

I took a moment to look for holes in his plan. As always, it really came down to me remembering when to keep my mouth shut.

I suppressed a sigh. "When's he coming here?"

"He'll meet you at 10:00 AM tomorrow, at Pierre's."

So much for me having a choice in the matter. "Okay. But anything Zach learns about Desjardins has to go to the police."

"Of course. Scout's honor." He snapped a two-fingered salute.

If Mike had been a Boy Scout, he'd know their salute uses three fingers. He'd just given me the Cub Scout sign, the little-kids' version.

***

The afternoon shift went quickly, as busy days do. I wrote one story about a car-theft conviction and another about ticket sales for the Rotary Club's annual August fundraiser, a rubber duck race down the Pennatucket River. Half an hour before the 6:00 PM wrap-up, the police scanner came alive with a car crash on the interstate's on-ramp. No fatalities, but a total fuster-cluck for traffic stuck in Winslow's brief afternoon rush hour.

I pounded away at the Selectric and dubbed sound bites from the AP feed while Keith spun his records and played commercial spots on the other side of the glass wall, and only Mike's recorded voice mentioned the murder.

When I left the radio station at 6:18, clouds were building over the hills again on the west side of town. My clutzy left foot was feeling better so I half-jogged across the parking lot's cracked asphalt and onto the pocket-handkerchief triangle of grass that marked the beginning of the Pennatucket River Trail, a narrow winding path along the mill pond above the falls. A restless wind kicked bits of trash into the water and a flock of mallards squawked and took wing as I approached their stand of cattails near the shore.

I found the designated bench and waited.

Marla came over the footbridge from the other side of the river at a fast walk, her hair tangled loose on her shoulders. She wore faded jeans, her wooden sandals, and one of Keith's old Harley-Davidson tee shirts. Not for the first time, I envied her those long elegant legs and slender feet, their symmetry and strength. She looked more like a teenager searching for her lost skateboard than a late-twenties mom-to-be.

She also looked nervous enough to snap a guitar string with a hiccup. She shot glances left and right, then sank down beside me. She was red-faced and breathing hard, and I wished I'd brought water. I moved to put an arm around her shoulders but she shifted away and flapped both hands, trying to fan air at her face.

"Too hot," she panted. "Give me a minute." Her breathing eased. "Okay, better. Whew."

I frowned. "Have you been drinking?" I could smell beer on her breath.

"Just one." She grabbed her mane of hair with both hands and twisted it onto the crown of her head. "Do you have a clip? Or a rubber band?"

"No, sorry." I've never wanted hair long enough for clips and barrettes. When I was little, the only way Gran could control my cowlicks was to lop everything off at the one-inch mark. I've followed that same technique ever since.

"Never mind, then." She quit fiddling and let her hair fall in a damp mass. She turned to face me. "Look, I—"

"Breathe. Just take another minute and breathe."

She shook her head and frowned. "No time. Look, AJ, I really need your help. This is big, so you can say no. But please say yes, and please please please don't tell anyone. Even if you say no."

"Okay, sure. Of course I'll help you. Whatever you need." Her anguish was painful to see. "I promise."

She glanced around again and dropped her voice. "That barn needs to be burned down. Right now."

I jerked back. "What barn? You mean the Grabtown barn?"

"Yes."

"Well, lots of people would agree, but—"

"It's an awful place, a real hazard." She spoke quickly, piling words on words to make her point. "It's been a danger for years. The fire department keeps saying they'll do a controlled burn, use it as an exercise for training the rookies. But the historical society says no, it needs to be preserved. Then nobody does anything. It's dangerous. Don't you remember what happened to Brenda Martinez?"

"That high school girl who hanged herself when we were in eighth grade?"

"Yes. We've got to make sure that doesn't happen again."

I tried to puzzle through her logic. Destroying the Grabtown barn wouldn't stop a determined suicide. There were so many ways, so many places.

I'd never been inside the barn, but I knew Marla had because she'd boasted about it in sophomore year. I'd heard the graphic details, whispered by gym lockers and picnic tables. Stories of booze, pot, sex. Girls who went too far and got caught, boys who claimed trophies and never got caught.

Marla brought me back to the moment. "Don't you see? Jimmy's dead. But all his stuff is still there. We've got to get rid of it. Now's our chance."

"What stuff?" I asked stupidly. "His farm equipment? The bales of hay? And what chance? A chance for what?"

"What I said before."

Which told me nothing. What was I supposed to remember now, from something she said earlier?

Her voice went fierce and low. "We have to destroy it all, AJ. Burn it all down. It will make everyone safer."

"You want me to help you burn down the old Grabtown barn."

"Yes!" She was breathing hard again. "Haven't you been listening? I'd do it myself, but I shouldn't be handling kerosene."

"Well yeah, but—"

"Kerosene's really toxic. I have to protect my babies." She said the last part slowly, like the words were new to her. "There's lots of things pregnant women shouldn't do. Don't scoop the cat box, don't take really hot baths." She touched her barely discernible belly bulge. "Don't handle petroleum distillates. Like kerosene and paint thinner and gasoline. Everyone knows this."

What about not drinking alcohol? But this wasn't the time to bring that up. All I managed was, "Well, no. I didn't know all that."

Marla had gone down some mad rabbit hole and I was still trying to wrap my head around the part where my closest friend was asking me to set fire to a building. I knew pregnancy could trigger some odd behaviors and strange cravings, but I didn't think barn-burning was on the list of *What to Expect When You're Expecting.*

I seized on the main point. "Marla, that's crazy. You're talking about arson."

A white-haired woman with a golden retriever appeared on the far side of the footbridge. Marla dropped her voice. "If the town asked the volunteer firemen to do it, no one would say it's crazy."

Abruptly, she stood and slapped invisible dirt off the seat of her cut-offs. A strand of golden-brown hair fell over one eye. She flung it back with a flip of her head and planted her hands on her hips.

"I should've done it myself, years ago." She raised her head to watch the woman and her dog wander by.

She turned back to me. "I already bought the kerosene. I paid cash and got three cans that look just like the ones Jimmy keeps under the shed at the back of the barn. That's where the fire should start."

Damn. She's going to do this with me or without me. And I still don't know why. Not really.

She went on, "And no, I didn't buy the kerosene in Winslow, smarty-pants. In case you were going to ask."

The "smarty-pants" stung. That's what she used to call me in high school, whenever I pointed out the flaws in her teenage schemes to right the world's wrongs. In her senior year, Marla had been a passionate crusader for a dozen causes: abused children and war refugees, underdogs and real dogs. Most of the time, her righteous ire was directed into protest marches, fundraising, and letters to the editor, but a few times she took more drastic action.

Once, she was determined to liberate a starving hound from a neighbor's yard. Another time, she decided a couple of local punks needed to suffer for vandalizing a synagogue. To rescue the hound, she took bolt-cutters to a chain-link fence. To punish the vandals, she dropped sugar cubes in their car's gas tank.

Both times, she'd acted alone, under cover of darkness, with mixed results. She freed the hound, but it escaped before she could take it to a shelter. The sugar escapade went off without a hitch but the typed note she left under a windshield wiper must have blown away, because there was no indication the boys ever connected their vandalism to the ruined engine.

I never had the nerve to join her in what she called her "justice missions," but I provided a few useful alibis. We both got good at keeping secrets, and she never got caught. After graduation, she threw herself into training as a physical therapist. Marla flew through her undergrad degree, three years of medical studies, the licensing exam, a one-year residency, and finally board certification. All that seemed to keep her busy and fulfilled, saving humanity one knee replacement at a time. All that time, I just puttered along, bouncing from a general humanities major to sociology, English, political science, and philosophy, wondering all along what sort of career I'd land in when I was done caring for Gran. Radio news reporter hadn't been on my list, if I'd ever had a list.

And here I was, sitting on a park bench while the friend I thought I knew—this self-appointed savior, still wrapped up in her quirks and passions—tried to talk me, her admiring sidekick, into her latest mission.

Now she paced a few steps up and down, then paused to pick at a cuticle. Watching the ducks and waiting for me to agree that yes, burning down an old barn was the right thing to do.

I was missing something. "Marla, why is this so personal?"

She dropped back onto the bench beside me and kicked the toe of a clunky sandal against the dirt.

She took a deep breath and began. "Those Friday night parties I told you about, in high school? There were usually six of us, sometimes eight. We went to the barn only on nights when it was clear and there was a moon. It was always dark inside, but the roof had holes in it where a little moonlight came through. Sometimes we remembered to bring a flashlight. Two of the boys said they'd been in there during the day, so they knew their way around.

"The big open part at the front is where they stacked the hay. Big mounds of it, in square bales but also stacks of loose hay that you could pile up to make caves and tunnels. About halfway in, before you got to the back wall, there was a big tarp hanging down from the beams. You couldn't see behind that, and we didn't go back there because there was a lot of junk scattered around. Old farm equipment, saws and shovels and stuff like that. No one wanted to trip and fall on that in the dark.

"Except once, when one of the boys got drunk and curious. He pulled the tarp back and I saw what looked like a tripod, like for a camera. We didn't go any further.

"Maybe a week later, one of the girls—her name was Katie Parker, maybe you remember her? She found a note in her school locker asking for money. Whoever wrote it said they had nude pictures of her and her boyfriend, together. And they'd show them to her parents and the principal if she didn't leave fifty dollars under a rock next to the barn."

I felt an involuntary shudder. "Oh god, that's horrible. What did she do?"

"What could she do? She paid, like the note told her to do."

"Then what happened? Did she figure out who did it? Did she tell the police, or her parents?"

"No! How could she? No one would believe her. Or they'd call her a slut and say she got what she deserved. Slut, slag, whore, whatever. You remember what high school was like."

Not really, I wanted to say. High school wasn't like that for everyone.

Aloud, I said, "But what if it wasn't true? I mean, if the photos weren't of her."

"Oh, it was true. I saw one of the pictures. It was kinda fuzzy but yeah, it was her and she was naked. So was the boy, but you couldn't see his face, just hers. And you could see everything else, too. Her body, his body, what they were doing. All of it." She rubbed her arms and shivered in the warm air.

I tried to work a bit of saliva into my mouth, which had suddenly gone dry. "Did the blackmail stop after she paid?"

"All I know is, her family moved away right after." She turned to face me. "But what if that wasn't the only time someone did that? What if it was going on for years? Maybe that's why Brenda hanged herself."

"But she died years earlier, right? And with Katie—what you're talking about now—it was a decade ago."

More cuticle picking. "Maybe we just never heard about the other times. Shit, maybe it's still going on. I've thought about it for ten years but I couldn't do it before, because people were using that barn to store stuff."

"You mean for hay and farm equipment? Jimmy's the only person who's using it now. Was using it."

She shrugged and dropped her hands back into her lap.

"Ah," I said. "You think it was him taking the pictures, don't you?"

"I don't know. Well, yes. It must have been, right?" She caught her bottom lip between her teeth and worked her jaw. "Because he took pictures of me, too. Once. But I was wearing my swimsuit," she added quickly when she saw my look. "It was at Bowman's Lake. Remember, at the camp? When we were ten. He said I should pretend I was a movie star. Try to pose like they did in those glamour shots, in the fan magazines my mom used to buy us."

She watched ducks for a moment. I stayed silent, resisting the urge to take her hand.

"Jimmy was very proud of those photos," she mused. "He gave me a few prints and said I should give them to my parents as a present. He said maybe that would make them stop fighting and then they wouldn't get divorced."

"Did you? Give them to your parents."

"No. It felt too weird. I wasn't exactly embarrassed by the photos, but I know I was vamping it up a bit, trying to copy the models' poses, and that felt wrong. Also, I couldn't see how giving my parents some pictures of me in a swimsuit would make them stay married, so I just stuck them away in my hope chest. I found them years later and threw them away."

"But you remembered."

"Of course. But the nude photos in Katie's school locker didn't look anything like the photos he took of me, the little kid in her swimsuit pretending to be a beauty queen." She rubbed her hands as if wiping off soil. "It doesn't matter now. He's gone."

"Of course it still matters," I said. "If there's anything there now, it may be evidence that the police will want. Help them find out who killed him."

"No." She shook her head hard and turned to face me. "What for? Jimmy's dead. The only people who can be hurt now are those kids who made stupid choices ten years ago. Sure, maybe there's evidence. Maybe there's even some old photos with names on them. But what good will it do to drag that all out into the open? No one went to the police back then, and no one is gonna want to do that now. They'll have their lives ruined.

"But right now," she insisted, "if there is anything there, we have a chance to get rid of it. Make it go away before the police find it. We've got to do it tomorrow morning, AJ. Early, before anyone else gets in there. You know that old dirt road in the woods? The one that runs behind the barn? We can drive most of the way in, then park in a place I know and walk down from the ridge."

Marla had it all figured out, I realized. All she needed was me, to light the match.

I thought of something else. "But who'd keep cameras and photos in a leaky old barn? If those this are still going on, they'd be in Jimmy's house."

"The barn's where he—or someone—took those blackmail pictures."

"Well," I finally said. "If it means that much to you, I guess it's worth a drive up there. Just to look, okay?"

She slid closer and gave me a quick reassuring hug, looking suddenly relieved. "I knew I could count on you, AJ. I'll pick you up tomorrow morning. Five-fifteen, okay? Don't worry, it'll be fine. We'll be fine."

Her arm dropped and she scrambled to her feet. "Now I've got to clean up for dinner. Keith's mom hates it when we're late."

Anyone listening would've thought we were arranging a brunch date, or our next trip to the lake.

I sat for a few more minutes, watching as she jogged back across the footbridge. Wondering if the "other girl" who'd been blackmailed was really Marla herself. That would explain why she'd quit her party-girl persona so abruptly in our junior year.

Thinking about photographs and secrets reminded me of what Evelyn Roland had told me about Jimmy Desjardins. His camera, and the little girls in the store.

But that incident, and Jimmy's photos of ten-year-old Marla in her swimsuit, happened almost twenty years ago. Long before the blackmail photos were left in a girl's locker. When those later photos were taken, Jimmy was a mid-thirties hardscrabble farmer with no wife, no children. He never made it past eighth grade, had probably never been inside the high school.

How would Jimmy know where someone's locker was?

**

The afternoon breeze is still coming in from the open window but Cassie's room has gone suddenly airless, as if all the oxygen has been sucked away by the weight of what she's just read. She leans forward with one hand pressed flat against her chest, struggling for breath and fighting to make sense of the words she's just read.

If this is a purely fictional story—if this is AJ's idea of a fun yarn, spun to entertain on a winter's evening—it's nothing but a cruel and terrible joke. The kind of sick fiction that uses real people's pain as entertainment, turning teenage trauma into bedtime stories.

Even as she thinks that, Cassie knows this wasn't written as any kind of joke. The details are too specific, too well preserved in AJ's careful, precise wording and annotated by Marla's own handwriting. This is confession disguised as story, wrapped in a thin gauze of narrative distance. Her mother—her quiet, compassionate mother who disliked fireworks and frowned at elbows on the table—had been victimized by a soulless predator when she was only a child.

Now Cassie knows what her mother and AJ have been hiding for four decades. Not just humiliating photographs that should have been buried with their mother's shame, but her strategy for revenge.

Cassie's hands tremble and she wants to fling the pages across the room, to unknow what she now knows. She's also feeling now the desperate rage that her mother must have felt. Rage against a system that objectified girls. Against a society that turned an indulgent eye on youthful transgressions and bad decisions. Against that "live and let live" community described by Dotty Kellerman.

Cassie can't pause here, there's too much at stake. She needs to understand exactly what was stolen from the frightened girl her mother used to be. She carries the unread portion of AJ's story downstairs again to the porch and sits where she can see her mother's geraniums.

CHAPTER FOURTEEN

AJ

~ 9 ~

At 5:10 the next morning, I was shivering near the mailbox at the end of my driveway, a flashlight in my hand and a pair of work gloves in the pocket of my denim jacket. The half-moon had set hours earlier. A clammy mist swirled and dripped from invisible trees.

Marla's Civic smelled sharply of kerosene. I hoped she'd wedged the cans securely in the trunk so she wouldn't have to explain any spills to her husband.

"What did you tell Keith?" I asked.

"I didn't, I just left a note saying I had to fill in for someone at the sports center in Hartford. They open at seven, so of course I left extra early."

Marla's PT work took her out of town occasionally, and Keith's afternoon-evening shift at the radio station meant he never had to get up before eleven. They often went a day or more without crossing paths until the evening.

But the casualness of her lie surprised me. I'd forgotten how much practice she'd had in high school, fabricating credible tales to conceal the truth during her justice-mission and party-girl days.

"Besides," she added, "Keith and Ryan were out late last night playing poker. They didn't get back until nearly one. They'll sleep until ten, at least. No worries."

We saw no other headlights on the five-minute ride from my house to the stop sign at the end of Turnbull Road. There, instead of going left onto Cherry Valley and heading past the Desjardins farm, she turned right to climb the ridge toward the abandoned village of Graves Parish.

About a quarter-mile along the paved road, a dirt track veered off to the left, sloping down a little from the ridgeline into heavy woods. More of a wide path than a road, it was peppered with weeds and washouts, where rain had pulled away the soil and gravel. The Civic's headlights bounced off rocks and tree roots, and I feared her car would bottom out, but she drove with expert caution, leaning over the steering wheel and finding her way as much by feel as by sight.

And practice, I realized. She'd been here before.

I couldn't have found the trail in the dark, but Marla had no problem locating it. She stopped at a wide spot on the gravel road where a narrow footpath led off to the left and, presumably, downhill to the barn.

"It's not far now." She switched off the Civic's headlights, plunging us into near-darkness.

"Maybe we should leave the kerosene here until we're sure," I suggested.

"Seriously? We're gonna walk all the way in, then walk back out for the kerosene?" She popped her door open.

The weak glow of the dome light sent shadows across her face. She wore a turtleneck sweater and a knitted watch cap with her hair tucked beneath. Everything black, like a cartoon cat burglar. But this was no cartoon. Smudge her face with charcoal, hand her an assault weapon, and she could've stepped out of a military recruitment poster or one of those commando movies that Keith loved so much. Like *First Blood*, but with a pregnant female lead.

I didn't know this person at all. Maybe I never had.

"Come on," she said. "Get your gloves on. It's almost daylight."

It wasn't almost daylight, not really, but I followed her out of the car. By the light of my flashlight, she retrieved three rectangular metal cans from the Civic's trunk and, in silence, we started down the trail.

She carried a fuel can in one hand and a heavy black flashlight in the other, swinging it behind her occasionally to point out a rock or fallen limb. I carried the other cans, keeping my flashlight pressed between my palm and the handle of a kerosene can. I tried to hold the light at an angle so I could see the trail, but the can was heavy and I was mostly moving blind. My uncooperative left foot, as always, found every branch and root to trip over.

Marla never looked back. She just strode on through the thick dark woods like she was force-marching her platoon. We walked for what seemed like an hour but was probably no more than ten minutes.

At last the trees thinned, the sky lightened from inky black to a misted charcoal, and we emerged from heavy woods into a stand of tall weeds and saplings. Two hundred feet beyond, at the top edge of Jimmy Desjardins' freshly cut hayfield, the silhouette of the

Grabtown barn emerged. Nearly three stories tall, clad in rough clapboard siding and moss-spotted shingles, it was at least half the length of a basketball court.

"Watch out for trash." Marla swung her flashlight beam toward a faint path through the brambles. "There's an old fallen-down fence under the weeds. Woven wire, barbed wire. Old tires and tractor parts and lots of other crap."

We moved carefully along one side of the fieldstone foundation, skirting a shed crammed with rusted farm equipment. Near the front of the barn, we set down the kerosene and directed our flashlights into the space where two big doors had once hung. The doors had fallen off their roller track and into the weeds long ago, leaving the interior open to the weather. Inside was a vast open floor, a high space that rose to hand-hewn beams and rafters, with a partial loft platform at the far end. Mounds of dry hay rose all around us, some loose and some packed crookedly in bales.

Everything smelled of mold, mildew, and a sharp animal musk that made my eyes water. Bat and bird droppings, probably. There was an undertone of urine, mostly animal but maybe human, and a base-note of whatever might have died in the walls or beneath the floorboards.

I couldn't see its attraction. Who'd want to camp out here? Lie in the bat shit, romp in the moldy hay? This place wasn't spooky or mysterious, just really filthy and repellent.

"Come on, AJ. This way." Marla was walking across a thick carpet of dirty hay toward the back wall, where a normal-sized door was set into an interior wall of wood planks.

I played my flashlight beam along the wall, and door, stopping to highlight the deadbolt hardware installed above the round knob. "Marla, did you know about this? It looks new. I thought you said there was just tarps hanging back here."

"Yeah, but that was years ago. Someone's been renovating, obviously."

She twisted the knob and gave the door a hard kick, with no success.

"Wait here." She turned and went back the way we'd come, moving quickly along the floor of the haymow. I stood in the dark, wondering if I should have followed her and wishing I'd thought to bring extra flashlight batteries. Nearby in the dark, something squeaked. A bat, or maybe a rat.

From the other side of the locked door, I heard thumps and the sound of breaking glass. I flinched, suppressing a yelp.

"Marla? Is that you?"

She gave a short laugh, muffled by the door. "Hunh. Of course, who else would it be?"

The door snicked open.

Inside was a workshop. In one wall was a double-hung window, its frame and panes broken. Below the opening, shards of glass littered the floor; above, a torn black curtain hung from a bent rod. The pale gray light of near-dawn filtered in, giving just enough light to see by.

Unlike the rest of the barn, these walls were finished with wallboard and painted an uneven blue.

An industrial-looking gray carpet covered the floor. In one corner, two Victorian-style floor lamps and a flood lamp on a tripod stood beside a small space heater and a portable generator.

There were chairs, an ornate wooden desk, a dorm-sized fridge, and, on the floor, a thin mattress spread with a pink velveteen blanket and tangled satin sheets.

"Someone's been living here," I offered.

"Or working here," Marla jerked her chin toward a set of bookshelves on the far side of the room. Bulging duffel bags rested on the bottom shelves, stacks of boxes on the higher ones. I carried my flashlight closer and read a few labels.

"Tri-X, VHS, Kodak Gold, FujiFilm. That's all photography stuff. Who's using this—"

"Over here." Marla's flashlight brightened a dark corner where the faint daylight couldn't reach. Two folded tripods leaned against the wall beside a four-drawer metal filing cabinet. She opened the top drawer and pulled out two folders, spilling the contents onto the gray carpet.

I crouched and stared at a pile of ten by twelve photos. Some were black-and-whites but most were in full color. As I nudged the photos apart with the tip of a finger and brought my own flashlight closer, body parts became visible. I saw rounded buttocks, the curve of a breast. A close-up of male genitals beside a wide red mouth and tongue.

I yanked my hand back and looked away. Took a deep breath and looked back.

Every photo showed explicitly positioned nude bodies, or parts of bodies, with splayed genitals. Most were female, shot mostly in close-up. I tore my eyes away again, only to realize that many of these shots had been taken in this room. There was the satin-sheeted mattress, the blue wall, the wooden desk.

A few of the photos made an attempt at artistry, showing a model partially clothed or shot from the back with the head turned demurely away. Most, however, were purely pornographic.

Many featured bondage or masochism. Women bound by ropes, handcuffs or chains, wearing hoods, tied to a folding chair—probably this chair, the one right here beside me. Some of the photos showed clearly recognizable features: blank faces twisted into a parody of lust, or frozen in shame or fear or pain. Many photos included young men coupling with the women, or being serviced by them.

And some of the women were clearly not women, but young girls. Adolescent, or younger. Maybe pre-pubescent.

I dropped the flashlight, stumbled to my feet, and shot out the door into the haymow, falling to my knees and vomiting into the moldy hay. All I could bring up from an empty stomach was a sour, stinging bile.

I heard Marla's feet rustling nearby. Then silence. Into the quiet, from somewhere outside, came the three-note, pre-dawn call of a Carolina wren. A second one answered, beginning their morning as always with music.

That's where I should be, I thought stupidly. *Walking in the woods, listening to birdsong.*

Marla dropped to her knees beside me and placed an arm around my shoulders. Her other hand pushed damp hair off my forehead. "Now you see why we have to burn this place down."

I wiped my mouth against the collar of my jean jacket and sat back. "That's all Jimmy's stuff, isn't it?"

"Yes. At least, I think so. Most of it."

"How did you know what was here?"

"I didn't know for sure. But after he died I remembered his camera. The tarp, the tripod, that blackmail note. What we just saw, though—it's way worse than I imagined."

"But what you saw was ages ago. More than a decade! What made you think something like that was still here?"

She dropped her hand from my shoulder and handed me my flashlight, then stood and hauled me up with a strong hand. "We'll talk about it later, AJ. Come on. We're running out of time."

"The police need to—"

"No police! That filing cabinet was full, did you see it? Did you see how many folders there are? They all have photos in them. There's hundreds of photos."

"I only saw a few."

"Each folder has a girl's name. Maybe they're real names, but probably not. There's VHS tapes, too, on the shelves. Boxes of them, with names like Baby Bambi Grows Up and Sweetie Pie and My Precious Darling."

She grabbed my shoulders and pulled me around to face her in the faint light. "Now think about what will happen to those girls if the police get hold of all that. They'll be asked a million questions, like why didn't they come forward right away and why didn't they tell their parents, and how could they let this happen? Because no one will believe they were forced into this.

"Jimmy's dead," Marla added. "So he can't be arrested. Whoever else is involved, if the cops ever catch anyone, it'll just be a he-said, she-said thing. No one believes what kids say. They'll be shunned and hated and kicked out of school, if they're still in school. Their lives will be ruined. Their families' lives, too. Maybe it happened years ago, but the consequences will happen right now. We're doing this for them."

"But—"

She pulled me closer and stared into my eyes. Her face was just inches from mine and for one brief moment I thought—absurdly—she was about to kiss me.

"No more buts," she urged. "We're going to stop it. We have to. You have to, because I can't. Dump the kerosene and light the match. Do it for me, AJ."

I stared, breathless and senseless. Then I closed my eyes. "Yes."

We moved fast then, carrying armloads of dry hay from the mow and piling it high in the workshop. Marla yanked boxes from the shelves and emptied the drawers of the filing cabinet. Then she waited outside beneath the trees while I soaked everything with kerosene and tossed the empty cans among piles of trash inside the shed.

I took the box of strike-anywhere matches she'd left on the windowsill and walked out the way we came in, stopping only to drop lighted matches on photos and dry hay.

Moving with my head down like a well-trained robot, thinking only of how much I loved Marla, because how else could I do such a terrible thing?

Then we stood together beneath a hemlock tree at the edge of the woods. Marla rested one hand on her belly and slipped her other hand around my waist. I wrapped an arm around her shoulders and we stood hip to hip, watching the sun rise as the barn burned.

Orange flames licked through broken clapboards and empty windows, as an oily smoke curled above the moss-spotted roof of the last building in Grabtown.

Chapter Fifteen

Cassie

Cassie lets the pages slide from her hand onto the porch floor.

Lurching back into the present, she's suddenly aware that the seat of the wicker chair has cut off circulation at the back of her thighs. Small spikes of pain stab each leg, though the rest of her has gone numb with disbelief.

She pushes herself out of the chair and stumbles to the porch railing. Pressing the heels of her hands against her eyelids, she tries to construct a new image of her mother at twenty-eight: patient wife, mother-to-be, hard-working medical professional, arsonist.

Impossible.

She holds the dusty railing, watching bumblebees tumble in the nasturtiums and stretching her legs, one at a time, until the tingling fades. The sun is low in the western sky and it's nearly dinnertime. Still half numb, but thinking she should call upstairs to Ana, she grabs the manuscript and opens the screen door. Changes her mind and pauses in the doorway, the door propped against her hip.

What will she say to her sister? Never mind, Ana, you don't have to read it after all?

Cassie's earlier rage, the fury burning bright on her mother's behalf, has been tempered now with the hard reality of arson.

She never thought Marla and AJ would actually set fire to the barn.

For the first time in her life, Cassie finds herself wanting to protect Ana. So, again: What to say? That she was wrong, that now she realizes AJ's novel is just a piece of sensationalized crime fiction?

But however she might try, she can't bring herself to deny or trivialize AJ's story, which is also her mother's story. And therefore it's their story, hers and Ana's.

With this thought comes a confusing flood of resentment, because it's their mother who's dropped it in their lap. How *dare* she leave the manuscript here, knowing they'd find it while they're cleaning out the house. When they're still raw and grieving, just days after her death.

Coward. AJ, too. They're both gone, so we can't ask questions. They can't explain or justify anything. Not the bad decisions, not the criminal behavior.

But her mother and AJ were most certainly not cowards.

She retrieves the manuscript from the table and clutches it to her chest. She moves to the screen door but pauses uncertainly, cycling through all the emotions.

Through the screen, she spots the pitcher of black-eyed Susans on the kitchen table. Desperate to focus on something else, anything else, her mind disconnects from the terrible knowledge she's holding in her arms.

Two days post-funeral, the wildflowers are drooping their heads and shedding yellow petals onto bank statements and a pepper grinder. Thinking to toss the spent flowers into the woods, she moves into the kitchen, drops the manuscript on the kitchen table, and grabs the pitcher instead. Her breathing steadies.

As she's carrying it outside, a black SUV turns into the driveway.

Paused on the porch with one hand holding the pitcher and the other grasping the flower stems, she watches as an old man climbs out of the driver's seat.

He's in his mid-seventies, at least. Clean-shaven, mostly bald, with only a short ruff of white hair fringing the base of his skull. His shoulders are hunched and there's a caved-in look to his chest, but there's also something military in his bearing, like he'd stand at attention if he could. He's wearing neatly pressed stone-washed jeans and a plain black t-shirt, the clothes of a younger man. He looks like someone coming to retrieve his wife's casserole dish.

He'll be disappointed. We haven't eaten anything the neighbors brought.

He moves gingerly between his car and the flower beds, careful to avoid a tangle of nasturtiums encroaching on the driveway. He stops at the base of the steps and turns mild brown eyes up toward Cassie.

"Good afternoon. You must be one of Marla's daughters." He nods at the pitcher she's holding. "I'm glad you kept that pottery piece. My wife was very fond of it. She found it at a studio on the west coast."

Cassie glances at down at the pitcher, then back up at him.

"Sorry," he says. "I should've said. My name's Carl Androski."

She freezes, her mind flying suddenly to the past and a forty-year-old arson. Then forward again to Wednesday, when she found the note in the flowers.

The weight of the pitcher is a heavy ache in her forearm. She recovers sufficiently to continue her task, dumping flowers and water into the narrow space between the porch railing and an overgrown azalea bush.

She holds his eyes in a level stare. "I'm Cassie Bousquet. Cassie Masterson, actually."

His lined face creases into a slight smile. "Cassandra. Of course. You look so much like your mother."

"Do you think so? Maybe you're thinking of my sister Ana? She's a lot more like Mom is—was—than me." She bends down to set the pitcher on the warped floorboards, close beside her feet.

"I was sorry to hear of her passing," he continues. "Your mother was a remarkable woman."

You have no idea, Cassie thinks. Or maybe he does, so she manages the semblance of a wary smile. "You were one of my mother's friends?"

The old man stretches his right hand up to where she's standing on the porch but it's too much of a reach, so she moves down the three steps to meet him on the flagstones and take his hand. Despite his age and the bent posture, there's an imposing bulk in his torso and still-broad shoulders.

His handshake is firm. "I'm more of a longtime acquaintance than a friend, I guess. And an admirer, though not in the way you might think."

Think? I don't know what to think. Cassie blinks, suppressing a shiver and the urge to pull back from his touch. Her eyes flick to his waist. No sidearm.

Damn. Where's Ana? Cassie knows if Ana sees this guy she'll ask him in and maybe start chatting about AJ's story, but Ana doesn't yet know about the arson. She won't know she should stay quiet. *I need to tell her —*

Releasing her hand, he peers at the jumble of flower stems she's dumped behind the azalea. "Your mother always loved black-eyed Susans. She called them —"

"—her ditch babies," Cassie supplies. "These were dropping petals," she adds in a rush. "I'm just going to pick some more."

She had no plans to pick flowers but now she needs something to get him away from the house and away from Ana, who, she hopes is still upstairs, reading.

He waves a hand agreeably toward the driveway. "I saw some growing by your road, a little ways back. Shall we take a walk?" He doesn't seem concerned that Cassie hasn't asked him in. "Let me just grab a hat from my car. Don't want to invite skin cancer on this scalp. Though I'm of an age where maybe it doesn't matter anymore."

He walks to his SUV and retrieves an old brown bucket hat from the back seat, moving easily if a little slowly. He tugs it onto his head with a gnarled hand.

Cassie forces her feet down the steps, trying to figure out why he's here.

What the hell am I doing, going off to pick flowers with a police detective? When last night I learned my mother and her best friend torched a building.

It happened four decades ago and her mother's dead now, but still. *What happens now? Do I say anything? Should I tell him I'm busy, ask him to leave?*

Too late. They're walking side by side along the gravel road now. The early evening air is cool and pleasant, there's no traffic in sight, and he's telling her about his wife Connie, their three children and five grandchildren. How in retirement they'd converted their garage into an art studio so Connie could work on her watercolors, and how he's been at a bit of a loss ever since her death six years ago.

Cassie remains quiet as they stroll beside a roadside culvert full of weeds and wildflowers, looking for black-eyed Susans. When she spots a cluster of blooms, Androski pulls a wood-handled pocketknife from his jeans and unfolds it.

He hands the knife to her, butt-end first. "Always carry a knife, my dad told me. Unless you're going through TSA at an airport. Or security screening at a courthouse, or a school, or—well, lots of places now, I guess. We never had to worry about that, when I started. Back when you were born."

Cassie smiles, acknowledging his small attempt at humor, and has to remind herself that he's not here just to pick flowers. *When will he ask about the arson?*

She steps down into a shallow culvert and cuts a fistful of black-eyed Susans, surprised at how easy it is to slice through the fibrous stems. The knife is sharp and thin, showing the wear that comes from honing a blade over many years.

"Other things have changed, too," he muses. "Like forensics. Big changes there. Forty-fifty years ago, we didn't have all the crime-solving tools we have now. I was a detective, you know. With the state police."

Ah, here it comes.

She climbs out of the ditch and back to the gravel road, brushing bits of milkweed floss from her shirt. She turns to face him, steeling herself.

Now his gaze holds hers. "Like when that Winslow farmer got murdered, back in 'eighty-five. James Desjardins. That one's still unsolved. Did your mother ever talk about it?"

"Not really." Cassie closes the knife and hands it back. She inspects the flowers for insect damage and discards two stems. "Like you said, it was a long time ago. I think Mom was pregnant with us when that murder happened."

"You and Anastasia."

"Yes."

"There was a reporter at the radio station who covered that murder. Agnes Porter. She lived here with you for a while, I believe."

Keeping her eyes on the flowers, she fishes for a suitably bland contribution. "She was Mom's friend. She preferred to be called AJ," she adds helpfully.

"Yes, AJ. She was our key witness to the murder, but we never had enough evidence to charge anyone, so she was never called to testify. She must have mentioned the murder."

"Not really. Ana and I were too young to remember AJ working at the radio station. She went to law school—I remember all those big books scattered around the house, she was always studying. She ended up working for a legal-aid group in Willimantic."

He doesn't push it. "Yes, I remember that." Another pause. "Is your husband here with you?" His tone is casual but he's watching her carefully.

"Marsh? No, he's overseas for a few days on business. Hong Kong." She discards another spent blossom.

"I'm sure that keeps him on his toes." He pauses, as if waiting for her to explain what Marsh's business is, but she has the feeling he already knows.

"Cassie, how well do you know Marsh's brothers?"

Startled, she looks up from the flowers. "His brothers?"

Androski waits. He seems to be very good at waiting.

"Very little. I've never met them. It's not a close family. Marsh said they helped him start his car company, but they had a business disagreement so he bought them out. That was decades ago, before I even met him." She drops her eyes to scan the roadside, pretending to search for more flowers.

He's fallen silent, leaving her to wonder why on earth he wants to know about her husband's brothers. If Androski was from the IRS, sure, they're always auditing Marsh's company—he says it comes with the territory when you run a business dealing in old cars, however fancy they are—but why is he asking about Marsh and his family?

The cat-and-mouse game is exhausting. She wants to yell, *Get to the point, dammit!* but that would be unwise. And why is he asking about the murder, not the burned barn?

Impatient to wrap up the conversation, Cassie starts walking toward the house. She keeps her eyes away from his. "The Desjardins murder, is that how you met our mom? I can't believe you're still looking into that. I thought you'd retired."

He matches her stride. "The victim was your mother's second cousin. We talked with everyone in the family, of course, and anyone else who knew him." He pauses for a beat. "And about the retirement thing. It's hard to walk away from an unsolved case. They never really go away, did you know that? There's no statute of limitations on murder.

"Once or twice a year, the chief drags out the old files and they take another look. He lets me help on this one because I always thought I knew the answer. I just couldn't find the evidence to prove it. But each year I get hopeful, because you never know. Sometimes there's a new lab test for old evidence. Or someone dies, and someone else finally comes forward, years later, with a new piece of information."

She meets his gaze. "Has that happened in this case?"

"No," he admits. "Not yet. This one was pretty thin to begin with. It's all circumstantial. Hints and hearsay, nothing I could hang my hat on."

Androski's eyes have gone watery, a little puffy and red around the rims. A fluff of milkweed drifts by and Cassie wonders if he has hay fever, or if he's just an old guy with rheumy eyes, lonely for company.

He stops to wipe beneath his eyes, one at a time, with a careful finger. "Do you have enough for your bouquet? Here, how about some Queen Anne's lace for contrast." He breaks off a spray of tiny white blossoms and flicks away a ladybug.

Queen Anne for Ana? She's reading too much into this. Maybe he just likes wildflowers.

They resume their walk back to the house, a little more briskly now as it's nearly half-past seven and the sun is setting.

Cassie feels awkward in what's become a long silence. They've walked farther than she realized. "You must have regrets about that cold case. About not solving it."

He considers this. "I hate leaving loose ends. But I've learned one important thing. Jimmy Desjardins was not a good man. I wish more people had come forward and told us what they knew about him. It would've saved a few lives, I think."

He glances at her, perhaps waiting for questions, but she's quiet.

When they reach his SUV, Androski pauses with one hand on the driver's door. He straightens a little, suddenly looking more official, almost military. He's switched back to his earlier formality. "I want to give you a heads-up, Ms. Bousquet. Someone else—another detective—may contact you with their own questions. It's just part of the routine."

"Who will that be?"

"I'm not sure."

"Do I have to talk to them?"

"No more than you're talking to me now. And you're always free to contact an attorney."

She takes a step closer and finds she has to look up to face him. He's old, but he's still many inches taller. "My brother-in-law is an attorney."

It's a bluff, because Jonathan is a real estate attorney. Criminal law is way outside his wheelhouse. Is that what Androski's talking about?

The creases around his mouth deepen into a smile. "It was good to finally meet you, Ms. Bousquet. As a grownup, I mean." He looks as if he's about to bow or touch his faded bucket hat. "And if you ever need to contact me about anything, that number your mom wrote down—it's still good."

"Thanks, but I don't think I'll need to— Oh," she remembers. "Your wife's pitcher."

He waves a hand. "Consider it a gift. It should stay with you, for your black-eyed Susans."

After he's gone, Cassie picks up the brown stoneware pitcher. She turns it over and smiles, recognizing the logo of a well-known pottery studio near her house in Palos Verdes.

Her smile dies. The house in Palos Verdes doesn't feel like hers anymore. It's just a place she's supposed to return to. Everything there is Marsh's. Always has been.

Her home isn't three thousand miles away, it's right here.

She also realizes that, for the first time in years, Marsh has been out of her thoughts for nearly a whole day. But now he's crept back in.

***

"Hey, where were you?" Ana's at the kitchen counter, chopping carrots and broccoli. "I found a chicken casserole in the freezer, and I'm steaming some veggies. You always say you're never hungry, but I don't care, I'm starving."

Her hair's piled untidily on top of her head and there's a smear of moisture across the front of her tee shirt. The microwave is humming and there's a covered pot oozing steam on a front burner. On the far wall, the small kitchen television shows a serious-faced young woman gesturing at a weather map. The domestic scene is so familiar, so comfortable—so normal—that for a moment Cassie sees her mother standing at the counter.

She finds her voice. Realizing that she is, in fact, hungry. "Ana, that sounds great."

Startled, Ana looks up from her chopping. "Since when are you—" She changes tack. "You were gone a while. I called your phone but you left it on the porch. Where did you go?"

"For a walk," Cassie says truthfully. "I picked more flowers. Have you been reading? How far did you get?"

"Like I said, I'm a fast reader. Let's eat first, talk later. Here, can you husk these?" She hands Cassie two cobs of sweet corn. "I've got fresh tomatoes, too, from the farm stand on the corner."

After dinner, they bring their separate pieces of AJ's story to the kitchen table, central to so many evenings of homework and craft projects.

"So," Ana says brightly, "It's got a real Kinsey Millhone vibe, doesn't it?"

Ana obviously hasn't gotten very far, despite her claim of being a fast reader. Cassie takes a deep breath and tries to match her sister's light tone. "No surprise. Mom and AJ loved those mystery stories. Sue Grafton, Sara Paretsky."

"Or Cagney & Lacey. Do you really think you can turn it into a screenplay? Or a movie script, that would be cool."

"Umm...How far have you read?" No spoilers, Cassie reminds herself. Ana still thinks it's a simple mystery that Mom's friend AJ is going to solve. AJ Porter, ace reporter and girl detective.

"I just finished chapter six. Where AJ loads her shotgun and brings it into the bedroom. *The* shotgun, right? The same one you found upstairs." Ana leans forward, her hazel eyes bright.

"I'm not thinking about turning it into anything right now," Cassie cautions. "First, we both need to finish reading." She realizes with a small start that yes, they do need to finish it. Because that's what their mother wanted them to do: read it and learn the truth, Ana and Cassie together.

"And that detective, Androski. Now I know who he was, the name in the old phone book. But why did Mom save his number?"

Cassie looks away. "I'm sure the police talked to everyone who knew the victim. Maybe she spoke with him more than once." She hesitates. "Ana, look. You need to know something. He was here today, while you were upstairs reading."

"Who?" Ana's eyes widen. "Androski? The same detective? Why?"

"He's the one who brought the black-eyed Susans. The first batch, from the funeral. Then he showed up this afternoon and we went for a walk and I picked some more flowers." She waves a dismissive hand. "Don't ask, that doesn't matter. He said he knew Mom, from the investigation into the murder. And now… Well, they never solved it but the case is still open. A cold case. Androski's retired, mostly, but he's still poking around, looking for information to help solve it."

"But we don't know anything. AJ's dead, Mom's gone now too, and there's nothing— Oh." She glances down.

"Yeah." Cassie taps the manuscript. "That's what this is about."

"Then we should give him a copy—"

"No!"

Ana jumps and immediately Cassie wants to walk it back, that forceful shout that startled both of them.

Reaching across the table for her twin's hand, she gentles her voice. "Ana, please. Don't tell anyone anything, especially not him." She squeezes Ana's hand, encouraging trust. "We have to read this all the way through, both of us, and then decide what to do. You're going to find out…in the next chapters, Mom and AJ do some awful things. There's other things, also, that they talk about. Sexual abuse, exploitation, and—well, you'll see."

Ana frowns and sits back, freeing her hand from Cassie's. "No spoilers, remember? But if it's something bad— No, I don't want to read anything bad about Mom. If that's in there, I don't need to know what she did. Or what happened to her." She eyes the two manuscript halves as if they're poisoned. "Maybe we should just shred it. Or burn it."

Cassie hears burn it and suppresses a shudder. "We both need to do this, Ana. You can't leave me alone with what I already know. Read it, then we'll decide together.

And don't tell anyone anything. No one, definitely not the cops. Not yet."

Don't tell anyone anything. Now she's repeating Marsh's words. She groans inwardly, trying to remember what she's told her faraway husband about the manuscript. *I could write a good adaptation*, she remembers. *And Ana needs to read it, too.*

Ana's staring down at the table, unable to meet Cassie's eyes. Her voice goes small and soft. "Maybe you could summarize it for me?"

Cassie pushes both hands through her hair, sending it helter-skelter. She used to think spiking it into many messy layers would make her appear taller. Now she suspects it just makes her look slightly deranged. Or feral, like she's lost in some pathless wilderness, which is exactly how she feels now. But there's only one way forward.

"No, Ana. We both have to read it. AJ's story is Mom's story, and they left it for us because they felt it was important to read. I know you can do this." At the risk of sounding trite, she adds, "Remember what AJ used to say? 'Don't ever underestimate your mother, girls. She's tougher than a boiled owl.' That's what we have to be, too. Tougher than boiled owls."

"Oh god, I hate that stupid expression." Ana groans and almost smiles, swiping at a tear. "Okay. But no more wine until we've finished reading. No more alcohol. Please, Cassie, promise me. I need you sober."

Cassie opens her mouth to protest but realizes she doesn't care about wine or anything else except finishing the story.

Silently, she hands Ana everything she's read and carries the remaining pages up to her room, readying herself for whatever comes next.

Chapter Sixteen

AJ

~ 10 ~

As we bumped out of the woods in Marla's Civic, the light of dawn grew stronger and the smell of smoke faded. I tried to piece together what she'd told me.

"Marla, that girl who got that blackmail note…that was you, wasn't it?"

She stopped the car and shifted into park. Doused the headlights and planted both hands on the steering wheel, staring blankly through the windshield.

Suddenly she glanced down, looking startled. Her gloved hands went to her abdomen and her eyes opened wide. "Oh! What was that? Ohmigod, something's moving! It's a baby!"

"How do you know? What's it feel like?"

She stripped off her gloves and splayed both hands on her belly. "Like a…goldfish. Like I've swallowed a live goldfish and it's flopping around in there. It's the strangest feeling…" She turned to face me, her hazel eyes full of wonder. "Here, AJ, give me your hand."

I pulled off a glove and touched her abdomen with tentative fingers but felt nothing except her body's warmth.

"Here." She shifted my hand a few inches to one side and pressed the palm firmly against the small bulge beneath her shirt.

"Are you sure?" I started to pull my hand back.

But then I felt it, a small ripple of inner movement. "Oh! Yes, I think so."

We held our breath, her hand on my hand, my hand on her belly, until the activity ceased.

She smiled, looking suddenly beautiful in her watch cap and dirty turtleneck. "Finally. Now I know they're real. One of them, anyway. How will I know for sure they're both moving? I wonder what it will feel like in a few months. Probably like I've swallowed a wrestling arena."

She straightened her shirt. "Damn, I nearly forgot. Give me your gloves, AJ."

She opened the driver's door and disappeared into the woods with both pair of gloves. In less than a minute, she was back.

"Jeez, it's getting late." She shifted abruptly into first gear and started too quickly, spinning the Civic's wheels in loose gravel. "We've got to shower and run all our clothes through your washer, right away. Can I hang out for a couple of hours at your house? Just until Keith's gone to work. I brought my scrubs to change into."

"Of course. Stay as long as you need to. But I've got to leave at 9:30 for a meeting in town. For work."

Mentioning work felt surreal, something from a distant universe. My other life, the part where I had a job and normal responsibilities and hadn't just burned down a barn.

I tried again. "That girl who found the note?"

She pulled off her cap, shook her hair loose, and sighed. "There were two of us. We both got notes. She told her parents, but I didn't. Dad and Mom were divorced by then and Mom was working two jobs to make ends meet. I sure wasn't going to bother her with something that was my own stupid fault. I'd been drinking and yeah, I had sex in that barn with a guy I thought I was in love with.

"So when I got that note and the photos, I kept my mouth shut. I didn't tell the police, I didn't get kicked out of school, and I didn't have to move away. I paid the money, quit drinking, ripped up the photos, and dumped the boy. Then I met Keith and everything got better." She glanced at me. "I know he's not the prize catch in the husband derby, but he's loyal and funny. A good, kind man who will be a wonderful father."

Her eyes filled with tears. "He doesn't know about the stupid things I did before I met him, and he absolutely is not going to know about this. Got it?"

"Okay." What else could I say? I was good at appearing stoic, lousy at offering comfort. "It's your information but it's our secret. Of course."

She nodded, looking relieved, and swiped at her face with the back of a hand. She drove in silence as I watched the morning landscape roll by, thinking about what we'd found and what we'd destroyed. It felt both right and terrible, all at once.

We stood in my driveway for a few minutes and watched a thickening cloud of black smoke billow over the ridge, three miles away. The first siren sounded from the nearest fire station, on the far side of the valley.

I checked my watch: 7:15. The volunteers would need another fifteen or twenty minutes to assemble, get the pumper trucks on site, roll out the hoses, and start to pour water on the blaze. We'd lit the fire about forty-five minutes ago, giving it plenty of time to develop into a full-on conflagration but not spread too far, I hoped, into woods and fields.

"Marla, if someone else hadn't spotted the fire by now, we'd have called it in, right?"

"Of course."

***

In 1985, Pierre's was Winslow's most popular greasy spoon. Tucked away on a side street two blocks from the radio station, the diner gained the bulk of its foot traffic from the small district courthouse next door. Its clientele was mostly a predictable mix of lawyers, police, and other courthouse denizens.

Fridays were usually quiet, especially in the summer when judges and lawyers liked to take off early, heading to Maine or Cape Cod for long weekends. Of the dozen or so customers hunched over coffee and toast, only one looked unfamiliar, a stocky man with a bushy brown mustache and wire-rimmed glasses sitting in a high-backed booth near the front window.

Not real tall, maybe five-seven or five-eight. Early forties, with collar-length sandy hair combed straight back and an angular, craggy face that didn't match the barrel-chested body. His crooked nose suggested a history in something pugilistic, hockey or boxing. He wore rumpled khakis and a long-sleeved blue twill shirt with the cuffs rolled up. Everything screamed old-school newsman even before I noticed the pens lined up in his shirt pocket.

"You must be AJ Porter. Zachary Stollman." He set down his mug, half-rose and leaned awkwardly across the table to offer a large hand.

I swung my handbag onto the table and slid onto the red vinyl seat across from him. "My boss says we should work together, but I'm not sure how I can help you."

His shoulders rose in a small shrug. "I'm just looking for some orientation and a few contacts. I've never been out this way before. Mostly, I spend my time chasing legislators in Hartford. Or visiting with Beemer owners in Fairfield County. You know, the gold coast."

His voice carried a soft drawl, which I didn't mind, and a slightly patronizing tone, which I did.

I bristled. "We have a few Beemers in Winslow. But it's different here. Nothing like that end of the state."

"This town doesn't really feel like Connecticut at all. It's more like Appalachia."

"It's nothing like that." Actually, many people who lived here called it exactly that. The northern version of a hillbilly is a swamp Yankee, but I wasn't going to tell him that.

He eased off. "It's nice and quiet, though. That's good."

"Quiet, yes. We roll up the sidewalks at eight. Most evenings, we listen to coyotes howl and watch the neighbors' cows walk out to pasture. City people stare at little fish in glass tanks, here we have coyotes and cows."

He flashed teeth in lieu of a smile and abandoned the small talk. "I caught a couple of your newscasts yesterday, AJ. Very professional."

"It's nice to know someone's listening." Remembering that Mike wanted us to work together, I tried a more earnest tone. "And I've seen your by-line.

The nursing home series? Good stuff, balanced but honest."

He ducked his head in acknowledgement. "Some people say it was a little too honest."

Crystal, everyone's favorite red-haired waitress, strolled over with a coffee pot and a second mug.

"Morning, AJ." She poured coffee for me and raised a curious eyebrow at Zach. He didn't look up and I didn't introduce him, so she topped off his coffee and turned to me.

"Hey, AJ," she said, "you hear about that fire this morning out by Graves Parish? That was on the air at nine o'clock."

All I could manage was a nod. I reached for my spoon, picked up the creamer, and stirred slowly as she talked.

Suddenly I smelled smoke and felt my nostrils flare. But it was only burnt toast.

Crystal's voice carried like a bullhorn but no one else looked up. "It was the Grabtown barn. Burned to the ground and good riddance, that's what I say. Pete said the fire department had to call in mutual aid from two other stations, Muddy Brook and East Winslow. They got it under control, and then they just let it burn itself out. A good training exercise, Pete said."

Pete was Pierre's owner, himself a volunteer firefighter. He must have been disappointed, being stuck behind the grill when the first alarm came in over his scanner.

Crystal switched topics. "And AJ, I heard about you finding Jimmy on Wednesday. That must've knocked you on your butt, right? I can't begin to imagine. My sister and I was talking, and she said Jimmy must've known whoever shot him, right? And I said—"

"Thanks, Crystal. But not now, okay?" I patted the hand she'd placed on my shoulder and tried to look somber. "I can't really talk about it."

She gave me a sympathetic smile and withdrew her hand to tuck a strand of coppery hair back behind an ear. "Of course, hon, I hear you." She moved on to the next table.

"Finding the body, that must have been a shocker," Zach said to me when Crystal was out of hearing.

"You could say that." I steeled myself for a flood of questions about the murder and prepared to repeat my "no comment" statement.

He surprised me. "Mike says you know this area really well. You've lived here for several years, right?"

"All my life, except for a couple years of college. I've got a place just east of town, out near the Rhode Island line." I almost added, *And how about you?* But this wasn't a social conversation. He was just establishing my bona fides.

"So tell me something about the farmers you know. How do people get into farming?"

I forced my brain to focus. "Most farmers are born to it. Usually they inherit the land. It's not an easy life. Some people say all it takes is a strong back and a weak mind, but they're wrong. To farm successfully, you've got to be plenty smart and keep learning the business. As for what they're raising, its mostly dairy and beef cows, poultry, and apples. Some blueberries, raspberries, strawberries. Crops include field corn, hay and alfalfa." I sounded like a farm-equipment brochure.

211

He fiddled with his spoon, looking bored. "And who are the lawbreakers?"

I peered at him over the rim of my mug. "What do you mean?"

"Who are the farmers who end up in jail? And for what things? Like if someone's exploiting migrant labor or growing pot in the back meadow. Hiding drugs inside apple boxes, maybe. Tell me something juicy." He raised his eyebrows at "juicy" and leaned forward over the narrow table.

I picked up my mug and sat back, putting distance between us. "That's what you're looking for? You'll have to talk with the police about that."

He shrugged and eased back. "Last year, I did a story about an operation on a hog farm. Down in Virginia, not up here, but still. They were using an old equipment shed and the warehouse to hide stolen cars and run a chop-shop operation."

"Well, yeah, cars get stolen and chopped pretty much everywhere. But the farmers I know are just, well, farmers."

The moment I said it, I thought of Jimmy Desjardins. He hadn't been just a farmer. My coffee threatened to slosh. I set the mug down quickly, before Zach noticed.

He asked, "And why did this guy die?"

I shrugged, not quite trusting my voice.

He went on, "I'm betting it's one of the usual. Money or drugs. Sexual jealousy, or someone in the family taking revenge for something. Do you know the wife?"

"Her name's Charlotte." I wiped my mouth with a napkin. "I've seen her around. I don't really know her."

"I can see the headline, and the lede." He raised both hands, palms out and fingers spread. "'The Killing Field: Life and violent death in the bucolic countryside.' Did he get killed because of shady business connections? Was there a scheme to falsify milk production records? Not many farmers get themselves murdered. There's gotta be a good reason."

I glanced around to see who might be within earshot. "I can't speculate for you, Zach. Not about this, and not here. You'll have to talk to the cops."

One eyebrow climbed high and stayed there. "You don't seem very interested in digging into this on your own, AJ. A big story lands in your lap in this sleepy little town, and you don't want to run with it?"

"Mike told you, right? I'm a witness. I can't talk about it." I hated being baited by this guy. He was so damned self-assured.

Pierre's was getting busy. Crystal eyed our table, needing to know if we were going to order something more than coffee.

I dropped my voice. "I'm also not interested in helping you pry into the sordid details of everyone's private life out here in the 'bucolic countryside.' It's your story, not mine. And this is my community, I live here. Privacy's still important."

"Murder isn't private, it's public." His voice rose. "People need to understand why someone gets killed. And they want the murderer caught and punished. You want that too, right?"

Conversation paused at several tables and several heads swiveled our way. Hoping, I thought, to see me discredit myself by demonstrating bias and chatting willy-nilly about the case with another reporter. In public, no less. That would provide fuel for a week or more of gossip.

I kept my voice low. "Of course. But justice is more complicated than that. And I *cannot* talk about it."

I bit my lip and turned to look out the window. How had the conversation worked itself around to this point? To hell with Zach Stollman.

The air grew warm and that feeling of being elsewhere settled in again. Instead of clutching a coffee mug in the diner, I saw myself scraping a match on a strike-here box, touching fire to a pile of old hay and file folders.

Someone in the next booth dropped a plate on the floor and the crash jolted me back into Pierre's. All around us people scrambled to clean up the mess. But Zach only sat and stared at me.

I grabbed my bag and slid out of the booth. "I have to get to work. Why don't you go talk with the police? Or Marge Bellevance at the library. And Bob Peckham, our first selectman. He can put you in touch with other people you can talk to. You don't need me."

"Hey, AJ, relax. We can work this story together. I promise, no more questions that you can't answer—"

"Shut up, Zach!"

Jeez, what part of "can't talk about it" didn't he understand?

I swung my bag over a shoulder and walked out.

***

When I stepped into the comforting machine chatter of the newsroom shortly after noon, Mike's car was already gone from WWCT's parking lot. Good. I really didn't want to disappoint my boss with a rundown on my meeting with Zach.

I shook off the morning and turned my attention to work.

The newsroom phone's message light was blinking so I checked that before tackling Mike's to-do list. The answering machine played back a newly familiar voice.

"Hey AJ," Zach said. "I forgot to tell you. I got us an appointment to go talk with Charlotte Desjardins tonight. Six-thirty at her house." He stumbled a bit over the name, trying to dredge up the correct pronunciation for Desjardins. "Leave a message at the motel if you can't make it. Green Valley Travelers, room eight. Otherwise I'll see you there."

He didn't need me to be there; he was certainly capable of interviewing the grieving widow by himself. But then I'd have to explain to Mike why I'd ducked out of the opportunity he'd set up.

***

I think I did an okay job that afternoon, but I was moving and speaking on autopilot so I couldn't really tell. If I'd taped an air-check and recorded each newscast, maybe I'd have admired the professionalism without recognizing my own voice. Or perhaps it was the voice that remained the same, while the rest of me built a brick fortress to house the remains. Either way, I continued to function.

Keith, spinning his hits in the control room on the other side of our big window, seemed unusually quiet that afternoon and I wondered if Marla had told him yet about feeling movement from the babies. That news would make him happy, but maybe it would also remind him of the great weight of fatherhood. Or maybe he was just hungover from a late night out.

The fire had bumped the murder from the day's top-story slot. But that was only temporary, because there were only so many ways you could say "A blaze took down a derelict barn. Volunteers responded from three units. No one got hurt. Investigators are investigating."

At 2:15 I recorded a hurried telephone interview with Winslow's town manager, the monthly update we do on topics I knew people probably cared passionately about. But not me, and not at that moment.

At 4:30 I made a follow-up call to the fire chief, learning nothing new about the arson investigation. Eventually they'd find the kerosene cans beneath the burnt timbers of the shed, but not today while firefighters were still dousing flare-ups.

They might find evidence of other crimes, too. Items that didn't belong in an old hay barn, like melted blobs of plastic and twisted metal that had once been file cabinets, tripods, video cassettes, cameras. But there'd be nothing left, I hoped, with recognizable names or faces.

The statute of limitations for the crime of arson was five years. That's how long evidence collected at the fire would sit in police records, waiting for an arrest or indictment. Then, unless it was connected to another serious crime, it would simply disappear.

CHAPTER SEVENTEEN

AJ

~ 11 ~

On my way to work at noon, I'd avoided driving near Jimmy's farm by taking a back-roads route into town. But now, at six-thirty in the evening, the farm was my destination.

Driving oh-so-carefully up Jimmy's rutted, rock-strewn driveway, I kept my eyes averted from the hayfield where he died and aimed instead for the milking barn, a single-story concrete building. I parked between a stand of goldenrod and a rusty red GMC pickup. The truck had a Rhode Island license plate and a bicycle in the bed. There was no sign of Zach.

It was only when I climbed out of my car that I realized that the Grabtown barn, or what remained of it, was clearly visible from where I'd parked.

Half a mile up the hill beyond the hayfield, the pile of charred timbers stood in stark relief against a backdrop of woods and blue sky. A faint stink of burnt wood, kerosene, and scorched plastic hung on the evening air. Jimmy's herd of black-and-white Holsteins grazed nearby, apparently unbothered by the sight and smell of the ruin or by the presence of the fire marshal's red station wagon parked nearby.

The fire on the hill had been thoroughly doused, but behind my eyes it was still burning hot and furious. Thirteen hours ago, Marla and I stood in those woods and watched it burning. Half the valley had a clear view of that hill, and someone must have seen it. Might have seen us, too.

But it was dark then. And no one had come forward.

Now the numbness threatened to return, along with a quick rush of panic. I gulped in a deep lungful of acrid air and felt an overwhelming urge to flee. To run wild somewhere—anywhere—that wouldn't include a view of that hayfield or the destroyed barn.

The milking barn would do for now. I found a well-worn path through the weeds and followed it to a wide doorway where loops of frayed bailing twine held back a pair of unpainted wooden doors.

As I rounded the corner of the building, a dark-haired boy, maybe eleven or twelve, looked up with a deer-in-the-headlights stare. He was standing beside a tractor, his hands at the front of his jeans. As he scuttled away, I realized I'd interrupted him in the middle of peeing. I thought about calling out "Sorry!" but he was gone.

I stuck my head through the barn doorway and was momentarily blinded by the sudden change from late-day sunlight to indoor shadow.

"Hello?" My voice echoed down the long aisle of the single-story barn.

I took a few steps inside, letting my eyes adjust to the gloom. The distant smell of ash disappeared beneath an overpowering odor of disinfectant fighting with cow urine.

I hadn't been in this building since I was a little kid holding onto Gran's hand, but the setup was familiar. On either side of a wide center aisle, metal pipe stanchions stood upright in a concrete floor that was capable of holding two dozen cows at a time for twice-a-day milking. Clear plastic tubes stretched overhead to carry warm, frothy milk from each cow to a big storage tank in the adjacent milk room.

The evening milking had just finished. The cows were back out at pasture, and the barn floor was steaming wet from a recent hosing. At the far end of the aisle, one man was uncoiling a black hose from a wall bracket while another used a shovel to scoop cow manure from a concrete trench into a wheelbarrow.

I was about to slip back outside when the man with the shovel looked up. I took a few steps in from the doorway and managed a smile.

"Hi, I'm AJ Porter."

Both men wore knee-high rubber boots, heavy gloves, dark shirts and dirt-encrusted jeans. They were lean and hard-looking, with dark shaggy hair and narrow faces.

The closer man leaned his shovel against the wall and walked toward me.

"Curt Duffy." He didn't offer to remove a glove or shake hands, for which I was grateful.

I returned his nod and said the first thing that came into my head. "I'm looking for Charlotte Desjardins. Do you know if she's home?"

"Didja check at the house?" He jerked a chin back toward the doorway.

"Not yet." I looked over his shoulder. "You're caring for the cows?" An inane comment, stating the obvious. But I didn't want to go back outside just yet.

Another nod. "Someone's got to, in the meantime. You heard about Jimmy getting killed?" He didn't wait for a response. "Auction's not until next Friday night, but cows can't wait for lawyers and such."

I had the feeling this was a long speech for Curt Duffy.

The other man came forward. He was younger than I'd first thought, perhaps fifteen or sixteen. A strikingly good-looking kid, he had full lips, lush eyelashes, and a mass of curls hanging over dark eyes. One of those James Dean wild-bunch boys who must have had all the girls in class swooning every time he lifted an eyebrow. The swagger and surliness seemed built-in.

"Hey," he said abruptly. "I seen you somewhere."

Something flip-flopped in my chest. Oh god. Seen me where? Carrying cans of kerosene through the woods early this morning?

"You're that girl on the radio," he went on. "You and that deejay came to school for career day. Back in the spring. Burrowtown," he added helpfully.

I exhaled. "Oh. Yes, I remember." Burrowtown was just over the line in Rhode Island, maybe eight miles away.

Curt nodded at the boy. "My son, Connor. He's been helping Jimmy here all summer. But he doesn't seem to know diddlysquat about cleaning a cow barn."

Connor started to protest. Thought better of it and revised his mouth into a sneer.

I said, "Were you here on Wednesday? When Jimmy was killed."

"Not me," Curt said. "Connor was, though. Or so he says."

The boy scowled at his father, then glanced at me. "I was sorta here." His eyes slid away. "I mean, I was on the farm, but I was up the hill near the old barn, fixing fence. I heard the shot but I figured it was just someone doing target practice. The cops already asked me about it." He paused, then added his opinion. "It was probably just some druggie whacked out on PCP or something, dontcha think? Like those drive-by shootings they have in L.A."

Curt fixed the boy with an unsmiling glare, then turned his attention back to me. "Sorry, Miss Porter, but we gotta get back to work. My wife's holding dinner, we still got a lot to do." He jerked his head toward Connor. "And this one wants to get back to work on some old junker he says he's re-building."

The boy flashed a dark look at his uncle. "It's a Mercury Cougar. A three-oh-two V-8, four on the floor. Not a junker. That's what I should be working on. I never signed up for this shitty job in the first place. This sucks, big-time."

"Connor," Curt snapped, "you been working here all summer helping Mr. Desjardins, and I never heard no complaints until this week. That's how you been earning the cash to fix that old car." To me he added, "Three boys, and not one wants to be a farmer. Gearheads, all of 'em."

"You got that right," the boy muttered.

The muscles in his father's jaw worked. "I got another boy here, too, somewhere. My wife's youngest, my stepson." He looked down the length of the barn. "Connor, go find your brother."

Connor only scowled.

"I think I saw him outside," I said helpfully.

"He's useless, too. Always disappearin' on me." He glared at Connor and reached for his shovel.

I said a quick goodbye and left them to nurture their grudges.

As I neared the doorway, Zach popped his head through.

"AJ? There you are."

His face looked pinched and tight, probably because of the smell. I skirted a soapy brown puddle near the doorway and stepped out into the evening light.

Zach led the way to the house. "Who are they?"

"Neighbors, helping out. A guy and two kids, taking care of the cows until they get auctioned off next Friday."

"Were they here the day Jimmy got killed?"

"The teenager was here, but he says he didn't see anything."

He looked miffed at having missed the interview opportunity. "I thought you weren't supposed to ask questions."

As we approached the farmhouse's front porch, Zach placed a hand on my arm to stop me. "AJ, wait a minute. You're going to let me do all the talking with Charlotte, right? You should be just a friendly face in the background, here to introduce me. I don't want this woman shutting down because we're hitting her with too many questions."

I made a lip-zipping gesture with thumb and forefinger.

"Also," he added, "don't act surprised if I mention Charlotte's brother, Will Collier. He's a real estate agent who specializes in connecting housing developers with farmers going bottoms up."

"When did you—"

"He's got an office in Manchester. I called him while you were at work and asked a few questions about what's happening to the farms around here. Developers wanting to turn farmland into housing developments, that sort of thing. He's kind of a sleazeball if you ask me. And very excited about getting his hands on this place. Says he's got a couple of buyers all lined up."

"How could they do that so soon?"

"I think Charlotte's been nagging Jimmy to sell, ever since she married him. Do you know about the state's farmland preservation bill?"

"It's a program for farmers to sell the development rights for their land. A farm owner gets some cash while the state places restrictions on the use of the land. They can farm it or turn it into open space, but no one can subdivide or build houses on it."

"Exactly. Will said Jimmy was looking into that so he could get some cash but keep the farm. But now he's dead and it's up to his widow. If Charlotte mentions it, we just let her talk, okay?"

"Okay."

Zach headed for the front step, a slab of granite set beside the farmhouse's front door. The Desjardins house was old-style colonial, with no front porch or overhanging roof. The grass in the yard hadn't been mowed in a long time.

It was my turn to grab his arm. "No, let's go around back. They probably don't even use the front door."

I led us back through the weeds. A pair of crumbling cement steps led to a small porch, where a screen door hung crookedly on rusty hinges. Two kittens peered at us from beneath the porch and a large orange tom sat with his tail twitching. Nearby, ants swarmed over dried cat food in a cracked blue dish.

The inside door appeared to be propped open and the screen door had no screen, so I called loudly into what I presumed was the kitchen. "Charlotte? Mrs. Desjardins?"

No answer. From somewhere inside, I heard tires squeal and then a loud rebel yell, delivered in a fake Georgia drawl.

I said to Zach, "Sounds like the *Dukes of Hazzard.*"

I raised my voice several decibels. "Mrs. Desjardins! Hello!" I knocked sharply, rattling the door in its frame. The orange cat hissed and slunk off the porch.

A girl's high voice filtered out. "In here."

I stepped back to let Zach go in first but he hesitated, as if wondering whether to open the screen door or simply climb through.

I reached around him to unlatch it properly and we moved into a cramped entryway, a six-by-ten alcove lit by a single overhead bulb. Along one wall was a line of pegs hung with jackets and hats, all smelling of cow manure and cat urine. On the floor, mud-crusted work boots gave off the same odor. On one wall, a long narrow shelf, set at waist height, held old coffee cans filled with nails, screws, nuts and bolts. Tools hung on a pegboard on the other wall; above those, cobwebs festooned with dust and fly corpses hung from a beadboard ceiling.

A gray cat leaped through the screen door behind us and began twining itself around my feet, probably smelling Pippin. Zach paused again.

I nudged him forward. "This is one of the oldest houses in East Winslow," I whispered. "The historical society wanted to get it listed on the state register, but Desjardins wasn't interested."

"The historical society is insane," Zach muttered. I think he was trying not to breathe.

"You wanted to do a story on farms, right? This is a farm."

"I should've looked for a prettier farm. This one's not pretty."

I poked his arm again. Keeping an eye out for cats, we moved carefully through the foyer-closet-toolshed and into the actual kitchen, where Charlotte Desjardins waited with one hip tilted against a cluttered countertop.

.

Chapter Eighteen

AJ

~ 12 ~

I remembered Charlotte from the few times I'd seen her as petite, almost doll-like. But I wasn't prepared for how small she actually was.

Her waif-like frame suggested poor nutrition, anorexia, or genetics. She'd compensated with a liberal application of makeup and hairspray. The bleach-fried hair, teased into a bright blond pile, cascaded around her small, heart-shaped face and across her shoulders in lacquered curls.

She wore a plain white tee shirt with no obvious need for a bra. A pair of boys' jeans sat low and snug on narrow hips. Big hoop earrings, a trio of gold bangle bracelets, and bright pink lipstick suggested a little girl playing dress-up.

Acknowledging our introductions with a clipped and wary "hey," she waved us around a kitchen table cluttered with pizza boxes and soda cans. The living room was low-ceilinged and too small for anything more than a coffee table, a lopsided sofa, and a media cabinet, topped by a big new color TV and piles of video cassettes, crowded against the opposite wall. Friday-night TV fare, replete with Prohibition-era cops and moonshiners, was blasting bright and loud.

A jumbo-sized Fritos bag had spilled its contents across the sofa cushions. As I debated whether and where to sit, a yellow cat slid out from behind the sofa, saw me, and hissed. A long-haired calico jumped onto the center cushion and began batting stray corn chips to the warped wooden floor.

Ignoring the cats, Charlotte swung a knee over one end of the sofa and sat, straddling its arm. She didn't indicate any seating for us, so I cautiously pushed the calico aside, brushed away a few Fritos, and sat on the farthest cushion. I kept an eye on the cats but also the chip bag, which appeared to rustle slightly on its own after the calico settled into meatloaf position beside my feet.

Zach assessed the room, went back to the kitchen and returned with a creaky wooden chair. Charlotte didn't protest when he switched off the TV. Either she didn't care, or she was accustomed to having a man make decisions for her.

She broke the silence without prompting. Her voice carried a nasal whine and the Valley Girl uptalk that had become popular with every teenager who watched *Square Pegs*.

"The cops have already talked to me, right?" she said to Zach. "Like about ten times? I don't have nothing else to say. I was at my mom's house, sleeping, when Jimmy got shot? I sleep late." The last comment came with a side-glance at me, as if I'd be more sympathetic to a girl's need for sleep.

She turned back to him. "So how will this help me, talking to you?"

Zach leaned forward and handed her his business card, which she dropped on the sofa next to the Fritos bag. He crossed his legs, balanced his notebook on a knee, and pitched his premise. "I'm writing a story about farming, how it's changing. Your husband's murder may be related, as a symptom or a result of those changes—maybe there's a big-city violence connection. I want to show a balanced view of the pressures faced by today's family farms, with a brief profile of your husband's life. Then, as a sidebar, try to figure out why he died."

I was impressed, thinking he must've practiced that. Big, important-sounding words that didn't say anything. Very smooth.

Charlotte's face pinched itself into a half-frown as she tried to make sense of his words. "You taking pictures of me?"

"Sure," he promised, "but not tonight. I'm just gathering background right now. See, when there's something tragic like a murder," he continued, "many times, people are quick to blame whoever benefits from the victim's death—often the husband or wife. They say things like, 'Oh, that never would have happened if she'd been a better wife,' or 'She'll be happy he's gone—look at all the money she inherits.' That shouldn't happen to someone who's grieving for a lost husband."

He'd given Charlotte the perfect opening to respond with something like, "Oh, yes, and I did love him." But she just sat there.

She turned to me, the puzzled frown still in place. "So why are *you* here?"

"I'm his assistant. Sort of a corroborator." I was fairly sure she didn't know what a corroborator was.

Her eyes narrowed. "Is that like a lawyer? Do I need a lawyer?"

I quickly reassured her. "No, no, I'm not a lawyer." After a beat, I added, "I'm the one who saw your husband get killed. And I'm very sorry for your loss."

"Oh, okay." She relaxed. "They said I didn't need a lawyer unless I was suspected of something? I ain't done nothing wrong. At least I don't think so? So that's all right then."

What was all right? That I wasn't a lawyer, that I'd seen her husband get shot, or that he was dead?

Zach regained her attention. "Mrs. Desjardins—"

"It's just Charlotte." She shrugged and flashed a crooked-teeth smile, shaking her head in a calculated gesture that swung hair forward over both shoulders.

"Charlotte, then. Please tell me about Jimmy. What sort of a person was he?" Zach held his pen at the ready. I'd have used a tape recorder, but tape recorders make a lot of people nervous.

"Oh, well, you know. He was a farmer?"

We waited, expectantly, but she seemed to feel she'd described her dead husband sufficiently.

"Okay," Zach said. "Was he a kind man, a good husband?"

"Yeah, he was all right, I guess. I don't know, I mean I never had another husband to compare him to." She giggled and rocked a little on the sofa arm, pleased with herself.

Zach prompted, "You must have been really upset when you heard about his death."

"Yeah, I guess. A little scared?" She spun the gold bangles on her arm. "But I guess we weren't, like, real compatible. My parents didn't want me marrying him anyway. Not at first."

Zach pounced. "So why'd you marry him?"

"Because he was nice to me, in the beginning. I'd just lost my job at K-Mart and I wanted to get away from my parents, but I didn't have any place to go. I'd sort of run away from home, see?"

She picked at the pink polish on a chipped nail. "My parents said he was much too old and I'd be real miserable. But Jimmy told me I could stay here, he had enough money for both of us. I thought it'd be kinda fun, living with him. My parents were pushing me to get a new job, find an apartment, but when I told him how awful they were, pushing me to do all this crap when I didn't want to? Jimmy said, hey, so we'll get married. And I thought yeah, that's what I'll do. Just to show them I could make my own decisions."

The quick tumble of words left her a little breathless. She paused and turned her raccoon eyes on me. "Could you get me a Tab? From the fridge? And check the time on the kitchen clock, okay? I've gotta leave at half-past seven."

Zach's eyes danced but he said nothing. I pushed myself away from the sofa and its Fritos to locate the fridge, which held nothing but three six-packs of Tab and a half-eaten pizza. I didn't bother to look for a clean glass, figuring she wouldn't expect it.

I handed over the Tab, informed her it was 7:10, and relocated the calico from my place on the sofa. At least it wasn't a hiss-and-spit sort of cat.

Zach asked, "And did you enjoy being married? Would you call it a happy marriage?"

"Oh god, no," she declared. "I was so wrong about that. He had this big farm, and he had money, okay? But he wouldn't spend it on me. This TV right here is the only thing he ever bought me. What a ripoff," she added darkly.

He segued. "Did he ever talk about selling some of his land, or maybe selling the development rights to the state?

"Oh, no. Jimmy swore he'd never sell the land. He got angry if anyone even mentioned it. And I don't know about that other thing, the rights."

"How do you know he had money?"

"Because he bought that new tractor. And some other new shit for the barn. His cows lived better than me. I mean, look at this place."

Zach and I glanced dutifully around the filthy room. I politely refrained from saying it wouldn't be so horrible if she threw away the trash, cleaned the floors, and kicked the cats out.

He said, "Did you help him with the farm at all? Keep the accounts, balance the checkbook. That sort of thing."

"No, I don't know nothing about that. My arithmetic's not so hot. Every month, Jimmy took his checkbook and a shoebox full of papers over to my brother's place so he could do that. That's how I met Jimmy, see, through my brother Will? He's good with numbers."

Zach nodded and made a note. "So what are your plans now, Charlotte?"

She laced her hands together across one knee and smiled. "I'm moving back in with my parents for a little bit, then when the money comes through I'm outa here. I got a girlfriend in Fort Lauderdale. That's in Florida, and she says I can get a job in a bar if I want. It's a good way to meet college boys at spring break, but maybe I won't have to work at all. That'd be cool. Way more fun than here, you know?"

The smile faded. She turned toward me, shutting out Zach. Her voice sank into a confidential whisper. "An old man for a husband, that's what I had. He talked a good line, but jeez Louise. Even at forty-two, he shoulda been able to do something in bed, dontcha think? More than just playing with himself, anyway, and wanting to take pictures all the time. He was kind of a weirdo, actually."

She gave a hiccup that might have been a laugh, then paused and glanced at Zach, who'd already closed his notebook. A dirty white cat rubbed against his pants and he looked down, scowling.

She leaned closer to me, seeming pleased to have my attention on a topic she understood.

"Jimmy wouldn't take me out anywhere, not even for dinner at the diner," she complained. "He wanted me all for himself, he said. But then he was never here. And when he was here, he mostly ignored me unless he was taking pictures. And he was always after me to wipe off the makeup, said it made me look too old. It turned him off." Her voice went lower. "And speaking personally, you know, girl to girl, that was okay with me."

I put on what I hoped was a look of friendly invitation and waited.

She shrugged. "Eh. Maybe he was screwing around, who knows? All I know is, he didn't like me acting like a grownup. No makeup, no beer. He got mad, said I was too young for beer. I had to sneak it in. Beer." She shook her hair for emphasis. "Can you believe that?"

Her eyes dropped for a moment and I glanced at Zach, hoping he'd help me out with a question or two.

He stayed silent so, in the most casual way possible, I said, "What kind of pictures?"

She snickered and leaned closer again. "Dirty ones. With me dressed like a little kid in pigtails and white socks and a ruffled dress. He'd tell me to lift my skirt, and I'd have nothing on underneath, and he'd take all these pictures? I thought it was kinda fun at first, like I was being naughty, but then it got boring 'cause mostly that's all he did."

She sat back and stared at him. "Sorry, you wanted to know about the farm. But I don't know anything about any of that, so I'm just shooting my mouth off. You gonna put that stuff in your paper?"

He blinked and shook his head, looking a bit stunned.

"Whatever." She shrugged. "I just want people to know it wasn't all a bed of roses being married to that guy. Though I was sorta sorry," she finally added, "when he got, you know, shot."

Zach recovered. "Mrs. Desjardins—Charlotte. We believe there was a life insurance policy? With you as sole beneficiary,"

She was unperturbed. "Yeah, I'm really glad my brother got him to sign up for that, cause it'll take time to get the farm sold. This way I'll be okay for money, like, in the meantime? Will's got a real estate license, see."

Zach made a note. "Who do you think killed your husband?"

"I told the cops it was probably just some druggie spaced out on PCP. Like you said, big-city violence." She fiddled with her bangle bracelets, losing interest in the conversation. "People here kinda left Jimmy alone. I never heard him even argue with anyone except with me, about the beer. And my brother. Him and Will got into a real screamer once."

Zach leaned forward, his pen poised. "When did that happen, the argument with your brother? What was it about?"

"Oh, money, I guess. Couple months ago? Will said Jimmy did something he shouldn't have with some money Will loaned him, and Will told Jimmy he was going to have to sell some land to pay it back and Jimmy said no way. They were yelling and sorta shoving each other around."

"You told the police this?"

"Yeah. They were interested in that. But Will couldn't kill Jimmy."

"Why's that?"

"He's scared of guns. If he was gonna kill someone, he'd run him over with his truck. But don't put that in your paper," she added quickly, "or I'll never hear the end of it. When's the article gonna be out, anyway?"

"That depends. I'm hoping the police arrest a suspect soon."

"Well, I can't help you with that. Oh, hey," she said suddenly. "I got to go."

She slid off the sofa arm and grabbed a can of hairspray from the coffee table. Without warning, she bent over, threw her yellow mane forward, and began spraying into the middle of the mass. Zach and I scrambled to move out of range as the calico hissed and ran from the room. Two other cats shot out from beneath the sofa and followed it.

When she straightened up, the hair stuck out another three inches on all sides, making the rest of her look even smaller. She was obviously preparing to go out on the town.

As she ushered us out, I got in one last question. "Did you know anything about Jimmy being investigated for child molesting?"

She narrowed her painted eyelids and stared at him. It occurred to me that she might need glasses.

"I don't know nothing about that." She'd gone sullen. "Nobody told me."

We excused ourselves and carefully navigated the paths through kitchen, mudroom, cats, and yard.

Zach paused beside his car, squinting west across the hayfield into the beginning of dusk. "What do you think of Charlotte?"

I fished in my pocket for car keys. "The grieving widow? So much for offending her. Or scaring her with too many questions. She didn't care what we talked about. Money, sex, whatever."

He took a step closer to me. "You didn't seem surprised when she talked about her husband taking those photos. And what was that about child molesting?"

He asked casually but the question came with a small head tilt.

Those photos. And suddenly I was staring again at photographs scattered on the floor of the barn. Spilling from folders with labels like Bambi and Precious Darling, just before I touched a match to them all.

Had there been a folder named Charlotte? Or Marla? I didn't see those but—

"Ow, dammit." I slapped at an imaginary mosquito and rubbed my arm, buying a few seconds and thinking how to respond.

"I heard this rumor about Jimmy," I finally said.

Using as few words as possible, I told him about the incident with the girls in Rolands' store. "Evelyn didn't think it was a big thing. 'Just Jimmy being Jimmy,' she said. Socially awkward, missing the cues. Kinda slow on the uptake."

He considered that for a moment, then nodded. "Yeah, photographers can be like that. You see a cute kid doing something interesting, you want to snap a couple shots. People can take it the wrong way. And with Charlotte—I mean, they were married. What happens in the bedroom stays there, right? Lots of married guys like to spice things up." He cocked an eyebrow. "And that's what a wife likes, right? That naughty stuff."

Zach stepped closer and I stiffened, holding his gaze and tightening my grip on the car keys. Pointy ends out, like Gran taught me.

"I wouldn't know what a wife likes." Trying to remember if I'd left the Chevy unlocked.

The smirk disappeared as he took a step back. One hand lifted away from his side, as if to calm me.

"I just thought it was a little weird," he went on. "That she talked so much to you about their sex life. Maybe she's just pissed he wouldn't take her to fancy places or buy her stuff. I guess she didn't get what she bargained for, marrying an old man."

Repeating what Charlotte said. I didn't need to respond; he'd found his own explanation.

He continued, "But she didn't seem angry enough to kill him, did she? Or capable. I don't see her driving a strange pickup and picking up a shotgun that weighs more than she does."

I countered, "She'll definitely benefit from his death."

"Sure, but my money's on her brother. He should be our next interview. Maybe tomorrow morning?"

"You don't need me for that, Zach. I've got a few things I need to do at the studio, anyway. Fill me in tomorrow."

Behind us, the screenless door slapped itself closed. We turned to watch as Charlotte clattered down the back porch steps in platform heels, with a strappy black purse swinging from one shoulder. She disappeared around the back of the house without a glance at us.

A blue Cadillac sedan with a dented rear fender reversed out from behind the house. I saw Charlotte's big hair and small face leaning forward over the wheel, fixed in concentration as she struggled for a second to find drive. The car bumped slowly down the track toward the road.

"Is that Jimmy's car?" Zach asked. "She must be sitting on a cushion. How does she reach the pedals?"

I was thinking the same. "I wonder if she's ever driven it before. Maybe he didn't let her."

We watched as the Caddy swayed around a gentle curve, flashing its brake lights. As I climbed into my car, Zach called to me.

"Hey, AJ. Are you up for following her? We'll take my car." He wore a hopeful grin. "Come on, it'll be fun. I bet she's heading for a bar. We'll have a few beers, get to know each other."

"And what, just leave my car here? Sorry, no. That's a really bad idea." I jerked my head toward the road. "Better hurry. You'll lose her."

The grin faded. "Okay. I'll let you know if I learn anything."

Driving home, I mulled over Zach's invitation to join him in tailing Charlotte. What was he hoping for, something he could call a date?

Please, dear god, no.

In my admittedly limited experience, males needed careful handling. What started as a professional relationship or a casual friendship could go sour at the drop of a hat. Give them a smile with their coffee and boom, they think they've been invited to a banquet. They bruise too easily and they hold grudges far past the sell-by date. So no, not interested.

But I needed to stay on my boss's good side, so tomorrow I'd try to be polite and helpful.

Or maybe it was time to start looking for a new job.

***

Cassie turns over the last page of Chapter 12. She slides off the narrow bed and stands, stretching and rolling her shoulders. It's a little after one AM, Friday morning. Her eyes are dry and itchy, and her whole body feels cramped from sitting too long with her back against the hard wall. She can shake off the aches, but she can't shake away the image of her mother and AJ, sitting together in the car after setting fire to the Grabtown barn.

We were there, Ana and me. That's when Mom felt our quickening, that first movement in her womb. Which one of us woke first and kicked against her ribs?

That's one of the questions in the baby books, isn't it? "When did you first feel the baby move?"

Now I know why Mom left that page blank.

The house is quiet, in that soft breathing way that old houses have. A living presence of wood that shifts minutely in every breeze, expanding and contracting with the rise and fall of warmth, moisture, and the weight of the people living there. Cassie holds her own breath, listening for any sound from Ana's room. She hears nothing. Is Ana asleep? How much has she read?

Everything felt jumbled. She tries to grab something to fall asleep with, a good memory or some solid, beautiful image from her childhood. But every thought is draped in fire and dread.

With sleep eluding her, she slips from her bed to locate the bottle of Xanax in her suitcase. She dry-swallows one and then a second, because she's pretty sure one won't be enough to quiet the chaos.

Tomorrow, or later today because it's already Friday, she'll open the box and read the last part of the story, the part with Ana's name on it.

Then, depending on what she learns—she's dreading this because she thinks she knows where the story is going—maybe she'll argue again for destroying it. She'll explain that the story is nothing but trash and Ana doesn't have to read the whole thing. She'll destroy it then, feed everything into the shredder or burn it. That would be fitting.

She has the power to do that, right? With *her* half, anyway. Because it's her name alone on the first part of the manuscript.

She's Cassandra, the truth-teller, the troubled child that no one believes. In Greek mythology Apollo gave Cassandra, a princess of Troy, the gift of prophecy to win her love. When she refused him, he placed a curse on her: Cassandra would continue to foretell the future, but no one would believe her prophecies of disaster.

Who will believe AJ's story? And what good can it do? If the truth can't fix something—if all it does is hurt innocent people—maybe you should just turn away from it. Shred it, burn it, deny it ever existed.

Chapter Nineteen

Cassie

Cassie jolts awake at 9:00 AM Friday morning, fighting free of the twisted sheets. She stumbles downstairs barefoot, wearing only the tee shirt and boy shorts she sleeps in. Steam rises from two mugs of coffee on the kitchen table. Ana's busy at the stove, her back turned.

She slides into a chair, takes a long swallow of coffee, and props her elbows on the table, cradling her mug in both hands and watching her sister move about the kitchen. Emptying the dishwasher, wiping down the counters. Even from this angle, Ana looks tidy and pulled together. She's probably been up for hours.

Through the kitchen window, Cassie can see a leaden sky leaking rain. On the counter near the toaster, their mom's old radio is on, with WWCT's too-cheerful morning deejay prattling about the weather. Intermittent rain, he declares. An early hint of autumn. But it'll clear tomorrow, and apple season has begun. He's practically singing.

"It's gonna be a great weekend, folks, for pick-your-own. So get on out there with your baskets, soon as this little rain clears up. Bring the family. And don't forget, we're only ten days away from the Woodstock Fair. Always Labor Day weekend, expanded this year to four whole days! Remember, the dairy exhibit's been moved to Sunday and pony pulling happens on Saturday this year..."

243

Cassie smiles in spite of herself, feeling somewhat amazed at the persistence of tradition.

Not much has changed, she thinks, since they were seven years old, showing their rabbits in the 4-H barn at the fair. The rabbits had been their father's idea, an exercise in responsibility. As always, Ana went along happily with the project but Cassie rebelled against the drudgery of feeding and cage-cleaning.

Now, however, she's remembering her lop-eared bunny with a nostalgic fondness.

Ana sets a plate of toast on the table and slides into the opposite chair. Cassie studies her sister carefully, waiting for Ana to broach the subject of the manuscript. They'd both been so quiet last night, reading in bed. How much more did Ana get through before falling asleep? Not much, Cassie concludes, or she'd be looking way more upset this morning.

Ana's face appears serenely untroubled as she calmly dips a spoon into a jar of homemade strawberry jam, one of many gifts from neighbors.

"Ana," Cassie says abruptly, "what happened to my rabbit, Floppy? And yours, Peter."

Ana raises a quizzical eyebrow and licks her spoon. "You don't remember? You decided animals shouldn't live in cages, so you got up one night and set them free."

"Oh." Cassie switches off the radio and returns to the table. "Yeah, I did that, didn't I?"

It had seemed like the right thing to do at the time. But she knows now that their tame rabbits probably didn't last more than a day in the wild. Hawks, owls, coyotes—the predator list is a long one.

"I was training Peter to use a litter box." Ana doesn't seem angry, only wistful. "So he could stay in my bedroom and he wouldn't have to live in a cage out in the garage. But you said that was wrong, too. So you liberated them. We never saw them again."

"I was awful, wasn't I? Is it too late to say I'm sorry?"

Ana blinks, thinks, and swallows a piece of toast. "There's no statute of limitations on regret, Cassie." She waves a hand. "But water and bridges, okay? You weren't awful, just...passionate. Compulsive, maybe. You'd discover something new and run with it, everything be damned. *Everyone* be damned. You were hard on everybody, including yourself." She's quick to add, "Just my two cents. I'm not trying to analyze you."

It's Cassie's turn to be gracious, something new and awkward for her. "Analyze away. Somebody needs to do a better job of it than me."

Ana tilts her head, considering. "Well. If you must know, I've always admired that passion of yours. Mostly, anyway. The way you'd just throw yourself out there. Taking risks, creating trouble, challenging everything. Doing the things no one else dared to do." She hesitates. "But now...what's happened? I thought you'd be some great writer by now." She sips coffee and smiles. "Someone I'd be reading about in *The New York Times*, releasing your latest experimental fiction or writing a blockbuster script that sets the world on its ear. You know, Pulitzer Prize material. But—where's your passion now? It's like it's just gone."

Cassie's left speechless. She had no idea Ana ever admired her for anything.

After a long moment, she finds an uncertain voice. "I don't know. I'm too comfortable, maybe. Marsh has plenty of money, so I don't have to work. Maybe that's it."

But she knows it's more than that. Her life is comfortable, yes, but also small. There's a claustrophobic aspect to the ordered, regimented existence that Marsh wants her to live. She's stuck in a beautiful prison, all creature comforts provided.

Her mind slides away from Marsh again, back to her childhood. "I never thought of my behavior in terms of passion, or anything positive. I just figured— Well, you were the good girl. Everything was easy for you. People always asked Mom, why can't that one be more like Ana? I couldn't be like you, I didn't know how. And once I got labeled—"

"Yeah, labels are tough. ADHD, oppositional defiant disorder, 'on the spectrum.'" Ana's fingers create air quotes. "Jonathan and I had to fight that battle for Scott and Julie, too. Did you know that? We had to deal with the labels and the stigma, but also get them the help they needed. Oh, they're both doing fine," she adds. "But I wish you you'd been around when they were younger. They'd have loved having an oppositional defiant aunt on hand, riding into battle with them. Scott especially."

A familiar guilt tugs at Cassie. "I wish I had been. At least AJ and Mom were always here for you. And each other."

At the mention of AJ and their mother, Ana's mood shifts abruptly. She blinks hard, fighting sudden tears, and Cassie realizes the serenity was a façade. Ana's barely holding it together.

Cassie starts to offer something consoling or sympathetic, but Ana cuts her off.

"Don't. Just don't."

They sit in a heavy silence as Ana picks up a knife and slaps more strawberry jam onto a second piece of toast. She's pressing hard enough to break it. "Shit." The toast breaks and crumbles to the placemat. Ana sags in her chair and covers her face with a napkin.

Silently, Cassie eases off her chair and returns with a dampened paper towel. She moves around Ana, scooping up pieces of toast from the table. She carries the placemat to the sink.

Ana lowers the napkins and looks up, her eyes wet and rimmed in red. "Cassie, what I read last night—"

She glances away, then back. "I finished everything you gave me, right through to where they—" She swallows hard, and now the words come fast. "Where they discovered the pornography. And burned down the barn. It took me hours to get through it. One minute I was crying because of all the horrible shit Mom went through, and the next I was furious with her for talking AJ into burning that barn. Then I got even more angry with AJ for going along with it.

"I was crying so hard I had to put it down and I was going to wake you up and tell you I couldn't read anymore, I just couldn't do it. But I didn't want to bother you and finally I told myself if you could read it, so could I. And I did."

"Oh, Ana, you should've come to my room." Cassie reaches across the table to rest a hand on her sister's arm.

Ana shakes her head and looks down. Her hands are twisted together, fingers clutching the shredded napkin. She shifts her gaze to the kitchen window and stares out at nothing. "You're tough like Mom, aren't you? The way she used to be, before she had us. Not the Mom I thought I knew."

"I'm sort of like her, I guess. The younger her, the impulsive part. But I've never had her courage. When I get in trouble, I cave. Or run. But she was positively fierce, wasn't she?"

Ana is silent for a moment. When she speaks again, her voice is slow and soft. "You know how ages ago people feared the devil would steal their baby, and leave a demon in its place? They called them changelings. I feel like someone swapped Mom with a dark, avenging angel. Does that make sense?"

"Yes." Cassie tries to make light of it. "But someone must have swapped her back, at some point. Because as far as we knew, she was just boring old Mom. Steady as a rock."

"Yeah. Except she's kept these secrets. AJ, too. They must have been working on this story for years. But no one else knew about it."

Cassie only nods. *Maybe, maybe not.*

Ana's still staring out the window. "And now I know where you get your grit, your defiance. All that passion."

Uncertain how to answer this, Cassie fixes her gaze on the black-eyed Susans at the center of the table.

Ana finally turns to face her twin. "Cassie, what are we going to do with AJ's story? I'm trying to think of who it could hurt, if other people learn about it."

"First, we finish reading it. We both have to know the whole story. Then we'll decide." Cassie drains her coffee. "I think we'll have two choices, give it to the police or shred it. But we have to agree. If either of us says 'shred it,' we have to do that. To all of it."

"But what if the story's not entirely true? That AJ made it all up? Maybe it's like a superhero origin story, and she and Mom were going to give all the characters different names later."

There's a note of desperate hope in Ana's voice that tugs at Cassie's heart. "I had the same thought." Her voice steadies. "There's always the question of how reliable a first-person narrative is. But Mom and AJ are confessing to a crime, not building a fantasy fiction. They're trying to explain the arson, to justify it, so we understand. And the arson's connected somehow to the murder."

Ana flinches at "murder." Cassie adds, "None of that is fiction. The barn really burned, Jimmy Desjardins really got shot. There's also Detective Androski. He specifically asked if I knew anything about the murder. He exists, and he'll be back. Or someone will."

Ana nods. "Yeah, but if they don't know about the manuscript, and we don't say anything it—"

"Maybe AJ's story can stay a secret. I think a few other people suspect what happened—Dotty Kellerman, maybe, and definitely Androski—but they can't prove it. We just have to stay quiet."

Even as she says this, a finger of cold runs up the back of Cassie's neck. Because someone else knows about AJ's story. Marsh knows.

"What do I say to Jonathan?" Ana index finger is twirling her spoon in large lazy circles on the table. "I call him every night we're apart, did you know that? But I didn't call last night, because I didn't know what to say." She sniffles a little and wipes her nose with the back of her hand. "I need to call him this morning, or he'll worry. What do I say?"

"The truth, or part of it. Tell him we're still sorting through Mom's things. There's way more to do than you thought, lots of paperwork to read through. Have you told him we're postponing the estate sale? That's fine. We got a little sidetracked and you're sorry, you forgot to call last night until it was too late."

Ana nods, looking relieved. "Okay, I can do that."

Cassie's pleased with how glibly those words rolled off her tongue. She's had more practice at this than her sister.

Ana is silent. She's staring at a blank wall but Cassie knows she's also thinking. Planning, considering, choosing and rejecting options. Trying to forge a clear path while she charts the pitfalls. Because that's what her sister always does.

Ana squares her shoulders and lifts her chin. "Okay," she repeats. "You're right, it's what we need to do. Give me your chapters now, and you can get going on the rest of it."

Cassie rubs a hand through her short hair, feeling suddenly unwilling to tackle the last part of the story. She's a little startled that Ana agreed so easily. Now it's

Cassie who wants to issue a caution, give her sister another chance to refuse the unwelcome burden. She glances at the sink, where dishes are still piled from last night's dinner. "Okay. right after I clean up the kitchen."

"Oh, screw the dishes," Ana says. Cassie blinks in surprise, opening her eyes wide in mock disbelief. Ana offers a weak grin. "See? I'm trying to be more like you and Mom. The original version, Mom one-point-oh. Our secret super-hero."

Cassie smiles, acknowledging her sister's small attempt at humor in the midst of this madness, but her own thoughts are darker.

Our super-hero? I sure hope that's what she was.

CHAPTER TWENTY

Cassie

Ana and Cassie sit side-by-side on the patchwork quilt in Cassie's bedroom. Ana picks up the last three chapters from her sister's finished stack and nudges the unopened file-folder box, still sealed with frayed gray duct tape, toward Cassie.

Cassie peels off the tape. Inside is the second packet of typed pages, bound with wide rubber bands like the first. But this section is only half as thick, no more than a hundred pages. She removes the bands and sets it on the bed.

Ana says, "My paralegal's brain says we should take this somewhere and have it all scanned. Save it as a PDF and put it on a thumb drive. I couldn't sleep if something went missing."

"We can each keep a copy. I've got a new hard drive, I can save it on that. But let's finish reading first."

She's decided Ana's right, they should keep careful track of the manuscript until they've decided what to do with it.

"I'll be downstairs. Reading." Ana leaves, holding her portion away from her body as if it might sting.

Cassie digs through her laptop case and finds the new portable hard drive that Marsh gave her. Next to the manufacturer's name is a white adhesive label, where Marsh has neatly printed CASSANDRA in purple ink. She almost smiles, because purple was her favorite color when they first met and he still thinks it's important to her.

She switches on her computer and plugs the small storage device into a USB port. The familiar actions feel almost foreign. Back in Palos Verdes, she practically lived on this laptop. Checking email every half hour, roaming her social media accounts for the latest trivia about fellow writers, theater people, and social contacts. It was how she kept busy while her muse was avoiding her, which was most of the time.

Here, she's checked email only twice in five days and she's completely ghosted her social accounts. Life on the rural outskirts of Winslow is like living inside a time-capsule, drifting on unseen currents far outside the real world.

But she's not drifting, there's an undertow. She and Ana are being pulled down into this other story, mapped and controlled not just by AJ, but also their mother. AJ wrote the words, but Marla must have read, corrected—directed?—and approved everything.

Except the ending. Not the end of AJ's story, but the real-life ending. The what-to-do-with-this ending. That will be their choice, Cassie and Ana's.

Like those choose-your-adventure stories we fought over as kids. Ana usually opted for the safe, predictable finish in which the prince solves the puzzle, slays the dragon, and saves the maiden. But Cassie hated those sappy stories. She wrote her own endings, often choosing to raise an army of dragons and mount the prince's head on a castle turret. When Ana abandoned her fairy tales for teen romances, Cassie moved on to the darker stuff: Shirley Jackson, Joyce Carol Oates, H.P. Lovecraft.

How did we manage to share the same womb, much less an entire childhood?

Cassie double-clicks to open her new hard drive, expecting to see Marsh's usual encryption software. He's obsessive about digital security, always lecturing her about the importance of protecting their files from hackers and content pirates. "Anything worth saving is worth protecting," he'd say with that serious expression he wore when discussing business matters. If he's put his usual protections on the new drive, she'll know how to access it.

A window opens on her screen. She's assumed the brand-new, high-capacity, four-terabyte drive is blank. But it appears to be already full of data.

Listed below the system operating files, she finds two folders. One labeled Appetizers, and a much bigger folder named KPXXX2876.

Curious, she opens the larger folder. A password-request screen pops up and she confidently types in the password Marsh has assigned her.

ACCESS DENIED. FOUR ATTEMPTS REMAIN BEFORE CONTENTS ARE DELETED.

Confused, she stares at the warning. Has he changed her password? Or given her someone else's storage device by mistake?

That would be unlike him. Marsh is meticulous about everything.

Frowning, she clicks on the Appetizers folder, hoping there are a few miscellaneous files she can delete to make room for her own work. Though she can't imagine why her tech-savvy husband would create a business-related folder with such a casual, almost domestic name.

Six images arrange themselves across her screen like thumbnails of album covers. Clickable icons, linked to MP4 video files.

She blinks and catches her breath. Each image bears a title: DeepInDesiree, FireInTheHole, BeggingForIt. Below the English titles are what appear to be Chinese characters.

Each clickable thumbnail features a close-up of a naked Asian woman or man. All appear young, late teens or early twenties, with heavily made-up faces and provocative expressions. The images are small on her laptop screen, but she can see enough detail to make her stomach tighten—one woman brandishes a whip, another dangles restraints from red-tipped fingers.

It's an explicit invitation to something Cassie doesn't want to contemplate.

It's some kind of mistake. But that thought dissolves almost immediately. Marsh doesn't make mistakes with his technology. He's methodical, deliberate. Everything in his digital world has a purpose and a place. But why would he give her a drive filled with pornography just before she left for her mother's funeral?

The Marsh she married could be demanding, controlling even, but he's always been respectful about boundaries. Or has he? She thinks of all the times he's steered conversations toward his interests, the way he's gradually isolated her from friends and family. Because Ana's right, that's what he's done. Has she missed other signs?

Cassie hears Ana's footsteps on the floor downstairs. Moving quickly, she lowers the laptop lid and goes to the door, peering into the hall. Everything is quiet, so she eases her bedroom door closed again and returns to her desk.

Whatever she's about to discover, she doesn't need her sister peering over her shoulder.

Cassie mutes the laptop's speaker and reluctantly opens DeepinDesiree.mp4. The next moment, she's grimacing and clicking on the fast-forward button, skimming through content that goes way beyond ordinary porn. There's bondage, rape, bestiality...

The video is mercifully short—no more than five minutes—but it feels like an ugly eternity. At double speed, the action looks rudely absurd, but she's not laughing. When it finally ends, she rubs her hands on her shirt, unable to wipe away imaginary grime.

Feeling like an unwilling voyeur, she closes the first video and double-clicks on the next. The videos make her feel grubby—not only because of the content, but because it feels like she's spying on her husband. She's also feeling betrayed, manipulated in a way she can't quite name. After eighteen years together, why is she discovering this now? And why on a device he gave her?

In their years together, she's occasionally glimpsed porn on his laptop when he forgot to close a browser window—nothing shocking, just the usual mainstream sites depicting enthusiastic performers in predictable settings. She'd considered it normal, perhaps even healthy.

These videos are different. Minimal plot lines, spare settings, and lots of tight-focus camerawork on brutal, sadistic acts that seem to feature blood, terror, and screams. Faked, or real? She doesn't want to know.

And *why* is this on *her* hard drive?

"What on earth are you watching?"

Cassie leaps from her chair and slams the lid on her laptop, hard enough to make it jump an inch forward. "Shit, Ana! Don't sneak up on me like that!"

Ana stands a few feet away, the bedroom door open behind her.

"Sorry, Cass. The door was wide open. Well, not *wide* open," she corrects. "But it wasn't latched, either. I thought you were reading."

It's a simple statement, not accusatory, but Cassie recoils in defense.

"I am—" But Cassie clearly isn't reading. She rubs her scalp hard with both hands, knowing and not caring that her hair probably looks like she's stuck a fork in an electrical outlet. "I thought *you* were reading."

"I finished the last part you gave me, where AJ's gone back into PI mode, interviewing Jimmy's widow. But I'm done, so I came upstairs to see how far you got." She glances at Cassie's bed, where the final chapters still nestle in their box.

Cassie nods toward the computer. "What did you see?"

"It looked like porn," Ana says simply. "Is that what you do when you're being so quiet up here?" Her mouth lifts into a rare smirk.

"You weren't supposed to see that."

"Obviously, judging by your response. I wasn't sneaking up on you, by the way. Your door really was open."

Cassie shoots a glance at the offending door. "It's nothing, really, just some old files Marsh must have left on the storage drive he gave me."

"I thought you said it was a new drive. Isn't it empty?" She peers over Cassie's shoulder. "It's got your name on it. So let's see what Marsh left for you."

"I don't think— Oh, it doesn't matter." Cassie sighs. She opens her laptop and re-starts the second video.

In seconds, Ana has had enough. "Ugh. That is ugly stuff. Go to the end, let's see if they identify the actors in the credits. If it has credits."

Cassie has recovered enough to lift an eyebrow at her sister. "Why? See someone you know?"

Ana's face colors. "Just curious."

Cassie fast-forwards. But instead of a credit roll, they find something else at the very end. With the main characters locked in a mad frenzy of whips and body parts, everything splayed on a huge canopied bed, the camera pulls back and shifts focus to reveal another figure in the foreground. This new person—small, slender, seen only in shadows and from the back— remains perfectly still. Watching and waiting.

It's a brief scene, lasting no more than ten seconds before a final fade to black.

A preview of coming attractions? The next undiscovered superstar waiting in the wings?

Standing close beside Cassie, Ana grips her sister's shoulder hard. "Did you see that? It looks like a kid watching."

A kid? Wordlessly, Cassie pulls the slider back and re-plays the last few seconds of the video.

"See?" Ana points. "Look at those skinny shoulders. It's a child. And I think someone's hand is on their shoulder." She pulls her own hand away from Cassie.

They watch it a third time.

Cassie shudders. "I think you're right." She selects the next video, FireInTheHole. Grimacing at the title, she fast-forwards nearly to the end. They find a similar scene, with a partially hidden figure—a different one, with longer hair—crouched behind a potted palm.

Ana's voice catches. "That kid's even smaller," she whispers. "Younger. Maybe six or seven?"

Cassie's not a great judge of kids' ages, but even she can see this isn't just a small adult. Ana's hand has returned to her shoulder and the grip has become painfully hard, but Cassie doesn't shake it off. Grimly, she runs the second video again.

Definitely a child.

She swallows back a taste of bile rising in her throat. Closes that file, opens a third. Again, there's a silent, shadowy figure at the end of the film, concealed this time behind a half-open door. In this video, however, a portion of the child's face is visible—an eye, one small delicate ear, the side of a cheek, a corner of the mouth. As they watch, the lips curve into a parody of a smile.

Cassie's eyes water. Abruptly, she yanks the hard drive's cable from her laptop, and the screen goes blank. She shakes off Ana's hand and fumbles a wad of tissues from the box on her desk, catching a sour mouthful of half-digested coffee before it can spew onto her keyboard.

Her mind has gone as blank as the screen, except for a single thought: *Appetizers. That's what we just watched. Previews of coming attractions.*

So what's in the encrypted folder, the one labeled KPXXX2876?

All the blood drains from Ana's face as she touches a finger to the small, innocuous-looking portable drive labeled CASSANDRA.

"Do you think," Ana begins slowly, "your husband knew what was on this when he gave it to you?" She answers herself. "No, of course not. He couldn't, could he?"

Cassie's thoughts have shifted from numb to chaotic, possibilities rising and falling in a maelstrom. She's known Marsh for eighteen years. If he's attracted to rough sex and child porn, she'd know it, right? Surely he'd have let something slip.

She pushes back her chair, stands, and discovers she can't trust her legs to hold her up. But she needs to move. To run, or hide, or put her fist through a wall.

She tucks cold hands beneath her armpits and glances down at her bare legs. "I'm cold, I've got to get dressed." She collapses on the bed and yanks on her jeans.

Ana watches silently, her face white.

"I should call Marsh." Cassie fumbles her sandals from under the bed. "Give him a chance to explain."

When Cassie's on her feet again, Ana takes her gently by the shoulders. "No, you have to call the police. Regular porn, with consenting adults, that's one thing—

but we saw *children* on those videos. And some terrible brutality."

"The children were only at the end. We don't know—"

"Call the police, Cassie."

"I should give Marsh a chance to explain. Maybe there's a simple answer."

Someone else must have put those files on there, that's the only answer.

Ana lets go of Cassie's shoulders and tucks a loose strand of yellow-gray hair behind one ear. Her expression shifts from compassion to frustration. "Cassie—"

"I'll call Marsh first, then I'll take it to the police." Her voice wavers on the last word.

"And tell Marsh what? That you and I watched the videos, and now you're going to take it to the police?"

"No! I'll say it was just me. I saw the drive was full when I tried to use it. I'll tell him I didn't open any of the files."

"Cassie, think this through. Then he'll ask you to send it back but you won't have it, because you've given it to the police! Because you *are* going to do that, right? I don't know your husband very well but we both know he's got a temper. In what *universe* does telling him anything sound like a smart move?"

"I don't know, I'll tell him it was stolen. Or I lost it at the airport on the way home. Oh god, Ana! I can't fix this, I can't fix anything."

Now the word *home* is stuck in her throat because she's avoiding all thoughts of going home. But she'll have to, won't she? Marsh expects her to fly back to California as scheduled. *And then what?*

And oh god, she's still got to finish reading AJ's story. But this is more important. Isn't it?

And they need to clean out their mom's house and organize the estate sale and —

A sob breaks loose from somewhere deep in Cassie's chest. She collapses on the bed and curls into a tight, shuddering ball, unable to hold herself together. A second later, Ana folds down behind her, spooning her sister's trembling body and spilling her own stock of tears, grief, and shock.

Their arms and legs weave together, the way they must have lain in their mother's womb, entwined so thoroughly they no longer knew which heartbeat was which.

***

An hour later, Cassie's in Winslow. She can't remember much about the drive into town, but her face is washed, the tears are dried, and she's formed the semblance of a plan.

She finds parking close to the coffeeshop, the one with the excellent WiFi. The public library probably has good WiFi, too, and it would certainly be quieter at lunchtime. But even if she found a private corner there to make her calls, how could she discuss porn videos in the same reading room where Mom used to bring them every Tuesday for children's story hour?

She's decided to tell Marsh. Not about discovering the videos, only that the drive seems to be already full of someone else's data.

The coffeeshop is doing a brisk lunch business but most customers have chosen to sit outside beneath the festive market umbrellas, so Cassie easily finds an unoccupied table in the very back. She orders iced tea and a Caesar salad that she knows she won't eat, then plugs in her phone to charge it and sets her laptop case on the seat beside her.

In Winslow it's one PM on Friday, so in Hong Kong it must be one AM on Saturday. Delivery day for the Lamborghini. She wonders where Marsh will be when she calls. In his hotel room? With clients at a bar, perhaps, or a nightclub.

It doesn't matter. Marsh never discloses the details of his business ventures or his travels, aside from arrivals and departures and which luxury hotel he's booked into. All "their" money is his money. She's always been okay with that, because he's been so generous with gifts and a monthly allowance. Now she wonders how she's arrived at this point in her life, being what used to be called a lady of leisure, easily available whenever the lord of the manor wants some fun, or needs her presence at an important function. She's a kept woman.

Cassie wraps her fingers around the phone and feels the plastic warm against her palm. The café hums with quiet conversations and the gentle hiss of the espresso machine, but her world has narrowed to this moment. She stares at Marsh's contact photo, trying to decipher—not for the first time—the mind behind those sharp dark eyes. But all she sees in the polished surface of the phone's screen is the polished surface of him, the square jaw and full mouth set in a sardonic smile, the smoothly bronzed SoCal skin of the well-kept, highly successful businessman.

She taps the number that will connect her to him and waits, imagining the signal traveling halfway around the world.

Deep breath, she reminds herself. *You're puzzled, a little disappointed, and utterly clueless about what's on that drive.*

He picks up on the second ring.

"Cassie?" Marsh's voice comes through sharp, almost breathless. "I was just about to call you—"

"Hi. Sorry, I hope I didn't wake you." She bites her lip because that's not what she intended to say. *Don't start with an apology.*

She begins again. "Look, about that storage drive you gave me?"

Silence stretches between them, broken only by what sounds like traffic in the background. She imagines him on some busy street corner in Hong Kong's nightclub district, a dark figure paused amid the steamy heat and incessant noise, throngs of people flowing around him. A part of the city that really only gets going after midnight. His kind of place.

Though she's never been there, has she? He never takes her anywhere he goes for business.

When he speaks again, his voice is level, controlled, but there's a sharp edge underneath. "What about it?"

She forces her voice to stay conversational. "I was going to back up my files but there's no space left. I thought you said it was brand new, so it should be blank, right? But—"

His sharp intake of breath halts her chatter. "Did you look at anything? Cassie, this is important. Did you open any of the files?"

Her heart hammers against her ribs but the rehearsed lie comes easily. "No, of course not. I figured it was your work stuff." She tries to sound offended. "I wouldn't look at any of that, you know I wouldn't."

Another pause. She hears him exhale, long and slow. "Okay. Good." She can almost hear him running his hand through his hair, that familiar gesture that tells her when he's working through a problem. Now he sounds contrite. "Jesus, Cassie. I'm so sorry. This is exactly the kind of screw-up I've been worried about."

"What do you mean?"

"I've been having issues with one of the guys in IT. Derek, you remember Derek? I think he's been using company equipment for personal stuff." His voice carries that familiar mix of frustration and disappointment she's heard him use about incompetent employees. "I've been trying to build a case before I fire him, but if he's putting that garbage on drives meant for legitimate use—"

"What do you mean, garbage? What's on there?"

He goes silent. Realizing, she thinks, that he's told her more than she's admitted to knowing. She bites her lip.

"Have you told anyone else about finding it? Anyone at all?"

His question sends a chill through her veins, but she also hears what sounds like genuine concern.

"No." She adds a touch of annoyance. "I'll have to buy another drive. I just thought you should know I have it, in case you were looking for it."

Before she can stop herself, she adds, "What's so important about it?" Then catches her lower lip again between her teeth, wishing she could take that back.

"Client confidentiality," he says quickly. "And if word gets out that our systems aren't secure, that my employees are using company drives for their own shit, well—" She hears the disgust in his voice. "It could destroy everything I've built. The whole business could collapse."

His voice grows more urgent. "So keep it safe for me, okay? And don't tell anyone about it. I need to handle Derek quietly before this gets out."

Cassie closes her eyes. Unbidden, the images of those silent children flash through her mind. Terrifying, disturbing, wrong in every way. It makes her skin crawl.

He's blaming Derek. She remembers him, a little. A quiet guy in his late twenties or early thirties, who always seemed nervous around Marsh. But would someone really be that stupid? That reckless with company equipment?

Yet Marsh sounds genuinely angry. This is the same tone he used when he discovered a security breach with a custom-parts fabricator in Singapore. Controlled fury, mixed with injury, the voice of a man who trusted people and got burned.

But those children.

"When will you be back?" She tries to sound like any wife missing her husband.

"As soon as I can, so I can deal with this situation." His voice softens slightly. "Cassie, promise me. Don't look at those files! And don't say anything to anyone until I can handle this properly."

It's almost the old Marsh now. Protective, taking charge, trying to shield her from unpleasantness.

"Sure, I promise." She glances down at the rose gold ring on her left hand and realizes she's crossed her fingers. A silly gesture, one she'd over-used in childhood.

"Good. And Cassie?" His voice catches slightly, as if he's swallowed hard. "I'm sorry you got dragged into this mess. This is exactly the kind of thing I work so hard to keep away from you."

The apology sounds genuine, more like the man she married. He adds, "Hey, Cassie. I love you."

The words hit her like a slap. They rarely say that to each other, and his declaration feels loaded with meaning she can't decipher.

The line goes dead before she has to respond.

Cassie sets her phone aside as a server brings her lunch. She stares at the salad, then pushes the plate away untouched. The café continues its gentle rhythm around her.

She pulls the hard drive from her laptop case and turns it over in her palm. Such a small thing to carry such terrible weight.

CASSANDRA. She tries to rip the label off, but it's fastened with something that won't yield.

Derek, Marsh said. An employee using company equipment inappropriately. But it makes sense. Marsh is obsessive about protecting client information and his company's reputation. He's fired people for far less serious breaches. And he sounded genuinely disgusted when he talked about what was on the drive.

But then why does her stomach still churn with doubt? Why does some part of her mind keep circling back to how quickly he'd answered the phone, how he said he'd been about to call her first?

Her thoughts circle the possibilities. What if the Derek story is true, but Marsh knew about it all along? Or what if he's not the victim of an employee's misconduct, but something worse?

What if Marsh is complicit?

What if he's the one who *created* the videos?

And she's been sleeping next to him for years.

Her spinning mind settles on another chilling thought: What if he didn't believe her when she said she didn't look at anything?

Leaving the label and small black device intact, Cassie returns it to the computer case and pulls out a notepad. Flips a few pages forward and finds what she needs. On her phone, she enters the landline number she copied from her mother's old phonebook.

C. Androski. Her finger hovers over the call button, but then she sets the phone down again, staring blankly as the screen fades.

Buying herself time to think, she picks up her iced tea and uses a spare napkin to wipe condensation from the glass. Her ice has melted and the tea has gone thin and watery. She drinks it anyway, idly watching the café's other patrons go about their afternoon several yards away—reading newspapers, tapping on laptops, chatting over salads and sandwiches.

She's out of iced tea so it's time. She taps the phone to wake it up, then presses send before she can change her mind.

What does the law say about a wife testifying against her husband?

CHAPTER TWENTY-ONE

Cassie

On the phone, Androski is brief. "You need to speak with Detective Sergeant Meredith Clement at the barracks. She's part of the Eastern District Major Crime Division, the team I used to work with."

Cassie scribbles down the number for Detective Clement. "You can't meet me there? I'd rather talk with you."

"I'm retired, remember? They let me putter around with a couple of cold cases, but I can't work an active investigation. Trust me on this, Cassie. I think Meredith will be very interested. After you've talked with her, give me a call back if you want to talk, okay? Here's my cell."

She adds his cellphone number beneath Detective Clement's and reluctantly hangs up.

The phone rings only once. "Detective Sergeant Meredith Clement."

"Carl Androski said I should call you," Cassie blurts. She glances around the café and lowers her voice. "I've got something that might involve...child abuse. Maybe trafficking." She doesn't want to say the other words out loud: Child pornography, sexual exploitation.

"Your name and address, please?" The detective's voice is measured, professional.

"Cassie Bousquet," she says without thinking. "Cassandra Masterson, actually. I'm from Palos Verdes, California, but I'm here in Connecticut for my…" But that doesn't matter, does it?

"And what's the name of the person you think might be involved with this?"

"Marsh Masterson." She speaks more carefully now, knowing she's stepped over a line and there's no going back. "His middle name is James. Marshall James Masterson."

Cassie hears fingers tapping at keyboard. The detective speaks again with a new urgency. "Can you come to the Danielson barracks?"

"Right now?"

"Yes, if possible. I'll be here for another two hours. Ask for me at the front desk."

Cassie's hands tremble as she gathers her things.

The drive to the barracks takes twenty-three minutes, time enough for Cassie to second-guess herself. Time to imagine Marsh discovering what she's about to do, and wonder if she's making the biggest mistake of her life.

But each time doubt creeps in, she sees a child standing behind a half-open door. Watching.

From the outside, Troop D barracks looks exactly like AJ's description from four decades earlier: a boxy, three-story brick building. Windows freshly trimmed in white and a front entrance framed in square-cut granite, with an unexpectedly graceful iron lamp above the royal-blue steel door. The visitors' section of the lot is full, so Cassie parks in the Walmart lot next door. For a long moment she sits there, summoning courage and listening to the Volvo's engine ticking as it cools. She has a clear view of the barracks through the windshield and for a moment she just sits, watching uniformed officers coming and going. Their movements are purposeful and confident, and she envies their certainty.

There's a large sign on the front door warning her DO NOT ENTER with unauthorized weapons, biological materials, or hazardous items. For a moment, she flashes on the last line of coke she did at a movie premiere after-party, eight months ago. Are there traces of it still in her purse? No. She's carrying a different handbag now, a new leather cross-body.

Besides, she's done with that shit.

She removes the portable drive from her laptop case and slides it into the bag. She should have thought to wrap it in a tissue. Will Marsh's fingerprints, or maybe his DNA, still be on its hard-rubber shell?

But it's her fingerprints they'll find first. Hers and maybe Ana's. Her *name* is on it, so how will she prove it's not hers? Will they think she's part of whatever terrible thing this is?

Inside the small foyer, fluorescent lights glare from overhead and the sharp odor of disinfectant fills her nostrils. The floors are foot-square, gray and beige vinyl tiles, worn and chipped. Three walls are industrial gray, clearly bearing many coats of thick, washable paint. The fourth wall is made of dark smoked glass, impossible to see through. The desk trooper—she assumes there's someone behind the glass—is invisible.

She spots a sign directing her to pick up a wall phone. "I'm here to see Detective Clement," Cassie says, surprised by how steady her voice sounds.

"Please put your driver's license in the tray," a man's voice replies. "You'll get it back when you leave. I'll contact Detective Sergeant Clement."

She does as she's told and retreats four steps across the small room to perch on a hard plastic chair, her handbag in her lap. On the opposite wall, there's a bulletin board and a brochure rack displaying flyers and pamphlets. A booklet titled Domestic Violence Resources, others offering information on human trafficking, lists of elderly assistance and social services programs, animal control information, the fire marshal's burning permit program.

There's also a poster with the picture of a frightened child and a number to call if you know someone being trafficked for sex or labor. Cassie learns that, worldwide, an estimated four-point-eight million people are trafficked for sex each year. The U.S. is the largest market for pornography.

The horror of those statistics seeps in slowly, like poison through her bloodstream. Nearly five million, more than the entire population of Connecticut. Millions of human beings bought and sold like merchandise, their bodies treated as commodities and their lives reduced to profit margins.

The shadowy figures in those videos flash through her mind again. Each one represents not just a crime, but a life destroyed, a childhood stolen, a future obliterated.

She picks up a trifold brochure advertising the local rape hotline and reads something slightly more encouraging: "How to help if someone you love tells you they've been assaulted: 1) Tell them you are glad they confided in you. 2) Tell them you believe them. 3)

Don't blame them for what has happened. 4) Listen to them when they express fears, emotions, concerns."

Quick hot tears come to her eyes. This support hadn't been easily available to her mother forty years ago.

She returns the brochure to the rack and the minutes tick by. She catches her bottom lip in her teeth and worries it. *What will Marsh do when he finds out? What if—*

"Ms. Masterson? Or do you prefer Bousquet?"

Sergeant Clement is in her early forties. Medium height, deep brown eyes, near-black hair laced with gray and pulled back in a practical bun at her neck. She's carrying a spiral notepad and wearing an almost-uniform—black slacks, pale blue collared shirt, and an unbuttoned navy blazer. There's a badge on her belt and a service weapon at her hip.

She gives Cassie a clip-on visitor tag and holds out a hand. "I'm Meredith Clement. Please, call me Meredith. Let's talk somewhere private."

The detective leads Cassie through a narrow corridor and upstairs to a small interview room. In here, everything's beige: walls, window blinds, metal cabinet against the wall, four chairs, and a scratched metal table. Near the ceiling, two small cameras stare down with steady red eyes.

Meredith closes the door and gestures Cassie to choose a chair. "Coffee? Water?"

"No, thank you." She doesn't think she could swallow anything right now.

Settling into a second chair, Meredith folds her hands on the table, making no move yet to open her notebook. "You said you have something important to show me."

Cassie reaches for her bag, then hesitates. Once she hands this over, there's no going back. No pretending she never saw what she saw, no returning to her comfortably ignorant life with Marsh.

Her fingers find the rubbery case of the drive. She sets it on the table, its USB cable still attached like a short leash on a very small puppy. The white label with her name on it practically glows in the harsh light.

"My husband owns Masterson's Exotic Motors," she begins, "out on the west coast. Near Palos Verdes, California. He buys and restores rare vintage cars, then sells them all over the world. Really rare cars. Some of them cost over a million dollars." As if that's important. But maybe it is important, because Meredith raises an eyebrow, flips open her notebook, and makes a note.

Cassie's words come more easily now. "Marsh uses a lot of these portable drives in his business to back up data from his work, but also for marketing the cars with photos and videos. He gives them to clients and potential buyers. He says it's more secure than putting everything on the web and emailing stuff around." She places the drive on the table and looks down at it. Such a little thing, no bigger than a stack of business cards.

She pulls her eyes away and organizes her thoughts. "He buys these drives by the dozen. Before I left on this trip—I came here last Monday, I'm here for a week for my mother's funeral—he gave this one to me. To back up my work. It was supposed to be empty," she explains, "but there were... other things on it."

"What do you do, Ms. Bousquet? What kind of work?"

What do I do? Nothing important. "I'm a writer. Short stories, screenplays."

"And you're certain that your husband gave you this? Your name's on it. You didn't purchase it yourself? This is important, Ms. Bousquet."

"Yes, that's correct. He put the label on there. It's his handwriting."

"Did you see the receipt? When he purchased it."

"No, he just gave it to me. With the label." She knows she's repeating herself but it's important, the detective has to know that she's not involved.

"Okay. What did you find on it?"

"There are videos." Cassie's voice falters. "There's one big folder that's encrypted. I couldn't get into that one, but there's another directory—it's called 'Appetizers'—and I looked at those."

"And what did you see?"

Cassie takes a deep breath. "At first I thought it was just standard porn movies. Nothing unusual. I mean, that's not illegal, right? Unless it's a deepfake, where someone's using AI to put one person's head on another person's body."

"That's called weaponized porn. And yes, it's very much illegal."

"This is different. At the end of each video, the camera pulls back and there's a...a young child. Standing at the edge of the scene, sort of spying on the adults. Watching and...and learning, I think."

She stumbles to a stop. Shivers and wraps her arms around her body.

The detective's mouth tightens. "Where is your husband now?"

"Hong Kong. He flew there a few days ago to deliver a car to a Chinese buyer. It's a really rare Lamborghini."

Meredith tilts her head. "How was this car shipped?"

Cassie shrugs. "In a container, probably. The one he just sold cost over a million, so it went by air freight. There's pictures that show that on the company website. It's in a wooden crate, sort of a box within a box. They pack it with padding, put it into a container and strap it down, then load it onto a ship or plane. His company sells cars all over the world. He travels a lot."

She raises a hand and pops up her fingers like a little kid, naming Marsh's recent destinations. "Amsterdam, Rio, Caracas, Singapore. That's just a few."

"And how long has he been in this business?"

"Ever since I met him, eighteen years go. The business was much smaller then. Nothing overseas then, just North America. Now it's worldwide."

There's a bitter taste in Cassie's mouth. "It's the perfect cover for moving things, isn't it? Things, or maybe people, across borders."

Appetizers.

Cassie has never given much thought to how Marsh makes his money but now her stomach lurches. Shipping containers, taking cars all around the world. One legitimate payload and all documents in order, but with plenty of space for additional cargo. How could she be so stupid, so blind, for all these years?

Because she's pretty sure now Derek wasn't the one who put the porn on that hard drive. Or if he did, it was under Marsh's direction.

Using the tip of a pen, Meredith nudges the portable drive toward a plastic evidence bag she's pulled from her blazer pocket. "This could be evidence in an investigation, Ms. Bousquet. When you leave here, I'm going to contact the federal agencies, Homeland Security and the FBI in Boston. Things are going to move quickly. Are you prepared for that?"

"What do you mean?"

The detective leans a little forward, holding Cassie with hard eyes. "Your husband and others at his company will be investigated. Your life is going to change, and fast. We may have enough to get a warrant for his arrest and pick him up when he lands at the airport, but maybe not. You could be in danger."

Cassie pulls away from the sharp stare. "Do you have to tell him right away? That I gave it to you."

"No. But he'll know, won't he? When he comes home and asks for it? And you'll be called to testify if this goes to trial."

"You make it sound like the investigation's already started."

Meredith's gaze slides away. "Let's just say Marsh Masterson is already on the radar with the feds." She taps the drive again. "Who else knows about these files?"

"Only my sister, Ana—"

"Her too, then. You both need to think of a safe place to go. Some place your husband wouldn't know about."

"—and I told Marsh."

"*What?*"

Cassie twists her fingers together on the table. "I told him I found the files. I wanted to give him a chance to explain. He blamed it on a guy in IT named Derek, I don't know his last name. But Marsh knows what's on there, he as much as said so. Then he asked me if I looked at any of the files. I said no," she finishes lamely.

"So you believe your husband is directly involved?"

Cassie recalls Marsh's reaction when she mentioned the drive, the way his voice went hard and cautious. "Yes." Then she walks it back with a faint hope. "But I don't know for sure. Maybe not."

Meredith leans over the table, emphasizing each word. "Dammit, I'm serious, Cassie. No matter what his level of involvement, when he learns we have this, he's going to know exactly who to blame. If he's part of a trafficking operation, he will be coming for you. Him, or someone else. These people are ruthless."

She sits back again. "Anyone who can buy and sell humans—let alone children—isn't going to put up with ten seconds with an informer. Nothing will matter—not family, not your marriage, nothing. You need to be thinking—right now—about where you're going to hide. Then get there, fast.

"And I'm sorry," she adds, "but we can't provide protection for you. We can help with resources and referrals, but you'll have to vanish on your own."

Cassie thinks again of the children in the videos, of the files she couldn't open, of all the other children whose faces she'll never see but who are out there somewhere, suffering. She thinks of Marsh's quick anger when he's crossed, his ability to manipulate and control. Then she thinks about herself the way she used to be, before she met Marsh. She'd been so ready to rail against authority and whatever else needed challenging. That impulsive, passionate young woman wouldn't have hesitated.

Nor would her mother. Not the mother she thought she knew, but the one from way back, the one she now knows so much better. The question is simple enough: *What would Marla do?*

She blows out a breath. "Okay, what do I need to do?"

Meredith nods and sits back, looking grim but relieved. She slips the drive into the evidence bag and writes a few notes on the label. "I'll need a full statement from you. Dates, times. Everything you remember doing and seeing, what you said to your husband on the phone, his reaction."

"And Ana? She was with me when we looked at it."

"In your statement, you should mention that Ana was with you. But she'll need to tell us in her own words what she saw, too. And yes, she'll need to vanish also."

Cassie's eyes brim with sudden tears. She rubs a hand roughly over her face. *Oh god, what have I gotten Ana into? And her family.*

"What about my brother-in-law? And my niece and nephew, they're in college…they have no idea."

"The fewer people who know what's happening, the better. Marsh will probably try to keep this a secret from his bosses as long as possible, and he'll try to save himself first. But you know him better than we do."

Cassie drops her head into her hands for a moment. Obviously, she doesn't know Marsh at all.

When she raises her eyes again, the detective holds her gaze. "But I won't lie to you, Cassie. If your husband is involved in human trafficking at the level you're describing, then yes, these are dangerous people. He is dangerous. He has a lot to lose."

Cassie's stomach drops.

"But," Meredith continues, "we're going to be careful about how we proceed. Right now, your husband doesn't know you've come forward, correct?"

"No."

"Good. And he's still in Hong Kong. When will he be back?"

"Late Monday, or Tuesday morning. I have the details on my phone. But that's when he'll arrive in California, not here. Though he did say he's going to try for an earlier flight."

"Okay, that gives us a little time." Meredith frowns and leans back in her chair, considering. "Have you thought of somewhere safe you can stay? Family, friends, somewhere your husband wouldn't immediately think to look?"

"I'll have to think. I grew up here, but I don't know really anyone anymore. Ana lives in West Hartford. She'll know someone we can stay with."

"Good. The more remote, the better. Another question, is your husband tracking you with any devices?"

"You mean like AirTags? There's one on the key fob for my car, but I left that at home. I'm driving a rental. I don't know if there are any others."

"They're usually sold in four-packs, so if there's one there's probably more. Check your purse, laptop case, suitcases. And buy a couple of prepaid phones for yourself and your sister. Be very careful who you give those new numbers to. Then switch off your regular cells so he can't track those."

Cassie can't grasp the enormity of what they're doing. "Burner phones?"

"And don't waste time, move as fast as you can." Meredith pulls out a business card and writes on the back. "This is my direct number, and here's my cell. If anything feels off—if your husband calls, if you notice anyone following you, anything at all—call me immediately." Her worried look deepens, making Cassie wonder what similar cases the detective has worked.

"Cassie, has your husband ever been physically violent with you?"

Cassie wants to say no, wants to maintain the fiction that Marsh's control has always been subtle, more psychological than physical. But there was that time two years ago when she'd complained about one of his long business trips. He'd grabbed her wrist and twisted her arm so hard it ached for days. And there was the time she'd wanted to fly east for Scott's high school graduation. She'd just hung up after talking with Ana, when Marsh had grabbed her phone in a fit of pique and thrown it against the wall. He'd apologized later, saying he'd had a bad day at work or a big sale had fallen through. Something, she forgets which—

"A few times, maybe. But nothing really bad—"

Meredith nods grimly. "You'll need a place to stay for a month or two, maybe more. We'll move as fast on our end as we can, but..." She leaves the rest unsaid and becomes briskly efficient. "Ready to give us your statement?"

The detective centers herself in her chair and glances first at her notebook, then at an overhead camera. She says their names, the date, and the time. "I'm referencing a small portable computer drive, Samsung, about two inches by three inches." She pulls a magnifying glass from her blazer pocket and peers through the evidence bag at the miniscule lettering printed on the back of the hard drive. She reads off a serial number, then turns her attention back to Cassie.

"Ms. Bousquet, when exactly did your husband give this device to you? Please think carefully and repeat what you told me earlier. Every detail you can give me will help us protect others, as well as you."

CHAPTER TWENTY-TWO

Cassie

The drive back to the house passes in a blur of late summer countryside and churning thoughts. Detective Clement's words are stuck in Cassie's mind: *These are dangerous people. They have a lot to lose.*

About to turn into the driveway, she has to wait as a white van with a medical supplies logo on its side pulls out. Ana's on the front porch looking sweaty and distracted, a dust rag dangling from the waistband of her jeans.

"You were gone a long time, Cass. Did everything go okay with the police?"

"Yes. Well, sort of." Cassie watches the van disappear around a curve on their gravel road. "You sent the hospital bed back to the rental company?" Stating the obvious to buy a little time, before she has to tell her sister they need to switch off their phones and vanish.

Ana is brisk and businesslike. "One more thing checked off the list. I wanted to have it gone before the end of the month so you don't get charged for an extra month's rental. I appreciated your picking up the bill on that, and other things, too," she adds awkwardly. "You and Marsh."

Cassie flinches at the sound of her husband's name. Has Ana forgotten what they were just looking at?

Forgotten where it came from? Or does she simply not want to admit what they discovered?

Ana moves to the porch railing and reaches up to pluck a cluster of red florets, now gone brown, from a geranium. "Do you want me to send Marsh the confirmation that the equipment rental's been cancelled? Then he'll know his account shouldn't be getting billed anymore—"

"No!"

Ana jumps. She turns suddenly, the geraniums forgotten. Her eyes go wide and her mouth forms a small O as she stares at Cassie.

Cassie quiets her voice but the urgency remains. "Look, Ana, that's what we have to talk about. Don't say anything to Marsh, about the bed or anything else. Don't call him, send an email, text, nothing." She drops heavily into a wicker chair, then leans forward and plants her face in her hands for a moment.

Ana abandons the geranium stems and takes in her twin's posture. "Cassie, what's wrong?"

"We need to leave. Go into hiding. Tomorrow, or Monday morning at the very latest."

"Leave?" The furrows in Ana's forehead deepen. "What are you talking about?"

"And we need to stay hidden for at least a month. Maybe longer. We've got to pack up everything we can't live without."

Ana crosses her arms exactly as their mother used to. "Cassandra Bousquet, you're scaring me. What happened at the police station?"

Cassie takes a deep breath. There's no gentle way to say it. "I gave that storage drive to a detective, Meredith Clement."

"Okay. And?"

"She said Marsh is already 'on their radar.' She used those exact words."

"What does that mean? What for?"

"I'm pretty sure it's because of what we saw. Not just pornography but sexual abuse of…children. Maybe human trafficking. It's something big, it could get dangerous, and we're not safe. We have to leave."

Ana stares at her for a long moment, then lets out a short laugh. "Aren't you being a bit melodramatic?"

"No, I'm not." Cassie's voice breaks slightly. "You saw those videos."

"What I mean is, maybe there's another explanation. And why do we have to leave? Why can't the cops just handle it, pick him up when he lands in L.A.?"

Cassie closes her eyes, but the images of children remain. "The detective said these are dangerous people. There's no telling what Marsh is part of, or what he'll do—"

Ana sinks into a wicker chair beside Cassie, knowledge dawning. "My god, Cassie. Does Marsh know you found the videos on the drive? Did you tell him?"

Cassie bites her bottom lip, tasting blood. "Before I took it to the cops, I called him. I wanted to give him a chance to say he didn't know anything about it. He seemed to know about it, but he blamed it on a co-worker."

"That was—"

"Stupid of me?" Cassie throws both hands in the air. "Yeah, I know. But I didn't tell him we looked at it," she adds hastily. "I was hoping he'd say he didn't know anything about it. But he knew exactly what I was talking about. He blamed a guy in IT and said I absolutely should not open anything." She grabs her sister's hand. "Meredith—Detective Clement—says until they find and arrest him, we're not safe here."

Cassie reaches into her handbag and pulls out the two cheap prepaid phones she bought at Walmart.

"These are our new phones. Meredith said we should switch off our regular phones and use these instead. Put her info into the contacts and give the new numbers to Jonathan, but no one else.

Ana is quiet for a long moment, processing. When she speaks again, her voice is steadier. "Okay. If you're right—and I can't believe I'm saying this—where do we go? We can't just disappear."

"Maybe a hotel—"

"No." Ana shakes her head. "If we're talking about a month or more, we need somewhere private. Somewhere Marsh would never think to look." She pauses, then her expression brightens. "There's the cabin."

"What cabin?"

"Jonathan and I bought a little place in upstate Vermont, on a lake. It's pretty remote, no neighbors for miles. We were planning to use it as a summer retreat, but we haven't even spent a full weekend there yet. We closed on it three months ago."

Cassie feels a flicker of hope. "Who else knows about it?"

"No one. It was going to be a surprise for Scott and Julie. Part of our summer vacation. But then Mom got worse and…" Ana trails off. "I'll need to call Jonathan. Tell him what's happening."

"Can you trust him to keep this to himself?"

Ana bridles. "He's my husband, Cassie, and a lawyer. Yes, we can trust him." Her tone softens. "Besides, he's never liked Marsh. Jonathan always thought he was hiding something from his past."

"What will you tell him?"

"The truth. Jonathan deserves to know why his wife and sister-in-law are suddenly going into hiding."

"Then he should leave West Hartford and join us in Vermont, too. If he knows, he could be in danger, too."

Ana stands and walks a few steps away, then back. "This is crazy. Three days ago our biggest worry was where to donate Mom's china. Then we found AJ's manuscript, and now this…"

"I know." Cassie shifts in her chair, watching as Ana continues to pace the length of the porch. "And we still have that to deal with. The manuscript."

Ana stops and throws her hands up. "We don't have time to finish reading it now, or get it scanned. Let's just take it with us. If we're going to be stuck in a cabin for a month…"

"It won't take long to finish, there's only four chapters to go. I'll read it tonight, you can go through it tomorrow morning. And I'll get it scanned and copied in town tomorrow morning. Then we'll know what we're dealing with. That still leaves the afternoon to finish packing. Sunday morning, noon by the latest, we leave. I was thinking Monday would be okay but now I think we should just get away as fast as we can. That should give us plenty of time, even if Marsh catches an early flight back. I can drop my car off at the rental place on our way north. Then we take only the one car, your Subaru, to Vermont."

Ana considers this as she resumes pacing the porch floor. "Okay, that's doable. But before I switch off my phone, I need to call Jonathan." She pulls out her phone, then hesitates. "Cassie, what if we're wrong about this? What if there's a perfectly innocent explanation and we're running away for nothing?"

Cassie shrugs. "Then we'll have spent a month at your new cabin."

And my marriage will be over, either way.

Ana nods, leans against the porch railing, and dials her husband's number. She keeps her gaze on her sister as the phone rings. "Jonathan's going to think we've lost our minds."

"Better than losing our lives."

Ana turns away to focus on her call. Pushing her hair back with her free hand, she straightens her shoulders. "Jonathan? Hi, it's me. Listen, I need to tell you something important. You're probably going to want to sit down."

Cassie stands and walks to the other end of the porch, looking out at the peaceful landscape that no longer feels safe. In three days, her entire world has turned upside down. But she knows she's made the right decision.

Behind her, she hears Ana explaining to Jonathan about the videos, the police, and the need for the twins to disappear. The conversation can't be easy, but Ana's voice is steady and sure. Whatever happens next with Marsh, Cassie won't be facing it alone.

A few minutes later, they've switched off their phones and activated the burners.

***

That evening in her room, Cassie lifts the last chapters of the manuscript from the box. With her own life in danger, she feels now like the old crimes detailed in AJ's story are almost irrelevant. They're ancient history, fascinating in their revelations but not entirely relevant. The desire to uncover her mother's secrets has been replaced by the greater, more urgent need to find safety.

But it's only four chapters. She thumbs the stack quickly. Thirty-five pages, an easy read. It will be a good distraction, she thinks. Maybe help her sleep. Or she could just skim it quickly, to get the gist and learn the ending. Then she can pass it on to Ana and do a more thorough read when they get to the cabin.

She pauses on a page near the middle of the stack. Her eye lands first on a paragraph about the footbridge over the Pennatucket River, and then on a line of dialogue: "I don't want my children born in prison."

Her earlier sense of foreboding closes in and she's suddenly aware of the room's stuffiness. She gets up from her chair by the desk and shoves her window open, as wide as it will go, to let in the night breezes. A flash of lighting bounces briefly off a faraway hill, and she knows there's a storm brewing to the northwest. If the rain gets heavy she'll shut the window but for now she welcomes the fresh air.

Clutching the last of AJ's story to her chest, she props two pillows against the wall and crawls between the sheets.

CHAPTER TWENTY-THREE

AJ

~ 13 ~

I woke abruptly with cat whiskers brushing my ear. The unsettling remnants of a bad dream—something with fire and smoke, the desperate cries of children—danced at the edge of consciousness and then faded, leaving me only with a terrible desire to both confess and deny the arson.

I wanted to call Marla, but I didn't know what to say.

I should call Androski, but I was terrified of what I *would* say.

I called no one. Instead, I made breakfast as usual and drove into town by my regular route, passing the blackened ruins of the Grabtown barn and the field where Jimmy died. I drove steadily, keeping my hands light on the wheel and my eyes firmly on the road.

Everything gets easier with time and practice, Gran always said. Just keep at it.

At the radio station, I nodded to Tony the intern, pulling his fill-in shift in the control room, and headed for the newsroom to finish editing a pre-recorded interview for WWCT's weekend public affairs show.

In the break room, I surprised Mike and Peter Barlow, the sales manager, as I squeezed between them to store my sandwich bag in the fridge. They went awkwardly silent, but I'd already seen the little side-glances and heard a snippet of conversation from the hallway. The two had been talking, I knew, about a woman. Not me, I assumed—I'm too plain to draw that kind of unwanted attention, thank god—and I hoped it wasn't Peggy at the front desk, who's not very worldly and can be easily teased into an embarrassed blush.

But I knew they'd been comparing notes about someone, using their T&A body scoring system that was firmly entrenched in the "boys will be boys" culture long before Dudley Moore slavered after Bo Derek running down the beach in the movie *10*, that dumb male-fantasy flick from a few years ago. It's something women get targeted with when they crash the boys' club in the media business.

Pictures suddenly get stashed, sniggers get suppressed. But you still heard it, around the corners and behind the doors. A low wolf whistle and then a stage whisper, one man to another: "Whadya think about her, did she forget her bra today? Didja see her in that sweater?"

If I had more courage, I'd call them out: "Hostile-environment warning, guys. Remember the office memo we all got? Can it. Or maybe Peggy and I should hang out more, shooting the breeze about your butts and appendages. What merits a ten, Peggy? How would you describe Peter's ass for our female listeners?"

But that's just fantasy. I owe my job to Mike and my paycheck to Peter, who brings in the advertising dollars that pay our wages, so I kept my mouth shut.

Mike followed me back to the newsroom to tell me that the morning had been a quiet one. There'd been no news from the cops, or anyone else, about the Desjardins murder or the barn fire.

My pulse skipped a beat but I kept my voice casual. "Do they think the two are related?"

He gave a who-knows shrug, then flashed very white teeth in a smile that was mostly a smirk. "Hey, I hear Zach asked you out last night. You two planning some fun?"

I scowled. "No."

Mike raised both hands in defense. Adding, "Sorry, AJ, sorry. Just teasing. Okay, I'm leaving now. See you at the picnic. I invited Zach to come, too. Just in case you forgot to mention it to him."

"What picnic?"

But he hadn't heard. The door snicked closed, leaving me alone in the newsroom.

Then I remembered WWCT's end-of-summer barbecue, scheduled for this afternoon at the municipal park. Hot dogs, hamburgers, snow cones, splash pools for the kids, beer and softball for the adults, sunburns for everyone. Three o'clock, bring a lawn chair and a side dish. I'd have to go home for the lawn chair and pick up something from the deli at the A&P.

Marla would probably be there, too, with Keith.

How awkward could that be? Two sisters in crime, chatting together among happy picnickers and nosey journalists.

I managed to focus on the tasks at hand. I finished editing the interview on the reel-to-reel, added an intro, dubbed it all onto a cassette, and left it for Marie Pelka to play on Sunday afternoon. Marie was the gray-haired volunteer who, for twenty-some years, had given up her

Sunday afternoons to play three hours of polka music and twenty minutes of public service programming to a tiny but devoted fan club.

The phone rang as I was shutting down the equipment.

"AJ? Carl Androski."

Every instinct screamed *flee* but I managed to stay in my chair, swiveling so Tony, on the other side of the glass in the control room, couldn't see my face.

"Hi, Detective. What can I do for you?" To my ears, the words sounded like a choked squeak but he took no notice.

"I'm hoping you have a minute for a couple quick questions."

"Um, sure. Fire away." Wincing, I closed my eyes. *Did I just say that?*

"How well do you know Marla Bousquet? Her husband Keith works at the radio station."

Be careful, my mind was screaming. Be very careful.

"I've known her for maybe fifteen years. The three of us—me, Keith, and Marla—went to the same middle school and high school, along with Ernie Walters." Dropping the name of our local trooper couldn't hurt.

"Did you happen to see Mrs. Bousquet on Wednesday?"

I crossed my fingers and stared at the teletype, which had gone momentarily silent. I needed to get this exactly right.

"The day of the murder?" I figured I might as well get the topic right out there. "In the late afternoon, yes. She stopped by my house after I got home from work.

She wasn't there long, maybe twenty minutes. I was pretty busy. I had about half an hour to change, eat dinner, and go out again to cover a meeting. The board of ed."

"Was it a normal sort of visit? How did she appear to you?"

"No, of course it wasn't a normal visit." I didn't have to fake this response. "I saw someone get killed that morning, remember? She came over to see me because she's a good friend and she was worried about me. So yeah, we were both kind of shook. She's pregnant," I added, as if pregnancy should be an armor against suspicion. "You want to know how she appeared? Worried, concerned, anxious. About what you'd expect."

"Do you know where she was earlier in the day?"

"No, she didn't say. Her schedule's been kind of erratic lately." I paused. "Why are we talking about Marla?"

"Just routine. We're looking at the movements of anyone who knew the victim. Did you know they're related?"

"Yes, she mentioned it. A distant cousin."

"Does she hunt? Are there guns in the house?"

The topic change caught me off guard. I remembered our outing at the rod and gun club back in April, when Keith, Marla and I took turns shattering clay pigeons with Gran's little shotgun.

I felt a surge of adrenalin.

Just answer the question. Volunteer nothing.

"No, she hates hunting," I said carefully. "She doesn't own a gun. I don't think Keith does, either."

He thanked me for my time and hung up. And that was it: no probing questions about the barn fire or my Friday evening visit to Charlotte's house.

Needing something to lean on for a moment, I heel-walked the chair across the narrow room to the big window, propped my elbows on the sill, and dropped my forehead against the cool glass. I counted breaths and felt my heartbeat slow to a normal pace.

When I'd recovered enough to look up, I caught Tony's acne-pocked face staring from the other side of the glass. He blushed and paid attention to his turntable, suddenly very intent on sliding an LP back into its sleeve.

I wiped my forehead print off the window glass, resettled my glasses, and finished shutting down the newsroom.

***

Two hours later I hauled Gran's old lawn chair and a frayed serape across the dusty municipal baseball diamond to a row of willows on the bank of the Pennatucket. A few hundred yards upstream of the footbridge and falls, the water spread out in a slow, swampy expanse—the remains of an old mill pond.

Beneath the willows, Mike and George Grayson— WWCT's portly, balding owner—stood over a charcoal grill in crisp green butcher's aprons, poking at briquets with metal tongs as black smoke drifted across the river. Peggy Moran hovered near Mike, trying to catch his eye and smiling too much as she set out paper plates and plastic forks.

There must have been thirty people there, and more arriving. Small clusters of people I didn't recognize nursed Solo cups and chased their kids away from the Pennatucket's muddy shore. George must have invited everyone he knew, not just radio station personnel and alumni.

I set down my store-bought tabouli on a picnic table beside an array of homemade cole slaws, fruit Jellos, and potato salads, then went in search of Marla and Keith.

Zach intercepted me on his way in from the parking lot. He grabbed my elbow in one hand, my chair in the other, and steered us away from the crowd to a smaller, unoccupied willow where a red cooler and a brown leather duffel already lay. "AJ, wait 'til I tell you—" he began.

I handed him the serape and took back my chair, unfolding it before he could claim it. He spread the blanket on the grass.

I asked him, "Have you seen Marla and Keith?"

"I haven't seen Keith and I don't know Marla. But I caught up with Will Collier this morning. Charlotte's brother. You want a beer?" He pulled two brown bottles from the cooler, pried off the caps with a church key, and handed me one. "Here you go. Do you like Sam?"

I glanced at the label. Samuel Adams Boston Lager. "I've never had it. It looks pricey."

"Better than what everyone else is drinking."

I sipped, then took a longer pull. He was right.

"So you trailed Charlotte last night?"

"You didn't miss much. She hit a Southbridge biker bar, had a couple beers. Hung out with her girlfriends, flirted with some guys, then drove home. Big whoop."

"But you talked to Will, too?"

"Yeah. And get this." He rooted in the duffel, waved a stack of papers, and folded himself onto the serape beside me. "I found these in his office."

I frowned. "You stole them?"

"Of course not. I called him last night and set up a meeting for nine-thirty at his office. It's above a dry cleaner's, and the guy there had a key so he let me in early to wait in the office. While I was waiting, I spotted something in the trash and something else on a desk." He handed me the papers. "Didn't even touch his filing cabinets. I dug these out of the trash."

The first document was an application for the state farmland preservation program, describing Jimmy Desjardins's 240-acre Cherry Hollow Road farm. Except for a one-acre home plot, it was all crops, forest, and wetlands—eligible for up to $5,000 per acre if Jimmy sold the development rights to the state. The form was complete, except for an owner's signature.

I fanned the pages. "This looks complicated. Jimmy wouldn't know how to fill it out."

"That's why he asked Will. He's the one does Jimmy's taxes."

"Five grand an acre from the state. How much would a developer pay?"

"At least three times that much."

"Jimmy wouldn't sell, but Charlotte will." I turned pages. "What's this?"

"A listing agreement for sale of the farm. Look at the owner's name."

Charlotte Desjardins. The Listing Start date was noted as September 1, 1985. I stared at him. "They're moving fast. That's only a few days from now. All they need is a price and her signature."

I handed the stack back to Zach and he stuffed most of the papers back into his bag. "They're probably just waiting for the death certificate to be filed."

"Did you ever get to talk to Will?"

"Yeah. I pressed him about Jimmy and Charlotte, but he really couldn't give me anything. He's sorry Jimmy died, what a shock, no idea who did it. But he admitted it's a big windfall for Charlotte. She gets the farm, yeah, and also a big life insurance payout. Beyond telling me that, he gave me nothing but a poker face." He flipped over the last page and added, "However, I also found this."

On the back of the form, someone had penciled the names Benditto and McMurphy, plus a phone number with a Rhode Island area code.

"Who are they? Did you call?"

"Not yet. I rang a contact at the *Providence-Journal.* The two guys run a payday-loan shop. With possible organized-crime links."

I handed him my empty bottle and waved off a second. "How are you getting all that back into Will's office?"

"I'm not. I'll make photocopies and give the originals to Androski. Collier won't miss anything, he'll just think he misplaced them. Any agent can redo the listing in five minutes. And the farm preservation forms were in the trash. No one's interested, now that Charlotte owns the property."

A weight slipped quietly from my shoulders. Here was evidence of a motive for Jimmy's death. Simple greed. Follow the money.

"One other bit of info," Zach said. "I went back to Roland's and asked a few more questions. Did you ever hear about a girl who hanged herself, in that old barn that just burned down? Fifteen or sixteen years ago."

The mention of the barn sent a shiver up my spine again. "Sixteen years ago, I was twelve. In eighth grade…"

"Her name was Brenda Martinez," he prompted. "She'd have been a few years older, a sophomore." At my nod, he continued. "I tracked down her mother and called this morning. She lives down the other end of the state, in Ridgefield."

I raised an encouraging eyebrow but stayed silent.

"Mrs. Martinez told me Brenda killed herself over some photographs that someone was passing around at school. Pictures of her, naked, with her boyfriend. Kids at school were bullying her, sharing the pictures, scribbling her name and number on the walls. It got pretty ugly. She got called into the office, the parents got a call from the principal, and it all came out. Well, not all of it, but enough so her mom took one of the pictures to the police.

"The police said it was just a case of bullying, the school and the parents should handle it. And here's the thing: No one seems to have followed up to find out who took the pictures."

He paused, eyebrows raised, as I tried to form a response. What could I say? That I already knew about similar pictures, hundreds of them, stored in the Grabtown barn next to Jimmy's farm?

I said, "And then she hanged herself," as if I'd just figured it out.

He nodded. "She hanged herself, and her parents moved away." He paused for a moment as a breeze fluttered the willow leaves. "What do you think, AJ? You were hinting at this last night, weren't you? When we talked with Charlotte. But I can't see how it fits with Jimmy's death. Brenda was an only child. Her dad is dead and her mother is, like, in her late sixties."

I shrugged, deciding to fall back on my current best excuse. "I'm not supposed to speculate about Jimmy's death, remember? Witness conflict." But I felt bound to add, "Take it to Androski, let him figure it out. If he has two brain cells dancing together, he's probably already got that on his list."

I heard voices and turned to see three figures walking across the ballfield. Keith was already perspiring, his dark hair flopping over his damp forehead as he struggled to carry lawn chairs, a cooler chest, two fielder's gloves, and a bat. Marla, wearing a bright yellow sundress and a broad-brimmed straw hat, carried only a purse on her shoulder and a weary look on her face. The third person was unfamiliar, a man in a brown ponytail, full red beard, tie-dyed tee shirt and grease-stained jeans. He trailed behind with a second cooler, pausing mid-stroll to stub out a cigarette in the grass.

"Hey, can we join you?" Keith called as they approached. He began shedding gear as he approached our tree.

"Sure." Zach rose and took the lawn chairs from Keith's shoulder. He unfolded one and set it beside mine. "Hey, I'm Zach. And you must be Marla. Here, sit. AJ's told me all about you."

Busy with settling the chair on the uneven ground, she gave him a rote response. "Oh dear, I hope not. All my secrets…" She heard her own words and a slight flush climbed her neck.

She shot a glance at me, pausing for the briefest of seconds. "Thanks. Good to meet you."

She lifted a finger toward the bearded guy. "And this is Keith's friend, Ryan. He's visiting for a couple of weeks, helping us renovate the upstairs."

Ryan hitched up his drooping jeans before offering Zach a large square hand, the knuckles and nails blackened with grime.

He nodded at me, then pulled a beer from his cooler and hunkered down, his back against the willow tree, and directed a thousand-yard stare toward the river.

Keith loosened the top on a plastic bottle of lemonade and handed it to Marla. "You want one, AJ?"

I nodded and he passed a second dripping cold bottle to me. For a few moments, everyone paid attention to their drinks.

Into the silence, Keith spoke. "Hey, AJ, Marla says she felt the babies move this morning. For the very first time." His angular face was suddenly alight with a mix of delight, awe, and terror. Impending fatherhood seemed to have settled on him like a load he should have been eager to carry, but obviously wasn't.

Marla stirred. Her worried eyes held mine for a brief moment, just long enough for me to read her plea for my silence. She'd felt that first quickening yesterday, not today. With me sitting beside her in the woods and the stink of kerosene still on our hands.

Like I've swallowed a goldfish, she said.

I fashioned the biggest smile I could manage and pushed myself half out of the lawn chair, leaning into her for an awkward hug.

"Hey, man. I envy you, at least in theory." Zach offered his hand to Keith in a high-five. To Marla he added, "Congratulations, great news. Have you picked out names yet?"

Marla managed a smile. "Yes, now that I know they're real. We're calling them Anastasia and Cassandra." Her hand went to her belly again, in that universal gesture of protection.

Keith gave his wife a half-fond, half-fearful look. "Marla's been so worried about hurting the girls somehow, like forgetting to take her vitamins or playing music too loud. I keep telling her, they're well-protected in there. Nothing can hurt them." He directed a protective smile her way. "You should just slow down, don't work so hard. Put your feet up, relax. Take care of yourself and everything will be okay with the babies."

I said nothing about Marla's recent alcohol consumption nor her hike through the woods carrying thirty pounds of kerosene. Instead, I snuck another side glance at her. Beneath the hat, a lock of dark blonde hair had fallen over her face. Her eyes behind the sunglasses looked at no one.

Everyone went silent, the topic exhausted. Marla turned a little to stare at the slow-moving river, then crossed one leg over the other and began swinging a sandal-clad foot. Keith in his chair and Zach on my serape gazed toward the baseball field, perhaps wondering if it was okay to change the subject to sports. Ryan, his butt propped in a squat against the far side of the willow, had apparently dedicated himself to drinking as much beer as possible, as quickly as possible.

"So," Keith said in the same conversational tone, "the police stopped by this morning."

CHAPTER TWENTY-FOUR

AJ

~ 14 ~

I jerked in my seat. Cold lemonade splashed the front of my shirt.

"You okay, AJ?" Zach handed me a wad of paper towels from his duffel. As I mopped up the stickiness, I snuck a glance at Marla. The little I could see of her face, beneath the big hat and glasses, had turned pale.

"They came to your house?" Zach asked. "Why?"

"To talk with Marla about her cousin Jimmy. The guy who got shot on Wednesday."

Zach raised an eyebrow at me, then turned his attention to Marla. "I didn't know you were related."

She raised her head then so I could see her eyes, rimmed with red, and the dark hollows beneath. Her shoulders moved a little, more of a shiver than a shrug.

"Jimmy was only a distant cousin," she said to Zach. "We weren't close. Anyway, I couldn't tell them much."

They asked about Jimmy. Not the fire. I felt my breathing steady. I asked, "Who was it, Androski? What were they looking for?"

"It was Ernie Walters," she said to me. To the others she added, "We went to school with him, he's a state trooper. Ernie wanted to know about Jimmy. Who he hung out with, what his relationship was like with his

307

wife. The usual." Another shrug. "Then he asked me where I was on Wednesday morning, when I last saw Jimmy. Routine stuff."

She dropped her gaze to stare at the label on her lemonade bottle, then rotated it as if to read the ingredients.

"And did you?" Zach prompted. "See him."

I held my breath, feeling like this mattered more than it should. She'd said nothing to me about seeing Jimmy that morning.

"Yeah. I went to the farmers' co-op to buy some bags of mulch. Jimmy was there. He was buying a couple rolls of baler twine so he could finish haying. We chatted for a minute and then I went out the back door to get the mulch loaded. I didn't see him leave."

I felt the lawn chair's frame cutting into the underside of my thighs and realized I'd been leaning forward, focused on every word. I shifted a little to ease my legs and exhaled.

Ryan spoke suddenly from his squat against the tree. "Yeah," he grunted. "Then the stupid cop wanted to come out and have a talk with *me*. Hell, I didn't know nothin'. I never even met the dude."

"They wanted to know about Ryan's truck," Keith explained. "He's got a black pickup with Vermont plates, kinda like the truck they were looking for. But the thing's not running. Ryan's had it pulled apart in the garage. He's been doing repairs on it for two weeks."

"Except for one day," Ryan informed us morosely, "It was running for one day. Then, kaput again." He took a long swallow from his third or fourth beer. "First, I had to swap the distributor and the spark plug wires.

That fixed it, but then it just died again. Now I'm rebuilding the starter."

Zach rose from his seat on the serape and made a show if stretching his back, left and right. He turned to Ryan. "What day was that? The one day you say the truck was still working."

Beside me, I felt Marla tense.

Ryan shrugged his back against the willow's trunk, scratching a shoulder along the rough bark. "I dunno. Like I told that cop, I was kinda fuzzy on the days. Monday or Tuesday? Probably Tuesday. Anyway, he only asked me because I had the garage doors open and the cops were just walking by, that's how they saw the truck. But they weren't so interested when they saw I had the guts scattered all over the floor. It sure wasn't me killed that dude, so hey."

Zach turned away to rummage through the cooler again, apparently no longer interested in questioning Ryan. Keith tapped awkward fingers on the arm of his chair and Ryan remained focused on his beer consumption.

Marla resumed staring bleakly at the mill pond. She'd recited her piece about the police questioning, and now she was waiting, numb and silent, for—I didn't know what. All I wanted, desperately wanted, was to yank her out of that chair and carry her somewhere safe. Somewhere far away.

Instead, I sat in Gran's old lawn chair, watching a green dragonfly dart after insects and trying to connect uneasy thoughts about a pickup, old photographs, and a chance meeting in a farm store.

No one moved.

Into the uneasy silence someone on the far side of the baseball diamond shouted, "Softball, everyone! Let's play ball!"

Looking relieved, Zach scrambled to his feet and set his beer bottle against the tree trunk. "Who's playing what? Mike said we play first and eat after."

"You three go," I said. "Marla and I can hang out here in the shade and cheer you on from deep right field. Go."

Keith picked up his gloves and bat and they left, Ryan dragging on a fresh cigarette and trailing behind the other two. I stared at the river and tried to find a way to approach any one of the hundred questions I dreaded asking.

"AJ," Marla cried softly. "What do I do now?" It was a low wail of pure anguish, a desperate plea for help.

Chapter Twenty-five

AJ

~ 15 ~

Her cry tore at my heart. I stood and grabbed her hand, tugging her up from the lawn chair and toward the riverbank. We stumbled along the bank and down a slope to the mill pond.

I found a faint path near the water's edge and turned right, downstream. I hauled her along at a fast walk, heading toward the dam and the footbridge, just visible through a stand of young pine trees. The water flowed more quickly here. Below us, the river was sounding a muted roar as it went over the falls.

I stopped, released Marla's limp hand, and put an arm around her bare shoulders. She sagged against me, covering her face with both hands. Her whole body was shaking.

"We'll get through this," I told her. Not something I could guarantee, but the words seemed to help. When the trembling stopped, she wiped her face with the back of one hand, drew a deep breath and turned to face me.

"AJ, I need to tell you everything."

"Okay, but let's find someplace to sit."

A short way off the path, where young pine trees gave way to a dense wood with tall oaks and maples, we found a moss-covered log with enough room to sit side-by-side.

She sank onto the old wood, drawing in and wrapping her arms around her waist. "I killed him, AJ." As if in awe of the words, she repeated it. "I killed Jimmy."

I moved to hug her but she shook her head. She wouldn't meet my eyes, staring instead at a pile of brush and leaves mounded against our log.

She shifted her grip, splaying her hands wide over her belly as if shielding her future children from the conversation. "I had to, AJ. No one understands what he was like, what he—" Her voice cracked. "When he saw me at the feed store on Wednesday morning—I'd avoided him for years, but suddenly there he was, grinning—"

"Go slowly. Start at the beginning. Go all the way back."

She drew a deep shuddering breath and handed me her sunglasses so she could rub her knuckles against her eyes.

"Okay." But it was another minute before she could say more. I draped an arm over her shoulders and waited.

"AJ, do you remember that *Life* magazine photo spread? The 1962 issue, with Marilyn Monroe in the pool? The photo shoot from the set of that last movie she did. *Some Like It Hot*."

I must have looked as confused as I felt. "In 1962 we were only four years old—"

"My mother kept that *Life* magazine for *years*. She wanted to be a movie star. She idolized movie stars, and Marilyn was her absolute favorite. She kept a whole stack of magazines with articles about her."

"Your dad was in the Army then, right? Not around much."

"He was posted in Germany, then Korea. He came back every six months or so. They'd go out dancing, get drunk, fight, break up. He'd disappear again, and she'd go back to her job at K-Mart. I guess she did her best, but she always told me I could do better than her. I was her pretty little girl, and maybe I could be as beautiful as Marilyn. Mom had messed up and lost *her* chance at being a movie star, she said, but maybe I could do it." She sniffled and wiped her nose on a bare arm.

She resumed her story, "So when I was seven or eight, Mom pulled out that issue of *Life* and told me that Marilyn was the most beautiful woman ever born. I remember asking 'Where's her clothes?' and Mom said, 'If you look that good, you don't always need clothes.'"

"Maybe it was a body-beautiful thing?" I offered. "Like she wanted to make a point of telling you there was nothing shameful about being naked."

"Yeah, maybe. But what I got out of that was, this is how I was *supposed* to look. Sexy, and naked. In my mother's mind, Marilyn Monroe was the highest example of true beauty, the ideal we should all strive for. It makes me sick to think of it now, but back then...Anyway, when Cousin Jimmy showed up with his camera, I was *ready*. I'd practiced those poses in the mirror. I could strut and smile with the best of them.

"And yes, I took my clothes off for him. First when I was eight and later, when I was nine and ten. He didn't even have to ask."

A blind mixture of fury and heartache rose in my throat, choking back any words that I might have said.

She pulled away from me but I pressed in, trying to hold her for just a moment longer.

Finally I found my voice. "It wasn't your fault. You know that, don't you?" I thought for a moment. "Did your mother know you were posing for him?"

"She knew he was taking photographs of me in my swimsuit, I told you that before. She thought it was cute. Her little girl had such a beautiful smile, she was growing up so fast, et cetera. She never saw the nude photos. That was 'our little secret.'" She crooked her fingers into quotes. "We had a lot of secrets, Jimmy and me. And he was family, mom reminded me. He'd come to visit us when my father was away, which was a lot. We'd go for Sunday afternoon drives, sometimes the three of us but sometimes just him and me."

"How did he convince you to stay quiet?"

"He gave me things. Cheap jewelry,

"Did it get sexual, too?"

"You mean, did we fuck?" The brutal word sat in the air between us. She dropped her eyes and twisted her hands together in her lap. "Not quite. He said I was too little, he'd have to wait a few years. But he showed me how to do everything else. He jerked off while I watched. He made me touch myself in front of him."

She lifted both hands suddenly, crossing her arms so her hands clutched her upper arms. Abruptly curving her fingers into claws, she raked her nails down her bare biceps, creating instant welts. Drops of blood bloomed on both arms and I heard a low moan. She began shaking and fell against me again.

The hot rage rose in me again. If the man had been standing in front of me at that moment, I'd have gladly dug his heart from his body with my bare hands.

"You had no power," I whispered. "It wasn't your fault. But you managed to stop it, didn't you? Tell me, how did you stop him?"

She shook her head and pushed herself upright, wiping her eyes again. "It wasn't anything big, it was gradual. As I got older, I began to see my life wasn't normal, not like other girls. I learned the word 'predator' and heard stories about girls who'd been abused by the boys and men they thought they could trust. Not the way Jimmy had tricked me—what he did was way worse, because I was years younger—but I learned about all the ways boys try to manipulate girls. One day I said *no* to Jimmy and that was it. I think he'd started to lose interest, anyway. He likes his girls very young, and I was growing up."

She looked up. "You've met Charlotte, you see what she's like."

"Marla, you're lucky you got away from him. But you did it, you stood up to him."

"But you never get away from it, AJ. Not really. There's this overwhelming shame, the knowledge that if you'd just said something earlier. And then you're left with all the scars. You're *branded* with those early experiences no kid should have to go through. It's like you're wearing a sign on your back forever, one that says: please fuck me."

I made a clumsy show of peering at the back of her sundress. "Nope, nothing there. You must've pulled off that sign and burned it."

She attempted a weak smile. "We did, didn't we? Or we tried to. But it's still there, not very far under my skin."

She began plucking at the green-brown moss on the log where we sat. I watched her peel off a long strip, like it was a scab over the skin of the log. I heard birdsong, the trills of wrens and the chip-chip notes of a cardinal.

"Look," she said pensively. "Moss, bark, wood, everything in layers. The log we're sitting on feels perfectly solid on the outside, doesn't it? But beneath all these layers, there's rot eating away at the heartwood."

She tore the moss into pieces and brushed the crumbs from her hands. "Wednesday morning, when I saw him in the store, he smiled at me. He looked down at my belly and congratulated me, and then he smiled and said—" her voice caught, "he said, in a few years, he'd like to meet my girls and show them his camera, up there in the barn. They'd be two little princesses that he could love, just as he'd loved me…"

Everything went silent. The breath left my body.

She went on, "Later, I drove to his place to tell him I was going to get a restraining order." She shot a glance at me. "I was going to go to the police, see? But then he looked kind of hurt and said, 'But Marlie, you *liked* it.'"

My blood chilled.

She continued in that same steady voice. "He said he was only doing what I *asked* him to do, all those years ago. That's what he'd say, if I went to the police. So I killed him. But you know that, don't you?"

"Yes." I just hadn't known *how*. I ran my tongue around my lips, trying to find enough moisture so the words would form correctly. "You drove Ryan's truck, didn't you?" Trying to work it out. "Which was running okay for just one day. Ryan was wrong, wasn't he? it was Wednesday, not Tuesday, that his truck was still running. But you said you took the Civic to the co-op."

"I did, on the first trip. But I bought too many bags of mulch and it wouldn't all fit in my car. So I went home and swapped the Civic for his pickup. Ryan was working inside, upstairs. I heard him banging around and yelling at the plumbing, so I just picked up his keys and tiptoed out. He didn't see me."

"And the gun?"

"I found it under the seat of his truck, when I was looking for the lever to move the seat forward. It was a sawed-off shotgun. He'd left the safety on but it was already loaded. It was dangerous to have it rattling around in his truck. And illegal. You can get serious jail time for a sawed-off barrel." She missed the irony in her own words.

"Where's the gun now?"

"In that swamp off Reservoir Road. The spent shell, too. Then I drove home and vomited into the compost pile, twice. Wiped down the truck, unloaded the mulch, washed up, and made lunch for Ryan and me."

That one detail sent a chill up my spine: She'd had the presence of mind to wipe down the truck.

"Ryan didn't see you when you came back?"

"He was already on his second beer by the time I got back. I think he was watching a game show on TV."

Marla worried a cuticle for a minute, then turned to face me. The abrupt movement startled a chipmunk off the top of a nearby rock wall.

"Don't you want to know how it felt?" she said earnestly. "When I fired the gun. I was numb, at first, because my ears were ringing and my shoulder felt like it was on fire from the kickback. The whole world was reduced to this terrible clanging in my head. And I was horrified, not for shooting him, but for making my children hear the blast." Her hand dropped again to her belly.

"It was so loud. Everything in me went sort of upside down, and maybe that was my babies moving for the first time—the *real* first time—because it felt like everything jumped up into my chest. But I had to move, to get away. I almost stalled the truck and then I thought it was going to spin out and land me in the ditch—"

She paused, her nostrils flaring as she pulled in a heavy breath. "Then, as I drove away, it was like I heard voices in my head. Brenda, and Katie. Those little girls in Rolands' store, and a dozen other girls whose names I never knew. The ones in all the photos in that filing cabinet. They were all *cheering*. They called me a hero for doing what I did. For once in my life, I felt so *powerful*."

"What—"

But I'd forgotten what I meant to say, so we just sat there for a few minutes in a strangely comfortable silence, holding hands and listening to the birds. Marla appeared much calmer now, as if she was beginning to make peace with what she'd done.

But what would come next?

I heard the distant crack of a bat hitting a softball and someone applauded. It sounded like Keith, who was always a good cheerleader. He was that sort: a caring, dependable man who would be horrified to know what his wife had done.

As sat in the woods discussing unspeakable things, the picnic had continued without us. I imagined the last innings of the ballgame, the cheerful chaos of children running through sprinklers, and the smell of grilling hamburgers drifting from beneath the willow trees. Everything normal, everything innocent.

"We have to go back," I said. "Come on."

We brushed moss and bark from our clothes and walked back in single file, me in the lead and Marla trailing behind. As I turned off the path, heading for the willow tree, I heard Mike and Keith somewhere on the bank above us. They were arguing and laughing about an umpire's call, their voices rising in exaggerated outrage.

They hadn't seen us yet. I stopped and whispered, "What are you going to tell Keith?"

There was only silence. She was gone.

I spun back to the trail, catching a glimpse of her yellow dress moving through the trees along the shore of the mill pond. She was at least fifty feet away and striding away quickly, heading downstream toward the bridge and the falls.

She must've known I'd seen her because she broke into an awkward jog. I lost sight of her as the trail climbed over a tumbledown stone wall and curved left where the river narrowed.

Focused on the trail, cursing my unreliable foot and my heat-fogged glasses, I didn't waste breath trying to call out. The sound of the falls grew louder as the buildings of Winslow's business district came into view.

I lurched out of the trees onto a grassy bank, where the gravel trail forked. One branch continued downstream along the river, the other became the approach to the footbridge.

I saw her then, a hundred feet ahead on the bridge. She swerved around two kids wheeling their bikes and slowed to a walk. She'd lost the sunglasses somewhere and her hair hung loose and wild around her shoulders.

Halfway across the bridge, she stopped and leaned both hands on the railing, looking downstream at the boulders and the dam thirty feet below. A few people walked around her, but no one gave a second glance to the young woman in the yellow sundress contemplating the river.

By the time I limped onto the bridge to stand beside her, I was light-headed with heat and exhaustion. I planted my hands beside hers on the splintered wooden rail and heaved deep, rasping gulps of air until my breath and pulse slowed to near normal.

Before I could decide what to say, she spoke.

"Do you know what else I did, AJ? That afternoon, after I shot him." Her voice was low, but sharp and clear above the rush of the water below us. "I packed a suitcase. Toothbrush, hairbrush, shampoo. Clean underwear, pajamas. Keith thinks I'm getting ready—really early, obviously—for a trip to the hospital. An early labor or a C-section. Or, heaven forbid, a miscarriage. But no, it's not that. It's for when the police come to arrest me."

In her despair, I didn't have the heart to tell her that those things would be provided for her in jail.

She went on, "The police didn't ask me much. Just who Jimmy knew and what car did I drive, and where did I go on Wednesday." She glanced at me. "That was easy. I went to the co-op that morning, and then I was heading toward your house but I changed my mind. Went home and made lunch. All true, right? Then each day, it got harder to say the rest of it. This morning they questioned Ryan and it hit me. I realized that an innocent person could be arrested."

I placed a cautioning hand lightly on her wrist and she fell silent. A man in jogging shorts approached the bridge at a rapid walk, then passed behind us.

She continued in the same low voice, "But I don't see any way out now. The only thing I'm sure of is this: I don't want my children born in prison."

She paused and turned her attention back to the water, leaning forward over the rail to stare at rocks and a battered tree trunk caught at the top of the dam.

She said quietly, "His funeral is next Wednesday, did you know? Cousin Jimmy's." She grimaced at the bitter taste of his name. "And I'll be expected to go. I don't know if I can do it, AJ."

"I'll go with you. We'll do it together—"

"What if they arrest Ryan?"

"I don't think they will. They'll need a warrant to search his truck, and they'd have shown up with that already if they suspected him. Ryan didn't know Jimmy, he has no motive. They have no evidence. Their only witness is me, and I was compromised from the beginning. Androski knows that."

She thought about that for a moment. I heard distant voices, someone calling from beyond the trees we'd run through.

A stifled sob caught at the back of her throat. "Why are you trying so hard to save me, AJ?"

I took in her red-rimmed eyes and anguished face, full of shame and hurt. There was only one answer. "Because I love you more than anything. And I will do whatever it takes to keep you safe, you and your babies. You didn't force me into this, Marla. I made my choice yesterday morning, when you showed me those photos in the barn. I'd make the same choice again, ten times over. For you."

She merely stared at the water and said nothing. I wasn't sure my words had registered.

At some point, she'd kicked her sandals off. Standing barefoot on the rough planks, she shifted her weight heavily onto both hands, tilting forward over the splintered railing. She looked straight down. Her shoulders tensed and I felt her whole body coiling like a spring.

My left hand still circled her right wrist. I tightened my grip but I knew I wasn't strong enough to stop her. All I could do was keep talking. Trying to figure out how to save someone who might not want to be saved.

I raised my voice and threw every ounce of urgency into my words. "If you check out—if you cave—that asshole wins. Don't let him win, Marla. He hurt you but you *stopped* him. You're the bravest person I know. You can *do* this."

Finally she spoke. Whispering, "But do *what*? Do it *how*? When all I want to do is run away, where none of this exists. Dive into the river, or run over the next ridge and disappear."

"Do exactly what you've always done. One step, then another step. Keep your head up and stay strong." The words felt hollow but I had nothing better and she seemed to be listening.

Finally, she turned to look at me. Her hazel-green eyes were red-rimmed, bloodshot, and filled with uncertainty.

"How do I live with the secrets?"

"*We* will keep them safe. I'm right here."

"But it's different now. I'm a—" She couldn't say the word.

"You're a mother protecting her children," I said firmly. "That's what you are."

She didn't let go of the railing right away, but I felt her hand ease its grip. After a minute more, her whole body shuddered once. She gave me the ghost of a shaky smile, looked down, and began fumbling her feet into her sandals.

"Well, then," she said. "Let's see what happens next."

CHAPTER TWENTY-SIX

AJ

~ 16 ~

Androski called me on Monday morning with another warning about a witness's need to avoid even the appearance of a conflict of interest, but his heart wasn't in it. He seemed to know he'd lost that battle the moment I stepped back into the newsroom on Wednesday afternoon. And the testimony of one faraway witness wasn't worth much without forensic evidence, which he still didn't have.

Also on Monday, WWCT received word that Winslow's fire marshal had determined that the barn fire was "likely caused by arson," based on the probable use of an accelerant found where it shouldn't have been. But with no witnesses—and the entire Winslow town council expressing relief that they no longer had to decide what to do with the Grabtown barn—that investigation also was going nowhere.

On Tuesday, Mike Gorman learned that he'd been passed over for the TV anchor slot at Channel 14. He slunk home and stayed on as WWCT's news director for another six years, where he continued his reliable reporting of every local fender-bender and town budget controversy.

Ryan Jones finished, more or less, the renovation to Keith and Marla's upstairs, though he'd confused the water lines to the new bathroom sink. When Marla pointed this out, he corrected his error by sticking red and blue electrical tape on the wrong faucets to match the wrong water lines, and the Bousquets learned to open the right-hand spigot for hot water. A week later, Ryan put his pickup back together and headed south in search of over-winter construction work. He got stopped once along the way for a burned-out tail light.

Six months after the murder, I decided I'd wasted enough time as Mike's underpaid media flunky and decided to go back to college. The plan was to start part-time, finishing undergrad and doing my pre-law at Eastern Connecticut. Then I'd apply to UConn's law school with a focus on family law. Meanwhile, Winslow's new domestic violence program needed staff and volunteers.

The investigations continued. Zach kept digging but didn't find anything more he could use. Eventually, he published two lengthy stories in *The Nutmeg Insider*: a well-received piece on the hard challenges faced by family farms in a difficult economy; and an article on the stalled murder investigation, predictably titled "Who Killed Jimmy?" which never answered that question. Still, it lauded the hard work of the Connecticut State Police Eastern District Major Crime Squad and included two flattering pictures of Charlotte.

Charlotte sold the farm—no surprise—and moved to Ft. Lauderdale. Maybe she met Ryan Jones there.

The following spring, developers tore down Jimmy's house and barns and secured a permit to build a hundred new three-bedroom, bath-and-a-half tract houses. Dotty Kellerman led the protests at town meetings and a land-planning hearing, but Winslow had abolished zoning years earlier so construction went ahead anyway.

The Major Crime Squad did its best, but they never found enough hard evidence to link anyone to the murder. Every so often, Detective Sergeant Androski paid Marla a friendly visit to ask if she could remember anything more about the day her cousin died.

Her answer was always, "Not really."

Somehow, in the middle of it all, my friend charted her course through the scary turbulence of childbirth and motherhood. Her girls arrived a month early, as twins often do. The firstborn emerged smiling and serene, the second scowling and wailing at her very first breath. Marla declared them both perfect, the princess and the prophet.

In 1988, during a massive drought, the big swamp by Reservoir Road dried up and a hiker found a sawed-off shotgun. A police search also turned up a spent shot shell, the same gauge that killed Jimmy Desjardins. The gun was an older model, with no serial number. Its wooden stock had begun to rot and the barrel was too rusty to recover fingerprints.

One day about a year after that, Detective Androski invited Marla and me to a mid-morning cup of coffee at Pierre's.

We brought the twins along and parked them in a large booth with crayons and coloring books. One on each side of the table, so they wouldn't squabble.

We talked of nothing important for a few minutes. Then Androski said he thought we'd like to hear about the arrest of a man in upstate New York.

Connor Duffy, twenty years old and originally from Burrowton, Rhode Island, had been charged with three counts of sexually molesting a thirteen-year-old girl while he was working as a counselor at a summer camp. Duffy protested his innocence, and the case was set for trial, when investigators found, beneath a floorboard in his apartment, several photos and a videotape of the girl. He abruptly changed his plea to guilty and was sentenced to eight years in prison.

On Duffy's job application for the position of camp counselor, he'd noted his prior job experience. In the summer of '85, when he was sixteen, he'd been employed on a dairy farm in Winslow. He'd listed Jimmy Desjardins as a work reference.

Androski thought we'd like to hear about that, especially the part about Duffy's being convicted and sent to prison.

When he finished his coffee, he dropped a ten on the table for our coffee and muffins and got up to go. He paused for a moment, then, looking down at Marla and me with a faint smile.

"You two, you've done well," he said quietly. "I admire that, I want you to know." He glanced at Cassie, coloring neatly within the lines, and Ana, scribbling hard with a broken crayon. "What will you tell them, when they're older?"

"About my cousin?" Marla shrugged. "Nothing,"

"They should know how amazing you are. Both of you." He shifted his gaze to me. "There might be a story here, I think. And you should write it, AJ. You're a good writer."

— The End —

And there we have it, Cassie thinks. Our mother was a murderer.

The word sits heavy in her mind, foreign and familiar all at once. *Murderer.* She turns it over like a small stone in her palm, examining its weight, its sharp edges.

Outside, a steady rain is falling. A cool mist coats her bedside table and moisture pocks the windowsill.

When did the rain start? While she was reading, of course. While Cassie's entire understanding of her mother was shifting and cracking like ice on the Pennatucket after a hard winter.

Her hands shake a little as she shoves the sash closed, muffling the sound of the rain. She leaves the manuscript on her bed and pads softly to the bathroom for a towel to mop up what the wind has blown in, her feet moving automatically over the worn floorboards.

At the sink, she turns on the left-hand faucet and cups cold water in her palms. The left faucet should be hot, but this is the way Ryan Jones plumbed it forty years ago. They'd all learned to live with it.

Ana and I can learn to live with this, too.

Their mother refused to be a victim. Instead, she'd extracted a harsh but righteous payment from the man who abused her and then threatened the daughters she hadn't even met yet.

Cassie bends over the sink to splash her face. Cold water stings first her cheeks and then her arms where it runs down.

This is what love looks like, when it grows claws.

Their mother was a murderer, but she was also a protector. Cassie finds herself both proud and terrified, awed by the woman who raised them with such careful tenderness while harboring this capacity for violence.

As the water chills her cheeks and arms, Cassie wonders if Ana will see it the same way. From the bathroom doorway, Cassie glances toward the closed door of Ana's bedroom. All is quiet. There's no light under the door, no sound from within.

She retrieves the manuscript from her bed, squares the pages, and silently slides the bundle beneath her sister's door.

CHAPTER TWENTY-SEVEN

Cassie

Saturday's early morning light feels thin and sharp, like it's charged with electricity left from the overnight storm. Cassie feels she needs to match that energy. As if they're living on borrowed time, and she needs to move quickly. Though she's not sure what she should do first.

It's nine AM. They have less than thirty-six hours to pack and leave, but it should be plenty of time.

She stands in the kitchen doorway, shifting from one foot to the other and watching Ana pour coffee into two mismatched mugs.

"I still can't believe we're doing this," Ana says, not looking up from the coffee. Her voice carries the hollow quality of someone who hasn't slept well, if at all.

"We don't have a choice." Cassie accepts the mug and wraps her fingers around its warmth. The coffee is stronger than usual, Ana's way of preparing for a day that will require strength as well as energy.

Ana's expression suggests she's still processing the enormity of their situation. Twenty-four hours ago, their biggest concern had been clearing out their mother's house and reading an old manuscript. Now they're preparing to disappear into the wilderness for who knows how long.

"The cabin has electricity and water," Ana says, switching to the practical details that ground her. "But we'll need to bring everything else. Sheets, towels, pillows. Food for at least a week, maybe two. Jonathan says he'll join us in a few days. The nearest grocery store is at least half an hour away, and if we're really going into hiding—"

"We can't risk being seen too often," Cassie finishes. She moves to the table and sits, curling one bare foot beneath her like she did as a kid.

Centered neatly on the table is AJ's manuscript, wrapped with white cotton string tied in a bow like a tidy package. Like kite string, Cassie thinks. We could glue all those pages end to end and turn them into a couple of giant kites, one for Ana and one for me. Fly them over Vermont's Green Mountains and lose all those words to a wild breeze.

She touches the small bowknot with a single finger, wondering if all the pages are back in the bundle. If Ana really read all the way to the end.

"I'm sorry some of the pages are damp," Cassie says. "I had the window open last night while I was reading, and the rain blew in. I'll take it to the copy shop and get it scanned right after breakfast. Did you read…?"

Ana sets her coffee on the table and sits. "Yes, of course I read it. I was lying awake, waiting for you to push it under my door. The way you used to when we were kids, and you wanted me to read something creepy that you liked but I knew I'd hate, because I never wanted to read all the scary stuff you were into."

"But you were always curious, weren't you? You always read what I pushed under the door. Eventually."

"Most of it," Ana admits. "Some of the Stephen King was okay, like *The Green Mile*. But not all the real horror stuff. I didn't like anything by Clive Barker. Or that other British writer you liked so much, Ramsey Campbell. And Lovecraft, he gave me terrible nightmares. Still does. He's way too dark and creepy."

"What about this?" Cassie nods at AJ's manuscript. "Did it give you nightmares?"

Ana's holding her mug with both hands, her elbows planted on the table. She tightens her grip. "Yes. This is way worse. Because…"

"Because it's Mom, and it's real. But she saw no other way—"

"No, that's not it. The worst part is imagining what he did, the absolutely hideous way that monster preyed on people." Ana sets her mug aside, grabs her sister's hand and squeezes hard. "And maybe it wasn't only the two we know about, Jimmy and Connor. There were probably others, too. High school boys who left blackmail notes in the girls' lockers, and got other boys to bring the girls to the barn. Because they thought it would be such fun." She spits the word *fun*, her voice laced with bile. "Kids that they were grooming to do their dirty work for them. Think of it—all that equipment, the studio, all the photos and videos."

She releases Cassie's hand and pauses for breath, then wraps one more statement in a bitterness overlaid with pure fury: "I wish she'd killed them all."

This hard-steel aspect of Ana is new. It's something Cassie's never heard from her twin sister, the earnest nurturing woman who's always been compared to their own gentle, soft-spoken mother.

And that's exactly right, Cassie realizes. At their core, first and foremost, Ana and Marla were—are—something that Cassie has never been.

They're mothers. The fiercest of fierce warriors, protecting their children. Other people's children, too.

It occurs to Cassie that Ana has had time to think about the conclusion to AJ's story. Perhaps last night wasn't the first time she'd seen it.

"You read the ending earlier, didn't you? Before me."

Ana's face closes and her eyes drop to her mug. "Yes. Yesterday, while you were in town. That last part has my name on it, after all. So I wasn't really reading ahead, was I? I was just reading first. I read it a second time after you pushed it under the door last night."

And here Cassie was worrying that Ana might not be able to stomach the rest of the story. That she'd turn away and close her eyes, fingers in her ears, chanting *la la la* to drown out whatever mean thing Cassie was saying.

Ana pushes her hair back from her face, wipes angry damp eyes with a paper napkin, and changes her tone to one of reassurance. "We'll talk about it more as we're driving, okay? Here, I started a couple of lists. Things we need to buy, things we need to bring."

Of course you made lists, Cassie thinks. *My supremely competent sister. Because just like that, you're Ana the Girl Scout again.*

As a snarky teenager, Cassie would have laced those thoughts with snide sarcasm. Now she feels only awe and gratitude for the twin she used to think of as her insufferably prim and proper big sister.

They divide the tasks with little discussion. Cassie tosses dirty clothes into the washer, adds detergent, pushes buttons. The mundane activity should soothe her mind but it feels like a countdown, setting her on edge. They know what they must do and they have enough time, but she's certain there's something she's missing in their plan.

She selects a few of her mother's least-worn shopping totes, planning to go to the grocery store while the copy shop scans and duplicates the manuscript. She checks the items on Ana's Things to Buy list—a cooler chest, batteries, bags of ice, matches, shampoo, a first aid kit—and adds *thumb drives* and *prepaid phones*.

The Things to Bring list is longer: winter sweaters and cold weather outerwear, boots, raincoats and umbrellas. Cassie has none of these things. She lives in southern California and she's traveled with only a few changes of clothing, mostly breezy summer cottons and sandals.

They'll need pillows, towels, blankets. What size are the beds? The cabin has beds, right? Fighting down a quick rise of panic, Cassie tries to focus on the job at hand. She moves to the chest of drawers in her mother's room and pulls out a stack of sheets. The scents of lavender and gardenia, faint but immediately recognizable, waft into the humid summer air. She gathers the linens into her arms and inhales deeply.

Their mother will be going north with them, she realizes. In every old memory, but also in the new knowledge they now hold.

Cassie hears Ana's feet moving from room to room overhead, and she's prompted to move on. She dumps two sets of queen-size sheets into a large empty box, adds a patchwork quilt, and squashes a blanket and pillows on top. She sets the box on the floor near the front door, then abandons her packing to locate her purse and keys.

Calling upstairs to let Ana know she's heading into town, she grabs her things and leaves. Her thoughts are scattered, leaping from one item to the next. It feels wrong, this hasty rush to flee with supplies scrounged from their mother's closets, but Detective Clement's words echo in her mind: Get somewhere safe.

By noon, AJ's manuscript has been scanned and copied, all the pages neatly stored in a new document box and the digital files saved to a pair of new thumb drives. Choosing to scan and save their mother's story is another decision point, Cassie realizes as she pulls into the supermarket parking lot. *It's Mom's legacy, and we've decided to keep it.*

But who will they share it with, and when?

She moves through the aisles of Stop & Shop methodically, avoiding eye contact with other shoppers. Standing in the checkout line, she glances at her phone. There are no texts or emails requiring a response.

No word from Marsh. Has he been able to book a red-eye that will get him to California on Monday instead of Tuesday, or will he have to stick to his original schedule? She imagines he'll catch a flight to the east coast, Logan in Boston or Bradley near Hartford, as soon as he lands at LAX.

Either way, she's confident she and Ana will be far away by the time he can get here.

Her new phone vibrates with a text from Ana. *Can you get some $$$ from ATM? Get the max.*

Cassie types back: *Will do. On my way.*

She finds an ATM outside Stop & Shop. Now feeling like each moment spent is a moment lost, she feeds her debit card into the slot. Taps in her password and waits as the icon on the screen tells her *Processing...Processing...*

The machine buzzes and the card pops back out. Invalid password.

She scowls at the screen. Pushes the card in again, tries once more. Invalid password. Two attempts remaining before her account is locked.

Damn. She thumps the machine with her fist. One part of her brain tells her it's just a careless mistake, she's forgotten her PIN. But she knows the truth: Marsh has changed it. She's been cut off.

She grabs the useless debit card and hurries toward her car, suddenly terrified of what may happen next. Northern Vermont doesn't seem nearly far enough away.

She returns to find Ana's done her usual wonderful job of packing. Suitcases, boots, winter coats, and two bankers' boxes are arranged in a neat row inside the front door. The Subaru is parked close to the porch, doors and hatch open.

Ana stands in the living room, surveying the pile. "I've packed everything but your suitcases, Cass. I think we have what we need."

"Except cash." Cassie juggles two heavy bags of food and supplies. "I think Marsh has locked my account, or changed the passcode. I couldn't use my debit card."

Ana lifts two dripping bags of ice from the cooler and drops them into the refrigerator's freezer drawer with a frown. "You don't have your own account? Something he doesn't have access to?"

"No," Cassie confesses. "Everything's in his name, or in our joint account. It's never been a problem before. There's always been enough, I never had to worry about money. I do have my own credit card, but I never signed up for the cash advances. Never needed to." She hears the hint of a defensive whine in her voice and flinches.

"Which he pays off each month for you, right?" Ana shoots her a dark look. "That must be nice, never having to worry about money or a budget."

Cassie doesn't need Ana's sarcasm to feel stupid. "Well, if we need anything at the cabin, there's always Amazon," she says lamely.

Ana's still staring at her. "Actually, I'm not sure about that. Did I mention the cabin is kind of isolated? Maybe Amazon won't deliver."

Cassie turns, eyes wide. "Seriously? You and Jonathan didn't consider that when you decided to buy it?" A new panic surfaces. "If it's so isolated, what if there's an early snowfall? It's almost September. Northern Vermont gets snow sometimes in September. Definitely in October. Who's gonna plow us out?"

Ana looks momentarily off-balance. "I'm sure we'll be back by then."

But they can't be sure of anything.

With their supplies packed and stowed, Cassie hands her sister one of the thumb drives and a sturdy portfolio-style folder, heavy with the weight of AJ's story. "Here's your copy. I'll get my clothes into the dryer and figure out lunch. Then I'll pack, promise."

Ana stirs and moves toward the kitchen. "Don't bother with lunch, it's too late. We'll scrounge leftovers for dinner and then dump anything that's still in the fridge. Some things can go in the freezer, I guess—"

Their mother's phone rings its loud, insistent peal and Cassie jumps. As before, they freeze and stare, but this time neither moves to pick it up.

"It could be anyone," Ana says weakly. "There's no way to know."

The black desk phone goes silent after five rings. Both women exhale.

"Clothes in the dryer," Cassie says briskly. She avoids Ana's eyes. "Then packing."

Upstairs in her room, she moves first to the window and checks to be sure the sill has dried after last night's rain. Through the glass she can see her rented Volvo where she parked it, in front of the one-car garage. Where the police found Ryan Jones's pickup all those years ago, when they came looking for Jimmy's killer.

There's nothing in the garage now but cobwebs and rusty garden tools. She shivers a little and rubs her arms. So many little things had to happen in just the right sequence, back in August of 1985. The truck, the gun, the mulch. Ryan inside, drinking his beer, never knowing his truck was used in a murder.

And AJ, willing to hike through the woods in the dark with Mom. Willing not only to light the matches, but also to hear the darkest secrets and remain silent for four decades. To stay alive, to stay free.

Cassie reins in her wayward mind and glances at her watch, surprised to see it's nearly four o'clock. How long has she been staring out the window, thinking about the past?

Her last-minute packing is easy. She pulls her suitcase from beneath the bed and unzips it.

It takes her only a minute to find the tracking device, a small round disc taped into a corner between the removable lining and the case's frame. She sets it in a desk drawer and opens her laptop case.

Yes, there's one here, also. Marsh—or someone— has opened a small hole in an inside seam and wedged a second tracker into the space between fabric and padding, then restitched it with the same color thread. She can almost admire the careful, precise work.

Of all the things she's realized she doesn't know about her husband, here's one she never thought of: *I didn't know Marsh could sew.*

But it was probably Rosa, his loyal housekeeper, who'd done the carefully needlework.

The second AirTag joins its partner in the desk drawer as Cassie tries to recall what that second tracker told Marsh about her movements. The laptop case had gone with her to the café, twice, but otherwise it had remained in this house.

Except for the trip to the police station.

But I parked at Walmart. I left it in the car.

There's no way to know what her husband knows, so she turns to the third item that might hold a tracking device, her cross-body bag. She dumps everything on the bed and turns it inside out, inspecting each crevice.

There's nothing that doesn't belong. The bag is too new, or Marsh ran out of tags.

Cassie turns to her suitcase and begins packing, stuffing in everything she brought from California, which isn't much.

She's been living out of her suitcase for less than a week, unlike Ana, who's been staying in this house for three months. There's nothing else Cassie really needs to bring.

Except for AJ's shotgun.

They're heading north to the wilds of Vermont and it would be sensible to bring a gun, right? But she has no ammunition for it. And she'll have to be careful about traveling across state lines with a probably unregistered weapon. What are the gun laws in the states they'll be traveling through? Another complication to worry about.

Wondering if AJ might've had a gun license or proof of ownership stashed away where she found the gun, Cassie spends a few minutes searching the back corners of the closet, then turns to her old desk. In the lower drawer she finds a stack of printer paper and a box of paperclips. Behind the paperclips, tucked way in the back, there's a half-empty box of bright yellow, two-and-a-half-inch shotshells. After a moment's hesitation, she places three brass-capped shells on the desk.

The gun is still propped in the corner of her room. She lifts it, feeling immediately reassured by its heft and the smooth warmth of its wooden stock. She checks the chamber and magazine. It's empty, of course—the way she left it two days earlier—but she can still hear her dad's voice behind her shoulder: *Always check. Every. Single. Time.*

Keith Bousquet had his failings as a husband— frightened by the responsibilities of parenting, too easily impressed by pretty women and the perks of a fast-paced job in Boston—but he loved his daughters and tried his best to keep them safe. What would he have done if Mom told him about the abuse and the murder? Stood by her and kept her secrets?

Cassie suspects their mother was wise not to place that heavy burden in his hands.

She places the gun on her bed and begins to fold the old quilt over it, then unwraps it again and loads two shells into its small magazine. She drops the third shell into the firing chamber, clicks the safety back on, and returns the gun to its place in the corner.

***

Dinner is a scattered affair, a random process of grabbing a few bites as they toss perishables into trash bags. As usual, Ana's thought of everything.

"There's a dumpster at Roland's store," she informs Cassie. "They let Mom drop her trash in there when she couldn't get to the transfer station during regular hours. We'll just drop it off after the store opens at eight."

They're still stuffing suitcases and file boxes into Ana's Subaru at 11:00 PM. As Ana slams the car's hatch, the midnight crowd of cicadas, crickets and katydids is humming a full-throated chorus. The night air offers a light breeze, bringing a hint of autumn chill into the air. Cassie knows it will be cooler in northern Vermont, but she's looking forward to a new environment.

An entirely new life, actually. *I'll need a job, a place to live…* It hits her suddenly, the yawning gulf of unknown next steps reaching out before her. She's not ready to think about any of that yet. *Just leave. Get somewhere safe.*

"That's it," Ana announces as she climbs the porch steps. "Bedtime." She clicks the fob to lock her car and goes inside, reaching around her twin to switch off the porch lights. "Can you get the door, Cass?"

Ana's halfway up the stairs when Cassie says, "I just thought of something. What about Mom's geraniums?"

But Ana doesn't hear. She's in the upstairs bathroom, the water running.

The plants will have to be abandoned, left to die with no one here to water them.

On impulse, Cassie flips the porch light on again, steps back outside, and reaches up to unhook each pot from its chain. She steps off the porch and sets the plants one at a time beneath the azalea bushes, hoping the pots will receive enough rain and shade.

If they're back before the first frost, maybe the geraniums will survive.

CHAPTER TWENTY-EIGHT

Cassie & Ana

Cassie's still downstairs in the hall, the front door open and the porch light on, when she hears gravel crunching under tires. Headlights cut through the darkness and she glimpses the sleek dark hood of an unfamiliar car, big and black, pulling into the driveway.

The terrible thought crosses her mind that it's Marsh, somehow transported from Hong Kong all the way to Connecticut more than a full day early, cutting through their carefully constructed timeline like pruning shears.

Of course it's not Marsh. It can't be. There's no way he could leave Hong Kong on Saturday afternoon and arrive in Connecticut just after midnight on Sunday morning.

But her heart is hammering against her ribs and her mind is screaming, *Not now! Not when we're so close.*

"Ana," she calls softly, but her sister is moving now along the hallway upstairs, her footsteps quick and purposeful. Her steps pause at the top of the stairs and Cassie hears a sharp intake of breath. The sisters lock eyes through the banister spindles, Ana's expression mirroring Cassie's fear.

A car door slams. She hears it then, Marsh's tuneless whistle—that random play of notes he always makes when he's pleased with himself. The sound that used to make her smile now turns her blood cold.

345

There's still a small pile of their belongings by the door. Jackets piled on the cooler, her laptop in its bag. Too damning, he'll know they're planning to leave. But there's no time to hide anything.

She forces herself to move, to close the inside door and reach for the deadbolt lock, but she's too slow and he's too quick. He's at the screen door, pulling it open, then his foot is between the inner door and the jamb.

He fills the frame like a dark shadow, backlit by porchlight—charcoal suit wrinkled from the long flight, tie loosened, carry-on bag slung over his shoulder. The tousled black hair and a day's growth of stubble tell her he's driven straight here from wherever he landed. The faint scent of travel—dirt, sweat, airport soap—clings to him. She once found that windblown-rebel look charming, but now her instincts shout danger.

"Hello, Cassie." His voice is quiet. His mouth curls into a thin-lipped rictus, pretending to be pleasant.

She expects him to walk into the house like he's built it, because that's the way he enters every space. But instead of that usual easy saunter there's something different in his voice and posture, a tense exhaustion she's never seen before. Like a thin wire, stretched to the breaking point. Beneath his tired, rumpled exterior she sees his fear. He looks far older than fifty-two.

She exhales with something close to relief. To find a hint of vulnerability, but also to confront what's been haunting her.

His eyes sweep the room, taking in the packing boxes, the items by the door. He's been in this house only once before, years ago, and she can see him cataloging the layout, the exits. The faint smile falters and something colder slides behind his gaze. "Going somewhere?"

Cassie's mouth goes dry. She forces herself to breathe, to think. "Marsh. How did you get here so early? I thought—"

"I caught a ride on Li's private jet." He drops his bag and steps fully into the room, closing the door behind him with deliberate care. "We finished the Miura deal early. He was so happy he offered to fly me home. Lucky me, getting to cross the date line twice in one trip. The magic of time travel."

Of course. That's what had been niggling at the back of her brain. When you're flying east, Sunday in Hong Kong is still Saturday here.

"We were just—Ana and I were going to go away for a couple days. To Vermont. She and Jonathan bought a cabin—"

"You were planning to leave without telling me?" His voice cracks slightly, and for a moment he sounds genuinely hurt. "Without asking? Or at least letting me know?"

She lifts her chin. "I don't need permission to go on an overnight with my sister."

"Where's Ana now?"

Did he notice their two cars, the Volvo and the Subaru? But he wouldn't know which car she's driving. And the Volvo's parked around the side, beside the old garage.

She looks him straight in the eye. "West Hartford. She had to go home yesterday but she'll be back around nine. Then we were planning to leave."

"You should've told me, Cassie. I'm really sorry but you're in danger now. We're both in danger."

Does he know she's been to the police? But how? Her legs feel unsteady beneath her.

"I don't know what you mean. What kind of danger?"

"Don't pretend you don't know. You're a smart girl, Cass. By now, you must've figured out my real business. The real cargo."

Without thinking, she spits it out. "People, right? Children. Not cars."

He sighs and reaches into his suit jacket. Her breath catches. When his hand emerges, it's gripping a military-style knife with a black handle. He thumbs it open and the serrated edge gleams in the overhead light. A K-bar, she realizes with horrible clarity. The kind she's seen in all those commando movies he likes to watch. It's a hunter's tool, useful for killing and gutting a deer.

"Jesus, Marsh—"

"Quiet, now." The words might sound kind, in someone else's voice. His friendly mask drops. "You've been meddling, Cassandra. I hear the feds are looking for me. Do you have any idea what you've done?"

She thinks again, *How could he know?* But then she remembers what Detective Clement said, that they'd been watching Marsh even before she handed over the drive. Maybe he thinks she told them something earlier. But she didn't *know* anything before she opened those files.

A moot point, Ana's paralegal voice would say. It doesn't matter.

Where's Ana? Cassie's eyes dart toward the stairs, but there's no sign of her sister. She sidles a few steps into the living room, trying to put the coffee table between herself and the knife.

"The police came to see me yesterday," she lies, hoping to buy time. "They had questions about your business trips. About some files they found."

His face goes white. "You spoke to the police?" Every trace of vulnerability is gone.

"I don't know what—"

"Don't lie, Cassie!" With startling agility, he vaults over the coffee table and grabs her wrist. The flat of his knife presses against her neck, cold and sharp. "We've got to get out of here, right now. You're going to give me that stupid device and then you're coming with me. But we don't have much time."

"No—" She digs the nails of her free hand into his knife arm, but the blade turns, biting into her skin just enough to draw blood. Gasping, she thrusts harder against his forearm. The hand gripping her wrist tightens. They're locked together in a horrible tableau, his eyes inches from hers, blood tricking from her neck into her shirt.

She stares into his eyes for a sign, a flash of warmth. Some glimpse of guilt or remorse, something to let her know he remembers why he asked her to marry him, why she said yes. But there's none of it. Everything now washing over her is cold steel, like the knife at her throat.

He shifts the hand with the knife to the back of her neck, pulling her close. His breath is hot and stale and for one horrible moment she thinks he's going to kiss her. She breaks her gaze and tries again to twist away.

His voice drops into a chilling intimacy. "It's funny, isn't it? Years ago—just a couple days before he died, I think it was—Jimmy showed me an old photo of Marla and promised me I could have one of her twins. And I got one, didn't I? I was only twelve, but I remember that. So I watched and waited and finally I got you. But along the way, I fell in love. At least I thought I did. But now—well, some things are bigger than love." He's added a mocking twist to the word love. "Like survival. That's what we're looking at here, Cassandra. Survival, pure and simple.

"But now I'm thinking maybe I should've gone after the other one. She'd be more compliant, maybe. More obedient."

Her mind is stuck on the name Jimmy. Jimmy Desjardins, the predator her mother killed more than forty years ago. Marsh knew Jimmy? *What had Jimmy promised?*

"You're lying," she whispers. "You never loved me. You can't love someone and then do this."

"I'm giving you a chance to live, Cassie. A new life, a new identify somewhere. That says something, doesn't it?"

Her mind races. Once he has the drive, he doesn't need her. The truth will get her killed, but lies might buy Ana time to act. If Ana is even still in the house. Maybe she ran. Maybe she's calling for help.

"I made a copy," Cassie chokes out. "It's upstairs, in my laptop case."

"Good girl." His grip on her wrist tightens again, fingers digging deep enough to bruise. But the knife moves an inch away from her neck. "We're going to go get it now. And I want that story, too. Whatever your mom's friend wrote. Then we're going to take a little drive, just you and me. Somewhere private, where we can discuss your future."

He's not going to take her hostage. He means to kill her, she can see it in his eyes. The knife at her throat is just the beginning.

"Marsh, please—"

"Show me where it is. Move."

He drags her toward the stairs and up, the blade still close to her throat. It's an awkward side-by-side climb, and each step feels like she's climbing a gallows. On the top landing, he pauses, holding her tight and listening. The house is silent except for their breathing and the old floorboards creaking when he shifts his weight.

"Which room?"

"On the left." Her childhood room, later AJ's room.

The shotgun. It's still in the corner of her bedroom, not yet packed. If she can just get to it—

But Marsh is too smart and too careful. He pushes her through the doorway first and scans the room. He spots the gun immediately.

"Well, well. Planning to play soldier, were we? Hah. Sweet little Cassie with her daddy's rabbit shooter. Did you even remember to load it?"

He kicks the door and releases her, but only after pressing the knife once more into the soft flesh of her neck. "Sit on the bed. Hands where I can see them. Don't move."

She sits on the edge of her childhood bed, rubbing her wrist and fighting a wave of nausea. The quilt beneath her is one of a pair her mother made when the twins were ten—soft cotton patches in faded blues and yellows. The same quilt she planned to wrap the shotgun in.

Three strides across the small room and Marsh has retrieved the shotgun, keeping an eye on her as he checks the chamber with practiced ease. "Loaded. Good girl. Though I have to say, I'm disappointed. This little thing's just a toy. Still, it could be useful. When's the last time it was properly cleaned?"

Not expecting an answer, he pulls her along as he props it against the wall next to the door and turns his attention to her laptop case. "Get it. Give me the drive. And turn on your computer, too. I want to see if you made other copies."

She moves slowly to the desk, her hands shaking as she types in her password. He leans over and places his free hand on her shoulder, gripping it hard, as the screen illuminates and desktop icons populate the screen.

"I encrypted the files," she lies. "I'll need time—"

He presses the knife to her throat again, so fast she can't react. "You have thirty seconds to show me everything. And where's the portable drive?" He releases her arm and reaches into the case.

A floorboard creaks.

Marsh jumps and grabs Cassie's shoulder. He pivots sharply, staring at the door where Ana stands with AJ's shotgun in her hands.

"Let her go, Marsh."

Ana's face is ghostly white but determined. It's how their mother must have looked when she raised a different gun toward Jimmy Desjardins.

Marsh's laugh is strained. "Two for the price of one. How economical." He shifts position, swiveling Cassie's chair and moving behind her so he can hold her there and use her as a shield. His six-foot frame is in a half-crouch, keeping the knife at her throat. "Put the gun down, Ana. You don't want to hurt your sister."

Her voice is low and steady. "You're the one holding the knife."

"Do you think you can fire that thing before I cut her throat? Want to test those reflexes?"

The barrel of the shotgun trembles slightly, but Ana doesn't lower it. "I don't have to be fast. I just have to be close enough not to miss."

"Brave words. But we both know you don't have it in you. You're not a killer, Ana. You're soft. Weak, just like your dear mother."

The mention of their mother is a mistake. Cassie sees the change in Ana's face—the hardening of her features, the steadying of her grip.

Marsh sees it, too. "Oh, yeah." He grins. "I knew your mother. You didn't know that? All those pictures pinned up in the barn, just like a movie star. Jimmy made her a real star, did she ever tell you that? She was very popular."

"Our mother was the strongest person I've ever known," Ana says quietly. "And she taught me that sometimes killing is the only way to protect the people you love. She'd have shot you at the drop of a hat."

The word "drop" carries a slight emphasis, the tiniest of pauses.

Cassie dives below Marsh's arm, twisting away from the knife and shoving her chair hard against his legs. Down on her stomach, she scrambles to get beneath the bed, thrashing past the quilt's hem and shoving herself back toward the wall. She's ahead of Marsh by only a fraction of a second, but it's enough.

In an instant, he's grabbed the metal bed frame with his free hand. He upends it against the wall but it falls back when he lets go. Holding the bed up with his free hand, he bends down to slash at her kicking feet with the knife.

The shotgun roars.

Marsh yells a curse and the knife clatters away as he falls to the side. He grabs his right thigh with both hands and falls to the floor beside Cassie. The bed topples away from the wall again, dropping hard onto his shoulders. They're both trapped and thrashing beneath the metal springs.

Cassie squirms past him and fights her way free of the tangled bedclothes. Clambering to her feet, she steadies herself against the desk and gasps as a sharp pain stabs her shoulder.

Ana's holding the gun on Marsh's crumpled form. She racks the bolt action on the shotgun, ejecting the spent shell and chambering another round. The crisp mechanical sound is nearly drowned by his curses. His top half is jammed beneath the bed, but they can see his legs and the hands clutching his right thigh. Bright blood seeps through his fingers.

When he stops yelling to catch his breath, Ana says calmly, "The next one goes in your chest. Pull yourself out of there," she adds. "You're not dying yet."

Crawling awkwardly, dragging his bloody leg, Marsh pulls himself free of the frame and collapses against the nightstand, the right leg of his expensive suit shredded and soaked with blood. He's moaning, his face contorted with pain. Cassie sidles away from the desk and moves to stand next to her sister, careful not to get in the line of fire.

"You don't understand," Marsh gasps, "who you're dealing with. It's not just me. The people I work for—they'll kill you both. I had a plan, we could've gotten away. But now you—you can't stop them."

"But we've stopped *you*," Ana says. "That'll do for now."

Cassie retrieves her burner phone from her rear pocket. The screen's cracked but it seems to be working. Her face is wet with tears, her shoulder hurts, but her hands and voice are steady.

And she's getting a signal. Only one bar, but it's enough.

"Detective Clement? It's Cassie Masterson. Cassie *Bousquet*," she corrects herself. "Sorry to bother you in the middle of the night, but we need your help. "My husband, Marshall Masterson, is here. He has a knife and he tried to kidnap me. My sister had to shoot him." She pauses, listening. "No, he's alive. But he'll need an ambulance."

As she gives their address, she watches Marsh's face cycle through disbelief, fear and defeat. He slumps against her small table, still pressing both hands to his wounded leg.

"They'll find you," he whispers. "No matter where you hide. No matter how far you run."

"Maybe." Ana manages a shrug but keeps the shotgun trained on his chest. "But that's tomorrow's problem."

Moving carefully so she doesn't get between Ana and Marsh, Cassie retrieves the kicked-over desk chair and stands it on its feet, facing the door, so Ana can straddle-sit and rest the gun barrel on the back of the chair.

They wait, Cassie breathing hard from the doorway and Ana keeping watch from the chair, as Marsh emits an occasional groan. By the time they hear sirens in the distance, he's gone pale and quiet. The sirens grow louder, and they hear the added whoop of an ambulance.

Cassie looks at her twin sister, sitting guard with AJ's little rabbit shooter, and feels things she hasn't experienced in years. Love for her sister, and a fierce pride in the family that created them.

CHAPTER TWENTY-NINE

Cassie & Ana

Five days after Marsh is taken into custody, AJ's manuscript sits on Marla's kitchen table beside the coffee pot and a plate of croissants.

Carl Androski's weathered hands move with the deliberate care of an archeologist, setting aside a crumb-laden plate and fixing a pair of reading glasses on the bridge of his nose.

He begins turning pages, pausing only occasionally to read a dog-eared passage in depth. He finds the first of the key pages Cassie has marked—the arson—and stops abruptly, frowning. He re-reads a section, then glances across the table first at Ana, then Cassie. One eyebrow arches upward as if he's looking for confirmation of what he's reading. He flips ahead then to the last few pages, finding Marla's terrible confession on the footbridge.

As Cassie adds more coffee to Androski's mug, Ana rises to clear their plates, then returns to sit beside her sister. Through the kitchen window, Cassie can see that the sun has burned away the early-morning fog, bringing warmth and a cluster of white butterflies to the hedge of late-blooming lavender.

In the maple grove on the far side of the gravel road, the lowest branch on one gnarled tree is already sporting a hint of orange. Labor Day and the Woodstock Fair, those classic end-of-summer heralds, are only a few days away. In a week, big yellow buses will trundle down all the narrow back roads of Winslow, gathering schoolkids bound for weekday classrooms and, a few weeks later, senior citizens hunting the prettiest fall foliage.

The best season, their mother always said.

Ana returns to the table and the sisters remain quiet in a waiting silence. Ana watches Androski's face as he finishes the last few pages; Cassie thinks of nothing at all as she studies the dust motes in a stray sunbeam lying across the old oak table.

When he finally looks up and sets his glasses aside, something like peace has smoothed the deepest creases around his eyes.

"It's gratifying to know I wasn't entirely wrong about a few things."

Cassie abandons the sunbeam and straightens up. "About Mom and AJ protecting each other?"

"That, but other things also. Over the years, there'd been complaints about Jimmy and his photography. We talked with him every now and then, but no one would ever press charges. I always suspected he died for something deeply personal, and I was sure Marla and AJ knew more about it than they told us. But we never had the evidence to link anyone to it.

"And the arson." Androski places the flat of his hand on AJ's manuscript. "AJ was right, we dropped the ball on that. When the firefighters realized they had no people or animals to save, they turned the fire into a training exercise for the rookies. They had to be super cautious about moving in too soon on that blaze, because there were a couple of old tractors and a batch of dead batteries stored under the shed. The fire chief had everyone holding back until they could get it knocked down.

"It was more than a week before the investigators turned up some unusual items...a file cabinet, a metal bed frame, a tripod, and a few pieces they thought were parts of a camera. People store all sorts of things in old barns, so we didn't tie that to the murder.

"It was only later that I thought maybe your mother knew something about the fire, too. But I never pegged AJ for the arson. I thought she was just keeping secrets. That young woman had a hell of a poker face..." His expression is three parts chagrin, one part admiration.

Cassie allows a wry smile. "We had no idea, and we lived with them. They were both good at staying silent."

They sit quietly for a moment, then Androski pulls them back on track. "What questions do you have for me? I'll tell you what I can, but I'm not in the loop on everything."

"How big was it?" Ana asked. "The pornography operation. Detective Clement didn't have time to give us the whole history. And the guys from ICE and the FBI won't tell us anything. They're strictly need to know."

"I'll tell you what I can. It was pretty small at first. It started with Desjardins and, for a while, it was just one guy with a camera, taking pictures for himself." Regret wrinkles his forehead and scalp. "I wish more people had come forward at the beginning. We could've stopped him early on."

Cassie's skeptical. "You think so?" She taps the manuscript. "You said yourself no one would file charges. People mostly just kept quiet, even the victims." Her voice goes bitter. "Just 'Jimmy being Jimmy,' they said. But Mom told us, through AJ's story, exactly what it felt like, to be a victim of that shit. How nobody believed the few girls who dared to speak up. Because if you said anything, you were shamed and blamed, branded a slut and kicked out of school."

She shoots Androski a dark look. Adds, "Back then, was there even a sexual assault hotline in this town?"

"Sort of. There was a number you could call for counseling. I don't know how good it was."

His headshake is weary. "But you're right, no one talked about it. And no, there wasn't a lot of support available. The state's domestic violence coalition wasn't formed until that year, 1985. We had a few female troopers, but not many. And no one was really trained to handle sexual abuse cases. Not like today.

"We've had shelters for abused animals a lot longer than we've had shelters for humans, or even standard procedures in place. I like to think we're doing better now." He corrects himself. "I *know* we're doing better now."

Cassie asks, "When did Jimmy's...hobby... become big business?"

He pauses for a swallow of black coffee. "Jimmy was just a small-timer. At the beginning, he got girls to pose for pictures and learned to develop his black-and-white film in his basement. Then he got bolder about talking girls into what he wanted. After Connor and Shelby Duffy got involved, it escalated. A lot."

He hesitates, his eyes on Cassie. "Connor and Shelby Duffy," he repeats. "Marsh's older brothers. Half-brothers, actually."

"Marsh's *brothers*?" Ana turns to her sister, eyes widening. "Connor Duffy was the one in the milking barn. But the other boy AJ said she saw, outside the barn—he was eleven years old, I think—was that Shelby?"

"Shelby would have been older then, fourteen or fifteen," Androski says.

"It was Marsh." Cassie's voice cracks on the name. "He turned twelve in 1985."

"And he was part of that even *then*?" Ana's voice rises, incredulous.

Androski rubs a hand over his bald scalp and nods. "Yes. He might even have been one of the young…performers. At the beginning, anyway, before he graduated into the business end."

A look of horror crosses Ana's face. "Dear god."

Cassie reaches for Ana's hand and offers a bitter smile. "He hinted at something like that once. Said he'd had an 'early introduction to sex.' But I never imagined…"

Androski says, "In the early days, Connor worked the business angle, selling photos and setting up the blackmail. He built the studio, too, in the barn. The younger boys did whatever he told them to."

"But Connor Duffy went to prison," Ana says.

"For a few years. While he was there, he took some computer courses. By the time he got out, the internet was a thing and that opened up all sorts of possibilities."

He adds, "While Connor was inside doing his time, Shelby started a used-car business outside Providence. When Connor got out, the three of them ran it together. Later, they turned that all over to Marsh."

Cassie looks from her sister to Androski. "Marsh told me he and his brothers had a 'falling out.' I never met them and he wouldn't talk about his family. All I know is his dad disappeared when he was young. Then his mom remarried."

Androski shakes his head, "I don't think the brothers ever had a falling out. Or if they did, it wasn't for long, because all three were very much involved in the family business from the beginning. *All* the family businesses."

More lies, Cassie thinks. *I shouldn't be surprised.*

"And the business was obviously more than just running a garage," Ana says.

He makes no attempt to soften his words. "Pornography, plus trafficking. What Marsh really means when he talks about his 'transportation business.' And the side hustles, blackmail and money laundering.

"Who set up the blackmail scheme at the high school?" Cassie asks.

"Shelby first, then Marsh when he got old enough. First they targeted the older ones who'd already quit school, or the ones who were still in school but struggling. Marginalized, neglected, falling through the cracks. The ones who needed money for food, or drugs. A lot of those kids are looking for any way to get by. It doesn't take much to get them to just go along and keep their mouths shut.

"Later," he adds, "they got ambitious and targeted the younger ones. Middle-schoolers."

Ana shivers again but Cassie feels only a cold fury pushing against her throat.

"And Marsh went along with it all." She's found some distance, she's no longer stumbling over the sound of his name. *Marsh* and *my husband* feel foreign on her tongue now, like he's a character in a horrific tragedy someone else has written. "I can't believe I lived with him and *married* him. I'm so stupid."

"You didn't know, Cassie." Ana places a consoling hand on her sister's arm.

Cassie just shakes her head, wanting to say *I could have stopped it years ago! If only I'd paid attention.*

But could she? She's wearing a high-collared shirt to cover the bruises on her neck and shoulder, but she can still feel where Marsh had gripped her hard, holding a knife to her throat.

Shifting in his seat, the detective fixes his eyes on Ana. "When Marsh was young, I'm sure he admired his big brothers. They'd figured out how to turn cruelty into profit. But they didn't see it as cruelty, just a great scheme to make lots of money. Marsh probably convinced himself he was *helping* the local kids by giving them money. By the time Marsh was out of high school, the brothers were part of a nationwide network. And now it's global. A far cry from passing a few photographs around the schoolyard."

He pauses to rub a hand over his scalp. "These days," he adds, "anyone with a smartphone can make, or fake, videos and send them anywhere." He sighs and shakes his head. "I'm glad I'm out of it, frankly."

A fresh wave of nausea threatens Cassie as a new thought rises. She twists in her chair to stare at the detective. "I wonder—Do you think Marsh knew about our mother? Knew that she was one of the girls Jimmy had photographed, years earlier? Something that Marsh said, about Jimmy promising him he could have 'one of the twins.'" She shudders. "One of *us*."

The ugly phrase chokes air from the warm kitchen. Androski pivots away from them and fixes his gaze on something outside the kitchen window.

Then he turns back, his face hardened. "I guess it's possible. Marsh was twelve when Jimmy died. Maybe he sought you out because Connor wanted to know what your mother might have told you, or someone, about Jimmy, or the early days of their operation."

"So Marsh came looking for me," Cassie says, "when he found out I was at UC-Berkeley."

Androski taps the manuscript lightly with an index finger. "Which was essentially nothing, until you found this."

"Which was nothing, until this surfaced." Cassie taps the manuscript.

"But why," Ana asks, "did they think Mom was a threat to them?"

"Because she fought back when no one else did." He taps the stack of pages beside his coffee mug. "She confronted him in the feed store. Maybe Jimmy told Connor or Shelby about that when he got back to the farm, just before she killed him. Maybe one of them overheard that confrontation, or saw her kill him. According to AJ, Connor said he was somewhere on the farm that day, fixing a fence." He stares at Cassie, one eyebrow raised. "We never interviewed Connor. Never even knew he was there."

Cassie throws both hands up in anger at herself. "And last week, I told Marsh about AJ's story. That was dumb. I put us both in danger."

Ana protests. "But you didn't know! You told him about it before you read the whole thing. And you didn't know about his connection to Jimmy," she finishes lamely.

Cassie's still shaking her head. "Then when I found that hard drive, he really panicked." She turns to her sister. "I'm so sorry, all those horrible things I said to you. I was stupid to believe *him*, instead of you."

They sit in an uncomfortable silence until the detective shifts in his chair. "I understand he's taken a deal."

Cassie answers, feeling like anything pertaining to Marsh is her responsibility. "Yes. He's cooperating fully, pleading guilty to racketeering and money laundering. He's giving them names, dates, shipments, financial info. The other charges—trafficking, distributing CSAM—have been dropped." Cassie pronounces it cee-sam, the acronym for child sexual abuse material. One of the many new terms they've learned.

"There won't be a trial," she adds, "so I won't have to testify. He's also claiming that he's the one who turned over the hard drive. Says he had a change of heart about the whole operation." She sighs. "Another lie, I guess. But maybe he's protecting me?"

"Cassie," Androski says sharply. "Don't make him sound noble. Like he's found a conscience. He's mostly trying to save his own skin." He frowns. "I understand you're not pressing charges against him for the attack. Neither of you?"

They shake their heads. Ana says, "I wasn't hurt. He didn't attack me."

He narrows his dark eyes. "But he would have. He wouldn't have left you behind as a witness."

The sisters share glances. Cassie says firmly, "We don't want our names connected to this. And Marsh was trying to convince me to disappear with him. He could've killed me right away but he didn't."

"But he would have," he repeats. "Maybe not until after he knew what you knew. But eventually, yes, he'd have to kill you."

Ana catches her breath with a small whimper, but Cassie only flinches and steels herself. The brutal words have silenced whatever else she was planning to say.

His angry eyes drop to her throat and his voice gentles. "Cassie, he held a knife on you. You have the scars to prove it."

She colors. Her hand goes involuntarily to her shirt collar on the side where she can still feel the K-bar blade biting into her skin. The clothing she wore that night is stored now in an evidence locker, dark spots of dried blood—hers as well as his—still peppering its front.

Ana finds her voice first and rescues the conversation. "I'm still trying to figure out the money laundering part. How did that work?"

He explains how Marsh's vintage car business provides cover for the operation. "Each vehicle's a one-of-a-kind item, so the IRS can't say the prices are inflated, but of course they are. Some portion of each car sale purchase is legit, but the rest isn't. Large payments get broken into many small deposits, no more than ten thousand each, to avoid triggering an extra round of bank paperwork. Or buyers pay large amounts in digital currency, which is harder to trace.

"Then the buyer gets a kickback from a dirty-money stash, so he's happy. A few invoices for restoration work that never actually occurred, paid for in cash by a non-existent client, carries more of the dirty money into a 'clean' account. Or, Marsh might have claimed he won a lot of cash by gambling. Meanwhile, he paid his taxes faithfully, on time, every year."

Cassie says, "He liked to gamble. He'd come home boasting about his winnings."

Androski nods. "Then when a car is shipped, there's maybe something extra in the trailer or the container. Drugs or humans, or both."

His jaw tenses. "Remember that, Cassie. Marsh may not have been directly involved with shooting those videos, but he was in charge of delivery."

His voice goes harder. "Was your husband a monster? Maybe not, but he was a big part of something that *was* monstrous. Pure evil. Remember *that*, the next time you're feeling sympathetic toward Marsh."

"Believe me, I'm not—" Cassie's composure crumbles abruptly. She closes one fist over the other, trying to stop her hands from trembling on the table. Ana places a hand on Cassie's forearm.

What's it like, being locked in the back of a truck or a container? Trapped in the stinking dark for days at a time, crammed in with strangers, maybe, and a rich man's million-dollar toy. *Becoming* the toy.

The scar on her neck throbs. *Yes, I'll remember. How could I forget?*

Ana's grip tightens a little on her sister's forearm. All three sit for a minute in silence.

Androski's not done. "The portable drive you found wasn't just storage, you know. It was a marketing tool. A sampler, passed around to attract buyers to the 'hidden services' on the dark net. And there was live action. Delivered, perhaps, to a special club in some city. They're playing a cat and mouse game with law enforcement, but it's absolutely *not* a game when you consider the victims."

Another silence.

"I keep thinking about Mom," Cassie says at last. "About how hard it was for her to do what she did. But she did it anyway, to keep us safe. She was so courageous."

"She was that." He stirs, rises, and tucks the manuscript into his messenger bag. "Thank you for this."

The sisters rise also, but they're not quite ready to let him go. Ana asks, "What happens next? With your cold case file."

"Well, we can close that now, can't we? Everyone involved in the murder and arson—they're all gone." He shrugs. "I guess I'll go home, putter around the yard, plant some flowers. Maybe take up pottery."

Ana tucks a stray lock of hair behind one ear and offers him a relieved smile. "Somehow, I don't see you doing that."

"What are your plans?" he asks them.

Cassie and Ana share a glance. "First," Ana says, "we're going to disappear for a week. Go to Vermont, like we planned. We might as well. My Subaru's packed and Cassie's already arranged to turn in her rental car."

"You're okay to drive?" He looks pointedly at Cassie, reminding her of her bruised face and body, the angry red knife marks on her neck.

"I'm fine, really. Well, it's a little sore when I turn my head," she admits. "But it will be good to get away for a while. I think I'll sleep better there," she adds.

He asks Ana. "Is your husband joining you?"

"Yes. Jonathan raced out here on Sunday, the moment he heard what happened. He intended to stay for the week and drive to Vermont with us tomorrow, but he had to go home yesterday to put out some client fires. Virtual fires," she clarifies, though Androski doesn't look worried. "He'll join us on Friday."

"He's bringing groceries, and a satellite hotpot so we'll have cell service and WiFi." Cassie says. "He's convinced we're going to starve there without his intervention."

"What I meant was, what about long term? Will you go back to California, Cassie?"

"Absolutely not. There's nothing for me there." She glances at Ana. "First, I'll help Ana settle Mom's affairs. We're not in any hurry to sell this place, so I'm going to live here. For a year, maybe more. Do some home repairs, put together a new life, get to know my family better. Including Julie and Scott, the niece and nephew I've been neglecting."

Ana adds, "We also have to figure out when to tell them about all this. They should know who their grandmother really was, but it's a big topic. I'm thinking we'll tackle it over winter break."

Cassie says, "I'm also planning to volunteer at a local shelter, or the rape crisis hotline. Like Mom and AJ did."

"And your writing? You haven't mentioned that."

Her eyes slide away. "At some point I'll get back to it. I think for a while I've been afraid to write. Afraid of failing, and *really* afraid of Marsh's criticism. But now, maybe…I've got so many story ideas in my head, but they're all jumbled up. But yeah, at least I'm keeping a journal again."

He nods. "Good for you. It's a good start. What about *this* story?"

Cassie's eyes find Ana's. "We've decided to keep it in the family, for now." She shrugs. "Maybe, in a few years, we'll change our minds."

He turns to Ana. "And you?"

"After Vermont? Back to West Hartford, and Jonathan's law firm. Real estate, contracts, drafting wills and trusts. But I want to make time for the legal aid society, too. More pro bono work."

"Those sound like great plans." He walks to the door and starts to push the screen door open.

"Oh, hold on. I nearly forgot." Cassie returns to the kitchen and retrieves his stoneware jug, freshly filled with wildflowers: white and yellow daisies, frilly Queen Anne's lace, long-stemmed black-eyed Susans.

She holds the heavy pitcher in both hands like an offering. "For you. Mom loved all of these, but the black-eyed Susans were her favorites."

"I remember." The detective shifts his messenger bag to one shoulder, props the screen door open with one hip, and takes the pitcher. His hands are firm, but his eyes have gone a little misty.

He blinks a few times before speaking. "My wife Connie told me people used to assign meanings to different flowers, like a special language."

Ana joins her sister by the front door. "Mom told us that, too. Like, daisies are for innocence and purity."

Cassie slides an arm around her sister's waist. "And Queen Anne's lace means sanctuary, did you know? But black-eyed Susans, those are different. Those are for justice."

Epilogue

The plane banks sharply and Elena feels the familiar lurch at the beginning of a descent. The three girls stand in the dark and brace themselves against the wooden crate's rough wall. Elena wraps her arms around Carmen and Sofia, who claps her hands over her ears to shut out the whine of machinery directly beneath them.

Two bumps, and they've landed. A few minutes later, everything goes quiet. For long hours, nothing changes and the girls grow drowsy with exhaustion.

When bright light comes suddenly through the ventilation holes, their eyes fly open, darting quickly around the inside of their prison. Everything looks the same in the tiny space where they've been living for so many days: discarded granola wrappers, empty water jugs, dirty blankets, shabby backpacks. And the dreaded bucket, filled nearly to the brim with their waste. A small puddle of brown liquid has slopped onto the floor.

Even as she shrinks from all this, Elena tells herself: *Recuerda esto.* Remember this, because maybe someone will ask. She *hopes* someone will ask, someday. She must get the details right.

They hear voices. The sounds of a key turning in a lock, the big latches swiveling open. The doors swing apart as light floods in.

For a long moment, they are blinded. Then two people appear in the brilliant white space between the doors, a woman with jet black hair and a taller yellow-haired man, frowning behind her. Both wear black vests with radios clipped to their shoulders and the words *Guardia Policia Police* printed across their chests.

The girls scramble to their feet and shrink back against the big box. In the doorway, the woman sucks in her breath against the stench and mutters something. It's in an unfamiliar language, but it carries the weight of a curse.

The woman's face shifts quickly from disgust to compassion. She holds out a hand, palm up, and stumbles awkwardly through a few words of Spanish.

"Somos la migra. Ahora están a salvo, mis niñas. Están a salvo." She switches to English. "We are customs agents, we've come to help you. You're safe, girls." Emphasizing the last part: "*Están a salvo.*"

Elena steps back warily, still holding her sisters close. The woman pulls her phone from her pocket and scrolls quickly. She smiles warmly and turns it so the girls can see.

"¿Eres Elena, sí? You're Elena, right? Is this your mother? ¿Es ésta tu mamá? Look, here's a picture of her. She loves you, she's been looking for you."

Elena stares at the photo of their beloved mother. "Sí, sí, ella es nuestra madre." Through tears of relief, she finds the English word. "Yes, yes, yes!"

࿏

Read an excerpt from Sarah's 2024 debut novel:

DRAWN FROM LIFE

Thursday, November 18, 2015 - 2:00 a.m.

"Really, Em. You're being such a drama queen, all that moaning and groaning. It's not like you're dying. You saw the X-rays, it's just a little crack."

Lucy risked a glance away from the wet road to frown at her cousin Emma, huddled beneath a blanket in the passenger seat. "And, FYI, your shirt's buttoned all crooked. You look like a sad-ass refugee."

A gust of wind rocked the car. Sucking in her breath, Lucy tightened her grip on the wheel and braked. She hunched forward, squinting past thrashing wipers into inky blackness. Seeking a glimpse of slick pavement through the downpour.

Woozy with painkillers, preoccupied with tracking rain streaks on the side window, Emma blinked herself halfway into focus and organized a response.

"Next time," she began slowly. "Next time I break a bone…I'll dress better. I'll be dressed. No more…" She thought a bit. "No more posing nudely. Nudity? Posing nude."

Lucy shot her a worried look. "You don't mean that, right? You can't stop sitting for me. I need you, Em. You're my abso-fucking-lutely best model, always have been." Her eyes flicked to the road, then back to Emma. "You're kidding, right? Hey, Mouse. I *said* I was sorry."

Nudidity, Emma thought. There's a fun word. Who used to say that?

Radar O'Reilly, that's who. On *M.A.S.H.*, her dad's favorite show. She should call. Let him know she was okay. The broken collarbone was nothing, they'd still be there for Thanksgiving.

Call her dad, she amended. Not Radar O'Reilly. And not right now because it was like two in the morning.

Belatedly, Emma caught up to Lucy's words and worry. "But posing for you is dangerous. You saw it, right? That easel attacked me." She frowned. "My name's not Mouse. I hate that nickname. You should use my real name."

The pain meds were doing a fine job now of blurring everything except the mesmerizing swipe of the wipers. Emma rolled her head back toward the side window, careful not to jostle her left arm in its sling.

Lucy found the interstate's on-ramp and accelerated, risking a skid.

Emma wanted to say something about the perils of excessive speed on slippery mountain roads, but then she felt the Subaru's all-wheel-drive take hold and the moment was gone. The words weren't lining up correctly anyway.

Lucy exhaled loudly and relaxed her grip on the wheel. "That doctor said you'll be just fine, Em, all healed up in a week or two. So no one needs to know about this, right?"

Emma considered that. "I'll need an extension from Panetta. I've got a paper due Friday, the day after tomorrow. No, tomorrow. Today's Thursday already, right?"

"I'll call him," Lucy reassured her. "What's your topic? Never mind," she added quickly. "This is just me, faking an interest. I'm sure it's totally mind-numbing."

"The Roles of Women…" Emma frowned in concentration. "…in Sub-Saharan Village…Economies? …Maybe."

"Yeah, boring as fuck." Lucy swapped dismissal for persuasion. "Don't worry, I'll tell Panetta you got a doctor's note. But no one else needs to know. Right?" Fingers twitched on the wheel. "This is adulting one-oh-one, Em. We don't need to run to Daddy or Uncle Jerry with every little boo-boo, right? We solve our own fucking problems. Pinky-swear, okay?"

Only Lucy would say fucking and pinky-swear in the same breath.

Through the rain and inky darkness, Emma saw the flash of an exit sign and the lights of what might be a gas station. She wanted to remind her cousin about the Subaru needing gas but instead she fell asleep.

She woke to the crunch of tires on gravel and the growl of the Outback downshifting as it began the sharp climb to their cabin. On the car's instrument panel, the GET GAS NOW light glowed red.

A small panic jolted Emma upright. "Lucy, the gas—" She gasped as a sharp pain knifed her left shoulder.

Lucy scowled, her face inches from the windshield as she navigated a hairpin turn through the downpour. The wipers were slapping frantically now, running on high. At the second switchback, she slowed to a crawl and snapped on the high beams.

"Stupid headlights." One hand left the wheel to scoop back a shock of white-blond hair. "They're fucking useless! I can't see anything."

"Go back to low beams," Emma forced the words through clenched teeth. "It won't reflect off the rain as much."

"Really?" Lucy snapped. "Do you want to drive?"

❧

Drawn from Life, Grabtown, and other works by Sarah P. Blanchard, are available through all bookstores and online at bookshop.org, as well as through Amazon. They can also be ordered directly through the website at sarahpblanchard.com.

ACKNOWLEDGMENTS

Many people have contributed to the making of *Grabtown*. First, a big thank you to my wonderfully talented writers' group, hosted by one of my favorite bookshops and workshop spaces, Booklovers Gourmet in Webster, Massachusetts. Thank you to early readers Brynn Turner, Jess Andersen, and (from across the pond) the very talented Nora Rosenius. Karin Warinsky also provided thoughtful comments and a wise critique of several early-draft portions of this story, before it grew into coherence.

This story has been a long time in the telling. My good friend Tony Krulic provided a *very* early review of the first iteration of AJ's story, which was written more than thirty years ago.

I especially appreciate the assistance of Connecticut State Police Master Sergeant John Miller, Troop D Danielson, who answered my many questions about weapons and police procedures, and gave me a tour of his barracks. John also provided an eagle eye in catching the parts that I initially got wrong in depicting police procedures. If I still got something wrong, it's my own fault.

Thank you also to Alyssa Flori of Flori Fundamentals for her enthusiastic and savvy assistance in guiding *Grabtown* to market.

My dear friend Joan Weston offered her highly professional editorial scrutiny and excellent design commentary to improve several aspects of this work. Thank you, Joan, from the bottom of my heart.

My gratitude also to Rachel Graham in New Zealand, a gifted writing coach and fellow author who provided editorial comments and her enthusiastic support for my work.

The Weaverville Writers' Workshop in North Carolina and the Worcester Writers' Collective in Massachusetts have also been stalwart sources of enthusiastic support in my writing universe.

None of this would be possible without the constant support of Rich Valcourt, my husband and all-time favorite grammar grinch, who is always ready to celebrate every success or argue the necessity of an Oxford comma. Thank you for all you do, from the bottom of my heart.

࿔

Readers have asked me about the setting for *Grabtown*. While Winslow, Graves Parish, and the Pennatucket River are fictional, astute readers familiar with The Quiet Corner of Connecticut will note many similarities with the town of Putnam, a history-rich mill town on the Quinebaug River. (References to the Bradley Playhouse and the devastating 1955 flood are giveaways.)

However, anyone seeking a pedestrian bridge directly over Cargill Falls in the center of Putnam will be disappointed. There's a pedestrian bridge about an eighth of a mile downstream, but it spans a more placid section of the Quinebaug River and isn't quite what I needed for this story.

And yes, in another lifetime, I was a news reporter for Putnam's radio station WINY, 1350 on the AM dial. But I never had to provide news coverage for a shotgun murder, nor did I witness one.

I've invented all the names and many of the locations for this story because nothing this bad should ever happen in your hometown.

BOOK CLUBS

For information on bulk purchases or to download a readers' discussion guide for *Grabtown* or *Drawn from Life*, please contact the author through her website at www.sarahpblanchard.com

NOTES ON HUMAN TRAFFICKING

In the United States, the Department of Homeland Security oversees law enforcement efforts to halt human trafficking, which is defined as the use of force, fraud, or coercion to exploit people for labor or commercial sex acts.

All minors under the age of 18 who are induced to perform commercial sex acts are considered victims of human trafficking, even if no coercion is involved.

Human trafficking can occur in any community—urban or rural, rich or poor—and victims may be any age, ethnicity, or gender.

Traffickers look for people who are easy targets: those people, especially younger ones, who have a psychological or emotional vulnerability, suffer economic hardship, lack a social safety net, or have recently survived a natural disaster or a period of political instability.

Human trafficking is often a hidden crime. Language barriers and a fear of law enforcement can keep victims from seeking help. For many victims, the trauma can be so great that they don't look for help, even in highly public settings. Young victims, in particular, may be manipulated and groomed in such a way they don't even see themselves as victims.

I took some liberties with the depiction of the trafficked girls in this story. Unlike Elena and her sisters, the majority of child victims are living at home while they are being trafficked. And, contrary to popular myth, very few victims are transported in cargo containers—it's just too risky—but it can and does happen. We need to speak up more.

National Human Trafficking Hotline
www.humantraffickinghotline.org

Shared Hope International
www.sharedhope.org

Blue Hope Campaign
dhs.gov/blue-campaign

Connecticut Alliance to End Sexual Assault
www.endsexualviolencect.org

Connecticut Safe Connect
www.CTSafeConnect.org

Source: https://www.dhs.gov/blue-campaign/what-human-trafficking

ABOUT THE AUTHOR

A New England farmer at heart, Sarah P. Blanchard has also lived in Hawai'i and North Carolina, where her first novel, *Drawn from Life*, was set. Rural life and the natural world are always strong influences in her writing, as are the works of writers Barbara Kingsolver, Percival Everett, and Joyce Carol Oates.

Sarah holds a B.A. in English literature and an M.B.A. in marketing. Before turning her attention to writing poetry and fiction, she worked for many years in communications and marketing. On side journeys, she has been a volunteer firefighter, radio news anchor and talk show host, magazine editor, website developer, horse trainer, and a facilities supervisor for Gemini Observatory. She taught English and communications for several years at the University of Hawaii-Hilo and also taught fiction writing in the College for Seniors Program in the Osher Lifelong Learning Institute at the University of North Carolina-Asheville.

In her writing, Sarah is drawn toward flawed, compassionate characters who believe they must battle their demons alone, and complex antagonists who think they have nothing to lose.

Grabtown is her second novel. Her first, *Drawn from Life*, was an Independent Press Award silver-medal winner and was long-listed for *The Letter Review's* unpublished novel award in 2024. Many of her short stories, poems, and essays have been published in magazines and literary journals. She was a finalist for the 2021 Doris Betts Fiction Prize and the 2024 Porch Prize for short fiction.

She is also the author of a short story collection, (*Rift Zone*), and a poetry chapbook (*river, horse, morning*).

Follow the author
Website: sarahpblanchard.com
Facebook: @Sarah.P.Blanchard.author
Instagram/Threads: @sarahpblanchard
Tiktok: @sarah_p_b_author
Bluesky: @sarahpblanchard.bsky.social